$\mathcal{Do}$ you really wish to sleep in the chair that much?" he demanded in a tightly controlled voice.

"It is not that I wish to sleep in the chair; it is that I do not wish to sleep with you!" she hissed.

He was silent for a moment, as if he were somehow confused or surprised by that statement. Suddenly he moved away from her. "Mademoiselle," he began in an incredulous tone, "when exactly was the last time you bathed?"

"How dare you!" spat Jacqueline as she freed herself and sat bolt upright on the bed.

"I mean no insult," he swiftly qualified, "it's just that if you are worried about your precious virtue, I would like to set your mind at ease. My preference is for women who have bathed, at least sometime within the not-too-distant past." He turned away from her and adjusted his half of the blanket over his shoulder. "You may share this bed with me and rest completely assured that even if you were stark naked and willing, I would not have the slightest desire of laying a hand on you."

A mixture of humiliation and fury boiled up inside Jacqueline.

"Move over," she ordered sharply as she gave the pillow on what was to be her side a whack.

He sighed impatiently and moved a bit to accommodate her. Jacqueline lay down and primly drew the blanket up to her chin.

The space he offered her had already been warmed by the heat of his body. In fact, after a few minutes she found that she could feel the heat of him radiating across the few scant inches that separated them. It had been a long time since she had felt warm in bed. She allowed herself a muffled sigh of pleasure and unconsciously huddled closer to its source. . . .

BANTAM BOOKS BY KARYN MONK

Surrender to a Stranger
The Rebel and the Redcoat
Once a Warrior
The Witch and the Warrior

Surrender
to a
Stranger

Karyn Monk

BANTAM BOOKS
NEW YORK TORONTO LONDON
SYDNEY AUCKLAND

SURRENDER TO A STRANGER
A Bantam Book

PUBLISHING HISTORY
Fanfare edition / January 1995
Bantam Books mass market edition / December 1999

ISBN 0-553-56909-0

Published simultaneously in the United States and Canada

Bantam Books are published by Bantam Books, a division of Random
House, Inc. Its trademark, consisting of the words "Bantam Books" and
the portrayal of a rooster, is Registered in U.S. Patent and Trademark
Office and in other countries. Marca Registrada. Bantam Books, 1540
Broadway, New York, New York 10036.

PRINTED IN THE UNITED STATES OF AMERICA

OPM   10 9 8 7 6 5 4 3 2 1

To my dearest Philip,

who has always made me feel like I can do anything,

and to Lorraine,

who has wrapped me in the warmth of her love

all my life.

Surrender to a
Stranger

Chapter 1

November 1793

She stood tall in the dock, her hands resting lightly on the polished surface of the bar that separated her from her accusers. The wooden rail was warm despite the chill of the room, it sent heat into the icy flesh of her fingers, and Jacqueline wondered if the prisoner before her had gripped the bar in fury or in desperation. As she faced her five judges, who were yawning and shifting with weariness and boredom while the charges against her were read, she decided it was easy enough to feel both.

"Citizeness Jacqueline Marie Louise Doucette, daughter of the convicted traitor Charles-Alexandre, former Duc de Lambert, you are charged with being an enemy and a traitor to the Republic of France. . . ." read the public prosecutor. He went on to list the charges against her. Viciously attacking a member of the National Guard and thereby interfering with the execution of his duties. Engaging in counterrevolutionary activities, including the hoarding of gold, silver, jewels and food, and the illegal transfer of said money and jewels out of France. Assisting with the illegal emigration of members of her family, and conspiring with enemies of the Republic. Corresponding with émigrés and writing counterrevolutionary propaganda. The list went on, some of the charges accurate and some purely fictional. It did not matter. The trial was merely a formality. Her sentence was inevitable.

She pulled her gaze away from the judges, who instead of listening to the public prosecutor were busy arguing over how many cases they had yet to hear before they could retire for the day. Her eyes swept over the audience. The rough men and women who packed the courtroom were obviously enjoying the proceedings immensely. They shouted at her as her indictment was being read, calling her a traitor, a whore, demanding that she lose her head for her crimes. They laughed and jostled each other as they yelled at her, some spat on the floor to show their contempt, while others drank and ate and knitted as if they were watching an amusing piece of theater. She stared at them, dressed in their rough, greasy clothes with their red woolen caps and their tricolor sashes looped about their chests and waists. She was not upset by their hatred of her. She simply wondered how they could believe that her death, and her father's, and her brother's, could possibly make their miserable lives any better. Tonight, when she was lying stiff and cold in a pit of dead bodies, they would not have any more bread or wine on their tables than they had before.

"Citizen Barbot, would you tell us if this is the woman who attacked you as you were attempting to perform your duties to the Republic of France?" demanded the public prosecutor, Citizen Fouquier-Tinville.

"It is," replied the soldier in the witness box. He looked at Jacqueline and smiled. She could see the dark hole in his mouth where she had knocked out two of his teeth.

"And before she attacked you, did she make antirevolutionary statements?"

"She did," affirmed the soldier with a nod.

"Would you tell the Revolutionary Tribunal and the citizens of this court exactly what Citizeness Doucette said to you?"

The soldier paused and cleared his throat. "She said the National Guard was an outfit of thieves and pigs and that we could all go straight to hell." It was obvious even repeating such an antirevolutionary statement made him uncomfortable.

"It's that bitch that's going straight to hell," shouted a man from the back of the courtroom.

"Carrying her head in a basket," added another. The crowd in the courtroom burst into laughter.

Citizen Fouquier-Tinville waited for his audience to settle down before continuing. "And is it not true, Citizen Barbot, that Citizeness Doucette attempted to prevent you from entering her home, even though you showed her you had a legal warrant for the arrest of her brother, Citizen Antoine Doucette?"

"She slammed the door in my face," admitted the soldier, looking somewhat irritated by the memory.

"And what did you and your men do?" asked Fouquier-Tinville.

"We smashed the door down," the soldier replied proudly.

"What happened then?"

"We began to search the château, looking for the Marquis de Lambert, and any incriminating documents. We found Monsieur le Marquis in his room, in bed. He was evidently ill," the soldier explained.

"Made sick by his father's greed," called out a woman in the front row.

"Hiding under the covers," cackled another. Jacqueline fought the urge to step out of the dock, walk over to the woman, and slap her soundly across the face.

"And what did you do?" demanded the prosecutor.

"We informed the former marquis of his arrest and ordered him to get up. And he refused."

"He was sick with fever and barely knew you were there!" objected Jacqueline.

"Silence!" thundered the judge president. "The prisoner will not speak to the witness."

"What did you do when Citizen Doucette refused to comply with your orders?" asked the prosecutor.

The soldier shrugged his shoulders. "I had my men drag him from the bed and force him to his feet."

"Good for you!" shouted a spectator.

"He is a true republican," commented another.

"Is that when Citizeness Doucette attacked you?" asked Fouquier-Tinville.

The soldier nodded. "She came into the room carrying a dagger and told my men if they wanted me to live they should unhand her brother. My men laughed and let go of her brother, who collapsed to the floor. And that was when she attacked me."

"Weren't your men armed?" demanded the judge president.

"They were," replied the soldier. "We carried muskets and sabers."

The judge president appeared to ponder this for a moment.

Citizen Fouquier-Tinville continued with his questioning. "And what injuries did you sustain before you were able to restrain Citizeness Doucette?"

The soldier looked somewhat sheepish. "She lodged the dagger into my shoulder before I could strike her to the ground. And when I grabbed my shoulder to stop the bleeding, she got up and knocked out two of my teeth." He looked at the jury and wiggled his tongue through the ugly black gap in his mouth. The jury gasped in sympathy.

"Did she strike you with her fist?" asked the judge president, evidently amazed.

"No," replied the soldier. He shifted in his seat uncomfortably.

"With what then?" persisted the judge president.

The soldier scowled. "She hit me with Monsieur le Marquis's chamber pot."

The jury and the audience laughed.

The judge president rang his bell to silence the room, but Jacqueline could see even he was smiling.

"After Citizeness Doucette was restrained, you and your men made a thorough search of the château, did you not?" asked the public prosecutor.

"We did," confirmed the soldier. "We found several incriminating documents in the form of letters to Citizeness Doucette's sisters, who have either illegally emigrated or are in hiding. These letters denounced the Republic of France and called for a return of the monarchy. We also found that all of the former Duchesse de Lambert's jewels were missing, as were many valuables from the château. These undoubtedly have been transferred out of France to finance a royalist plot." This last statement was said with grave authority, as if merely making the accusation was proof enough that it was true.

"She's a spy!" screeched a woman in the audience.

"The whole family must be found and made to pay for its crimes!"

"Take her head as the first payment!"

The judge president rang his bell to silence the room. Citizen Fouquier-Tinville dismissed the soldier from the witness box and turned his attention to the prisoner.

"Jacqueline Doucette, is it true you attacked Citizen Barbot while he was performing his duties as a captain of the National Guard?"

Like many prisoners, Jacqueline had chosen to represent her own defense. When her father had been arrested earlier that year, he had engaged a lawyer to prepare his case. The man had charged a fortune and done virtually nothing to help him in his fight for his life. Jacqueline knew many lawyers were becoming rich on the assets of their unfortunate clients. Even though the Château de Lambert and its contents would be seized by the state after she was condemned, she had no desire to pay someone for the charade of a defense.

"I was trying to help my brother," she replied.

"Your brother was being arrested. You were interfering with an official act of the Republic of France," Fouquier-Tinville informed her.

"Was it an official act of this Republic that he be savagely kicked after he collapsed to the floor?" she demanded furiously.

"You noblesse have been kicking us for years," shouted a voice.

"Maybe he needed a good kick to get him up again," added another.

Fouquier-Tinville smiled and faced the jury. "Citizeness Doucette, the measures which the National Guard is forced to take as they bravely struggle to protect our Republic are not at issue here. What is at issue are your actions, which clearly demonstrate that you are a traitor to your country." He paused and turned to look at her. "Where are your two younger sisters, Suzanne and Séraphine?"

"They are staying with friends," Jacqueline replied.

"Are these friends in France?" demanded the prosecutor.

"No."

"You realize, of course, that makes your sisters émigrés, and therefore traitors to this Republic?"

"I realize that makes them far away, and therefore safe from bloodthirsty murderers like you and the members of this tribunal," Jacqueline calmly told him.

The audience and the jury gasped. Even the weary judges straightened up in their chairs. The prosecutor looked slightly disconcerted. He was obviously not accustomed to being called a murderer. He cleared his throat.

"So you admit that you arranged the escape of your sisters across the border of France?" he persisted.

"That's exactly what it was," agreed Jacqueline. "An escape."

Fouquier-Tinville smiled. "Where are the jewels that belonged to your mother, the former Duchesse de Lambert?"

"I sold them earlier this year."

"Then where is the money?" he persisted.

"I spent it."

The prosecutor looked at her in disbelief. "All of it?" he asked incredulously. He shook his head. "The De Lambert jewel collection was worth a fortune. Do you expect us to believe you could go through so much money in such a short period of time?"

Jacqueline looked at him with contempt. "In a country where the currency is not worth the paper it is printed on? Where the maximum prices fixed on grain and flour mean you have to pay ten times the legal amount to get someone to sell you what they are hoarding?"

Disgruntled murmurs of agreement could be heard from the audience.

Fouquier-Tinville interrupted them. "You cannot expect the members of this court to believe you went through what must have been an extraordinary amount of money over a period of just a few months. You transferred the money out of France, didn't you?" he demanded.

"Either way, I don't have it anymore," she replied indifferently. She knew the revolutionary government was in appalling debt, and relied heavily on the money and properties confiscated from émigrés, condemned criminals, and the church to help finance its massive war effort and ailing economy. She would not leave them one more *livre* than necessary.

"Did you write these letters Citizen Barbot found in your home when he was arresting your brother?" the prosecutor asked as he waved several sheets of paper in her face.

"No."

"Come, come, you have not even looked at them," he protested. He held one up for her to see. "In this one, which is to your sister Suzanne, you lament the loss of your father and pray for the death of the revolutionary government. In this one, to your sister Séraphine, you call France 'a great scaffold which is sustaining itself on the blood of the weak and the powerless, all in the name of the law.' You speak longingly of the day when the royal family will be restored to the throne. Do you deny that you wrote these?"

Jacqueline reached out and took the letters. They appeared to be documents in progress and were not signed. She examined the writing. She was relieved to see it was not Antoine's. She handed the letters back to the prosecutor.

"I would never be so stupid as to put such comments into writing for your esteemed National Guard to find," she told him. "Also, I do not find the subject matter suitable for correspondence with eight- and ten-year-old children. Do you?" she asked sarcastically.

Fouquier-Tinville was not disturbed by her denial. "If they are not yours, Citizeness, then they must be your brother's. Thank you for confirming this." He turned to place the documents back on his table.

"Antoine would never write something like that!" she burst out furiously. "And he has been too ill these past weeks to hold a quill to paper!"

"Citizeness Doucette, these letters were found in your home. If neither you nor your brother wrote them, pray tell us who did?" asked the prosecutor with mock curiosity.

Jacqueline glared at him. She did not know who had drafted those letters and planted them for the National Guard to find. As former aristos and the family of a condemned traitor, she and her brother had many enemies. And the Château de Lambert with all its holdings was a fine prize for the state, so anyone who sought to improve their status with the revolutionary government might be only too willing to denounce them. That was all it took to make an arrest. There was no need for any proof. Just someone else's word against your own. But the arrest warrant had only been for Antoine, not her. If she had not attacked that odious captain, who tramped through her home giving orders for his men to tear the place apart as they searched for Antoine, and then laughed as his soldiers each took a turn kicking her poor brother on the floor, she might never have been arrested. These letters were meant to be found as evidence against Antoine, and the fact that someone had taken the trouble to write them meant they wanted to be sure he would not return.

"Any ideas?" prodded Fouquier-Tinville.

Jacqueline hesitated. There were several possibilities, but without proof she would not denounce anyone. The action could not save her life anyway, but it would undoubtedly extinguish another. She shook her head.

"Send her to the national razor!" cried out a woman over her knitting. "She is an enemy to the Republic!"

The public prosecutor nodded with satisfaction. "Perhaps the jury has heard enough to render a verdict. I could continue with my questioning, but in light of the evidence already presented against the defendant—"

"Has the jury heard enough?" demanded the judge president.

The weary members of the jury nodded that they had, and were quickly removed to an adjoining room to discuss their verdict. Normally the prisoner would also be removed from the courtroom so the Tribunal could continue with its session, but as the last prisoner of the day, Jacqueline was permitted to remain standing in the dock.

She scanned the audience as she waited for the jury to return. It was getting late, and the men and women who had enjoyed the painful ordeal of the prisoners who faced the dreaded Revolutionary Tribunal that day were packing up their belongings to head home. She searched the crowd for someone she knew. She suspected that Henriette was there somewhere, for her loyal maid would not be able to stay away, even though Jacqueline had expressly forbidden her to come. She did not see François-Louis anywhere, and he would surely stick out in such a rough-looking crowd. His absence did not surprise her. Her betrothed was not a man who took unnecessary risks, and he undoubtedly feared his association with her would soon be called into question. She was sorry for that, and despite her disappointment that no one was there to offer support through their presence, she could not fault him for his desire to be cautious.

For the most part the members of the audience ignored her as they gathered up their food and drink and discussed her fate among themselves. Her eyes came to rest upon an old man who was sitting at the back of the courtroom. He did not speak to anyone around him, apparently uninterested in sharing their harsh enthusiasm over what was certain to be a guilty verdict. He was dressed entirely in black, and his head was covered with a battered, low crowned hat that bore a revolutionary cockade. The scraggly hair spilling out from underneath his head dress was snowy white, the sallow skin that sagged upon his face spotted and lined with age. He hunched forward on the bench, his pale hands gripping the top of a cane that was evidently very much needed to give his ancient, fragile body support. He stared vacantly into space, apparently oblivious to the coarse remarks about "the aristo whore" who would soon find herself lying down for Sanson, the executioner. Someone jostled him and laughingly asked him a question while pointing at her, and the old man smiled and nodded. He turned his eyes to her and appeared surprised to find her looking at him. They locked gazes for the briefest of seconds, and Jacqueline found herself transfixed by the intensity of his stare. Then he turned abruptly and made some remark to the burly man seated beside him, which caused the lout to shake with booming laughter before wiping his nose on his sleeve. Jacqueline looked away.

The jury returned after a few minutes with a verdict of guilty. The audience cheered.

"Citizeness Doucette, you have been found guilty by this court of committing crimes against the Republic of France. Do you have anything you wish to say in your defense before you are sentenced?" asked the judge president.

Jacqueline gripped the bar of the dock as she looked at the judges and jury with contempt. "You have found me guilty of trying to protect my family from the cruelty and corruption that has hooked its claws into France," she began, her voice tight and frigid. "You have already murdered my father, and undoubtedly you will soon do the same to my brother. Do you think I believe you would have stopped there? By attacking the scum who invaded my home, I merely saved you the time and expense of sending another party to the Château de Lambert to arrest me later." She paused and stared hard at them. "My advice to you, my fellow citizens, is that you enjoy today, and tomorrow, and the day after that, because your days are sadly numbered. By murdering the noblesse, and the wealthy bourgeois, and anyone who has the courage to speak out against you, you cannot solve the enormous problems that are choking the breath out of France." She gestured to the men and women in the audience, who had settled back into their seats to listen to her. "It is only a matter of time before these people to whom you have promised so much grow weary of your fancy rhetoric," she continued. "Ceremonies of liberty and reason and the constant chop of the guillotine do not put food on a table or clothing on a body." She looked at Fouquier-Tinville and smiled. "Even you, fellow citizen, will not be exempt," she told him with certainty. "But my sisters will be safe. And when reason and justice have been restored to France, they will return."

"Citizeness Doucette, the hour grows late and your political opinions are no longer of interest to this court," interrupted the judge president impatiently. "Since you do not seem to have anything to say which would alter the verdict of this jury, I find you guilty of the charges laid against you, and hereby sentence you to death by the guillotine. This execution will take place immediately," he added as he began to shuffle together the papers on his bench.

The audience, which had been relatively quiet during Jacqueline's speech, began to cheer and applaud the court's decision. One of the court clerks laid down his pen and pulled out his watch to examine the time. He motioned to Fouquier-Tinville to come over to him. After exchanging a few words, the public prosecutor shrugged and turned to face the bench.

"It would appear the last tumbril departed for the Place de la Revolution some half hour ago," he informed the judge president.

"Then Citizeness Doucette may be returned to her cell in the Conciergerie until tomorrow," amended the judge. "But the sentence is to be carried out within twenty-four hours."

Four members of the National Guard stepped up to

the dock to escort Jacqueline out of the courtroom. They surrounded her as she walked down the aisle. The crowd around them began to surge in, cursing and trying to grab at her clothes and her hair.

"Pretty hair—too bad Sanson will have to cut it so the blade can find your neck—" sang out one toothless hag who shot her hand in between the guards and gave Jacqueline's hair a yank. The pins came loose and the rough coiffure she had managed to fashion before she left her cell sagged down around her shoulders.

"See how proudly the bitch walks," commented a man with a face reddened by too much cheap wine. He spat at her. "Take that, bitch."

"Let's see how proud she is tomorrow when she lies down and puts her head through the republican window," said a skinny youth whose bony shoulders slumped forward at an unnatural angle as he laughed.

"Or when the tart's body is tossed headless into the pit," added another with a sneer.

Jacqueline kept her eyes straight ahead and used the comments to fuel her sudden hatred of these people. The soldiers closed ranks around her so no one else could touch her, and she was grateful for that. She had heard stories of atrocities committed against arrested people who never made it as far as the court, or even the prison, for that matter, and she supposed she was grateful that she had not been openly butchered by an angry mob. At least the guillotine was quick and, she hoped, painless.

The new Republic of France, birthplace of Liberty, Equality, and Reason, was a world gone mad. The men who had wrested power from their king, insisting that even a monarch who ruled with divine right was answerable to his people, had quickly discovered they were no better equipped to feed or clothe millions of angry, starving peasants than Louis XVI had been. It was a sobering realization. They blamed the soaring inflation and lack of food on a royalist conspiracy, and removed Louis's head. But then the wars against Great Britain, Holland, and Spain began, spiraling the national debt out of control, and the crops continued to fail. The people, now proudly called citizens, continued to starve. And so they removed the head of their former queen, Marie-Antoinette. And still they were freezing and miserable. Surely someone was to blame?

The former noblesse, who for centuries had made their fortunes on the sweat and misery of others, were undoubtedly the cause of so much want. They were leeches, traitors, enemies of the revolution. True, they had already been stripped of their titles and their privileges. But now they must pay for their crimes with their blood. France must be purged of her enemies. And thanks to the new Law of Suspects, any loyal citizen could denounce another and cause their arrest without the slightest trace of evidence. The fifty-odd prisons of Paris swelled with elegant inmates who had no hope of escaping the razor-sharp justice of the guillotine. Their deaths did not feed the population, but somehow the constant river of blood that flowed out of the Place de la Revolution made the people feel something was being done.

The prison called La Conciergerie adjoined the Palais de Justice in which the Revolutionary Tribunal held its sessions. The severe, imposing castle dated back to the end of the thirteenth century and had served as a prison since the 1500s. Dark, cold, damp, and evil smelling, the Conciergerie was widely recognized as the worst prison in Paris. As Jacqueline walked with the guards along twisting corridors and up narrow staircases, their way lit only by the faint glow of an occasional torch mounted on the thick stone walls, she could hear the scratches and squeals of rats scurrying out of the way of their feet. She had grown used to those sounds and was no longer terrified by them. The one time a rat had decided to invade her small cell she had consolidated fear with fury and smashed the loathsome creature over the head with her soup bowl until it lay dead. She decided if she was to die in prison, it would not be from the plague.

The fumes that assaulted her as they reached the floor of her cell made her stomach wrench and her throat constrict. The hallway was thick with the stench of sewage and sickness, of unwashed bodies and fouled floors. She lifted her hand to her nose and tried to breathe through her mouth, but the fetid air was so bad it threatened to choke her. She pressed her lips together and forced herself to take small, shallow breaths. It had taken her days to grow used to the stink when she first arrived here. Her short trip to the Palais de Justice had been an almost welcome reprieve from her miserable surroundings, and her nose had quickly grown used to inhaling cleaner air. As she was only staying here one more night, she doubted she would be able to adjust to the stench again.

"What's she doing back here?" demanded Citizen Gagnon, the jailer of the wing they had come to.

"She is sentenced to death, but it was too late to take her to meet Sanson," commented one of the guards indifferently.

"Missed the last cart, did you?" asked Gagnon, his voice heavy with sarcasm. He lifted a torch from the wall and stood before Jacqueline. He was a huge bear of a man, with enormous shoulders and thick, strong arms straining beneath the dirty, ragged clothes he wore. His skin was black with years of grime, and when he smiled he exposed an uneven set of brown, rotting teeth. Unlike most of the prisoners, who tried to wash themselves and their clothes as best they could in the icy water of a fountain located in an open courtyard below, the jailers were quite accustomed to their own filth.

"Well, my beauty, you're in luck, because your room is still available," he joked as he led them down a hall while sorting through an enormous iron ring of keys.

He stopped in front of a wooden door with a tiny grille window and inserted a key into the heavy lock. The door swung open with a groan to expose a small cell, perhaps nine feet square, accommodating a trestle bed with a coarse woolen blanket, a table, and a chair. Jacqueline raised her chin, drew her shawl up around her shoulders, and calmly stepped into the room. She could hear the hasty footsteps of the soldiers retreating down the hall. Undoubtedly they were as anxious to leave the foulness of the place as she was. She examined her surroundings for a moment and then turned to face her keeper.

"My candle is gone," she pointed out. "I would like it back."

"Certainly, certainly," replied Gagnon agreeably. "You remember the fee?"

"I paid for the one that was in here," Jacqueline stated flatly.

"Ah, but I was not expecting you to return, so I sold it to another," he told her with a shrug. He slowly looked her up and down, causing Jacqueline to draw her shawl even tighter around her shoulders. "Have you any money?"

"I will write my maid and instruct her to bring some tomorrow," she replied.

The jailer shook his head. "Tomorrow you will expose your pretty little neck to the hot blade of the guillotine. How do I know your maid will come and pay me?" he demanded.

"Because she is a woman of honor and she will see to it that the debts I acknowledge are paid," answered Jacqueline impatiently. The cell had no window and was oppressively dark. If she had to spend her last night in blackness, unable to write a letter to Antoine or make out the shape of a rat that may have invaded her tiny space, she felt sure she would go mad.

Citizen Gagnon appeared unconvinced. "She might pay me," he agreed, "and she might not." He scratched his head thoughtfully as he studied her. "Have you anything you could give me?"

Jacqueline considered for a moment. She had no jewelry, and the gown she wore, which had once been a pretty blue silk day dress with fine lace trim, was now nothing but a filthy, tattered robe. Her black knitted shawl was still in good condition, but having no cloak, she would need it tonight and tomorrow for warmth. She shook her head.

"Well now, maybe we could work out something," Gagnon mused as he stepped toward her. He reached out a grubby hand to touch her hair, which was half falling down her shoulders. He wrapped his massive fist around a thick lock of it and examined the golden strands between his filthy fingers. "Very nice," he murmured appreciatively. He looked at her, still holding fast to her hair. "We'll make a trade," he announced. "Your hair for a candle."

"Absolutely not!" replied Jacqueline, thoroughly disgusted by the idea of this man owning something so intimate of hers. She tried to move away from him, and felt a burning pain in her scalp as he continued to hold her hair.

"Don't be so hasty in deciding," he whispered, pulling her face close to his. The stench of his breath was overwhelming. "Either you cut it, or Sanson will cut it for you. This way at least you get something in return," he argued reasonably.

Jacqueline shuddered. She knew the executioner insisted his victims' hair be shorn off the neck so the blade of the guillotine had a clear path in which to cut. Perhaps it was less messy that way. She was not sure. But prisoners awaiting execution often arranged to cut their own hair and left it to their family as a small token by which they might be remembered. Otherwise it was roughly hacked off and thrown away by the executioner. She had thought perhaps she would leave her hair to her maid, Henriette, who would somehow get it to her sisters. After almost three weeks in prison it was far from clean, but even this brute of a keeper could obviously see that her hair was unusually thick and luxuriant. Ever since she was a child people had commented on the beauty of her hair. The humiliation of having to cut it so this man could carry it as a prize or give it to his wife for a wig was totally repugnant to her.

"Keep your damn candle!" she spat as she slapped his hand off her and moved away from him.

"It's up to you," returned Gagnon with a shrug. He

stepped out into the hall carrying his torch and shut the door. The cell was plunged into darkness.

Jacqueline moved over to the bed and sat down on it. The sounds of sobbing and moaning filtered through the thick walls of her chamber. Somewhere a woman was pitifully screaming that she was innocent. Somewhere a man was being sick. A few of the prison's many dogs were barking. Perhaps they had spotted a rat. Jacqueline pressed her lips together and fought to retain her composure. These were, after all, only the normal sounds of the Conciergerie.

She wanted to cry, but she could not. After the arrest of her father she had wept for days, so terrified was she of what would happen to him. He was kept in prison for three months, but not in a place of misery and death like this one. He was incarcerated in what was called a *maison de santé*, a relatively comfortable house of arrest intended for the wealthiest prisoners. The rooms at the Luxembourg were clean and airy, and if one was able to pay, and all of its inmates were, one could dine on seasoned mutton, veal, and duckling, and wash it down with fine French wine. The prisoners there had servants who brought them fresh clothes, books, paper, and ink, and their rooms were cheered with the addition of carpets, paintings, tapestries, and furniture brought from their homes. Many inmates continued to manage their financial affairs from the prison, as they were permitted to have notaries, financial agents, brokers, and auctioneers come to do business with them. Jacqueline and Antoine were regular visitors there, and had been assured by their father that his living conditions were far from intolerable. The former Duc de Lambert found his companions in the prison most pleasant, and spent his days reading, writing, managing his investments, and preparing for his defense. In the evening the prisoners enjoyed card games, lively discussions, and often organized a little play or poetry reading to present to their fellow inmates. It was a world away from life at La Conciergerie.

When Jacqueline first arrived she was placed in a common cell, about fifteen feet square, which she shared with two other women. One was the wife of a military officer whose husband had been executed because his last campaign was not successful. Such failures were highly suspect and deemed counterrevolutionary. The other was a prostitute who had complained to someone that her trade was suffering miserably since the revolution. That was clearly an attack on the government. Both women had been in prison for months as they waited for their case to come before the Tribunal. They slept on beds of straw on the floor and were heavily infested with lice. Two days later Jacqueline was moved to this small cell, where for the rate of twenty-seven *livres,* payable in advance, she could have a bed for a month. She was grateful for the move and did not mind being placed in solitary confinement. The only visitor she had was Henriette, who was permitted to visit her mistress once and had been practical enough to bring some money.

Her eyes were adjusting to the dim light, and so far she could not see anything moving in her cell. Feeling cold and tired, she sighed and lay down on her bed. Tomorrow she would be executed. She supposed she ought to feel terrified, but in fact she was relieved. Her trial had come up relatively quickly, and she thanked God for that. The idea of rotting in this cess pit for months before facing the Tribunal and its inevitable sentence had haunted her.

Her only fear now was for Antoine. He had been sick with a cough and fever for more than a week when the National Guard came to arrest him. Antoine was only a year older than she, and had not been blessed with good health. When they arrived at the Conciergerie they were immediately separated, and despite Jacqueline's constant inquiries no one seemed able or willing to tell her anything about his condition. She prayed his accommodation was cleaner and warmer than hers. She had no doubt he would also be sentenced to death, but she did not want him to suffer before his execution.

A key scraped in the lock and the door groaned. The jailer stepped aside and the tall figure of a man stepped into the darkness of the cell. For a brief instant his face was lit by the weak torch her keeper held.

"Bring a light in here immediately," he snapped as he removed his hat and flung it on the table. Gagnon hastily retreated from the door to do his bidding. Nicolas stared through the shadows at her as Jacqueline rose from the bed.

"Mademoiselle de Lambert, I hope I find you well," he drawled sarcastically as he swept into a low, mocking bow. He straightened up and pretended to examine her surroundings with interest. "But what a terrible turn of events this is, to find you in such a dismal environment." He clucked sympathetically.

"Get out," said Jacqueline in a low voice.

He looked at her with feigned surprise. "Mademoiselle, you astonish me. Have you forgotten your gentle manners, which were always such a clear reminder of your fine, noble breeding?"

"Neither my manners nor my breeding are any concern of yours, Monsieur Bourdon. Get out."

At that moment the jailer reappeared, carrying a thick candle which he set down on the table. "Will there by anything else, Inspector Bourdon?" he asked. It was obvious to Jacqueline that her keeper was much impressed by her visitor.

"No," replied Nicolas. "Leave us." Gagnon nodded and left the cell, locking the door behind him.

"It would appear I must remind you that you are no longer the idolized daughter of a wealthy duc, holding court in the magnificent salon of the Château de Lambert," Nicolas remarked as he slowly stripped off his gloves. He raised his dark eyes to her. "I am not some humble peasant who must bow and scrape before you, Jacqueline. You have no power here. I would advise you to remember that." He smiled. Evidently he was enjoying the reversal of their roles immensely.

"What do you want of me, Nicolas?" she demanded. "Undoubtedly you have heard I am to face the guillotine tomorrow. Does that not please you enough? Or did you come to savor my humiliation as I cried and begged you to use your influence with the Committee of Public Safety to save me?"

He looked at her with what appeared to be genuine regret. "I did not intend for *you* to be arrested Jacqueline," he told her softly.

His words hung on the filthy cold air as a mixture of surprise and fury flooded through her. "It was you who denounced Antoine," she whispered slowly. "That means you must have written those letters," she concluded, recalling the papers the National Guard claimed to have found in her home.

"None of this would have happened if you had only accepted my suit," he complained bitterly. "If you had married me, I would have protected you and your family."

"Marry you?" Jacqueline gasped in disbelief. "You can still suggest such a thing after you have demonstrated the kind of man you are? After you arrange for the arrest of my brother when he was so ill I feared for his survival?"

"I did not realize he was so sick," Nicolas protested. "The arrest was to have been simple and orderly, the way most arrests are. It never occurred to me that you would attack a member of the National Guard and get yourself arrested in the process." He shook his head in disbelief, as if the very image of such an act was utterly beyond his imagination.

Jacqueline stared at him, her body rigid with loathing. "What's the matter, Nicolas? Did I spoil your plans for me?" she asked sarcastically.

He shrugged his shoulders. "They have been altered, but I remain confident we can reach an agreement," he replied nonchalantly.

Jacqueline looked at him and began to laugh. It was a harsh, bitter laugh, but it was the first time in many months that anything had even slightly amused her, and she indulged in the feeling. "An agreement?" she repeated mockingly. "Oh, but certainly Monsieur Bourdon, do let us negotiate. Shall I arrange for some refreshment while we work out the terms?" she asked politely as she motioned for him to sit in the chair. "I must confess I am not sure what to order, for the Conciergerie is not well-known for the quality of its food and drink, but no matter. Pray, tell me what you will have?"

"You." His answer was curt and businesslike. It was impossible to mistake its meaning.

She stared at him in outraged disbelief. "Are you mad?" she demanded. "Tomorrow I am going to be executed. My father is dead, and my brother is either dying or already dead. I blame our murders on you and your damned revolutionary government. Can you honestly think I will give myself to you on the eve of my death?"

"Perhaps," he replied with a shrug. "If it means you can save your precious life." He removed his heavy brown coat and draped it over the chair. "You have heard, I am sure, of women who have managed to escape the blade of the guillotine, at least temporarily, by revealing that they are pregnant?"

"I am not," protested Jacqueline indignantly.

"Of course you are not," Nicolas agreed. He removed his brown jacket and carefully laid it over his coat. "Convicted women who declare themselves pregnant are removed to the Tribunal hospital at the Maison de l'Evêché near Notre Dame," he continued conversationally. "They are kept there until it can be determined whether or not they are actually pregnant. Once their condition is confirmed, they are permitted to avoid their execution by carrying to term and giving birth."

"And what happens to them after that?" demanded Jacqueline.

"Then they are executed," he admitted. "But the Tribunal hospital is not a fortress like the Conciergerie. During the months in which you are staying there, an escape might be possible."

Jacqueline looked at him incredulously. "Are you suggesting that you get me pregnant tonight so I can cheat the guillotine of another victim tomorrow?"

"We may not be successful tonight," Nicolas qualified.

"But I can tell the Tribunal that as an acquaintance of the family, I am aware you have had a lover for some time, which will make your plea of pregnancy more credible. The lover, of course, could not be me, for that would make me suspect. In my capacity as an inspector for the Committee of Public Safety, I can, however, arrange to visit you at the hospital, under the pretense of needing to further investigate your case. During these meetings we can make sure my seed has more opportunities to take." He smiled at her, evidently looking forward to that prospect.

"Get out," commanded Jacqueline, her voice low and full of loathing.

Nicolas sighed. "As always, you continue to disappoint me, Jacqueline." He stepped toward her and grabbed hold of her hair, then roughly jerked her into him.

Jacqueline struggled to free himself as he wrapped his other arm around her and held her tightly against his chest. "Did you really think I would be stupid enough to believe you wanted to help me?" she grated out. "All you want is to strip me of my dignity by tricking me into finally giving myself to you. That would please you, wouldn't it, you loathsome bast—"

He released his arm and cracked her hard against the face. She would have staggered back from the impact, but he still held her a prisoner by her hair. His face dark with fury, he reached into the neckline of her gown and tore down in one violent motion, ripping away the delicate silk bodice and exposing her breasts.

"Do you know what you are now, Jacqueline?" he drawled as he let his hand roughly wander over her. "You are nothing," he spat, shoving her back against the cold stone wall. "You noblesse have been stripped of your titles and your rights, and now it is up to us if you are allowed to live." He reached down and began to pull up the skirts of her gown as he pinned her against the wall with his body. "Tomorrow you will die," he stated viciously, "but tonight, my sweet, you will finally be mine." He lowered his head and savagely ground his mouth against hers, stifling any cries she might have made.

Jacqueline strained against him, clamping her mouth shut as she frantically scratched at his face and tried with the other hand to stop the rise of her gown. She could feel him pressing against her, holding her a prisoner as he brutally squeezed her breast. His hand was groping her thigh, she struggled and tried to lift her knee to strike him in the groin, but to her horror this action only served to speed his hand's ascent. He was there, roughly probing her with his fingers in the most intimate of places, hurting her, laughing, and she wrenched her mouth away to scream, knowing full well that a woman's screams for help in the Conciergerie would bring absolutely no one.

"Oh, er, pardon me, I was not aware the citizeness was entertaining company," said a frail, gravelly voice before dissolving into a hideous fit of coughing.

Startled, Nicolas released Jacqueline and stepped away from her. Jacqueline quickly pulled together the torn remnants of her bodice and grabbed her shawl up from the floor, covering herself before she turned to face the welcome intruder.

"Who are you and what do you want?" demanded Nicolas harshly, obviously infuriated by the interruption.

The old man Jacqueline had noticed in the courtroom waved his gnarled hand at Nicolas as he continued to cough, a horrible, wet, choking sound that made it quite impossible for him to reply. A scrawny youth of perhaps fifteen or sixteen, who had been standing in the shadows by the door, stepped into the cell and pulled the chair that held Nicolas's coat and jacket over for him to sit on. With great effort the old man leaned on his cane and slowly lowered himself into the chair. The boy reached into a pocket of the enormous black cape the man wore and produced a relatively clean handkerchief. The old man accepted it with one hand and proceeded to hawk into it noisily. It sounded to Jacqueline as if he might expire at any moment.

"His name is Citizen Julien. He's an agent of the

court," explained Gagnon apologetically from the door. "Here to see about her personal affairs."

"Debts to be settled, last letters to write," managed the old man in a wheezy voice as he fought to control his coughing. "Distribution of personal effects, scraps of clothing, locks of hair. The lad here, Dénis, and I will see that they are safely delivered to loved ones, all for a modest fee. I am also able to take last statements or confessions of any counterrevolutionary activities, names, places. It is my duty to admit I do have some access to our most eminent public prosecutor, Citizen Fouquier-Tinville, and might even be able to get a final confession or denunciation to him if the information provided is worthwhile. Perhaps you have something to tell me, young lady, that might affect your sentence, hmm?" he said suggestively, with one thick white eyebrow raised in her direction."

Jacqueline wanted to laugh, so grateful was she for this interruption. She was aware prisoners were entitled to settle their affairs in the brief hours before their execution, but did the Tribunal really believe she would denounce others who opposed the new Republic to try to save herself?

"I am afraid, Citizen, your timing is not ideal," stated Nicolas in a tightly controlled voice. "The citizeness and I have a personal matter to resolve. You can come back later." He folded his arms across his chest and waited for the old man to excuse himself from the cell.

Citizen Julien ignored him and motioned to the youth, who handed him a thick leather case. He laid it open on the table and moved the candle closer, pulled out a sheaf of papers, and began to mumble as he rifled through them. "Saint-Simon . . . Rabourdin . . . de Crussol . . . Pontavice . . . Coutelet . . . La Voisier . . . Dufouleur . . . aha!" he called out triumphantly. He separated a sheet of paper from the pile and held it beneath the light of the candle. "Jacqueline Doucette, formerly Mademoiselle Jacqueline Marie Louise de Lambert, daughter of the convicted traitor Charles-Alexandre Doucette, former Duc de Lambert," he read from the document with squinting eyes. He reached back into the case, took out a quill and a little pot of ink, and began to set them up on the table.

Nicolas took a step toward him, clearly annoyed. "Citizen, I said you will have to come back later," he bellowed into his ear, obviously thinking the man must be deaf.

The old man slowly lifted one pale, spotted hand to his ear and shook his head, as if the sound was rattling around in his brain. He looked at Nicolas impatiently. "No need to shout, boy, no need to shout," he bellowed back. "I'm old, not dead," he grumbled irritably as he turned his attention again to his papers.

"Actually, I have a number of matters to discuss with Citizen Julien, and would prefer to do so now," interjected Jacqueline. As long as the old man remained in her cell, Nicolas would be unable to touch her.

"Citizen, if you would come back in about an hour, Citizeness Doucette and I will have concluded our business and you may talk with her for as long as you like," suggested Nicolas pleasantly. He gave Jacqueline a warning glance that told her if she dared to speak again, it would be far worse for her once they were alone.

"Can't do it," said the old man as he began to write something on the paper before him. "Unfortunately, Citizeness Doucette is my only client at the Conciergerie. I have five others to see before the night is out, and they are divided among three different prisons." He lifted up what appeared to be a note to himself, cleared his throat, and began to read: "One at La Conciergerie." He lowered the note and looked at Nicolas. "That is here," he informed him. He lifted the note again. "Two at La Force." He lowered the note and looked at Jacqueline. "Not a very nice place, La Force." He paused and looked around the cell. "Not a very nice place here, either," he commented absently as he lifted the note again. "One at L'Abbaye." He lowered the note and looked at the jailer, who was still standing in the doorway. "Ever work at L'Abbaye?" he inquired pleasantly.

"Enough!" ordered Nicolas in exasperation. He reached behind the old man and yanked up his jacket and coat.

"Two at Sainte-Pelagie," continued Citizen Julien, obviously unimpressed by Nicolas's outburst.

"I will return in one hour to finish what we started," Nicolas ground out to Jacqueline. "I trust you will be waiting for me?" he drawled sarcastically. He turned abruptly and left the cell.

"Excitable fellow, that one," commented the old man as he looked up from his paper. He fixed his gaze on Jacqueline. "He seems unusually fond of you." He stared at her meaningfully.

"Call me when you want out," said Gagnon as he closed and locked the door.

"Now then, Citizeness, what can I do for you today?" asked Citizen Julien brightly as he set a clean sheet of paper before him and dabbed his quill in the pot of ink.

"If you cheat me, I promise you will regret it," stated Jacqueline in a warning tone. She had heard stories of dishonest agents who made a comfortable living by simply keeping the valuables they collected from their condemned clients. It was bad enough they were living off the misery of others, but then to charge prisoners for services they had no intention of rendering, and to sell or discard the last precious items bequeathed to their loved ones, was utterly despicable.

"Citizeness, er . . ." The old man paused to squint at his note, "Doucette, you need have no fear of my integrity. You may mount the steps to the guillotine with complete peace of mind, confident that your last wishes will be carried out to the letter," he told her with pride.

"Very well," conceded Jacqueline. She stood in the middle of the cell and thought for a moment.

The old man sat poised at the table waiting for her instructions. The boy Dénis, who like Gagnon was covered with years of grime, made himself more or less comfortable by sitting on the floor and leaning against the wall. His loose, dark trousers, short, coarse jacket, and red cap was the typical outfit of the new sansculottes, revolutionaries who scorned the tight, knee-length breeches and long jackets aristocratic gentlemen had favored for most of the century. He folded his arms and closed his eyes, evidently undisturbed by the filth around him.

"Since our honorable Republic has, in its infallible wisdom, decided to confiscate all of my father's investments, including my home and everything in it, my bequests are somewhat limited," Jacqueline stated sarcastically. "I wish to send a letter to my maid, Henriette Mandrou, and with it I shall include my hair. She will know what to do with it."

"Henriette," repeated the old man as he began to write. With a shaking hand he slowly scratched the letters onto the paper, using long, embellished strokes. When he had finished he paused and stared at the name, as if trying to remember why he had written it. After a moment he smiled and looked up. "I knew an Henriette once," he told her conversationally. "A dairymaid. Wanted me to marry her. Only difference between her and her cow was the cow smelled better." He chuckled and looked back at his work.

"I would also like you to cut my hair, if you think you can hold your scissors steady enough to do it without slashing my throat," continued Jacqueline, irritated by his cheerful attitude. She pulled the pins from her hair and shook it loose, running her fingers through the blond cape to feel its silky texture one last time before it was removed.

Citizen Julien stared at her as she did this, holding his quill in midair, the smile on his face quite gone. It appeared to Jacqueline that the sight of her hair had startled him, and his reaction made the impending loss even more painful.

"It is only hair," she told him bitterly. "Tomorrow it will be my head."

His response to that statement was to burst into another terrible fit of coughing, so deep and choking he dropped his pen and began to gasp for air. Concerned, Jacqueline rushed over and began to pat him lightly on the back. The boy leapt to his feet, pushed Jacqueline aside, and proceeded to give his employer a solid thumping.

"He's having one of his fits," Dénis explained.

"Medicine—" wheezed the old man in between wallops. "Need—medicine."

"Where is it?" demanded Jacqueline.

"It's in his bag, downstairs," Dénis told her. "We carry a lot of people's stuff with us, and the wardens don't usually let us take it up to the cells. Afraid we'll smuggle in poison, or a gun maybe," he explained.

"Gagnon!" shouted Jacqueline through the grille on the door. The old man's coughing and wheezing was becoming more severe. "Citizen Gagnon!"

"What is it?" snapped the jailer as he unlocked the door and stepped inside. He looked at Citizen Julien, who was huddled over gasping for air while the boy continued to bang on his back. "Here now, what's his problem?"

"He needs his medicine, which is in a bag downstairs," explained Jacqueline urgently. "The boy must go and fetch it."

"Go on then," said the jailer, motioning to Dénis. "And be quick about it."

The boy raced out of the cell, leaving the old man to the care of Jacqueline.

"A drink—" he managed weakly before heaving into another fit of choking.

"Perhaps you should fetch some water, or wine maybe," she suggested to Gagnon as she helplessly watched the old man hacking and spewing phlegm into his handkerchief.

"No wine!" wheezed Citizen Julien in between coughs.

"Water then," said Jacqueline with a nod to the jailer.

"Do I look like your servant, Citizeness?" he demanded.

The old man let out a horrible, agonizing moan and clutched his chest, gasping for air.

"Please!" begged Jacqueline. "It won't look very good if an agent of the court dies in your wing while you are on duty," she added desperately.

Gagnon scowled. "I'll be back in a minute. I'll leave the door open for the boy, but don't you be thinking about wandering off anywhere, Citizeness," he warned. "If I have to go searching for you, I will demand payment for my trouble, and I might not be satisfied with just your hair. Maybe I'll try some of what Inspector Bourdon came for." He grinned at her, exposing his jagged, rotting teeth before leaving the cell.

He went to his table at the far end of the hall and was irritated to find that the bucket of water he kept there was empty. The old man's dreadful hacking continued to echo through the vaulted corridor. Gagnon decided he had better do what he could to keep the poor bugger from croaking, so he grabbed the battered cup from the bucket and went off toward the east wing, hoping the jailer of that ward had some water handy. He was not concerned in the least that Jacqueline would escape. The Conciergerie was crawling with guards who would take great pleasure in stopping a woman prisoner and punishing her for wandering from her cell.

He returned after a few minutes with the battered cup full of murky water. Citizen Julien's coughing had subsided considerably, and when Gagnon entered the cell he could see the boy had returned with the medicine. The old man, apparently somewhat recovered from his attack, was wheezing as he bent over Jacqueline, who was now lying huddled on her bed.

"There, there now, my dear, it is nothing to be concerned about, a little faintness and chills on the eve of one's execution is perfectly normal," he soothed in a raspy voice. He adjusted the blanket around her shoulders and sighed.

"What's the matter with her?" demanded Gagnon.

The Republic did not approve of its prisoners dying in prison. To do so was to cheat the guillotine of another victim.

"Citizeness Doucette is in need of a little rest," explained the old man. "I fear the excitement of the day has been too much for her."

Gagnon snorted loudly. "Tomorrow she'll be getting all the rest she'll ever need," he joked.

"Quite so," agreed Citizen Julien. "In the meantime, the lad and I will give her a few moments to collect herself before we resume our business." He turned his attention back to his papers and began to read one of them by the dim light of the candle. The youth Dénis, who had been standing in the darkness staring at the woman lying on the bed, sank to the floor, bent his head into his chest, and prepared to take a nap.

"Call me when you want out," said Gagnon with a shrug. He pulled the door shut and locked it.

After a time he could hear the sound of Jacqueline's voice as she dictated a letter to the old man, evidently recovered from her spell. Citizen Julien read the letter back to her, and she pointed out several missing words. Then followed a very loud argument over the price of the old man's services, which nearly sent him into another fit of coughing. The issue was finally resolved, at which point Gagnon could hear Jacqueline begin to sob. Evidently a compassionate man, Citizen Julien fussed over her again as he told her to lie down. A few minutes later the old man called for Gagnon to let him out.

"She is resting again, and should not be disturbed by anyone," said Citizen Julien in a low, grave voice. "Especially that rather volatile young man who was here earlier. Clearly his presence is not welcome," he stated with a raised white eyebrow.

Gagnon shrugged. "Citizen Bourdon is an inspector for the Committee of Public Safety and can see whoever he wants. What he does in this cell is none of my business."

The old man looked at him in disgust. "Citizeness Doucette is sentenced to die tomorrow. Until then she is under your care, and if I hear of any impropriety when I return tomorrow to cut her hair, you can be sure I will report it to Citizen Fouquier-Tinville. Our public prosecutor is a man of the law, and he does not approve of the mistreatment of prisoners who are in the custody of the new Republic."

"You did not cut her hair?" demanded Gagnon with interest. He squinted through the darkness and could see Jacqueline's hair spilling out from underneath the black shawl wrapped around her head and shoulders.

"She was too upset," explained Citizen Julien with a sigh. "I offered to come back and cut it tomorrow so she would not have to suffer the loss of it tonight."

"That was kind of you," murmured Gagnon thoughtfully. Perhaps he would own that golden mane after all.

"Kindness is an act which is too little seen in these difficult times," commented Citizen Julien as he collected his papers and put them into his leather case.

"Careful, Citizen," warned Gagnon. "Lest your words come back to haunt you."

"If they do, I will know who felt they were worthy of repeating, won't I?" said the old man. "Come, Dénis," he called, motioning to the boy. "We have four more clients to see before the night is out."

Dénis handed Citizen Julien his cane, accepted his leather case, and then stood close beside him so he could lean heavily on his shoulder. "I fear I am getting too old for this," Citizen Julien muttered irritably as they slowly shuffled out of the cell.

Gagnon looked at the candle on the table, which had burned down to almost nothing. Citizeness Doucette was sleeping and therefore unaware that the light of her precious candle was being wasted. Gagnon decided to wait until it had burned itself out before coming back to waken her. Then they could make a trade, he thought with satisfaction.

It was not to be. Barely ten minutes later Inspector Bourdon returned and demanded to be let into Citizeness Doucette's cell.

"She had a fainting spell and took to her bed," Gagnon told him as he unlocked the door.

Nicolas peered through the darkness at the sleeping form of Jacqueline, whose glorious hair was down and flowing like a river of honey across her back. He had never seen her with her hair down. The sight of her sleeping peacefully, unsuspecting and vulnerable, made him hard with desire. The candle on the table sputtered and went out.

"Shall I bring you another candle?" offered Gagnon.

"No," replied Nicolas abruptly. "Get out."

The cell was plunged into total darkness as the door eclipsed the faint light of the torch Gagnon held.

Nicolas held his breath as he removed his hat, gloves, overcoat, and jacket. He slowly unfastened his waistcoat and loosened his trousers, savoring the anticipation of finally having what had been denied to him for so long.

"Jacqueline," he called softly as he moved toward the bed. He stood towering over her, clenching and unclenching his hands. "I have returned to finish what we began," he whispered, bracing himself for the pleasure of the struggle that was about to begin. He reached out and touched the silky hair that adorned the thin, coarse blanket covering her. She did not stir. "I am glad you did not cut your hair," he told her as he held her hair in his fist. "It would have marred your beauty, and when I remember you begging me to stop, I want you to be just as perfect as always."

He yanked down hard on her hair, intending to waken her with pain.

"What the—"

He stared in confusion at the golden skein dangling lifelessly in his hand, tied at one end with a length of ribbon.

"What in the name of God—"

He tore away the blanket and wrenched her up from the bed. A terrible roar of rage echoed through the halls as Nicolas realized he held nothing but a tattered silk gown, stuffed with fetid straw and a shapely puff of fine linen petticoats.

Chapter 2

The streets of Paris were unfamiliar to Jacqueline.

Until her father's arrest she had only been in the great city once before, years ago when the Duc de Lambert had taken her and Antoine to see a play at the Comédie-Française. They had arrived in their magnificent carriage, all scarlet and ebony and gold, with the lavish De Lambert crest proudly gracing its doors. Although Jacqueline was only fourteen at the time, her father had permitted her to have her hair elaborately dressed and powdered for the occasion, and she had to be extremely careful as she got in and out of the carriage not to knock the stiff curls that rose in a rigid bouquet somewhere above the top of her head. Her gown was a cumbersome affair of the snowiest silk, richly embroidered with threads of silver and gold. The low-cut, fitted bodice was decorated with a lavish stomacher, a triangular piece heavily encrusted with pearls and sapphires. The beauty of the gown made Jacqueline feel like a princess, and in her heady excitement she imagined meeting a prince who, unaware of her tender years (for she was quite certain she did not look her age), would immediately drop to his knee and profess his undying love at first sight of her. She carried a little white-and-gold lace fan, which she had practiced opening and closing with an accomplished snap in front of a mirror for days. After listening to his wild declarations, she intended to give it to the prince as a token of their meeting, tearfully informing him that despite her womanly appearance, she was in fact too young to marry.

Her father looked magnificent that night as well, gloriously outfitted in a gold brocade jacket, ruffled shirt, white satin culottes, and silk stockings. He carried a gleaming sword at his side with graceful ease, as was expected of an aristocratic gentleman. Even Antoine, who had become rather tall and lean at fifteen, was particularly fine in his blue velvet jacket and silvery waistcoat. Their excursion to Paris was an attempt on the part of the duc to pull himself and his two eldest children out of the self-imposed mourning that had gripped their lives for over a year. Since the unexpected death of Jacqueline's mother, the Château de Lambert had become a quiet, sad place, with little reason for merriment or celebration.

The opulence of that evening in Paris was unlike anything Jacqueline had ever experienced. After the theater the duc took his children and some friends to a fashionable restaurant, where they were attended to by a flock of waiters. A sumptuous five-course meal was ordered, beginning with velvety truffled foie gras and iced oysters, then on to a selection of elaborate dishes made with veal, mutton, duckling, squab, rabbit, beef, capon, partridge, and quail, and finally ending with fresh fruit, compotes, ice cream, cheeses, and pastries. The gay melodies of a string quartet drifted pleasantly around them as the happy group laughed and talked and quenched their thirsts with bottle after bottle of sparkling champagne. When dawn was painting pink-and-gold patterns against the sky, the De Lamberts climbed back into their carriage and returned to their magnificent hotel, where a respectful staff was only too anxious to cater to their every whim. For Jacqueline, Paris was a magical, glittering world of dazzling gowns and exquisite jewels, of theater and music and fine food, of wealthy people enjoying themselves and perfectly content servants seeing to their every comfort. It made life at the Château de Lambert seem rather quiet and provincial by contrast. Not any less enjoyable of course, but not nearly so exciting.

That was in 1788, a year before the start of the revolution. The next time Jacqueline came to the magical city of Paris, it was to see her father in prison.

It was the spring of 1793, and the world that Jacqueline had known had literally turned upside down. In their quest for a new social order, educated, idealistic men like the Duc de Lambert had disputed the absolute power of their king, Louis XVI. In doing so, they introduced a whole new philosophy of society, one based on equality rather than the rigid social hierarchy that had been in place for centuries. The new National Constituent Assembly, of which her father was a member, abolished the ancient system of feudalism and the collection of seigneurial dues and services, and drafted a Declaration of the Rights of Man and the Citizen. As the liberal ideals of equality and liberty took root, the assembly went on to eradicate the age-old privileges of the nobility, including exemption from the *taille* or tax, the use of hereditary titles and coats of arms, the monopoly on high office, and the wearing of the sword. The new France was to be a freethinking society of "citizens," all equal under the law and not burdened by the accident of their birth. It was a romantic, poetic vision, started by aristocratic philosophes like her father and members of the wealthy new bourgeoisie, men who never dreamed that their ideas would quickly race out of control, manipulated and interpreted and perverted into something oppressive and tyrannical. It was not until the National Convention voted to chop off the head of their king, who ruled by the will of God and was supposed to be their partner in the new order, that the former Duc de Lambert realized something was going terribly wrong.

"Stop looking around and keep your head down," commanded Citizen Julien.

Jacqueline obediently snapped her head down and watched her heavy wooden shoes dragging along the cobblestone street. Its broken surface was treacherous, and made more so by the refuse and slops that were carelessly strewn over it. The avenues they were taking were narrow and dark, without any sense of order or logic. They twisted up and down, circling around ancient, decrepit buildings that seemed to house many families, sometimes leading to a tiny square where a small, crumbling church pointed up to a dim patch of sky, and then heading off again into another dank, foul alley that never enjoyed air or light. Jacqueline could hear the screeching and scurrying of rats foraging through garbage. If she closed her eyes she could almost imagine she was back in the halls of the Conciergerie, except that the stench was not quite as oppressive.

When they first left the prison Jacqueline had wanted to run, simply to release herself from the steady grip of the old man and move one foot in front of the other and just run and run, as fast and as long as she could, until she was sure that the guards of La Conciergerie and the jailer Gagnon and the members of the Tribunal and Nicolas Bourdon were far behind her. After passing all those guards and gates in such a slow, shuffling pace, with the terror of discovery churning wildly within her, and Citizen Julien pausing to exchange inane pleasantries with each and every guard they encountered, the exhilaration of walking away from that chamber of death almost made her shriek with excitement. She had started to move faster, and immediately felt the firm pressure of Citizen Julien's ancient hand on her shoulder, restraining her from exceeding his tortoiselike pace.

"Walk," he told her firmly as he continued to shuffle along beside her. Jacqueline realized that Citizen Julien was unable to run, and as he seemed to have some destination in mind, and Jacqueline did not have the faintest idea where she could go to hide from the National Guard that would be sent searching for her, she decided to slow her pace and stay with him, at least for the time being.

The streets were not crowded, and Jacqueline supposed that as it was late, most people were at home taking their supper. The few men they did pass were mostly drunk, hanging about gulping from bottles and glaring at whoever happened to pass by. The men seemed to eye her and the old man with interest, as if they knew there was something peculiar about the duo, or perhaps they were debating whether or not to accost them. Jacqueline felt herself shiver and told herself she was being ridiculous. In her ragged sansculotte outfit, dressed as a boy accompanying a frail old man, it was clear that neither of them could possibly have anything of value. Still, if they were stopped for any reason and it was discovered that she was a woman, she wondered how she would protect herself. Citizen Julien was far too old and feeble to render her any assistance, despite his planning and quick action during their escape.

After Gagnon had left the cell in search of water, Jacqueline was startled to see her elderly patient, still coughing and wheezing hard enough to burst a lung, rise from his chair and quickly open his enormous black coat, revealing a series of deep pockets bulging in the bottom half of the lining. From each pocket he produced an article of clothing that he threw at her, motioning for her to change into them quickly. Momentarily stunned, she simply stood clutching the garments to her chest, and was prodded into action only when he stepped behind her and deftly removed her shawl and unfastened the back of her dress. Without pausing to see if she was indeed going to change, he turned his attention to her bed, which he stripped of its blanket and began to fill with filthy straw from the floor. As Jacqueline stepped out of her gown and petticoats, Citizen Julien scooped them up and proceeded to stuff the dress with the soft linen. He created a rather well-endowed form, which he laid on the bed, carefully arranging the skirt of the gown over the mound of straw. Jacqueline continued to don the filthy, coarse outfit he had provided her, realizing by now that the clothes exactly matched those worn by Dénis. Citizen Julien artfully wrapped her shawl around a clump of straw before placing it at the head of the bed and pulling its edges over the shoulders of her gown. He then reached inside his coat and produced a pair of scissors and a piece of ribbon. Still coughing and wheezing away, he knotted the ribbon around her hair and hacked off a length of perhaps fifteen inches or more.

Jacqueline watched with a twinge of regret as the old man tucked the end of her hair under the shawl and then fanned the rest of it out so it spilled gloriously over the shoulders and back of her silk gown. He reached into two pockets near the hem of his coat and produced a pair of sabots. Jacqueline removed her silk brocade high heels and pulled on the clumsy wooden shoes as Citizen Julien placed hers at the edge of the bed where they could be seen. Having lost almost two inches in height, Jacqueline now closely matched the stature of the boy. She stuffed what remained of her hair into the red woolen cap as Citizen Julien generously applied some dirt to her face, neck, and hands. He then turned and pulled the blanket up over the sleeping form on the bed, fussing and wheezing just as Gagnon walked into the cell carrying a cup of water.

Jacqueline froze, waiting for Gagnon to see that she was not the boy. But the jailer ignored her. He seemed much more concerned about his prisoner in the bed than the youth who stood in the shadows watching. Jacqueline had to admit that in the dim light the figure lying on the bed was rather convincing. Citizen Julien calmly returned to his papers and Jacqueline decided to sit on the floor and pretend to nap. Gagnon, evidently feeling that all was well, shrugged his shoulders and left the cell.

What followed was sheer torture for Jacqueline. Instead of waiting a few minutes and then asking to be let out, Citizen Julien continued with his assignment as if nothing had happened. He made Jacqueline dictate a letter to him, then slowly read it back to her before engaging in a loud argument over his abilities and his prices. He told her to sob and once again went through the motions of fussing over the sleeping form on the bed before finally asking Gagnon to let him out. Despite her terror of being caught, Jacqueline could not help but admire the old man's calm presence of mind. As they left the cell and shuffled slowly down the hall, Jacqueline expected at any moment that Gagnon would call out for them to stop. With every guard and gate they passed she was certain she would be discovered. But the guards were evidently accustomed to the coming and going of visitors, and as Citizen Julien's official papers for himself and the boy were all in order, no one seemed interested in delaying the passage of the coughing, wheezing old man and the filthy, ragged youth who accompanied him.

They were walking along a street that enjoyed considerably more activity than the others they had taken. Lively music was spilling out from a café at the end of the road, and colorfully dressed women were standing in doorsteps calling out to the men stumbling drunkenly along the street. A fleshy woman, fairly bursting out of the wrinkled red satin dress she had somehow squeezed herself into, left her post at the side of the street and approached Citizen Julien.

"A chilly night, isn't it, Citizen?" she asked as she dropped the thin cloak around her shoulders to reveal a bulging bust. She stank of wine and too much cheap perfume.

"It is indeed," agreed Citizen Julien, who kept his gnarled hand on Jacqueline's shoulder and continued walking.

"Perhaps you need someone to warm you up," the woman said suggestively.

"I am afraid, my dear, that I am too old to accept such a kind offer," replied Citizen Julien.

Undaunted, the woman pulled up her cloak and began to walk with them. She fixed her gaze on Jacqueline.

"Pretty boy," she remarked. Jacqueline could see that the woman's wig was in much need of a dressing, and her heavily painted face made her look old beyond her years. "You done it yet, lad?" the woman demanded as she grabbed Jacqueline's grubby hand and pressed it to her ample breast.

With a stifled cry of horror Jacqueline wrenched her hand away. She felt Citizen Julien wrap his arm tightly around her shoulders, and the woman laughed.

"Shy, are we?" she snorted. She turned her attention back to Citizen Julien. "It's been a slow night. I'll do the boy for half price."

"That is very generous of you," acknowledged Citizen Julien with a nod. "But the lad and I are in a hurry and simply cannot spare the time. Perhaps another evening," he suggested as he continued to steer Jacqueline down the noisy, crowded street.

"To hell with you then," snapped the woman, clearly insulted. She turned away in a swish of crushed satin and cheap perfume.

Two men who had been watching the exchange now started to follow them. One of them carried a half-empty liquor bottle, which he lifted high to drink from with every few paces, while the other mimicked the hunched and shuffling gait of Citizen Julien, much to the amusement of the prostitutes who watched from the side of the street. It was obvious to Jacqueline that the men were drunk and looking for a little distraction. Citizen Julien ignored them and continued to guide her down the street. The men and women standing outside the café began to call out to the little procession, laughing heartily at the antics of the two burly men behind them. Fear began to creep up Jacqueline's spine. She wondered if the men would soon tire of their game and want to do more than simply mock them. If they were attacked, Citizen Julien was far too old and frail to protect either himself or her, and she did not think she could defend herself against two men. If it was discovered that she was an escaped aristocrat, she did not want to consider what this crowd might do to her.

Citizen Julien did not seem to notice the two drunken, heavyset men behind them. He continued to shuffle along in a slow and steady pace, keeping his grip on Jacqueline and leaning heavily on his cane. They came to the end of the street and started down another empty alley. The men followed them, and Jacqueline wondered how Citizen Julien could not be aware of their threatening presence.

"Citizen Julien," she whispered nervously as she leaned in to him, "I believe we are being followed."

"What? What's that? Followed?" he cried out loudly, looking around in obvious confusion. He turned, noticed the men, and smiled. "Oh, good evening, Citizens," he said pleasantly. "Going our way?"

One of the men stepped forward, took a long draft from his bottle, and then wiped his mouth on the sleeve of his stained jacket before speaking. "Seems to me you and the boy insulted Lucille," he drawled out. "What do you think, Georges?"

"Saw it with my own eyes," agreed the other in slow, slurred words. "She looked mighty upset."

"Good Citizens, no insult was intended, I can assure you," rasped Citizen Julien hastily as he released his grip on Jacqueline's shoulder and slowly moved in front of her. "If I have offended either of you, please accept my sincerest apologies," he continued humbly.

The man named Georges burst out laughing. "Apologies?" He sneered in disbelief and took a menacing step forward. "Tell you what, old man. Give us your money, and we'll just forget the whole thing."

Citizen Julien considered for a moment and then sighed. "These times of change are difficult for all of us," he remarked sympathetically. "How can I refuse to share my meager earnings with a fellow citizen in need?" He reached inside the deep folds of his enormous overcoat and produced a small, worn leather purse. He opened it up and calmly extracted a few notes.

"All of it," commanded the man with the bottle.

Citizen Julien stared at his purse regretfully a moment, and then tossed it onto the ground, where it lay at the feet of the man named Georges. He bent and greedily snatched it up to examine its contents.

"I trust we may go now?" asked Citizen Julien, still appearing quite tranquil as he leaned heavily on his cane.

"Not just yet," said the man with the bottle. He stared at Citizen Julien. "That looks like a very warm coat you're wearing, Citizen. Give it over."

"He will freeze!" protested Jacqueline, outraged by the man's demand.

The man shrugged his shoulders. "That's his problem,

not mine." He stepped closer to her and spat on the ground. "I'll have your jacket, too, boy. And your shoes."

Jacqueline hesitated. She had no idea how much further they had to go, but without her shoes and with Citizen Julien freezing in the November night air, she did not think they would make it.

"I said hand them over boy," repeated the man menacingly. "Now."

"No," she snapped, her heart racing with fear and fury. She realized she had no choice. She would have to fight these men, and she looked about desperately for something to use as a weapon.

"Now, now, Jacques, let us not be selfish," interjected Citizen Julien in a soft, scolding tone. "Such behavior is unworthy of a true citizen."

Jacqueline stared at him in disbelief. He actually seemed to be more concerned about her behavior than about the fact that they were being robbed of their money and their clothes. She wondered if perhaps his mind was weak from age.

"It is evident to me the needs of these men outweigh our own. We must try to help them," he soothed as he slowly began to undo the buttons on his coat. "After all, what is a coat or a pair of shoes between brothers of the revolution?" he asked philosophically.

"Shut up and be quick about it," snapped Georges.

Citizen Julien appeared to be having some trouble with his buttons. "I fear my fingers are too aged to manage the last few," he murmured apologetically. "Perhaps, my friend, you would be kind enough to assist?" he asked the man with the bottle.

The man stepped toward him, leaned down, and began to fumble with the last few buttons. As soon as he bent his head to see to the task, Citizen Julien swung his cane high above his head and brought it crashing down on the back of the man's skull. The man groaned and slumped onto the ground.

"What the hell—" shouted his companion furiously as he lurched toward Citizen Julien.

Jacqueline reached down and grabbed the liquor bottle the other man had dropped. As Citizen Julien pulled his pasty fist back to drive it into the face of his attacker, Jacqueline lifted her weapon into the night sky and then smashed it down on the assailant's head. The bottle broke, blood gushed into the wool of the man's red cap, and without the slightest murmur he fell to the ground beside his friend. Citizen Julien, his fist suspended in mid-air, stared at her in amazement.

"It would appear you really did attack a captain of the National Guard with a chamber pot," he remarked with surprise.

Jacqueline turned over the body of Georges and searched his pockets for Citizen Julien's purse. She put it back into Citizen Julien's coat and quickly did up his buttons. "Let's get out of here," she said as she grabbed his arm and offered her support. "They may have friends who come looking for them."

They hurried down the dark alley and wove their way up and down several more. No one followed them. They trudged along together in the cold for what seemed like miles. Freezing and exhausted, Jacqueline was about to ask Citizen Julien if perhaps he was lost when he finally stopped in front of a narrow, decrepit building. Its stone front was pocked and crumbling, the shutters over its windows were peeling and hanging at haphazard angles. A sign indicated that it was an inn, although if not for the sign, Jacqueline would never have believed people actually paid to stay here. Citizen Julien banged the knocker against the cracked wood door, and after a few moments a thin, mean-looking little man appeared. He stared at them suspiciously a moment, his eyes shining in the light of his candle like two tiny black beads, and then an expression of recognition crossed his face.

"So you're finally back," he muttered irritably as he held the door open for them.

"Unfortunately, Citizen Dufresne, the work my grandson found took longer than we expected," explained Citizen Julien apologetically. They followed the innkeeper to a small desk in the hall, where he opened a drawer and selected a key.

"Water's up there, like you ordered, but it's cold by now." Dufresne shrugged. His tone indicated he had absolutely no intention of reheating it.

"That is fine," replied Citizen Julien with a nod.

The scrawny innkeeper lifted his candle high as he led them up the stairway. "Did you hear how many heads they cut today?" he asked.

"No," replied Citizen Julien.

"Thirty-two," Citizen Dufresne told him with satisfaction. "Thirty-two heads in just twenty-five minutes. The people's ax grows more efficient every day."

"So it would seem," agreed Citizen Julien.

The innkeeper unlocked a door, stepped into the room, and lit a candle on a small table beside the bed. He turned, holding his candle at his chest. The dim glow it threw onto his sunken face gave him a ghoulish look. "My wife went down to watch. Said it was beautiful. A whole family of aristos brought to justice. Husband, wife, and all their brats. Said the mother insisted the children go first, so they wouldn't have to watch their parents die. Sanson refused to let the mother accompany them onto the platform, so she stood and sang to them from the steps." He laughed, a whining, nasal sound that made his bony frame quiver with enjoyment. "Can you imagine that?"

"No," whispered Jacqueline in horror.

Dufresne looked at her with amusement. "You should take the boy down to have a look one day," he told Citizen Julien as he moved toward the door. "Toughen him up."

"I'll do that," agreed Citizen Julien. "Good night, Citizen." He closed the door and locked it.

"I cannot stay here," Jacqueline announced the minute they were alone. "I will not sleep under the same roof with that horrible man and his evil wife."

Citizen Julien slowly turned from the door, leaning

heavily on his cane. "You have no choice," he stated calmly.

"I would rather sleep on the street," she protested.

"I doubt that," remarked Citizen Julien as he walked past her. He laid his cane on a wooden chair beside the bed and removed his black felt hat.

"At least on the street one can fight back," argued Jacqueline angrily as she paced the floor of the small room. "And as you have seen, I am quite capable of defending myself," she boasted, thinking back to their skirmish with the two drunks.

"You did not do such an admirable job of defending yourself before the Tribunal today," commented Citizen Julien as he began to undo the buttons on his heavy overcoat. "I seem to recall you being sentenced to death."

"That was different," Jacqueline returned irritably. "My sentence was a matter of the corruption of the law, predetermined before I even stepped into the courtroom. Surely you can see that is not the same as fighting in the streets."

"Mademoiselle de Lambert," began Citizen Julien, using the ancient title that had been banned from usage for over three years, "what I see is a roof over our head and a bed that has relatively clean sheets. On that stand is a pitcher of clean water and a basin to wash in. Since this room is fully paid for, and since we do have a choice about sleeping in the streets or not, I believe I would prefer it if we decided to stay." Without waiting for her to respond, he began to unbutton his jacket and tugged on the end of his cravat.

"Perhaps you are right," conceded Jacqueline as she looked longingly at the basin of water. A threadbare towel with a sliver of soap lay on the stand beside it. She suddenly remembered that she was covered with filth from the prison floor, and the idea of removing it was overwhelmingly appealing.

"Of course you must have the bed," she offered generously as she poured some water into the basin, knowing full well that the old man would never accept.

"If you insist," replied Citizen Julien as he sat on the mattress and removed his boots. He looked up to see her holding the jug and staring at him in surprise. "Naturally, you are welcome to share it with me," he amended, gesturing to the side against the wall. "I can assure you that you need have no fear of your honor. Other than ourselves, no one will ever know of our sleeping arrangement." He dropped his heavy boot to the floor.

"Very well," replied Jacqueline slowly as she turned away from him. She did not like the idea of sharing a bed, but the bare floor was cold and hard and she did not believe that under these extremely unusual circumstances the rules of propriety could be applied. After all, Citizen Julien was old and arthritic, and she really should not expect him to sleep on the floor. They would both simply keep their clothes on and there would be nothing improper about it. Somewhat assuaged by that thought, Jacqueline removed her woolen cap and jacket, rolled up her shirtsleeves, and set to the task of washing herself.

"I would like to thank you for freeing me from La Conciergerie," she told him as she closed her eyes and soaped up her face and neck with the harsh-smelling sliver provided. "I never dreamed that anyone would be sent to rescue me."

"It seemed fortunate I arrived when I did," commented Citizen Julien.

She knew he was referring to Nicolas attacking her, but she was too embarrassed by the incident to discuss it. She splashed herself with cold water and soaped up her skin again, convinced that one washing would not remove the stench. "Of course I realize, Citizen Julien, that you must have a plan in mind, but if you intend for me to leave Paris, I should tell you there is something I must do before I can go. As you are aware, my brother Antoine was arrested at the same time I was. I will not leave until I find out whether or not he is alive." She rinsed herself a second time with water and then began to rub her skin vigorously with the coarse towel. "If he is alive, then I intend to rescue him. Naturally I do not expect you to risk

your life for my sake yet again. Although you were successful today, I hope you will not be offended if I tell you
that perhaps you are too old to be engaging in such dangerous ventures. The need to move quickly is vital, and I
am sure you will agree that your advanced age does not
allow you to—" She stopped suddenly and stared, confused by the sight that greeted her.

Citizen Julien had removed his snowy-white hair and
was raking his hand through a length of growth that was
obviously his own, hair that held not the slightest tinge of
gray. It was fair in color, not quite blond, and not quite
brown, but rather an even mixture of the two, with
threads of copper liberally mixed in. He stood with his
back to her, and Jacqueline noticed that his stooped, fragile body was now perfectly erect and bore no resemblance
to the hunched frame he had affected just moments before. Citizen Julien was actually very tall, with enormously broad shoulders. He had removed his jacket and
waistcoat and stood only in his shirt and trousers, revealing a firm, narrow waist and long, powerful legs. Unaware of her watching him, he wearily rubbed the back of
his neck and slowly lowered his head from side to side,
grunting with satisfaction at the loud cracking sounds that
rewarded his efforts. Then he undid the buttons on his
shirt and began to shrug out of it, revealing a muscular,
bronzed back and arms that contrasted sharply with the
pale, spotted skin on his hands. He turned suddenly, perhaps finally having noticed that the room had gone very
quiet, and found her staring at him, her eyes wide with
shock.

"I am, perhaps, not quite as old as you seem to think,"
he suggested. His eyes held just the barest hint of amusement as he met her gaze before continuing with the removal of his shirt.

"Who are you?" stammered Jacqueline, her mind racing with confusion. His face was still wrinkled and white
like his hands, but it was no longer a face to match the
body that carried it. His expression had changed, softened
somehow. His eyes seemed larger and the deep grooves

around them and in his forehead were now but hints of wrinkles that were yet to come.

He ignored her question and walked past her to the washstand. He took the bowl to the window and heaved its contents onto the ground before filling it from the jug and bending over to wash his own face, neck, and hands. He took his time, making sure to use the soap right up into his hairline and down his neck to his collarbone. When he had finally finished and stood there toweling himself off, Jacqueline could only stare, amazed by the transformation that had occurred.

Gone was the frail old man with the pale, wizened skin, white, scraggly hair, bent, arthritic frame, and slow, shuffling gait. In his place stood a handsome man of strength and vitality, who towered above her and seemed to fill the tiny room with an intense, restrained power. His eyes were an indescribable color, perhaps blue, but then again perhaps more green. His face was ruggedly cut, with definition to his cheekbones, a perfectly straight nose, and a strong, square jawline. Fine lines were etched in his forehead and around his eyes, lines that had appeared far deeper and more numerous with the skillful application of cosmetics. They might have been lines of laughter, but something in the intensity of his gaze told Jacqueline they were more likely to be caused by anger, or perhaps pain. His massive chest and narrow waist were well defined by thick layers of muscle; his heavy arms looked like they could easily crush a person in their embrace. He ignored Jacqueline as she continued to stare, walked over to the bed, and drew down its covers.

"Who are you?" she repeated, having gotten control of some of her surprise.

He shrugged his enormous shoulders. "Tonight I am Citizen Julien. For now, that is all you need to know." He lay down on the bed, pulled the covers up, and closed his eyes, obviously deciding the conversation was over.

"Why did you save me?" demanded Jacqueline.

"Because you needed saving," he replied indifferently as he rolled over and faced the wall.

Jacqueline stood and stared in confusion at him. How could she not have seen that he was not what he appeared to be? Of course the cell and the streets had been very dark, and his voice and mannerisms were most convincing. But once they were well on their way, how could she not have noticed that despite his maddeningly slow and shuffling gait, his grip on her shoulder always remained firm, his steps never faltered, and he never seemed to require any rest. Most of all, why did she not wonder at the strength he exhibited when he brought his cane down on the thug who tried to rob them, or the ease and confidence with which he drew back his pasty fist to smash it into the face of the other? These were not the actions of an old, frail man. These were the actions of a young, strong man in an exceptionally clever disguise. A man who knew his way around a prison. A man who spoke easily with guards and jailers and could offer authentic-looking identification papers. A man who risked his life to save condemned aristocrats. Understanding plunged into her like a knife.

"You are the one they call the Black Prince!" she exclaimed in a whisper. "I heard the guards and prisoners talking about you. You snatch condemned and persecuted aristocrats and their families out from under the nose of the National Guard and the Committee of Public Safety and smuggle them out of France. You are never accurately described because you have never worn the same disguise twice. Your escapes are a legend among the ancien régime and counterrevolutionaries. They even say you are related to King Louis the Sixteenth himself, through the bloodlines of one of his grandfather's secret bastards." She stared at his massive form lying on the bed, her voice clearly filled with awe.

He turned toward her and carelessly propped himself up on one elbow, his eyes again reflecting a trace of amusement. "You flatter me, Mademoiselle. Although I must admit, at this particular moment I almost wish that I could be this character, this Black Prince you evidently so admire." He paused and slowly swept his gaze over her from head to foot, as if he were trying to imagine what she looked like under her loose and filthy sansculotte outfit. "It would perhaps be interesting to see how a true aristocrat like you would show your gratitude to a man driven by such pure and noble intentions."

His tone was grossly sarcastic, and the leering way he looked at her made her uneasy, embarrassed, causing her to fold her arms across her chest. She must have made a mistake. The man known as the Black Prince was rumored to be a distant cousin to the royal family, perhaps not a duc, but at the very least a marquis. A gentleman of noble birth would not speak so to a lady, nor was it proper for any man to ogle her in such a way. She lifted her chin and gave him a condescending look, determined to put him in his place. "If you are not he, then who are you and why did you put yourself in such peril to rescue me?" she demanded in a properly frigid voice.

Evidently finished with his scrutiny of her, he fell back against the pillow and wearily closed his eyes. "Unfortunately, Mademoiselle, I am merely a man of business, without any royalist sympathies or bloodlines lurking in my background to lend chivalry to my actions. And you, Mademoiselle, are my business."

"What do you mean?" Jacqueline asked, still confused. "Almost all of my father's properties and investments were confiscated by the revolutionary government when he was condemned. The Château de Lambert had already been transferred to Antoine's name before my father was found guilty, but I am sure those crooks have taken it over by now as well. Since I no longer own anything and I have no money, how can my escape possibly aid your business?"

He yawned and rudely turned away from her. "I said *you* are my business," he told her impatiently. "You are a package I have agreed to deliver." He adjusted the blanket over his shoulder and prepared to go to sleep.

"A package?" repeated Jacqueline in confusion. Understanding dawned on her. "Do you mean to tell me that you are rescuing me for money?" Her incredulously haughty tone indicated what she thought of that reason.

"Not noble enough for you?" he drawled sarcastically. "Strange, but I would have thought that keeping your head attached to your neck would have been all that interested you."

"Naturally I am grateful for your services," Jacqueline allowed. "It's just that you are making your living out of the misery and suffering of others, and such a career could hardly be described as admirable."

"It could just as easily be said that I am making a career preventing the misery and suffering of others, and such a career is a hell of a lot more admirable than taxing hardworking peasants into a state of starvation so that you and your family can live in grandeur."

Jacqueline gasped in outrage at his insolent remark. "It was a system that had been in place for hundreds of years, a system created by God!" she told him heatedly.

He turned to look at her. "How utterly convenient," he drawled, "for you."

She glared at him. That the man would dare to criticize her class, in the face of this evil revolution, and on what had been the eve of her execution, was simply unbelievable. It was obvious he was not of counterrevolutionary or royalist sympathies, and in her mind that made him dangerous. If he was only saving her for money, undoubtedly because Sir Edward Harrington, her father's friend in England to whom she had entrusted the care of her sisters, had hired him, could he not just as easily be swayed to give her back to the revolutionary government if the reward was large enough? Of course that would damage his reputation among those who sought his services, but he might be clever enough to make it look like she was recaptured as they tried to escape Paris. She wondered if Sir Edward had been foolish enough to pay him in advance.

"Are you coming to bed?" he demanded irritably.

"You cannot expect me to share that bed with you!" she blurted out, momentarily distracted from her thoughts.

"Suit yourself." He shrugged. "Although I do not believe you will find the floor to your liking." He raised himself up to blow out the candle and the room was drowned in darkness.

"I believe good manners dictate that I should have the bed and you should have the floor," pointed out Jacqueline, deciding to leave the possibility of him betraying her aside for the moment. She was very tired, and if he did intend to return her, he would probably not do so tonight. He would wait to see what kind of reward was offered first.

"I believe logic dictates that since the bed is large enough, we share it," he replied shortly.

The idea was preposterous. The act of lying down beside an ancient old man, whom Jacqueline had considered feeble and arthritic and incapable of posing any threat to her, was bad enough. But to stretch out beside a strong, vital man, who undoubtedly had the same uncontrollable, animalistic urges that Nicolas did, was utterly impossible. He might even interpret her willingness to share a bed as a sign that she would welcome his advances. "I will not get into that bed with you!" she snapped.

"Then don't," he remarked in a tone of complete indifference.

Jacqueline stood and stared at his dark form on the bed with growing fury. She knew that since the revolution, good manners had become suspect and largely a thing of the past, but the idea that this man, who was being paid to save her and should be considerate of her comfort, would not give up the bed for her was truly galling. Resigned to spending the night in the chair, she stomped toward it in the darkness, and let out a yelp of pain as she banged her shin against its hard wooden leg.

"Keep it down," grumbled the stranger sleepily.

Infuriated beyond measure, at both him and the offending chair, she snatched his clothes and cane up from it and pitched them to the floor. The cane landed with a heavy clatter and rolled noisily to the other side of the room.

"Do you mind?" he muttered, half sitting up. "Some of us require at least a minimal amount of sleep," he grumbled before settling down again.

"Pardon me," bit out Jacqueline as she seated herself in the chair. It was hard and extremely uncomfortable. She twisted and turned in it a few times to see if she could find a more restful position. She could not. She curled her legs up onto the chair, but found this left her knees painfully wedged between the supports of the arm. She tried to sit in the chair sideways, with her legs draped over the arm, only to find the hard edge of the other arm digging into her spine. She repositioned herself again, leaned back, folded her arms across her chest, and gritted her teeth, determined that, comfortable or not, she was going to sleep. Within a few minutes her whole body began to quiver. Now that she had stopped moving, she realized the room was unbearably cold. She would have to stumble around in the dark again to find her jacket, which was coarse and filthy and smelled offensive.

Loud snoring was rising from the mound on the bed. It was quite evident that Citizen Julien, or whoever he was, had not encountered the least bit of difficulty in falling asleep. Despite the fact of his bare shoulders, he was evidently quite comfortable. Of course, he did have the advantage of a sheet and blanket.

Noiselessly slipping out of her wooden sabots, she crept through the darkness over to the bed. Citizen Julien did not stir, but continued his deep, even snoring. Jacqueline could see that he lay on his side, with one heavy arm casually draped against his waist, pinning the blanket to his body. She reached out hesitantly and grasped hold of the blanket below his arm. Slowly, carefully, she began to ease the woolen fabric down along the length of him, holding the sheet in place with her other hand so he would not waken with the sudden sensation of cold air. She was surprised and pleased to find she could feel his warmth retained in the blanket. Evidently he manufactured a great deal of heat on his own and would probably not miss the blanket at all. She had almost moved it down to his waist when suddenly he rolled over onto his back, made a low, irritated growl, and yanked the blanket back up over his chest. Jacqueline froze, terrified that she had been discovered. But he gave no sign of having awakened. His snores once again became deep and even, and his eyes remained firmly shut. Jacqueline let out a small breath of relief.

The problem was that now his hand actually gripped the blanket, making it impossible for her to move it without his knowledge. She would have to get him to release his hand before she could proceed. She took a step closer to him and bent down low. With one hand firmly grasping the blanket and her lips positioned just inches away from his ear, she shaped her mouth into a tiny circle and very gently began to blow, a soft, fluttering little breath that made the length of hair lying against his ear begin to dance and tickle him. At first he merely frowned, his eyebrows knitting together in profound irritation. She blew a little harder, and to her delight his hand released the blanket and moved up to scratch the offending ear. Quick as a whip she yanked down the blanket and clutched it to her chest. His tickling problem solved, the stranger sighed and contentedly laid his arm once again on his chest. Barely able to contain her smugness, Jacqueline turned from the bed to wrap herself in her prize.

Strong hands clamped around her waist with an iron grip, and before she knew what she was about, she was sailing through the air and landed with a thud on the mattress beside him, still clinging to the blanket. The stranger held her down with one hand and looked at her with amusement.

"There are two lessons you have learned tonight," he remarked. "The first, never assume your opponent is sleeping, unless you have personally drugged him or knocked him over the head. The second, if it is at all possible, make sure you get a decent night's sleep." Still holding her down, he disentangled her from the blanket and arranged it over both of them. Then he lowered himself to the mattress and casually flung his arm over her, effectively pinning her to the bed. "Now be a good mademoiselle and show me how well you have learned the second lesson," he finished, in much the same tone one would use on a naughty child.

"Let me go!" hissed Jacqueline as she struggled against his hold and tried to sit up. His response was to tighten his arm around her and haul her even closer against his body.

"It was warmth you were seeking, was it not?" he demanded roughly. "You waste your energy and precious sleep with this nonsense. We still have far to go before you are safe. Lie still and go to sleep." Evidently thinking the matter settled, he closed his eyes.

Mere seconds later a sharp pain assaulted his shoulder, and his eyes flew open to see Jacqueline hanging on to him with her teeth.

With a soft oath he grabbed her by what remained of her hair and yanked her head back so that she was forced to release his shoulder. She let out a cry of pain and then glared at him furiously as he gripped her by her hair.

"Do you really wish to sleep in the chair that much?" he demanded in a tightly controlled voice.

"It is not that I wish to sleep in the chair, it is that I do not wish to sleep with you!" she hissed, her eyes smarting from the pain in her scalp.

He was silent for a moment, as if he was somehow confused or surprised by that statement. Suddenly his grip on her hair relaxed and he moved away from her. "Mademoiselle," he began in an incredulous tone, "when exactly was the last time you bathed?"

"How dare you!" spat Jacqueline as she freed herself and sat bolt upright on the bed.

"I mean no insult," he swiftly qualified. "It's just that if you are worried about your precious virtue, I would like to set your mind at ease. My preference is for women who have bathed, at least sometime within the not too distant past. I realize your friend who visited you before me was not quite so discriminating, and perhaps that is what has given you cause for concern." He turned away from her and adjusted his half of the blanket over his shoulder. "You may share this bed with me and rest completely assured that even if you were stark naked and willing, I would not have the slightest desire of laying a hand on you."

A mixture of humiliation and fury boiled up inside Jacqueline. It was true, she realized, she was sorely in need of a bath. But the rooms at La Conciergerie did not include hot water and a maid service, she thought sarcastically. How dare this vulgar, low-minded lout comment on the miserable state of her hygiene, or tell her boldly that he did not desire her. He was discourteous beyond belief. Still, she had to admit, it did make her feel a little safer. Perhaps in her present condition she truly was offensive enough to repel a man. Well, if so, that suited her perfectly.

"Move over," she ordered sharply as she gave the pillow on what was to be her side a whack.

He sighed impatiently and moved a bit to accommodate her. Jacqueline lay down and primly drew the blanket up to her chin. The space he offered her had already been warmed by the heat of his body. In fact, after a few minutes she found that she could feel the heat of him radiating across the few scant inches that separated them. It filtered through the coarse wool of her shirt and trousers and warmed her chilled flesh. It had been a long time since she had felt warm in bed.

At home, Henriette used to heat the icy sheets of her enormous bed during the winter with a long-handled brass pan filled with hot coals. That was very nice, but inevitably during the night the effect would wear off and she would find herself huddled beneath a mountain of blankets trying not to move out of the last remaining warm spot. During her long nights at the Conciergerie, she had tried unsuccessfully to control the terrible chills that assaulted her every time she crawled into her rickety little trestle bed, fully clothed and with only one thin blanket to offer her any comfort. This unfamiliar sensation of heat was absolutely delicious. It made her very sleepy. She

allowed herself a muffled sigh of pleasure and unconsciously huddled closer to its source.

"Good night, Mademoiselle."

The unexpected voice jolted her back to wakefulness.
With a little gasp she rolled over, moving as far away
from him as the limits of the bed would allow.

Chapter 3

When she awoke the next morning she was cold. The room was washed in a dull gray from the sun that had filtered its way through the cracked wooden shutters over the window. A stream of dust motes lazily floated and twirled in the soft shafts spilling across the bare floor. Jacqueline closed her eyes and sleepily burrowed her face back into the pillow, idly wondering where she was and how she had come to be here.

She was alone.

That was the realization that forced her eyes open again and made her look around the room. There was no sign of him anywhere. His clothes, his hat, his great heavy overcoat, his cane, everything about him was missing. Citizen Julien was gone.

She threw back the covers and leapt from the bed, telling herself it could not be. She scanned the room for a note of some kind, telling her that he had only gone out for a moment, and not to be concerned, he would be returning for her shortly. There was none. A small feeling of panic began to grip her. For the first time in her life, she was utterly alone. He knew she had no money, no food, and no identification papers. How would she be able to find Antoine and rescue him if she could not even feed herself? And why would Citizen Julien, or whoever he was, desert her like this after taking such immense risks to save her? Surely his contract required him not just to liberate her from the prison, but to actually deliver her to someone. Sir Edward undoubtedly would have wanted her to go to a relative or friend in another part of France until the political situation was restored to normal. The possibility of the stranger's betrayal leapt back into her mind. Perhaps he really did intend to return her to the Conciergerie after all. It was possible he was out negotiating the terms of his reward with the Committee of Public Safety this very moment. If she was arrested again, she would be guillotined before the day was out, of that she was absolutely certain. The people who attended the daily executions would undoubtedly take great pleasure in watching one who had almost escaped have their head triumphantly thrust through the "Republican window."

She snatched up her jacket from where it lay on the chair and began to stuff the remains of her hair back into the red woolen cap. Her fingers slowed as they touched the raggedly chopped ends of what was once considered a precious asset. Her hair had always been gloriously thick and long, flowing down to the base of her spine. Since she was a child people used to remark on its unusual weight and shine. When she was very small her mother would weave it into a tight braid after her bath so the next day it could be brushed into a honey gold cape of ripples. The pitifully cropped locks that remained barely touched her shoulders. It could have been your head, she reminded herself impatiently as she yanked the rough cap low over her forehead. If you succeed in keeping yourself alive, it will grow back.

She wrenched down the handle on the door and found it was locked. She rattled it a few times to make sure. The fact that he had left her a prisoner by locking her in made her suspicions more credible. If Citizen Julien's intentions were purely to rescue her, why then would he find it necessary to lock her up? And why would he sneak out without telling her where he was going? Perhaps his plan was that while she slept he would go out and fetch the National Guard. Right now they were probably on their way, thinking to arrest her in bed. Well, they would not find her there.

She considered banging on the door and yelling until the innkeeper Dufresne came to let her out, but quickly decided against it. It would be risky to draw such attention to herself, and Dufresne might wonder himself why her "grandfather," or whoever it was Citizen Julien was supposed to be, would lock the boy up when he went out. She did not need anyone slowing her down with their suspicious questions.

She rushed to the window, banged it open, and threw the shutters wide. A blast of icy sharp air flooded the room. Jacqueline looked down to see a tiny enclosure, which might once have been a yard of sorts, but at the moment it was nothing more than a mess of dead weeds, broken bricks, and garbage. Haphazardly strung ropes crisscrossed between the buildings, heavy with faded, much-mended laundry, which had been abandoned overnight and was now stiff from the frigid air. She was only on the second story of the inn, but the drop to the ground was considerable. She leaned out to look at the building next to the inn. It was a single story, and its roof almost touched the side of the inn. A narrow ledge ran below her window right to the edge of the wall, and she felt almost certain that she could carefully step along it without too much risk. Once she reached the corner she could climb down onto the next roof, and from there she would figure out a way to get to the ground. She checked to see if there was anything she could hold on to. The battered shutters that hung from all the windows looked like they would probably be strong enough to offer her sufficient support as she shuffled along the ledge. She braced her hands on the windowsill and took a deep breath, preparing to swing her leg over.

"Do you find it too warm in here?"

With a startled gasp she leapt from the window and spun around. Citizen Julien had returned. He was standing in the doorway scowling at her, once again fully made up as the old man. He stepped into the room and the immediate effect was that the space became smaller somehow, as if whoever designed it had never planned on such a large visitor. He shut the door and locked it before slowly straightening up from his bent, arthritic position.

Jacqueline realized it must be difficult for him to remain hunched over like that for hours at a time. He twisted his head from side to side and rolled his shoulders before looking at her.

"I went out to get a few supplies," he told her curtly, as if he knew she had found his disappearance suspicious and was annoyed at her for that.

"Why didn't you waken me?" she asked as she nonchalantly closed the window.

"You needed your sleep." He deposited several packages onto the bed. "I felt it was better for you to rest than to traipse around after me." He began to unwrap one of the packages.

Jacqueline stepped over to the bed to see what he had bought, feeling only partially appeased by his explanation. She could not trust anyone, she reminded herself. From now on her life depended on her alone. Nevertheless, she could not help but experience a pronounced twinge of guilt over her accusing thoughts as she saw the gifts he was laying out for her.

On the blanket sat a loaf of dark bread, a thick wedge of cheese, some cold, sliced beef, several apples and pears, and two freshly made apricot tartlets, glistening with a sugary glaze. Knowing how scarce bread and meat were in the city, Jacqueline could not imagine how he had managed to procure such a feast, or what it must have cost him. He added a bottle of wine and another bottle of clear liquid, which she supposed was a harder form of alcohol, to the pile. In another pile he unwrapped a modest dress of dark blue wool, a collection of female undergarments, and a warm-looking gray cloak with a matching bonnet. The clothes were extremely plain, without the tiniest frill or ornament, but the fabrics looked soft and serviceable and would be eminently warmer and more comfortable than the scratchy shirt and trousers of her sansculotte outfit. In a third pile he unwrapped a small pair of dark leather boots, a rose-colored bar of fragrant soap, and finally a book.

"I wasn't sure of your size," he told her, his voice a

little hesitant as he watched her stare in silence at his purchases. He cleared his throat. "They are undoubtedly not what you are accustomed to wearing, but anything finer would call attention to you, and that is precisely what we want to avoid."

Jacqueline reached down and ran her hand over the warm fabric of the cloak. It was a heavy, soft wool, with a pearly-gray satin lining. She picked up the waxy-smooth bar of soap and examined its delicate rose marking before lifting it up to her nose and inhaling its sweet fragrance. A brief sensation of sheer pleasure washed through her. Closing her eyes, for one small second she was reminded of the long, languid baths she used to indulge in at the Château de Lambert. She opened her eyes to find Citizen Julien watching her.

"Would you do something for me?" she asked.

He hesitated for a moment. "If I can," he replied carefully.

She looked down at all the wonderful gifts spread out for her on the bed. To ask for something else at this moment seemed almost ungrateful. But she had to ask.

"The next time you have to go out and I am sleeping, would you leave me a note?" she requested softly.

He looked at her with genuine surprise. "Did you think I would leave you, Mademoiselle?"

The words hung motionless in the air as she stared at him, confused by the unmistakable concern in his expression. For the first time she noticed that his eyes were a mixture of blues and greens and grays, which made them look a totally different color from one moment to the next. There was an intensity to them, a keenness that spoke of an ability to act quickly, and a controlled wariness that told her he trusted no one. In his business these were obviously necessary traits. She found herself wondering what it was that had driven him to pursue such a dangerous profession, where every assignment he took might be his last. Underneath his disguise he was a handsome enough man. Did he have a wife or lover waiting somewhere for his return, anxiously counting the hours, agonizing over the dangers he faced as he earned his living? What kind of a woman could possibly endure such constant fear, knowing that each time he left her he might not be back? He regarded her quizzically. She suddenly realized she was staring at him and she turned away.

"Of course I knew you would return," she told him lightly. "You have been hired to rescue me, and I assume that does not mean abandoning me with no money or food in a run-down inn in one of the worst sections of Paris." She gave a tiny, shallow laugh, as if the mere idea of such a thing was totally ludicrous.

The room was silent for a moment. She could feel him staring at her back. She wanted to say something more to assure him that she had not been the least bit concerned, but somehow no words came.

"I will always come back for you, Mademoiselle."

Silence hung between them, making the words seem more like a solemn pledge than what they were, a simple attempt to reassure her. She knew she was merely the object of a contract to him, and nothing more. As he had told her last night, she was a package that had to be delivered. If she was not safely delivered, then he would not be paid. Theirs was strictly a business arrangement. But somehow his promise was strangely soothing. It was as if he had relieved her of an unbearably heavy weight, and for a brief moment she felt oddly safe and secure.

He cleared his throat and broke the spell. "For as you have pointed out, I have been hired to see you safely delivered," he continued matter-of-factly. He hesitated. "However, since my absence evidently caused you concern, the next time I shall remember to take the time to leave you a note."

She turned. "Thank you."

He gave her a curt nod and gestured toward the food laid out on the blanket. "Eat something."

She needed no further invitation. She seated herself beside the feast on the bed and immediately tore into the loaf of bread, stuffing great chunks of it into her mouth in a manner that could be described as anything but ladylike.

She did not care. Graceful, restrained table manners could not possibly be applied here. The food at La Conciergerie had been barely edible, and she had not eaten since the previous day. She was absolutely starving, and was preoccupied with trying to fit a massive chunk of bread with a slice of the cold beef and a piece of cheese into her mouth when she noticed that Citizen Julien was moving toward the door.

"Where are you going?" she demanded, her mouth full.

"I have some business to attend to before we can leave here," he replied vaguely. "I will return in about an hour. Eat as much as you can and then pack everything up, including your new clothes. You will be leaving here as the boy."

"But where are we going?" she asked. She disliked the fact that he still had not told her of his plans.

He sighed. "Mademoiselle, I cannot tell you exactly how or by what route we will be leaving, any more than I can tell you who I am. If you are captured, the less you know the better," he told her firmly.

Jacqueline scowled. "First of all, I have absolutely no intention of allowing myself to be captured," she informed him flatly. "But if I am arrested again, I will be executed regardless of what I know, so what does it matter if you tell me of your plans?"

"I was not thinking of your protection," he qualified. "I was thinking of my own."

Not terribly gallant of him, although she had to admit there was some logic to his reasoning. If questioned, she could not give much information about a man she knew virtually nothing about. And if there were others helping with her escape, as the boy Dénis had, she did not want to put their lives at risk any more than was necessary. Nevertheless, she did not enjoy being kept so ill informed. It gave her the sense that she had no control over what was happening to her, and after these past few weeks helplessness was a feeling she no longer intended to endure.

"Surely there would be no harm in your at least telling

me where we are going?" she persisted. "If something happens to you and we become separated, it would be helpful if I at least knew what direction I am headed in."

He hesitated a moment, weighing the validity of her words. Finally he relented. "I am taking you to England, to live with your sisters and Sir Edward Harrington."

She looked at him with pure dismay. "But I cannot go to England," she protested. "I cannot leave France. Not yet. Not until I have found out what has happened to Antoine. If he is alive, and I am certain that he is, I am not leaving Paris without him. We must find him and free him. I told you that last night."

She turned her attention back to her food, fully expecting him to argue with her. After all, it was obvious he had overlooked Antoine's fate, and would probably not be happy about having to change his plans. She waited for him to inundate her with all the reasons why they should flee now, without trying to rescue poor Antoine. But he said nothing. The meaning of his silence slowly wrapped itself around her.

"No," she whispered, finally looking up at him. She shook her head in denial as a mixture of horror and grief began to well up inside her.

"Mademoiselle," he began, his voice soft and hesitant. He knelt before her and reached up to take her hand.

"No!" she screamed abruptly, flying off the bed and racing over to the window. She stood in front of the frosted glass and looked out, not seeing anything, wrapping her arms tightly around herself and shaking.

He moved to stand behind her. She trembled violently as she tried to get control of her fear, unwilling to ask the question. She stared out through the lacy gaps in the frosted pane, at the gray lines of laundry that were frozen stiff, and the garbage that littered the ground. It was cold. Surely that was why she could not stop shaking. It was November, after all, and she could not remember a November ever being as cold and gray as this one.

If she had been home, she would have ordered one of the few remaining servants to throw more wood on the fire. Every room at the Château de Lambert had a huge, magnificent fireplace, with intricately carved mantels of the finest Italian marble. Some bore the De Lambert crest, while others sported fanciful designs of naked angels fluttering in stone carrying garlands of flowers and grapes. The fireplace in this room was tiny and black, and choked with powdery ashes that were cold and gray. She wondered absently how much one had to pay in a place like this for a fire to be lit. She remembered it had been very cold in her cell. She wondered if Antoine, who was so sick when they came to arrest him, was cold. A sob of deep, pure grief escaped her.

She sensed his hand rising up to touch her.

"Don't touch me," she choked. "I don't want you to touch me."

He withdrew his hand and silently moved away. Jacqueline continued to stare out the window. She could not cry. She felt she should. She wanted to. But something inside her would not let the tears come, something hard and dark that filled her with a grief and despair so heavy it threatened to crush her from within. She ground her jaw together and reached out with a thin, trembling hand to touch the frosty lace on the windowpane. The icy glass chilled her fingertips, making them tingle and burn from the cold. And then, slowly, the heat from the pads of her fingers melted into the frost, leaving five little clear ovals in the grainy white glaze.

"Did they execute him?" she finally asked, her voice barely a whisper.

"They did not have to."

She stared vacantly at the frozen laundry, letting the meaning of his words sink in. Antoine had been very sick, too sick to possibly endure the hardships of a freezing cold cell and rotten food. And of course those soldiers of the National Guard had all taken a turn kicking him at the time of his arrest. It was possible he died of an internal injury. It did not matter. Either way he was dead, as dead as he would have been had he mounted the steps to the guillotine. And for that there was only one person to blame. Nicolas.

"Why didn't you tell me last night?" she demanded suddenly as she turned around to face him.

He regarded her calmly. "Because you were exhausted and I wanted you to get some sleep."

A simple, practical answer. She could not fault him for thinking in practical terms. That was his job. "Was it not possible to rescue him?" she asked quietly, fighting to keep her voice steady and controlled.

Citizen Julien let out a harsh sigh. "When Sir Edward originally told me of you and your brother's arrest, I planned to rescue both of you. I found out where you were easily enough, but I could not locate Antoine. There was a record of his arrest, but no one seemed to know where he had been imprisoned. The Republic's record keeping leaves much to be desired, and with so many arrests these past few months it is difficult to get hold of the proper paperwork," he explained in frustration.

"The proper paperwork," she repeated absently, as if something in those words would help her to understand Antoine's death.

He began to pace the floor. "It was clear he had not yet gone to trial. But given his illness at the time of his arrest, I thought perhaps he had been sent to a prison hospital, or at least to a prison with better living conditions than the Conciergerie. I checked into the rosters at all the hospitals and prisons, and finally I found an inmate registered under the name Lambert. But when I went to see him, it turned out he was an old man, a common forger, and his correct name was Lavert, not Lambert." He stopped pacing and looked at her. "Spelling mistakes and errors in the rosters are common."

"A spelling mistake," she repeated with a nod, as if that somehow explained everything.

He began to pace again. "Several days ago I adopted the character of Citizen Julien, and used him to get into the Conciergerie so I could casually question some of the prisoners to see if any of them knew of your brother. I decided that since you were being held there, it was possible Antoine was as well, despite the fact that he was not listed in the records. After a few days I finally found someone who remembered seeing a young man being half carried, half dragged down the hall to a cell on the same evening you and Antoine were arrested."

Jacqueline clenched her hands until her nails bit deep into the palms. "What happened to him?" she whispered.

He stopped pacing and looked at her. "He died that night. He was buried in a common pit the next day." His voice was soft, apologetic, as if he felt that somehow it was his fault.

Jacqueline shook her head. "There is no proof that it was Antoine," she told him firmly. "It could have been someone else. You cannot be sure." Her denial made her feel better. If there was the slightest hope that he lived, Jacqueline would find him.

He took a step toward her. "Mademoiselle," he began in a low voice, "it was he. The prisoner heard the jailer who had guarded him boasting to another of the fine ring he removed from the body before they came to take it away. A gold ring bearing a crest with a lion, a fox, and a bird."

The flicker of hope she had nursed for those few seconds went out. He had just described the De Lambert crest. "The bird is a dove," she whispered raggedly. "That I may rule with strength, wisdom, and peace." She turned away again and rested her forehead against the icy cold pane of the window, struggling to accept what he was telling her. Antoine was dead. Her wonderful, handsome, intelligent brother, who had always been so gentle and good, except when he was teasing her or playing childish pranks as a boy, was dead. It did not make any sense. Nothing made any sense. She tried to focus her thoughts on something simple and tangible.

"The ring was my father's," she told him quietly. "He gave it to Antoine when he was in prison. He said that Antoine should keep it safe for him until he was released." She said the words calmly, as if she was telling him about something that happened to another family, or describing people who were quite distant to her.

She leaned heavily against the windowpane and tried to understand what had happened to her life. Antoine was dead. And her father was dead. She was supposed to be dead, but she was not. Suzanne and Séraphine were safe, far away in England, a place where the evils and bloodshed of this hateful revolution could not touch them. Jacqueline was glad of that. At least she had had the foresight to send them away as soon as her father was arrested, as risky as that move had been. The Château de Lambert and all its artwork and furnishings would be confiscated, as were her father's investments and bank accounts. She had nothing. It did not matter. She had been spared. Her life was a bonus. All she had to do was decide what she was going to do with it.

The answer came to her easily.

"I want you to help me kill someone," she announced calmly as she turned around to face him.

He looked at her with a mixture of surprise and pity. "Mademoiselle, you are upset," he told her, his voice calm and soothing. "You must realize you cannot bring this revolution to an end on your own. A political assassination would only martyr your victim and secure your own death."

She shook her head impatiently. "I am not interested in plunging a knife into Robespierre," she replied, referring to the powerful member of the Committee of Public Safety who was a major force in purging France of her enemies through terror and bloodshed. "Although I must confess the image of it does give me a certain amount of pleasure. The vengeance I seek is on a far more personal level."

"Who is it?" he asked, his curiosity piqued.

"His name is Nicolas Bourdon." She spoke the name harshly, bitterly, as if it was acid on her tongue.

"The man who attacked you in your cell?"

She nodded and turned her attention back to the window. "He was a friend of my father's," she ground out, her voice filled with loathing. "Or at least that is what he led my father to believe. He came from absolutely nothing. He must have thought himself very clever indeed to fashion a friendship with a man as great and powerful as the Duc de Lambert."

"That matters a great deal to you, Mademoiselle, doesn't it?" he observed. "The background a person comes from."

"Until my father became involved in philosophy and politics, I never thought about it very much," she informed him brusquely. "There was a system in place that had been created by God, and everyone knew where his place was. I am no more responsible for the fact that God made me the daughter of a duc than for his making another the daughter of a peasant. That is simply the way of things. It certainly isn't my fault they are poor." She realized her tone was defensive, but years of revolutionary rhetoric had made her sick of constantly feeling she should apologize for her birthright.

"Mademoiselle, have you ever met a peasant?" he asked curiously.

"Of course I have," she shot back. "What would you call those foul pigs who have watched over me in prison these past few weeks?"

"But before the revolution," he qualified. "Did you ever leave the grounds of the château and see how the families who rented land from your father and paid dues to him actually lived?" His tone was not accusing, merely one of genuine interest.

She thought for a moment. "Not really," she admitted indifferently. "Once a year my father would have a party on the grounds for all the peasants, and they would come with their wives and children and eat and drink and celebrate the arrival of spring. And sometimes Antoine and I would go riding in the fields and that would take us past their cottages, but we were usually in too much of a hurry to stop and talk to them."

"And while you were out enjoying yourself by riding through their fields, did you ever stop to consider that two horses trampling at great speed through a planted field might destroy part of its crop?" he demanded.

"In the first place, they were my father's fields," she pointed out defensively. "And seigneurial law permits the landowner access and right of way whenever he chooses. Secondly, with crops planted for miles around, there was more than enough to compensate for the small amount of damage we may have done."

He shook his head. "No, Mademoiselle. There was not more than enough. Between the harshness of the weather, the inefficient farming techniques, and the constantly increasing rents, dues, taxes, and tithes collected by your family, the church, and the state, the peasant farmers barely had enough left over to keep their family in a state of semistarvation and seed their fields the following year."

"I did not create the system," she informed him bitterly. "God did. And it seemed to work well for hundreds of years."

"From the point of view of the nobility, I suppose it did," he agreed, his tone blatantly sarcastic.

"Citizen Julien, you have been hired by my father's friend to rescue me, and I will not tolerate a mere employee lecturing me on the perceived evils of my class," she snapped furiously.

His jaw tightened and his expression grew dark. It was obvious she had insulted him, but she did not care. There was a moment of taut silence, and Jacqueline sensed that he was fighting to control whatever he was about to say to her. Then, as if by an act of will, his expression softened to one of amusement and his whole body seemed to relax.

"Then with your permission, Mademoiselle," he drawled out as he swept into a low, mocking bow, "I will leave you to continue the task I was hired to perform." He started toward the door.

"Wait a minute," she ordered.

He hesitated, but did not turn to her.

"You have not yet told me if you are going to help me kill Nicolas," she reminded him.

Slowly he turned to look at her. "No," he replied in a low voice. "I am not."

"Naturally you would be paid for your services," she quickly assured him. She realized she probably should have discussed the issue of his fee before asking if he would accept the job.

He looked at her with amusement. "So you wish to employ me now, do you, Mademoiselle? How very interesting." He paused, as if he was considering this turn of events. "And what, may I ask, do you propose to pay me with?" His tone was infuriatingly mocking.

She thought for a moment. She had absolutely nothing. All of her father's assets had been confiscated. She had been careful enough to hide what remained of the family's jewels and silver in the château, knowing full well that if the National Guard ever did decide to pay her and Antoine a visit, they would help themselves to whatever they wanted. The jewels were well hidden, but to make a trip out to the château to recover them was impossible. There would undoubtedly be guards there waiting to arrest her the moment she set foot on the grounds.

"Well?" he prodded.

"I have nothing to pay you with at the moment," admitted Jacqueline, "but when we get to England I can draw on the fund I set up with Sir Edward to pay for the care of my sisters. Providing your fee is not unreasonable, I should be able to pay you on our arrival."

His expression shifted from amusement to disbelief. "Come now, Mademoiselle, surely you can do better than that. Do you actually think that I will risk my life to murder a man I have absolutely nothing against, on the understanding that should I survive the incident, and not be captured, and somehow make it safely back to England with you in tow, that then I will accept payment based on what is left in a children's fund you have established with Sir Edward?" Much to her irritation, he actually began to laugh.

"Well, why not?" she demanded heatedly. "My word is good. If I say you will be paid, you will be paid."

"Oh certainly," he agreed as he attempted a serious look. "Providing we both survive and make it back to England." He shook his head. "I am afraid, Mademoiselle, that in my line of business I find it necessary to demand payment in advance."

Jacqueline looked at him with disgust. "That is most unreasonable of you. What if you do not succeed in your mission?"

He shrugged his shoulders. "Then I am dead." Once again he turned toward the door. "I will be back in about an hour. Make sure you are ready to leave."

She straightened her spine. "I am not going with you," she told him firmly.

He turned around and looked at her incredulously. "I beg your pardon?"

She folded her arms across her chest and stared at him, enjoying the cool sense of purpose that was fast growing within her. "I said I am not going with you," she repeated. "I have no desire to abandon my country and flee to England. Not until I have avenged the deaths of my father and brother. Nicolas Bourdon was responsible for their arrests, and I am going to make him pay with his life."

He appeared unimpressed by her bravado. "Mademoiselle, you cannot possibly succeed," he told her flatly. "Already we have stayed here too long for it to be safe, and by yourself you have absolutely nowhere you can go." Evidently thinking the matter settled, he moved once again toward the door.

His casual dismissal infuriated her. Did he really think she could be swayed that easily? "I have friends I can stay with, and a few loyal servants who would be willing to help me until I develop a plan," she informed him heatedly.

He turned abruptly and pinned her with his gaze, his patience clearly at an end. "Do you realize that at this moment at least four detachments of the National Guard have been sent out looking for you?" he demanded. "They have already torn apart your beloved château, and right now they are fanning out to question and arrest any remaining relatives, friends, or servants they think might have conspired with you in your escape. For you to go near one of them is to condemn them to certain death. Is that what you want?" he demanded harshly.

She hesitated for a moment. She had to admit she had not actually thought about anyone else's safety. Once Nicolas was killed, she did not care what happened to her. But to put a relative or servant at risk because of her need for vengeance was not justifiable. She realized she would have to manage on her own. "Then I won't go to anyone I know," she conceded. "I will simply stay at hotels like this one." How she would pay for them she had absolutely no idea.

"A fine plan," he remarked dryly. "Except that a poster is being circulated with a detailed description of you, offering what to most people is a remarkable reward. What innkeeper, tradesman, or street vendor do you think is going to pass up the opportunity to do his patriotic duty by turning you in while collecting a little money at the same time?"

Jacqueline clenched her fists in exasperation. "Well, what do you expect me to do?" she demanded furiously. "Simply forget about what Nicolas has done to me and my family and run away to England while he and men like him continue to butcher innocent people and destroy my country?" The idea was impossible.

"Yes," he replied evenly. "I expect you to leave this hatred and bloodshed behind. I expect you to come with me and make a new life for yourself and your sisters. Surely they do not deserve to have another family member sacrificed to the cause of the revolution, however noble or just you may think your mission is. What they need is someone they know and love to help them deal with the pain they have already suffered."

Jacqueline did not like to be reminded of her sisters. The thought of them clouded her anger, and made it hard for her to focus on the task at hand. "My sisters will be just fine without me," she assured him. "Sir Edward and his wife were good friends of my father and mother in their youth. I am secure in the knowledge that they are capable and devoted guardians."

"Indeed they are," he readily agreed. "But do you believe that is all Suzanne and Séraphine deserve? Good guardians who speak broken French and have no real understanding of the world your sisters have lost, or the trauma they have been through?"

"They are young," countered Jacqueline quickly. "They will learn English and they will forget the past." The thought of it filled her with a mixture of relief and pain.

He regarded her curiously. "Mademoiselle, are you aware that Séraphine has not spoken a single word for some three months?"

She looked at him, appalled. It had been just over three months since she wrote to them of the death of their father. "No," she whispered. "I did not know that."

"After she received the news of her father's death, she cried in her room for three days," he continued in a low voice. "No one could get her to come out. Trays were brought to her, but she would not eat. Suzanne and Lady Harrington spent hour after hour trying to reason with her. Finally they got her to leave the room. But despite everyone's efforts, Séraphine simply will not speak."

"I did not know," repeated Jacqueline weakly. "No one wrote to tell me." The anger and pain within her grew heavier, intensified by the knowledge that her sisters were suffering far more than she realized. She had sent them away so they would be safe. But sending them away could not protect them from the agony of having their father murdered. She had not been able to stop his execution, just as she had not been able to protect Antoine.

"Your duty now is to your sisters," Citizen Julien was saying authoritatively. "So put aside your thirst for vengeance and focus on getting safely to England. That is where you are needed, Mademoiselle."

She nodded absently and sat in the small wooden chair. Citizen Julien went to the door.

"I will be back as quickly as I can. Do not leave the room for any reason, and be prepared to depart as soon as I return."

She nodded again and continued to stare vacantly into space. The door of the room slammed shut and the key scraped in the lock. She listened to his slow, shuffling steps as they receded down the hall.

She sat staring at nothing for a long time. Her father and brother were dead. Her sisters were irreparably traumatized. Her family's home and assets were gone. Her entire world had been shattered, and nothing would ever make it right again.

The need for vengeance was great.

He moved along slowly but steadily, not daring to go any faster than would be acceptable for a man of his apparent years. He was tempted simply to hire a carriage to take him to his destination, but such a move would undoubtedly attract attention. As the revolution became more and more paranoid almost everyone learned to walk. To show that you had the money to pay for a carriage was foolish indeed, for it immediately marked you as someone with money to squander, unless of course you were an official of the revolutionary government. And so even those who could still afford the convenience of a coach opted instead to buy a sensible pair of sturdy, low-heeled shoes and joined their fellow citizens on their feet.

People looked at him as he shuffled by, but only with passing interest. He was just another old, bent man walking in the streets of Paris. There was nothing unusual about him. Still, he would not be able to wear this disguise much longer. Already the story of the old man who helped an aristo escape from the Conciergerie disguised as a boy was filtering through the streets, thanks to a report released from the prison early that morning. A reward was being offered for any information leading to their arrest. He wondered how many young boys and old men would be denounced and dragged into the prison for questioning. He tried not to think about it.

He continued to make his way through the twisting, narrow streets, methodically going over his plan again, evaluating the risks, looking for holes where something could happen. The possibilities were endless. Usually the mental exercise of analyzing the countless ways his plans could go wrong and what action he would take when it did kept his mind sharp and alert. Today it simply annoyed him, making him impatient to complete his task and get back to Mademoiselle de Lambert. After demonstrating her apparent lack of concern for her own well-being this morning, he did not like having her out of his sight. Although he was quite certain he had convinced her to abandon her suicidal quest for revenge, she was obviously suffering from intense feelings of anger and pain, and such a combination could be dangerous for both of them.

Most of the people he had rescued were in a state of shock, a condition that, in combination with their fear, left them eager to obey his directions. It was almost as if by his saving them, whether from prison or from imminent arrest, they were so surprised and grateful they immediately trusted him, making the challenge of secreting them out of France that much easier.

Mademoiselle de Lambert was not in a compliant state of shock, however. The news of her brother's death had affected her deeply, and the calm, methodical way in which she told him she would not be leaving Paris so that she could murder someone revealed a woman of considerable strength and will. This was no typical, sheltered, gently bred girl who was given to tears of sorrow and fits of the vapors, although that girl might once have existed. The woman he was in the process of rescuing was filled with a terrible, bitter rage that was constantly boiling below the surface of her relatively calm exterior. That was what enabled her to lodge a dagger in a captain of the National Guard before knocking out his teeth with a chamber pot, and to smash a bottle over the head of a drunken thug easily twice her size. It was a rage of anguish, and pain, and fury at feeling helpless, and he understood it well. Unfortunately, however, it made her unpredictable, and that made her dangerous, both to herself and to him.

He quickly scanned the candlemaker's shop from the window for other customers before entering. The proprietor was just finishing with a young woman, and Citizen Julien lowered his head and pretended to study some of the candles on the long, wooden counter as he waited for her to complete her purchase and leave.

"I believe, Citizen, that you have a special order for me?" he asked the man at the counter in a gravelly voice after the door had closed.

"Just finished it this morning," replied Citizen Gadbois as he went to lock the door and placed a sign saying CLOSED in the window. "Come into the back."

Citizen Julien slowly followed the man behind the counter and through the door that led to the workshop. The room was heavy with the smell of hot tallow. Bits of wick and hardened wax littered the floor. Citizen Gadbois stood on a stool and pulled down a wooden box that was sitting among a pile of candles on a shelf. He carried the box over to the workbench and opened it, producing two perfectly matched cheap yellow candles.

"The documents are rolled in stiff paper and encased inside," he told Citizen Julien in a low voice. "When you are ready for them, simply cut off the ends of the candles. They should slip out easily." He began to wrap the tapers in a sheet of paper.

Citizen Julien reached into one of the pockets of his heavy overcoat and produced a small leather purse. He dropped it onto the worktable, causing it to make a heavy clinking sound.

"In silver, as we agreed," he told Citizen Gadbois. "You may count it if you wish."

Citizen Gadbois quickly made sure his fee was complete before handing over the candles. "Not that I do not trust you, Citizen," he said apologetically, "but these are difficult times for all of us." He tucked the purse into a drawer of the worktable and locked it.

Citizen Julien nodded, not in the least offended by the man's desire to be cautious. "Have you heard any news today, Citizen?" he asked.

Citizen Gadbois looked around nervously, as if he expected someone at any moment to burst through the door that led to his shop, or perhaps emerge from a secret panel in the walls. "There is talk of an escape from the Conciergerie last night," he whispered. "The daughter of the former Duc de Lambert. They say she was helped by an old man. Some say he was a loyal servant, while others suspect it was the work of the Black Prince."

"What does the National Guard think?" asked Citizen Julien calmly.

Gadbois smiled. "They prefer to think it was simply an old servant. Apparently the jailer swears it was an old man who was in the cell with her before she disappeared. He told the public prosecutor that not even his own father could have given such a convincing performance. Of course Fouquier-Tinville is trying to prove that the jailer was in on it."

"Maybe he was," commented Citizen Julien. He turned to leave the workshop.

"A word of caution, Citizen," continued Gadbois. "The word is out that this particular aristo is to be found at any cost. They say she is a spy, and if she gets to England she could divulge secret military information that would enable the British to massacre thousands of loyal French citizens."

"Is that so?" remarked Citizen Julien. "And do you believe that?" His tone was one of amusement.

Gadbois shrugged. "I am not in the business of believing or not believing," he replied indifferently. "All I know is that the reward for her capture is high. The National Guard is searching for her as we speak, and everyone who leaves the gates of Paris is being questioned thoroughly." He looked at him intently. "If someone is helping her, they will both have to exercise extreme caution at all times."

Citizen Julien acknowledged his warning with a nod. "Thank you for the candles, Citizen," he replied.

Jacqueline lay on the bed, staring at the dozens of cracks that webbed the ceiling. She had packed up all the food and gifts Citizen Julien had brought her. The action of packing had briefly taken her mind off everything else. For a few moments all she had to think about was what should be wrapped in which piece of paper, and whether there was a sufficient length of string to tie the packages together into a neat bundle. Once that was done there were no simple chores left to occupy her, so she lay on the bed to consider the major changes in her situation, and the options those changes had created.

Basically she had two choices. She could stay with Citizen Julien, who would try to get her safely to England and reunite her with her sisters. Or she could remain in Paris and see to it that Nicolas Bourdon did not live.

The idea of being with Suzanne and Séraphine again was extremely tempting. She had not seen them in over five months, and the thought of wrapping her arms around them and holding them close filled her with pleasure. When she had sent them away, her thoughts had been only for their physical safety. They had not wanted to go. They both cried and protested pitifully during the few days it took to make the arrangements. They told Jacqueline they were afraid to leave their father, brother, and sister, afraid that they might never see them again. Jacqueline hushed them with soothing words that trivialized their fears, telling them it was only for a month or two, that as soon as Papa was released and things had settled down in France, she would arrange for their return. Suzanne, who was ten, asked her if those bad people who had taken her papa away were going to kill him. Jacqueline scolded her severely, telling her not to think such silly thoughts. Everything was going to be fine. She and Antoine would help Papa make those people see that arrest-ing him was a mistake. Papa would be released and then they would all be together again. She promised.

But she had not been able to keep that promise. In a sequence of events that seemed more like a nightmare than reality, her father had been found guilty of the charges laid against him. He was guillotined that same day, and she and Antoine were not even permitted to spend a few moments with him before his execution. In the brief hours before he climbed into the cart that would take him to his executioner, he wrote Jacqueline and Antoine a letter of farewell. He asked them to find it in their hearts to forgive his enemies, as he had. He did not doubt that their actions were motivated by a genuine belief in the creation and preservation of the new order of France, and it was not up to him to be their judge or to find fault in their zealousness. God alone could judge them. He asked his children not to cry and, despite their pain, not to hate.

It was a request Jacqueline found impossible to fulfil.

Her father and Antoine were dead. There was nothing she could do to change that. And her sisters were now orphans, lost and lonely in a strange land. It was evident they needed someone to help them through the loss of their family and the life they once knew. Jacqueline would have liked to believe she was that person. It would have comforted her to think she could go to them filled with wisdom and love, and be able to quietly and patiently help them heal, slowly restoring their faith in the good-ness of life and mankind until they could see only bright-ness and hope in the dawn of each day, instead of anguish and loss. But deep inside she knew she could not. A dark and painful fury was growing within her, festering into something hideously virulent and caustic. It seemed to swell and stretch with every breath, weighing down her body and her spirit, making her desperate with the need to rage, to scream, to cry, to take any action that would somehow help to relieve her suffering. She knew she could not cry. Her father's arrest and death had cured her forever of that empty, futile gesture.

If she accompanied Citizen Julien to England, what help could she possibly be to her sisters? Since she herself was so overcome by hate and rage, how could she help them with the challenge of dealing with their loss, of putting the past behind them and having faith in the future? How could she ask them to forget and go on to a new life, when she had absolutely no intention of doing so herself? Her sisters were young, only six and ten. Everyone knew children could heal. There would be scars, of course, but eventually time would fade them. Their memories of their father and brother would become cloudy and distant, their recollections of life at the Château de Lambert no more than a pleasant, blurred series of small, unimportant moments.

Jacqueline knew this with a certainty that made her heart bleed. When her mother died giving birth to Séraphine, Jacqueline was sure she would never enjoy another moment of her life again. For months she devoted herself totally to looking after Suzanne, who was four at the time and as devastated by the loss as Jacqueline. But while Jacqueline could not abide to be in the same room with the new baby, whom she regarded as the instrument of her mother's death, Suzanne was totally enchanted by little Séraphine and wanted to be with her constantly. When Séraphine started to walk, Jacqueline found she could no longer ignore her. Séraphine would toddle away from her governess and throw herself at Jacqueline, wrapping her chubby arms around her legs and refusing to let go. Eventually the needs of her own anger took second place to the needs of this motherless child. And although Jacqueline talked about their mother often, little Suzanne began to have more questions about her than actual memories. Even for Jacqueline, time gradually managed to stanch the flow of pain that poured from her heart each day.

So Séraphine and Suzanne would eventually recover. But Jacqueline would not. This time she was an adult, and the pain was not just that of a tragic death, but of an entire family destroyed by corruption and injustice. For Jacqueline, even time could not heal this kind of agony. Nothing could.

She made her decision. She would not flee to England. She was too consumed by hate and anger to have anything good to offer her sisters. So she would not join them. But if it was the last thing she did, she would see to it that Nicolas Bourdon did not live. Perhaps that was why she had been given a reprieve from her execution. She did not doubt she would be captured after she murdered him. It did not matter. As long as Nicolas was dead, her own survival meant nothing to her.

The sound of heavy, booted feet stamping across the floor below jerked her from her thoughts. A voice, harsh and authoritative, rang through the inn. Jacqueline strained to listen, but she could not make out what the man was saying. A quiet, hushed voice responded, presumably Citizen Dufresne's. She sprang from the bed and rushed across the room to press her ear against the door. The sounds were still muffled. She twisted down on the door latch, only to find it locked. She did not have a key to let herself out. Citizen Julien had taken the precaution of locking her in once again, perhaps thinking to protect her, but the innkeeper probably kept a second set. If he did not, it would be easy enough to break the door down. Citizen Dufresne and the man downstairs seemed to be arguing, and Jacqueline could hear the sound of furniture being overturned and doors banging open. Her heart froze in her chest as the heavy thump of boots began to move up the stairs.

For a few seconds panic gripped her with such violent intensity she was unable to move. They had found her. She was going to be arrested and taken directly to the guillotine. How monstrously unfair that she should have cheated death for just a few short hours, only to be dragged back and thrust once again into its icy black grip. Vengeance would not be hers after all. Nicolas would live, and she would die. There was no justice after all.

She spun around suddenly, frantic with the need to do

something, but not quite sure what. Her eyes came to rest on the lacily frosted windowpane.

She tore across the room and yanked the window open. Then she hauled her legs up and over the sill and lowered herself down until her feet touched the narrow ledge below. She tentatively exchanged her grip on the sill for a hold on the shutter, terrified that the ledge would not accept her weight. It did. Her wooden sabots were large and clumsy on the narrow shelf, so she had to inch her way slowly along toward the next window, hanging on to the shutter for as long as she could with her left hand as the outstretched fingers of her right reached out to touch the corner of the next one. She couldn't quite grab it without letting go of the first shutter, and for a few interminable seconds she struggled not to scream as she felt herself almost lose her balance. She ground down on her teeth and clung with desperate hands to the flat, crumbling surface of the building, her face pressed so closely against the pockmarked brick that she was sure it was crushed into her skin forever. With a grunt of determination she forced herself to release her right hand from the wall and reached out to grab the next shutter. Dry, splintering wood bit into her fingers. She ignored the pain, pressing down on the wood to test its strength before inching her way along again. Past that set of shutters, and on to the next, moving as quickly as her fear and her balance would allow, until finally she had reached the edge of the inn. The low roof of the next building began not far below her; still, it took a will of iron to make her let go of the shutters and leap down onto it. She landed with a heavy thud on her knees and hands, and then she was up and scurrying across the roof to a corner that overlooked a pile of debris and garbage. A gasp of fear escaped her as she jumped off the roof and landed in the center of the icy stiff mound. It did not cushion her fall as well as she hoped, and she found she was limping slightly as she bolted around the building into the dark, narrow passageway that ran between the buildings out to the street.

The front of the inn was crowded with people who had stopped what they were doing to watch a detachment of the National Guard make another arrest. Jacqueline quickly pulled her cap down low over her forehead, buried her face into the collar of her jacket, and ambled out into the street to lose herself in the middle of the curious mob. Eight horses were waiting patiently near the door of the inn. One soldier was watching over them, which meant that it had only taken seven brave men to go into the inn to arrest her. Obviously her previous encounter with the National Guard was known. She looked about slowly to see if anyone was staring at her. The street was filled with men and boys of all ages dressed in outfits similar to hers, so she did not stand out. Citizen Julien had been wise in his choice of costume for her.

She started to move gradually toward the back of the crowd, intending to lose herself in the steady stream of traffic up ahead that was either uninterested or unaware of the commotion happening inside the inn. The sight of a carriage rounding the corner at the end of the street stopped her. It flew along at a speed that was dangerously reckless on such a narrow and crowded street, causing the tightly pressed assembly to split into two great waves to accommodate it. Fortunately for Jacqueline she was caught up in the swell that moved farther away from the inn to the other side of the street. The carriage rattled to a halt in front of the inn, the door swung open, and out stepped Nicolas.

The wave of absolute hatred that washed over her as she looked at him was so intense it made her feel nauseated. He paused to speak briefly with the soldier standing outside before entering the inn. Every impulse in her told her to run, to get off that street and out of that area as fast as she possibly could, but instead she remained firmly rooted to the spot, listening to the jeers and yells of the crowd as they waited impatiently for the soldiers to come out with their prisoner.

A few minutes later Nicolas emerged from the door, a look of dark fury and disgust on his face. The innkeeper

Dufresne followed behind him, wringing his hands and protesting apologetically. The remaining soldiers of the National Guard filed out of the small doorway and returned to their horses, looking irritated and sheepish. They mounted quickly and rode away, obviously embarrassed at having failed in their mission. Nicolas strode toward his carriage, but before getting in, he paused, taking a moment to scan the crowd. It was almost as if he could sense she was near, that he knew she was watching, and if he just looked long enough he would find her. If he did, she had little confidence that he would be fooled by her disguise. Once again a feeling of panic began to grip her, making her hunch further into the depths of her jacket. She casually stepped behind a huge, burly man, who effectively shielded her from Nicolas's gaze.

The crowd's calls for arresting the prisoner had now deteriorated into a blistering mockery of the National Guard. Nicolas gave the crowd a savage glare, effectively silencing the people closest to him, who undoubtedly feared that if provoked, he might decide to arrest them instead. Evidently satisfied that he had been able to cower at least some of them into respectful submission, he jerked open the door of the carriage and climbed inside. Jacqueline let out a breath of relief as the carriage began to roll away.

She could not believe her good fortune. Not only had she not been discovered, but Nicolas had practically been delivered into her hands. She began to move quickly through the crush of the crowd, past jostling elbows and shoulders, intent on following his carriage until it eventually took him home. The excitement of purpose hastened her steps. Once she knew where he lived, it would be easy to return there tonight and gain entrance. She would convince him she was alone and afraid, and desperately needed him to hide her somewhere. She would tell him that in exchange for his assistance she was willing to become his mistress. Whether he agreed to her bargain or not, she had no doubt he would want her, there and then, as a way of asserting his power over her. All she needed was a few seconds alone with him, his guard lowered by his need for her, to plunge a knife deep into his heart. If he did not fall immediately, she would draw it out and plunge it in again. The first time would be for her father, the second for Antoine. Their deaths would be avenged. She smiled at the thought.

"Watch where you're going, boy," snarled a voice. Jacqueline looked up at the tall, scraggly youth she had accidentally walked into.

"I beg your pardon," she apologized. "I was in a hurry and did not see you." The apology made, she moved to be on her way again. She did not want to lose sight of Nicolas's carriage.

Two filthy hands grabbed her firmly by her shoulders. She looked up indignantly at the boy who held her. His mouth split into a nasty grin of rotted teeth, at least three of which had been knocked out. His bony fingers dug painfully into her as he stared down in amused disbelief.

"Got a fancy mouth on him, hasn't he?" he demanded as six of his friends moved in to form a tight circle around the two of them.

"Sure does," agreed another who cuffed her roughly on the back of her head. "Hey brat, where'd you get such a mouth?"

"Let me go," demanded Jacqueline forcefully as she struggled to free herself from her captor's grip. She could hear the sounds of Nicolas's carriage growing fainter and fainter, and she was determined not to lose it.

"Giving orders now, are we?" asked the youth with a smirk. He abruptly released her shoulders and gave her a solid shove that sent her flying backward toward the other boys. She stumbled before she fell into them. Several pairs of hands reached out and shoved her back toward her tormentor, who laughed as she came crashing into his chest.

"You need some lessons in how to be a good citizen, boy," he remarked as he caught her by her shoulders. "It's lucky for you we aren't busy."

Jacqueline twisted and turned in an effort to free herself from him. "Let go of me you filthy swine or I'll—"

"First lesson, no calling the teacher a filthy swine," the youth sneered as he raised his hand and brought it down sharply across her face.

She staggered back from the impact while the other boys cheered. A warm trickle began to ooze from the corner of her mouth. She shook her head to clear it and touched her fingers to the side of her lips. She pulled her hand away and examined the blood on her fingertips with horror.

A maelstrom of sheer rage exploded to the surface, extinguishing any ability to maintain control over her actions. How dare these worthless street thugs think themselves in a position to bully and brutalize someone who was alone and weaker than they? And they had delayed her, causing her to lose Nicolas's carriage, so she might not be able to find him tonight. The fury that burst within her as she launched herself at the youth and started clawing viciously at his face was not solely directed at him and his spineless accomplices. It was directed at the injustice of a world gone mad, and her burning need to get even with some small part of it.

"Get him off me!" yelped the boy as he tried unsuccessfully to shield his face and neck from Jacqueline's ruthlessly determined attack. Six pairs of hands and arms grabbed her all over to peel her away from him. Jacqueline shrieked and abandoned her efforts as soon as she felt someone's hands grab her breasts.

"He's a girl!" stammered one boy in amazement while two others held her by her arms.

The leader who had started the incident stared at her in confusion, tenderly rubbing his cheek where she had succeeded in making several deep scratches. He stepped toward her, reached up and yanked off the red wool cap. The ragged remains of her blond hair spilled down onto her shoulders. Apparently still not convinced, he reached out and painfully squeezed her breast. Jacqueline let out a furious curse, telling him in no uncertain terms what a filthy, despicable son of a whore he was. His scratch-marked face split into another grin of rotted teeth.

Within seconds they were surrounded by a shoving, cursing mob, fighting to get a look at the escaped aristo the boy was triumphantly yelling about.

Chapter 4

Pure, cold terror seized her, rendering her unable to fight, to scream, to move. She was going to be butchered by the mob. She was certain of it.

The bloodthirsty violence of a Paris mob was infamous. In September 1792, enraged citizens viciously hacked to pieces over fourteen hundred helpless prisoners in various Paris prisons. Men, women, and children fell to the relentless blows of axes, hatchets, sabers, knives, and pikes. The Princesse de Lamballe, who was imprisoned at La Force, was subjected to a mock trial before being brutally hacked to death, stripped of her clothes, and grotesquely mutilated. Her executioners then cut off her head and carried it triumphantly through the streets on a pike to the Temple, to present to her friend Marie-Antoinette. None of the perpetrators of the September massacres were ever pursued or punished. Such atrocities, while not openly endorsed, were seen by the republican government as unfortunate, but completely understandable. The message was clear. A citizen acting as part of a mob need have no fear of retribution.

"Take her to the guillotine! Sanson is waiting for her!"

"What about the reward?"

"Why wait for the razor? Let's kill her now!"

"She's mine! I saw her first!"

"Aristo whore!"

The crowd was crushing itself around her, reaching out and grabbing her hair, her clothes, her arms, her shoulders, her breasts. She tried to raise her arms to protect her head and face, but the boys held her fast, keeping her from collapsing as the mob slapped and punched and shoved and pushed, their faces twisted with evil, malevolent hatred. It was as if they believed that she alone was the source of all the misery in their lives, and that if they could destroy her, their suffering would somehow instantly come to an end. She had told herself she did not fear her own death, but in that moment the terror she felt was unlike anything she had ever known. She bowed her head and screamed, praying for it to be over quickly.

The deafening blast of a gun cut through the roar of the enraged mob. Startled, everyone froze, groping hands arrested in midair, looking about to see who had fired and who had been killed.

"Move away, all of you!"

The savage authority with which the order was given was not lost on the crowd. Slowly their groping hands returned to their sides, their hateful, contorted expressions shifting to looks of wariness and uncertainty.

"Back away—now!"

Some of them hesitated, torn by their thirst for blood and their fear for themselves. They looked around to see who was giving these instructions, as if that would determine whether or not they would obey them. And then, slowly, they started to move away.

The boys who held Jacqueline did not relinquish their painful grip, but most of the mob retreated, opening up the space around her. Her chest heaving as she fought to regain her composure, she lifted her head to see who had managed to bring the raging crowd under control.

An imposing captain of the National Guard sat tall on a magnificent black horse, his pistol drawn and ready to fire at the first person who dared to violate his orders. His military uniform of striped trousers and blue coat with filthy white lapels and frayed epaulets was ragged and ill fitting, as was typical of the day, but its shabby appearance did not diminish the stature and power of the handsome man who wore it.

It was Citizen Julien.

His eyes locked with hers, silently commanding her to

say nothing. Then they swiftly moved down, taking in every detail of her condition. With her bloodied lip and torn clothes she realized she must look a sight. A flicker of pure rage crossed his features for the barest of seconds, to be instantly replaced by a mask of total indifference. The control he exerted over his emotions was so absolute she felt certain she was the only one who had noticed. He looked at her calmly, giving not the slightest indication that he was anything but perfectly composed and serene, as if the situation at hand was merely a minor interruption to an otherwise orderly day. He shifted his gaze to the three boys who were holding her.

"Release her."

The boys hesitated, looking at each other in confusion.

"We found her," objected the youth she had first knocked into. "She's an escaped aristo. There's a reward for her capture and we want it." He said the words firmly, but there was a hint of uncertainty in his tone. It was clear he did not want to get into an argument with a captain of the National Guard.

"Release her," repeated Citizen Julien softly, "or I will arrest the lot of you for obstruction of justice."

Reluctantly the boys let go of her.

"Come here," commanded Citizen Julien.

Jacqueline hesitantly took a step forward.

He studied her for a moment. "Are you Citizeness Jacqueline Doucette, formerly Mademoiselle Jacqueline de Lambert, who escaped from La Conciergerie last night?" he demanded. He stared at her intently.

"No," she replied, feeling almost certain that was the response he wanted to hear.

"Of course she is!" yelled out someone from the crowd.

"My name is Louise Fournier," blurted out Jacqueline, trying to think fast.

Citizen Julien looked at her skeptically. "Do you have any identification papers?" he demanded.

Jacqueline hesitated. "No."

"Anyone here who can swear to your identity?" he suggested.

"No."

Citizen Julien sighed. "Then it is my duty to inform you that you are under arrest. You will be taken directly to La Conciergerie, where you will be held until it can be determined whether or not you are this escaped aristo we are looking for."

"What about my reward?" demanded the youth, clearly not liking the idea of having his prize removed from his keeping.

Citizen Julien regarded him impatiently. "If she is the escaped aristo, then you shall be paid the reward. What is your name, boy?"

The youth straightened his shoulders and lifted his chin a notch, visibly insulted at being called "boy." "Marc Gauthier," he replied stiffly.

"Very good, Citizen Gauthier," said Citizen Julien, nodding. "Come to the Conciergerie at six o'clock tonight. Ask for Inspector Nicolas Bourdon. Tell him you are there to find out if the woman brought in earlier was indeed Citizeness Doucette. I will leave word with him that you were responsible for finding her and releasing her to my authority. If she is the aristo, I have no doubt that Inspector Bourdon will want to commend you personally."

The youth nodded eagerly. Jacqueline almost felt sorry for him. Nicolas would not be pleased to learn she had escaped a second time, and he was certain to vent his rage on this youth who had caught her and stupidly let her slip away. Given the way Citizen Julien was glaring at him, she suspected that was his intent.

Citizen Julien turned his attention back to Jacqueline. "You will ride with me, Citizeness."

She stepped over to his horse and in one easy motion he lifted her up in front of him. The firm wall of his chest pressed against her back as he reached forward to adjust the reins around her. She was surprised by how much comfort she suddenly felt just from the nearness of him, from the iron-hard feel of his chest and thighs and arms as they positioned around her, from his unbelievable confidence as he performed his masquerade in front of this thoroughly duped crowd. Only moments earlier they had been eager to tear her limb from limb. Now they were calmly giving her up to someone they believed was a figure of authority, on the basis of nothing more than his costume and the fact that he exuded power.

"All of you back about your business," Citizen Julien commanded sharply as people continued to stare at them.

Reluctantly the crowd began to disperse, obviously disappointed at having the incident conclude in such an orderly manner. Citizen Julien turned his horse and slowly guided him down the street, ignoring the jeers and taunts that people called out to Jacqueline as they rode by.

"We'll see you at the chopper, you aristo tart!"

"Try to escape again and you will beg for the mercy of the people's ax!"

"Traitor!"

"Harlot!"

The cries were loud and thick with loathing. Still shaken, Jacqueline forced herself to keep her spine straight and her chin up. She would not give them the satisfaction of seeing they had managed to terrify her. For all they knew, she was not even the aristo they were looking for. It did not seem to matter. She was guilty by suspicion, and according to the laws of the new Republic, that was enough to condemn her, both in a courtroom and on the street. She hated all of them. She bit down hard on her lip to keep it from trembling.

Citizen Julien kept the horse moving at a steady, purposeful pace. They traveled up and down at least a half-dozen streets before they finally lost the last few members of the mob who had decided to follow them. Now the people who crowded the streets looked with only passing interest as they rode by. It was not clear that Citizen Julien was a captain making an arrest. If anything, it looked more like he had rescued a scruffy youth from a street brawl and was taking him home. They had originally headed off in the direction of the Conciergerie, but once Citizen Julien felt certain that no member of the original mob was with them, he changed his course.

"Where are we going?" whispered Jacqueline.

"Keep your eyes down and your mouth shut," he snapped.

She thought his reply outrageously rude, but did not dare tell him so while they were in public. The minute they were alone she would tell him in no uncertain terms that she would not tolerate an employee speaking to her so.

They rode for perhaps another half hour, winding along narrow, quiet streets that gradually led north to the district known as Montmartre. Finally they came to a short, deserted avenue of narrow, crumbling houses called rue de Vent. Citizen Julien turned their horse down a tiny lane that led to a small coach house. He placed the horse in an empty stall before taking Jacqueline to the back door of the home to which the coach house belonged.

He rapped on the door in what seemed to be a code, three rapid knocks followed by two long ones. After a minute the door swung open. A handsome young man with wavy blond hair and striking green eyes stared at them in surprise and then hurriedly ushered them into a small kitchen. He quickly shut the door and looked at Citizen Julien with concern.

"I was not expecting you. Are you all right?" he demanded.

Citizen Julien nodded. "I'm fine."

The man's attention shifted to Jacqueline. "Is he?"

Citizen Julien looked at her, and Jacqueline thought she saw a hint of a scowl cross his face, but it vanished almost as quickly as it appeared. "He is also fine," he replied. "He just needs some cleaning up."

"Are they not expecting you tonight?" asked the man, evidently relieved that there was no medical emergency at hand.

"Yes," confirmed Citizen Julien. "Unfortunately my plans have been somewhat delayed."

The young man nodded. "What do you need?" he asked seriously. The way in which he spoke made it obvious to Jacqueline that this man was ready to do anything for Citizen Julien.

"For the moment, just a room. I need a few moments alone with the boy. Then I will let you know if there is anything else."

"This way, my friend. My home is yours."

He turned and led them through the kitchen doorway into a hall, then up a narrow flight of stairs. He opened a door leading into a small bedroom and stood aside as Jacqueline and Citizen Julien entered.

"I will heat some water so you and the boy can wash, and prepare some food. Call me when you want the water brought up." He closed the door.

Citizen Julien removed his military hat and flung it on the bed. He stood with his feet braced apart, folded his arms, and glared at Jacqueline. "I thought I ordered you to stay in that room," he began, his voice low and menacing.

She looked at him in disbelief. Was he actually insinuating that it was her fault she had almost been beaten to death by a mob, because she did not blindly follow his orders? Fresh hot anger bloomed within her, pushing aside the fear and tension that had been gnawing at her nerves for the past few hours.

"In case you aren't aware, Citizen, after you left me the National Guard decided to pay a visit to that particular inn, and I was lucky to get out when I did," she informed him furiously. "They were practically through the door as I was climbing out the window, and were it not for the fact that I am not unduly afraid of heights, we would not be standing here at this moment having this conversation, because my head would no longer be attached to my neck!" she blazed.

He looked at her with surprise. He had not known about the National Guard. Up until this moment he had thought she left the inn of her own accord. He had been convinced she nearly got both of them killed because of her need for vengeance with this Nicolas Bourdon, and he was only one short step away from saying to hell with it and letting her go. He did not intend to get himself killed while trying to save some spoiled little aristocrat who did not give a damn about her own life. There were too many others who were desperate to live that could use his assistance. He regarded her suspiciously, still not convinced she was telling him the truth.

"When did the National Guard come?" he demanded.

"About an hour after you left," Jacqueline told him sulkily. If the man had been hired to rescue her, why had he left her alone for so long in the first place? The fact that while she was alone she had decided not to go with him to England, and might very well have climbed out that window even if the National Guard had not shown up, was conveniently pushed aside.

"How many were there?" he continued, still trying to decide if she was lying to him.

"Eight," she replied. "Once I made it out the window and onto the ground, I went to the front of the inn and watched them leave. I thought I would have a better chance if I mixed in with the crowd." She felt a little foolish as she said that. Her plan had severely backfired, to say the least.

"You should have stayed in the room and let them arrest you," he informed her brusquely. "At least then I would have known where you were. As long as I knew where you were, I could have taken measures to rescue you again. Out on the streets, how would I ever have found you?" His voice was shaking with rage.

"How should I know?" she flung back at him heatedly. "You're the one who is supposed to be doing the rescuing, not me."

The two of them locked glares. She noticed that when he was angry his eyes flashed like brilliant chips of silver, obliterating all trace of the blues and greens she had seen in them before. Momentarily fascinated by this discovery, she focused on those intense silver chips, and forgot what they were fighting about.

"You are right," he finally conceded. He pulled his gaze away from her in a conscious effort to keep his anger sharp. For some reason her glare had softened, losing its icy determination in favor of a more curious, questioning look. Her pale gray eyes had suddenly become younger, more naive, as if for a fleeting moment all the pain and suffering that had made her as she was today was washed away, revealing a girl who was gentler, younger, unscarred by anger and hatred. This glimpse of her unsettled him. He preferred it when she was angry.

"I should not have left you unattended for so long," he admitted. "Rest assured, it will not happen again." It sounded more like a threat than an assurance.

"I am not a child that needs to be watched every moment," she pointed out tartly, wondering how she could possibly have found anything in that cold, hard glare of interest. Once again there was a need to put him in his place. She summoned her frostiest demeanor. "The fact that you have been hired to rescue me does not place me under your control."

"You are wrong, Mademoiselle," he countered evenly. "The fact that I am risking my life to get you the hell out of here places you exactly under my control, and you would do well to remember it."

She found his rudeness appalling, but she reminded herself that she would not be in his company much longer. Perhaps until they parted ways it would be best simply to ignore his obvious lack of breeding. She regarded his outfit curiously. "Why are you dressed like that?"

He looked down at his ragged uniform with irritation. "It was my plan to appear at the inn and arrest you myself," he told her dryly. "It was the safest way I could think of to remove you from the inn."

She looked at him with astonishment. "Then it is just as well you did not tell me of your plan, or I would have sat there and calmly waited for you to appear behind the seven guards who came to make the arrest."

"None of them could have made a positive identification of you," he pointed out. "They would have had to take you back to the Conciergerie, and I would have returned to get you out."

There was something in the finality with which he said the words that made her feel strangely confident that was exactly what he would have done.

"Nicolas was with them," she reflected. "He would have made the identification and I would have been taken straight to the guillotine." The thought of Nicolas inflamed the anger within her once again.

He shook his head. "No, Mademoiselle. They would have taken you in for questioning first. I am sure they are most anxious to find out who helped you to escape in the first place."

"Well, if they had, I would have told them nothing," she assured him defensively.

"Perhaps," he allowed with a shrug. "But then again, thus far there is very little of value that you could tell them." He began to undo the tarnished buttons on his jacket. "At any rate, I have no intention of letting you come so close to being caught again. We are leaving for the coast tonight. We should reach Boulogne by tomorrow evening, and if the winds are with us, we will set foot on English soil the following day. Then you will be safe."

The time had come. She had to make her intentions clear to him. "Citizen Julien, I am not going with you to England," she informed him calmly.

Annoyance darkened his eyes. "We have been through this before, Mademoiselle," he told her impatiently. "I do not have time to discuss it again. You are coming with me." He turned to leave the room.

She shook her head adamantly. "I do not belong to you, Citizen. You have saved my life and for that I am grateful. But it is up to me to decide what I will do with this new chance you have given me. And I have made my decision."

He looked at her with disgust. "Then your decision is a poor one. It would be far better for you to help your sisters heal than to sacrifice your life to this empty cause of vengeance."

"How easy that is for you to say, you who cannot possibly understand the losses I have endured!" she burst out furiously. "Can you not see that I have nothing left to give my sisters, except for pain and rage and a hatred so intense it threatens to crush me beneath its unbearable weight?" She wrapped her arms around herself and began to pace the length of the room. "What could I bring to them but anger and resentment? How could I ask them to heal when I myself cannot?" She stopped pacing and faced him squarely. "Feeling as I do, what good could I possibly be to them?"

"Perhaps," he mused quietly, "they would be good for you."

"I do not want them to be good for me," she snapped. "I do not need anyone to be good for me. What I need is to kill Nicolas Bourdon, and after that, I truly don't care what happens."

He studied her for a moment. He realized she was deadly serious. And that was going to make his task considerably more difficult.

"I will write a note for you to give to Sir Edward, informing him that you did rescue me from the Conciergerie and that you should be paid your entire fee," she continued, pacing again. "I will make it clear that remaining in France was entirely my decision. You can tell him I have gone to stay with friends. He need not know what my intentions are."

"You will be killed."

She stopped pacing and looked at him calmly. "I know."

Perhaps it was the peaceful tranquillity that surrounded her as she spoke the words, almost as if the idea appealed to her. Or maybe it was the fact that as she stood before him, her back straight and her head held high with purpose, he found himself imagining her in another time and place, wrapped in a beautiful silk gown, with her hair pinned up amid delicate sprays of fresh flowers. In her ragged clothes, with her coarsely chopped hair and her swollen, bloodstained mouth, there was an unmistakable quality to her, a resolute determination, a firmness of spirit and daring that, were she a man, would have been applauded as courage. But she was a woman, and her need for vengeance was impossible, reckless, desperate. He did not doubt that were she given the opportunity, she would not hesitate to kill this man on whom she had decided to focus her rage. But he also knew that regardless of whether she was successful or not, she would be captured. And executed. He could not let that happen. He did not risk his life to save people so they could take his gift and throw it back into the jaws of death. He had taken on the task of saving her, and like it or not, she was damn well going to be saved.

"If you please, Mademoiselle," he said firmly as he grabbed hold of her arm and began to walk with her to the door.

"Where are you taking me?" she stammered, suddenly confused.

He did not answer, but gripped her forcefully as he escorted her down the stairs.

"Justin!" he called out when they reached the main floor.

"Citizen Julien, I insist you unhand me," ordered Jacqueline as she struggled to free herself.

His response was to increase his grip until it was painful. "Justin!" he repeated loudly.

The young man who had let them in appeared from the kitchen, wiping his hands on a towel. "I was just preparing some food for you—"

"Where is the cellar?" interrupted Citizen Julien.

Justin looked at him in confusion. "Through a door leading off the kitchen."

"Any way of entering or exiting other than the door in the kitchen?"

"No," replied Justin blankly.

"Any windows?"

Justin shook his head.

"Perfect," commented Citizen Julien. "Would you be kind enough to lead the way?"

"You cannot mean to lock me in there!" protested Jacqueline, staring at him in shock.

"Only until I return," replied Citizen Julien calmly.

"No!" she cried as Justin held the door open. "No, you cannot do this! You have no right!" She began to squirm wildly in an effort to break his hold on her.

"Justin, I think perhaps we will need a candle," suggested Citizen Julien as he pinned both of Jacqueline's arms behind her back and forced her to walk in front of him down the dark stairs.

The air in the cellar was musty and damp, but not foul like the air at the Conciergerie. Citizen Julien continued to hold her as they stood in the darkness waiting for Justin to appear with a candle. She decided to quit her struggling and try reasoning with him.

"Citizen Julien, you cannot keep me down here forever," she began.

"Of course not," he agreed pleasantly. "This is merely an unfortunate precaution so I can be sure you will still be here when I return."

"But I am not going with you."

"Well now, that is where I have to disagree. As far as I am concerned, you are coming with me, whether you like it or not."

"All right then," she hastily agreed. "I will go with you to England. Now can we go back upstairs?" she asked sweetly.

"Come now, Mademoiselle, you will have to do better than that," he told her with amusement. "To fool your opponent you have to be convincing, not simply tell him what you think he wants to hear."

"No, truly," she protested, desperate for him to believe her. "What you have said makes sense. I belong with my sisters. They need me. So I will go with you to England." She was certain her voice rang with sincerity.

"I am glad to hear it, Mademoiselle," he responded dryly.

"Besides, I doubt that I would be successful in my mission," she continued, with what she felt was just the right amount of feminine helplessness. "I don't think I could ever actually kill someone. I would probably faint." She tried to make her voice sound a little weak on that last part. She had never fainted in her life, but she knew that lots of women did, or appeared to anyway.

"Now that was truly marvelous," he told her with admiration. "Right up to that last bit, you really were most convincing. The only problem, Mademoiselle, is that I was at your trial, and I heard what you did to that captain of the National Guard." He felt her stiffen in his grip and he had to struggle to keep from laughing. "Also, during our skirmish with those thugs, I watched you smash a bottle over that poor chap's head, and I must say, fainting looked to be about the last thing in the world you would do. Ah, here is Justin with your candle."

Justin descended the stairs with a candle and placed it on an overturned crate. "Will there be anything else?" he asked Citizen Julien, his eyes completely avoiding Jacqueline.

Citizen Julien released his grip on her and stood so his massive body blocked her access to the staircase. "No," he replied. "The boy will be fine down here until I return." He motioned for Justin to mount the stairs ahead of him.

"I will not stay down here!" shouted Jacqueline. "You have no right to make me! I am not your prisoner, Citizen!"

Citizen Julien ignored her as he shut the door, plunging the basement into darkness, except for the meager glow of the candle.

"Come back here! Wait!" shrieked Jacqueline. She raced up the stairs and grabbed hold of the handle. It was already locked. She beat her fists against the door.

"Do not open the door for any reason," said Citizen Julien loudly. "If he does not settle down within five minutes, you have my permission to take a stick to him when I get back."

Jacqueline listened as his heavy boots thudded across the floor and a door banged shut.

"Justin, you have to let me out," she pleaded. "This is all a terrible mistake. Citizen Julien is kidnapping me. Please, you have to let me go!"

"Save your breath, boy," replied Justin. "Whatever he tells me to do, that's what I do. It won't do you any good to make a noise about it." She could hear him begin to walk away.

"If you let me go I will see to it that you are rewarded," she cried out desperately. His footsteps stopped. "I have some valuables hidden away. If you help me they are yours." How she would get them she had no idea. The most important thing was to get out of this house before Citizen Julien returned.

"You're not listening, boy," replied Justin. "I only follow his instructions. And he said you were to stay down there." His footsteps receded into another part of the house.

Temporarily defeated, Jacqueline slowly descended the stairs and looked for a place to sit. She started to dust off the top of an old trunk with her sleeve, but quickly decided that given how filthy her clothes already were, a little more dirt could not possibly harm them. She sat down heavily, crossed her arms, and stared into the faint glow of the candle.

Being locked in the cellar was a delay to her plans, nothing more, she told herself flatly. Regardless of Citizen Julien's plans for her, two things remained certain. She was not going to England. And Nicolas Bourdon was going to die.

The candle had burned down low by the time Jacqueline heard the door at the top of the stairs creak open. Stiff and sleepy, she opened her eyes to see the tall, dark silhouette of Citizen Julien filling the doorway.

"Come, Mademoiselle," he called down to her. "The

hour grows late and we have work to do on you before we set out."

With a little groan she slowly sat up on the trunk and rubbed her aching neck. She had not meant to fall asleep. For the longest time she had waited to hear the sounds of Justin entering the kitchen again so that she could try once more to persuade him to open the door. But he had not returned to the kitchen, and finally she had curled up on the trunk and closed her eyes. The events of the past two days had obviously left her more tired than she realized.

"Make haste, Mademoiselle, we do not have all night," said Citizen Julien impatiently.

"I'm coming," she muttered crossly as she dragged herself up the stairs.

She had to squint as her eyes adjusted to the late-afternoon light in the kitchen. She judged that Citizen Julien had been away for two to three hours at least. With a little frown of irritation she turned to complain to him about leaving her locked in that cold, damp cellar for so long.

One look at him made her eyes grow wide and she forgot all about her irritation.

Gone was the handsome, imposing captain of the National Guard who had single-handedly rescued her from a bloodthirsty mob. Citizen Julien had been transformed into a filthy, aged peasant. His hair was his own, she was sure of it, but it had been carefully dusted with powder until it was as gray as ashes. A mixture of carefully applied cosmetics gave his complexion a ruddy, weathered appearance, and his facial lines had been enhanced by smudges of dirt. He wore a loose-fitting coarse woolen shirt, trousers that had been mended at least a half-dozen times, a ragged blue coat, and a filthy red cap that was pulled down low over his forehead. He smiled at her, revealing an apparently rotten mouth, with several teeth so completely black they appeared not to be there, and the ones that remained so brown they looked like they should come out any moment. He was truly a work of art.

"Why a peasant?" she asked curiously as she continued to study him. She had to admit, the man was certainly
a master of disguise.

"Because every night the peasants who have come into
Paris to sell their produce during the day must pass the
city gates to return to their cottages in the country. Each
one of them is questioned, and some wagons are searched,
but if we play our parts right, we should be able to make
it past without incident," he explained.

"And what part am I to play?" she demanded. "That
of the farmer's son?"

"Too predictable," he replied with a shake of his head.
"The authorities know you have been disguised as a boy,
so they will be highly suspicious of any youth trying to
leave the city. I am afraid we will have to be a bit more
creative than that." He smiled. "For the next twenty-four
hours, Mademoiselle, I intend to turn you into a proper
farmer's wife." He lifted a coarse brown dress, yellowed
blouse, and shapeless petticoat from the back of a chair
and held them out in front of him. The dress was at least
twice as wide as he was.

"I will never fit into that," she protested.

"With a little padding you will," he assured her.
"Come, we have work to do." He held open the door to
the hallway and gestured for her to go first.

For a moment she hesitated, wondering if she should
just make a dash for the back door and try to escape him
now. But Citizen Julien was right, after her encounter
with the mob this morning, the sansculotte outfit she wore
was probably no longer an effective disguise. She decided
it would be to her advantage to let him create a new identity for her. Then, once they were outside and headed
toward the city barricades, she would find a way to get
away from him.

"Mademoiselle?" he inquired with a lifted eyebrow.

With a little start she focused on the task at hand and
preceded him out the door. She mounted the stairs and
entered the bedroom before turning to take the garments
from him so she could close the door and change. Much

to her surprise Citizen Julien stepped into the room and closed the door, and then handed her the clothes as if he expected her to put them on right in front of him.

"Citizen Julien, I require privacy to change," she pointed out.

"And you shall have it," he remarked agreeably. "If you turn around, you will see Justin has been thoughtful enough to install a screen in here so your modesty can be protected. I must say, though, I did have a devil of a time convincing him you really were a woman."

"But why is it necessary for you to be in here with me?" she demanded. She could see a jug filled with steaming water had been set on the washstand in the corner, and she longed to give herself a more thorough washing than she had the night before.

He sighed and went over to the washstand to examine the contents of a smaller jug beside the basin. "Unfortunately, Mademoiselle, given the remarkable talent you demonstrated today for climbing out of windows, I find myself in the rather difficult situation of not being able to let you out of my sight." He picked up the jug and sniffed it before stirring it with the spoon that was resting in it.

"But I have already made it clear that I will be going with you to England," protested Jacqueline lightly, trying to trivialize his concern. If Citizen Julien did not leave her alone, even for a minute, how would she get away from him before they left the gates of Paris?

He put down the jug and regarded her seriously. "No, Mademoiselle, it is *I* who have made it clear to *you* that you are going to England," he corrected. "You, on the other hand, have lied to me about your intentions, and then turned around and tried to bribe poor Justin into letting you out with some fanciful story about how I was kidnapping you. I must say, he was most upset about your allegations." He walked over to the bed and stretched out on it, his massive frame causing the mattress to sag heavily under his weight. He laced his fingers behind his head and closed his eyes. "I think perhaps you ought to apologize to him before we leave," he suggested. "Justin does not take criticism of me lightly."

"He is lying," replied Jacqueline indignantly as she turned away from him. "I did no such thing." It was most important that she get Citizen Julien to believe she could be trusted. That way there would be a moment when his guard would be down and she could get away.

His leap from the bed was so swift it startled her. His hands clamped around her arms like bands of steel, and he spun her about with a force that made her teeth chatter.

"Don't ever, ever lie to me about someone I trust," he warned in a soft, savage voice. "Do you understand?" He gave her a violent shake.

She wanted to deny that she was lying, but the furious intensity of his stare made her think better of it. "Yes," she stammered. "I understand."

Abruptly he released her. "Good," he replied curtly. "Now get changed."

She rubbed her arms where he had held her. Then she picked up the jug and basin on the washstand and carried them with her behind the screen.

Several minutes later she had washed as best she could and donned her new peasant outfit. If it was at all possible, the rough dress and blouse was even coarser and scratchier than her sansculotte outfit. She found herself wondering how the peasants could stand to wear such uncomfortable clothing. She was certain her skin was going to be rubbed raw before the evening was out. She stepped out from behind the screen.

"Much better," commented Citizen Julien as he looked at her critically. He had removed his coat and rolled up his sleeves. "Come and sit here." He gestured to the chair placed in the center of the room.

Jacqueline obediently sat in the chair and waited for him to start applying the cosmetics he had laid out on the washstand. Instead he moved behind her and she felt a comb start to rake through the tangled remains of her hair.

"I wish I could wash it," she remarked wistfully as Citizen Julien lifted a lock and began to work through the tangles.

"Unfortunately there isn't time," he replied. "However, if you are not overly tired when we board *The Angélique,* I will order a hot bath for you."

"*The Angélique?*" repeated Jacqueline.

"That is the ship we will be taking across the channel."

"Is it Sir Edward's ship?" she asked.

"No," he replied. "She is mine."

She turned and looked at him in disbelief. "You own a ship?"

The faintest trace of amusement lit his eyes. "Does that surprise you, Mademoiselle?" His tone was lightly mocking.

"I suppose it does," she admitted. She turned around again. "The rescuing business must be good," she commented dryly.

He gave the tangle he was working on a sharp tug, causing her to yelp.

"Sorry," he apologized, his tone not particularly convincing.

He worked on her hair a few more minutes until all the tangles were gone. Then he lifted it up and draped a towel around her shoulders.

"What are you doing?" she asked as he went to the washstand and picked up the small jug.

"I am going to change your hair color," he explained as he stirred the contents of the jug.

"To what?" she demanded, not at all sure she liked the idea and at the same time wondering why it mattered to her. She was not going to live much longer anyway. Who cared what color her hair was?

"To a dark brown." He began to drizzle spoonfuls of the liquid in the jug over her head. "The authorities are looking for a woman with short blond hair. It is too dangerous to leave you fitting that description." He began to massage the foul-smelling solution through her hair with his fingers. "You need not be concerned, the color will wash out when you have your bath tomorrow night."

The bath she was not going to have, because she was not going with him. Illogically, that struck her as unfair. Because of Nicolas, she was not going to finally have a bath. She added that to her list of grievances against him.

"We'll let that set for a bit while I do your face," said Citizen Julien as he deposited the jug on the washstand. He washed the brown dye off his hands before picking up a small jar and a sponge.

For the next fifteen minutes he sponged and stroked and blended and powdered, staring at her critically each time he paused to put down one jar and pick up another. Every now and then he would ask her to smile, or raise her eyebrows, or pucker her face into a frown, and as she did these things he would fill in the lines her expressions created with a tiny brush. Jacqueline found herself most curious about the new face he was creating for her. It was clear from the disguises he had made for himself that he possessed an unusual degree of skill.

"Where did you learn so much about cosmetics?"

He was busy painting a dark shadow around one of her eyes. "A friend of mine taught me," he replied vaguely.

"Was he an actor?" she asked.

"It was a she," he corrected. "And yes, she is an actress. Close your eyes."

She obeyed and the small brush began to make feathery-soft strokes across her eyelid. The heel of his hand rested ever so lightly on her cheekbone as he worked, and she found herself uncomfortably aware of the heat and power contained in that hand. She was not used to having a man so close to her, performing such intimate tasks as combing her hair and applying cosmetics. She could sense the strength and form of his body as he leaned into her, and suddenly he seemed too close, too masculine, too intimate. She shifted restlessly in her chair.

"Stop moving," he ordered as he firmly grasped her

chin and set it at the angle he needed to work. He resumed the feathery dusting of her eyelid.

"Is she Angélique?" she blurted out, trying to fill the quiet space between them with conversation.

His brush stopped in mid stroke. "Who?"

"The actress," she replied, wishing she had asked a different question. This one seemed far too personal, as if she had some interest in who he named his ship after, which she most decidedly did not.

He did not answer. She knew he was studying her, she could feel it, but she kept her eyes firmly shut.

"No," he replied after a moment. "She is not."

There was a finality in his tone that told her not to pursue that particular line of questioning.

Neither of them spoke again. He finished with her face, neck, and hands, and then he rubbed her hair with the towel, removing all the excess dye and causing it to matt and tangle all over again. He patted it down and plunked an ugly cap on her head before standing back to survey his work.

"Well," she demanded curiously, "how do I look?"

He smiled at her with evident satisfaction. "See for yourself."

She went to the mirror that hung on the wall above the washstand and gasped with surprise.

Nothing about her seemed familiar. Her pale, translucent skin was rough and reddened, and filled with lines that spoke of years of hardship and exposure to the elements. Her eyes seemed to be set closer together than they really were, and one of them was blackened and bruised. Her normally bow-shaped lips were pale and thin, her cheeks were flat and lacking in definition. Everything about her face looked tired, worn, and slack. Her darkened hair hung in ratty clumps underneath the filthy little cap, looking like it had never been washed or combed. There was no doubt about it. She looked absolutely awful. She spun around with delight.

"Not even Nicolas will recognize me like this!" she burst out enthusiastically.

"He won't get a chance to," he remarked, his voice slightly threatening. He held out a little pot. "Your teeth are too white. Rub some of this on them."

She took the pot and began to rub some of its contents on her teeth while Citizen Julien tidied up the jars on the washstand and packed them into a little leather pouch. Then he went to the bed and removed one of the feather pillows. Pulling out a knife from the back of his waistband, he made a small cut in each corner of the pillow and then threaded a sash through the slits.

"Tie this around your waist underneath your petticoat," he ordered as he held it out to her.

"Is it really necessary that I be with child?" she asked delicately. The idea was repellent to her.

"Farmers' wives are almost always pregnant," he told her matter-of-factly. "And citizenesses who are expecting are admired as breeders of the new generation of free citizens. That could be helpful if we are stopped along the way."

With a little sigh she retired behind the screen to tie the pillow around her waist. She emerged a few minutes later, her slender shape totally transformed by the round swell of the pillow.

"Well?" she demanded. Something in the intense way he was staring at her made her uncomfortable.

"Remember not to move too quickly," he instructed her. "The extra weight you carry is heavy and cumbersome. Your movements must reflect that."

Thinking back to the memory of her mother's swollen shape when she was pregnant with Séraphine, Jacqueline arched her back and slowly padded across the room.

"Much better," Citizen Julien commented. "Your name is Thérèse Poitier. You are nineteen years old and you are expecting your third child. I am your husband, Jean. We have spent the day in Paris trying to sell what little is left of our turnips and potatoes. Now we are headed home. I have traveling documents for both of us. You will not speak to the guards when we are stopped, unless you are asked something directly. Is that clear?" he demanded.

She nodded, wondering how far it was to the city gates from here. She had to get away from him before they were near any guards.

"Good." He opened the door for her. "After you, wife."

Justin was in the kitchen packing food into a basket. As Jacqueline walked in he stopped what he was doing and stared at her in disbelief. "You really are a woman," he stammered in amazement.

"Of course I am a woman," she snapped, somewhat insulted that her previous disguise had been quite so convincing. She was used to men being overwhelmed by her feminine beauty when she walked into a room, not gaping at her as if she was some kind of freak.

Citizen Julien tossed her an old cloak and shawl. "Put those on," he ordered. He shrugged into a tattered blue overcoat and shoved a heavy pistol into the waistband of his trousers. Then he turned to Justin.

"My friend, I am indebted to you for your assistance," he said, his voice low and serious.

"Never," replied Justin as he reached out and gripped Citizen Julien's shoulder. "It is I who will forever be indebted to you." The words were heavy with emotion.

They stared at each other a moment, a hard, intense look that spoke of some secret understanding, of some bond that united them in their game of danger and intrigue. If Justin was ever suspected of helping an escaped prisoner, he would be executed. Jacqueline found herself wondering what it was that drove him to risk his life to assist Citizen Julien. Perhaps it was money, but somehow she did not think so. She reflected on how angry Citizen Julien had been when she told him that Justin had lied. *Don't ever lie to me about someone I trust,* he had told her. Given the dangers inherent in his line of work, trust was not something to be treated lightly. It was a matter of life and death. These men obviously shared some experience that had earned that trust. Suddenly Jacqueline felt deeply ashamed for having accused Justin of lying.

"The cart is out in the back," Justin was saying as he handed Citizen Julien the heavy basket he had packed. He turned to Jacqueline. "I wish you a safe journey, Citizeness." He bent low and kissed her hand, an act of gallantry that had all but disappeared under the new Republic. Such courtesies were considered courtly and therefore suspect.

"Thank you, Citizen Justin," she replied. "Your good wishes for my welfare are greatly appreciated." Regardless of whether I am on my way to England or not, she added to herself.

"Come, Mademoiselle," said Citizen Julien. He swept into a low, mocking bow and gestured grandly toward the door. "Your carriage awaits."

She followed him outside into the yard. The leaden sky was shadowed with dark clouds, casting a pall over what little remained of the day. An ancient gray horse with bony ribs and a scruffy winter coat stood patiently waiting in front of a rough farmer's cart. Jacqueline could see that the cart was about one third filled with decrepit baskets of moldering turnips and potatoes.

Citizen Julien walked around to the other side of the cart, placed the basket inside, and climbed up onto the seat. He grabbed hold of the reins and looked at her.

"Are you coming?" he demanded abruptly.

She looked at him incredulously. "Are you not going to help me get up?" she asked.

"You are Thérèse Poitier," he reminded her. "You do not require assistance."

She stamped her foot on the ground. "I am practically nine months gone with child," she pointed out indignantly. "Any gentleman would offer his assistance, and I would certainly expect no less from my husband."

He shrugged his shoulders and spat on the ground. "Your husband is a peasant farmer, not a gentleman. And he expects you to get yourself on this cart. Now."

With a little huff of annoyance she walked over and awkwardly hoisted herself up onto the cart.

"That's better," he remarked. "Now listen to me, Mademoiselle. From this moment until we reach Boulogne you will act exactly as you would if you were Thérèse Poitier, is that clear?" he demanded.

"Perfectly," she replied, reminding herself that it would only be a short while before she was free of him.

"Good." He snapped the reins and they began to move slowly down the lane.

For the next while neither of them spoke. Jacqueline focused her thoughts on finding the right moment for her escape from Citizen Julien, but an opportunity did not present itself. The cart moved slowly through the streets, not attracting any attention whatsoever. She knew that if she jumped off the cart and began to run, Citizen Julien would simply stop the cart and run after her, so that was not an effective plan. She considered asking him to stop so she might look after her personal needs, but since they were in the midst of the city and the streets were crowded with people, that hardly seemed like a credible request.

Before she knew it they were approaching the gate. Already about a dozen carts were lined up to pass through. Several soldiers of the National Guard were performing inspections under the watchful eye of their sergeant. They questioned the men and women driving the carts, examined their loads, and usually demanded that a cask or crate be opened or a basket overturned so they could make sure nothing and no one was being smuggled out. The sight of them made Jacqueline experience a fresh wave of fear. What if she changed her mind, and decided not to stay and kill Nicolas? What if she chose to give up the fight and to flee with Citizen Julien to a new life in England? And what if, after making that decision, she was caught at the gate and arrested? She would be returned to the Conciergerie and guillotined tomorrow. Nicolas would be informed of her arrest and would undoubtedly visit her tonight, anxious to finally slake his lust for her before she was removed from his power forever. She would be degraded and then executed, and Nicolas would be left to live. The idea was intolerable. Panic began to grip her. She could not risk discovery. She could not pass through that gate.

"Citizen Julien," she whispered frantically as she turned to him.

"Don't call me that," he snapped between clenched teeth. He fought to keep his self-control. If this little idiot made that mistake when a soldier was near, it would cost both of them their lives. He should have smuggled her out hidden in something, preferably bound and gagged.

"Jean," she began again tentatively, realizing her mistake.

He looked at her. She seemed extremely agitated, and he realized she was terrified of being discovered as they went through the gate. He was surprised by this sudden show of fear; it seemed incongruous with the courage and daring she had exhibited thus far on their escape. But of course she was a woman, and perhaps underneath her adopted bravado and moments of instinctive defense she was just as helpless and vulnerable as most women. Once again he found himself wondering what she would have been like in another time and place, before the terror and bloodshed of the revolution had torn her from the sheltered walls of her château. He reached out and took her slender hand in his. Her thin fingers were chilled to the bone. He cursed himself for not having thought to supply her with a warm pair of gloves.

"Fear not, Mademoiselle," he said in a whisper meant only for her ears. "If we play our parts right, we will get through. Have faith." He gave her hand a little squeeze.

She shook her head and yanked her hand away from his. "I am not going through," she told him abruptly. "I cannot leave Paris." She quickly moved to step down from the cart before any of the guards noticed her, knowing he would not risk a scene so close to the gate by trying to stop her.

She was wrong. His hand shot out and snaked around her wrist, yanking her back into her seat.

"You are not going anywhere," he informed her brusquely, anger rising within him as he hauled her up against his side and crushed his arm against her. How could he have thought, even for a moment, that what he saw in those luminous gray eyes was fear? This little aristo was too damned stupid to be afraid of anything, except not getting a chance to murder a man who would probably throw her to the ground and toss her skirts up over her head before she knew what she was about.

She struggled to remove his arm from around her waist. "Let me go," she bit out. "It is not up to you to decide what I do with my life." She tried to pry his fingers off of her, but his grip remained strong and sure.

"You would not have a life at this moment were it not for me," he grated out savagely. "So sit still and shut up before you get us both arrested. Unlike you, I am not quite ready to die." He squeezed his arm around her so tightly she could barely breathe, much less break free and disappear into the evening light.

"You have no right to force me," she blazed as she punched him hard in the side of his ribs. The knuckles in her fist crashed into a rock-hard wall of muscle and bone, sending a streak of pain up her arm.

His other hand dropped the reins and reached up to roughly grab her face. "One more move like that and I'll—"

"No, no, I beg of you, this is all a mistake!" The desperate cry cut through the air and distracted him from completing his threat.

His arm still clamped firmly around her, they ceased their struggle to look up and see what was happening.

An elderly man whose cart was being searched stood wringing his hands beside one of the guards, who had evidently discovered something in one of the wine casks he had opened.

"Come out of there now," snapped the sergeant into the darkness of the cask.

Everyone watched as a young man crawled out of the opening and stood defiantly before the guard.

"Well now, my friend, would you like to explain why you choose to travel in a wine cask?" drawled the sergeant sarcastically.

The man shrugged. "I rather liked the peace and quiet of it," he answered flippantly.

"That is lucky for you," said the sergeant, unimpressed by his evident calm. "Since I can almost guarantee that soon you will have all the peace and quiet in the world."

The man acknowledged the threat with a small bow of his head. "The driver was unaware of my presence," he informed the sergeant. "He is a loyal citizen of the Republic and should not be charged."

The sergeant nodded to two other soldiers, who left the carts they were inspecting and enthusiastically took hold of the old man. "His innocence must be proven," said the sergeant. "Until then he is also under arrest. Take them away." He turned to the remaining guard. "Get an ax and chop up the remaining casks," he ordered.

"No!" cried both the prisoners in unison.

The sergeant looked at them and smiled with satisfaction. "Would you like to tell me which other casks to look in?" he suggested pleasantly.

His face stricken, the young man stepped forward and moved several casks out of the way before opening one that was situated in the middle of the cart.

"It's all right, my sweet," he said gently into the dark hole. "Come on out." He reached his hand in to offer assistance.

A frightened young woman in her early twenties emerged from the black cavern. The man wrapped his arms around her protectively as she sank against him and buried her face in his chest. "It will be all right," he murmured soothingly. "Trust in God and try to be brave."

"There is no God anymore, Citizen," laughed the sergeant, "or hadn't you heard?" He spat on the ground. "Take them away."

Jacqueline watched as the woman turned in her husband's arms. Her delicately chiseled face was white with terror and sorrow. She knew there was no escape. They had tried, and they had failed. She looked up at her husband and managed a small smile. Jacqueline felt a tightening in her chest that cut off her ability to breathe. She knew their moments together were at an end. They would be separated and imprisoned, and then they would be executed. It was that simple.

"You must do something," she whispered urgently to Citizen Julien.

He watched the pathetic little party being led away by the soldiers, anger and frustration churning within him. Yet he managed to keep his expression perfectly neutral, as if the incident was not his concern and therefore of no interest to him.

"What would you have me do, Mademoiselle?" he whispered harshly. "Shall I go over and have a word with the sergeant and tell him that he has made a mistake? Shall I barter with him, and offer him you in exchange for them? Or do you think I should race in, kill all the guards and everyone watching, and then ride away to freedom with four escaped prisoners in tow?" He turned to look at her. "Which plan do you think will succeed?" he drawled sarcastically.

"We cannot just sit back and watch!" she protested with helpless fury. "They are going to die!"

"Yes," he agreed. "They are. And there is nothing we can do." His arm tightened around her, effectively pinning her against the hard length of his side. "But like it or not, you are going to live, Mademoiselle, so keep your mouth shut and let me do the talking." He snapped the reins against the old horse's rump and the cart jolted forward to take its place in the line.

It was fear that made her obey him, rather than any change in her desire to stay and kill Nicolas. The sight of those people being arrested stunned her into a temporary state of submission. She realized she had waited too long to escape from Citizen Julien. She could not make any move here that might attract the attention of the soldiers.

She wanted to kill Nicolas more than ever, but to do so she had to stay alive and out of prison.

"Your papers, Citizen," demanded the guard who had come over to inspect their cart.

Citizen Julien released his grip on her and reached into his coat to produce the required documents.

"When did you come into Paris, Citizen Poitier?" the guard asked as he examined the papers.

"Just after dawn," replied Citizen Julien gruffly. "Didn't sell as much as we hoped."

The guard walked around and looked at the few baskets of vegetables in the back of the cart without much interest. He lifted his bayonet and shoved it into one basket, and then another, damaging some of the produce. Evidently satisfied that there was nothing in there except turnips and potatoes, he returned the papers to Citizen Julien.

"Quite a catch we just made, was it not?" the soldier demanded with a mixture of arrogance and pride. It was obvious his mind was still on the previous arrest, and he wanted to be congratulated as if it was he who had made the discovery.

"Indeed it was," agreed Citizen Julien enthusiastically. "Those cursed aristos will try to sneak out in almost anything these days, won't they?" He spat on the ground to show his contempt.

"None of them get past this gate," the soldier boasted. "We have a nose for them. One look at a driver and we can tell if something is amiss. That's how we caught the Comte Rabourdin and his entire family last week. The comte and his wife tried to make us believe they were simple servants traveling with their children to find work outside of Paris."

"And what made you think they were not?" asked Citizen Julien with interest.

"They did not look like servants," explained the soldier. "Oh, their outfits were convincing enough, but none of those lily-white hands had ever done an honest day's work." He looked over at Jacqueline. "Now, your wife there, that is a woman who knows what it is to work for a living," he said with authoritative approval.

Citizen Julien glanced at her without much interest. "She pulls her weight," he agreed. "Although, thanks to me, she now has twice as much weight to pull," he joked crassly. He reached over and rubbed her familiarly on the stomach.

Momentarily forgetting her terror of being discovered, Jacqueline lifted her head to glare at him.

The soldier snorted with laughter. "On your way, Citizen Poitier, so I don't have to listen to your wife yell at you." He waved them on with his hand.

"As you wish, Citizen," replied Citizen Julien with a dramatic sigh.

He snapped the reins against the bony rump of the horse and the cart rattled slowly through the gate and beyond the barricades of Paris.

Jacqueline moved as far away from Citizen Julien as the cart would allow and bit down hard on her lip. I will be back, she promised herself as she watched the lights of the city recede into the darkness.

This was only a delay. Nothing would keep her from having her revenge. Nothing.

Chapter 5

Jacqueline felt herself falling, as far and as fast as if someone had pushed her off a cliff, and then her cheek came to rest against something warm. She sighed and nuzzled her face deeper into the padding that had cushioned her fall. The tremendous weight of her head was more than she could bear. She lifted her hand to adjust the mysterious pillow that was providing such delicious relief.

And sat bolt upright as she realized she was resting against Citizen Julien's shoulder. She ground her fists into her eyes and shifted farther away from him.

"We still have a few more hours. You should try to get some sleep," he told her gruffly.

"I am not the least bit tired," Jacqueline informed him. In truth she was utterly exhausted, but she did not want to admit that. Especially since Citizen Julien showed no sign of being tired whatsoever.

He looked at her skeptically, noting the dark circles that had formed under her eyes. He knew he was driving them at a grueling pace, but it was essential they reach the coast as swiftly as possible. Still, when he delivered her to Sir Edward, he did not want her to collapse with exhaustion. "You can lean on my shoulder if you like," he offered.

"No," she replied stiffly. She pinned her gaze on the endless expanse of road and countryside ahead, willing herself to stay awake.

It was the afternoon of the following day. When they had started out, Jacqueline assumed they would drive for a few hours and then stop somewhere for the night, which would give her the perfect opportunity to sneak away from Citizen Julien while he slept. To her dismay, she quickly discovered that Citizen Julien was determined to make it to the coast without stopping. When they were about ten miles out of Paris, they were met by a rider who appeared out of the darkness leading two strong horses that could easily pull their light cart at a swift and steady speed. Their ancient nag was unhitched and the new horses were quickly strapped into place. Citizen Julien was a skillful driver, guiding them through the darkness and around ruts and holes in the road with apparent ease. But as the horses tired and Jacqueline assumed that they would stop at an inn to rest for the night, another mysterious rider appeared out of the trees with two fresh horses. And so it went, with Citizen Julien relentlessly pushing on toward Boulogne, and a series of men meeting them at prearranged stops with fresh horses every few hours.

When Jacqueline complained of hunger, Citizen Julien reached into the back of the cart and produced the basket Justin had packed for them. It was loaded with cold chicken and beef, cheeses, breads, fruit, two bottles of wine, and three bottles of some other clear drink. It was undoubtedly more than enough to feed the two of them on their journey. When Jacqueline delicately asked if they could stop so she could attend to her personal needs, Citizen Julien calmly got down from the cart and escorted her into the woods. He then pointed out exactly which tree she might use for privacy and waited patiently for her to reappear. The trees he selected were always slightly isolated from the others, so Jacqueline found she could not possibly slip away and quietly disappear into the darkness of the woods without him noticing. Every hour took her farther and farther from Nicolas, and with every hour she grew more anxious and determined to escape. She feared that if she allowed herself to be reunited with her sisters and placed under the care of Sir Edward, she might find it difficult to escape the peace and safety they offered and return to France to have her revenge. She was afraid her hatred might start to ease, and her fury over the horrendous injustice dealt to her and her family might somehow gradually fade in the light of a new and tranquil life. She would not let that happen. She could not. The lives of her father and brother demanded vengeance. The destruction of the world she once knew could not go unpunished. She knew she could not destroy the revolution. Nor could she reverse the despicable evils it had inflicted on her country and her people. But she could kill Nicolas. And with that relatively small, simple act, something in her would be assuaged. She had to get back to Paris.

"Citizen Julien, I need to stop for a moment."

He sighed and pulled in the reins. He leapt down from the cart and waited for her to climb down before leading her into the woods to find a satisfactory spot. The forest they had been traveling through was particularly thick with evergreens at this particular point, and it was difficult to find a tree that was relatively solitary from the rest. Jacqueline stood patiently as Citizen Julien considered where to send her.

"Find a place over there somewhere," he ordered as he waved his hand disinterestedly ahead of them. "And be quick about it." He seated himself on the ground and leaned wearily against a tree as he prepared to wait for her.

She walked forward into the woods and critically evaluated the breadth of several trees before finally stepping behind one that was very wide and quite a distance away from where Citizen Julien was waiting. Directly behind this tree were two thick evergreens, and with a few hurried steps she had disappeared behind them. Fairly certain that he could not see her, she quickly started to make her way deeper and deeper into the forest. Her heart was racing as she silently threaded her way through the dense growth, knowing in just a few minutes Citizen Julien would call out for her to hurry and would expect some kind of response from her. While she realized she could not expect to outdistance him in a few minutes, she hoped she could at least hide herself in the thick forest. Since Citizen Julien would have no idea which direction she had taken, he would not be able to find her. Pressured by the constraints of time, he would eventually be forced to abandon his search and continue toward Boulogne alone. Jacqueline would wait until she was absolutely certain he was gone, and then return to the road and start her journey back to Paris. No doubt a coach or cart would eventually pass and be able to take her at least part of the way. She did not think anyone would be suspicious of a young farm girl on her way to find work in the city. Certainly no one would ever suspect her of being an escaped aristo who was trying to get back into Paris. How she would eat, where she would sleep, these things were of no concern to her. The most important thing was to return to Paris and kill Nicolas. Nothing else mattered.

She continued to weave her way through the woods, wondering how many minutes had passed since Citizen Julien had left her. She paused for a moment and hid behind a tree, her heart pounding in her chest as she listened for the sound of him calling for her. The forest was quiet except for the occasional trilling of birds. There was nothing to indicate Citizen Julien had even noticed she was taking an inordinately long time to see to her personal needs. Perhaps he had fallen asleep as he sat and waited for her. If so, so much the better. She could quietly make her way even farther into the woods without being noticed. Hardly able to contain her excitement, she looked about as she considered which direction she should take next.

"Lose your way, Mademoiselle?" drawled a sarcastic voice.

With a startled gasp she lifted her head just in time to see Citizen Julien swing himself off the branch he had been sitting on and land gracefully in front of her. He stood with his feet braced apart and his hands planted firmly on his hips, the scowl on his face telling her in no uncertain terms that he was absolutely, unconditionally furious.

"Citizen Julien, thank goodness you found me," stammered Jacqueline awkwardly as she took a few steps back.

He looked enraged enough to throttle her, and a strong sense of self-preservation told her that a little distance between the two of them would be in her best interest. "I was trying to get back to the cart, but these woods are so dense I could not find—"

"As always, Mademoiselle, you are a remarkably poor liar," he interrupted, his voice low and furious. "But your relative ineptitude at lying is nothing compared to the contempt with which you treat your life." He reached out for her as he said this, roughly grabbing her by the arm and jerking her into him. "I believe what you need, Mademoiselle de Lambert, is for me to take you over my knee until I succeed in beating some sense into you, or at least make you think twice before trying to escape me again." The hard, grim set of his mouth told her he was deadly serious.

"Don't you dare touch me!" spat Jacqueline, her heart racing with a mixture of fear and aristocratic indignation.

He ignored her order and clamped his enormous hands painfully about her shoulders, holding her still as he stared into her eyes, two shimmering gray pools of righteous defiance that glared back at him with a fury that quite possibly matched his own.

"I have tried to be patient, Mademoiselle," he began, his words slow and measured, as if he was trying to rationalize whatever he was about to do. "I realize your actions are in response to the tragedies that have been inflicted on you. I am sympathetic to your shock over the loss of your brother and father, and I understand your need to blame and your thirst for vengeance—"

"You understand nothing!" she burst out furiously as she struggled to free herself from his painful grip. "You are not part of the noblesse. You are a bourgeois merchant who trades in human cargo, making a living from those who have been unjustly thrown into prison, saving only those whose families or friends can afford to pay your fee. Then you return to England, where you sit safe and smug until your life necessitates that you take on another assignment, like me. What do you know of honor, or duty, or the agonizing need to avenge the ones you have loved?" Her voice was thick with loathing and contempt.

His expression became hard. "You know nothing whatsoever about me, Mademoiselle," he ground out tautly. "Do not dare presume to judge me."

She stared at him in silence for a moment, wondering for the briefest of seconds what he was alluding to. His gaze seemed clouded, as if the pain of some memory had suddenly pierced through his anger and he was fighting with every ounce of his will to suppress it. She watched as he struggled, and was aware of the exact instant when he had succeeded in subduing whatever thought or memory had disturbed him. Once again the sharp focus of his anger returned to her.

"But we were speaking of you, Mademoiselle," he reminded himself softly, staring at her with renewed interest.

He released his hand from one of her shoulders and raised it to lightly trace the contour of her jaw. The day was crisp and cold, yet his fingers were warm against her cool skin, the strength that they so brutally exerted on her shoulder mere seconds earlier restrained in favor of a lighter touch.

"Such a delicate, aristocratic neck," he commented softly. The tips of his fingers slowly burned a path from the line of her jaw to the point where her pulse was beating rapidly in her throat. "What a tragedy it would be for such a perfect column to be laid bare beneath the sharp blade of the guillotine, warm and dripping with the blood of those who placed their necks under it before you." His fingers continued to lightly caress her skin as he spoke, causing a warm, tingling sensation wherever they stroked. Jacqueline felt a shiver shoot all the way down her spine. She told herself it was because the air around them was so cold.

"Then again," he continued, his fingers traveling upward to absently caress her cheek, "it is possible you would be arrested before you ever got to Paris." His other hand released its hold on her shoulder and moved to cradle the side of her face. He held her steady as he gazed down at her, his eyes the color of a summer day, all field greens and sky blues. "Do you know what would happen to you if you were arrested in a village?" he asked softly, his thumbs lightly brushing over her cheeks, inexplicably causing them to grow hot and flushed with the sensation of his gentle touch. "They would take you prisoner, and they would lock you up while they decided whether or not it was worth their trouble to take you all the way to Paris," he told her, his voice low and strangely hypnotic. "And it is possible, Mademoiselle, that the men who guarded you would see that underneath all of this filth and cosmetics, there lies a hidden beauty." His words were low and strangely hushed, as if he was speaking to her from far away. He stared at her intently, holding her prisoner now only by the gentle touch of his fingers and the husky whisper of his voice. Jacqueline gazed up at him, listening to the rhythm of his words and accepting the exquisite heat of his touch, and the animosity between them seemed to disappear, or rather stop, as if it was suddenly suspended somewhere high above them and no longer relevant. She stared into those turquoise summer-day eyes, burning in their intensity, and found that she could not move, could not speak, could not even understand what it was he was saying. All that seemed to matter was that they were alone, together, in the middle of a forest where time and place and who they were had suddenly ceased to matter.

"I have seen your portrait, Jacqueline," he murmured, his hand reaching around and threading into the hair behind her neck. He spoke her name slowly, sensually, as if it was a glorious piece of music that must be treated with care. Jacqueline was vaguely aware that it was the first time he had called her by her given name, and an unfamiliar sense of pleasure flowed hotly through her.

"I wonder," he whispered, his head moving down toward hers, "if there is anything left of that innocent girl in the portrait."

His lips touched hers, warm and firm and gentle, coaxing rather than demanding, igniting an unfamiliar flame within her that heated her blood and stirred the need to respond. She did not move, but held her breath and allowed his lips to taste hers, slowly, leisurely, filling her with an accepting languor that blocked her ability to think. She sighed and moved her lips against his, enjoying the warmth and strength he exuded. He responded by wrapping his arms around her and lightly tracing her lower lip with the tip of his tongue.

Suddenly sheer panic flooded through the very core of her being. He was too close, too powerful, he was trapping her as surely as Nicolas had trapped her against the wall of her cell, and the overwhelming, terrifying maleness of him cut through her lethargy and shattered the spell he had been weaving over her. Responding by pure, unchecked instinct, she clenched her hand into a solid fist and drove it in an upward motion as hard as she could, smashing it into the underside of his jaw and causing him to grunt with pain and stagger back.

He looked at her with genuine amazement as he lifted his hand to his jaw. She stared back at him defiantly, her fist still clenched and ready to hit him again if necessary.

"Don't ever touch me again," she managed, her voice soft and trembling. "Or I will find a knife and plunge it clean into your chest."

He studied her a moment, his jaw aching from where she had struck him. The girl certainly knew how to throw a punch, he reflected soberly. He could not imagine what in the name of God had possessed him to make him want to kiss her. With her filthy, haggard face, her matted hair, her swollen, pregnant shape, and her ragged clothes, one could not exactly describe her as a great beauty, even with the veiled memory of what was obviously an extremely flattering portrait. Beyond that, it was simply not his custom to make advances on a woman who was in his care, even though many had been attractive and, perhaps in a somewhat euphoric state at having been rescued from death, more than willing. It had been a long time since he had indulged himself in the pleasures of a woman. But until this very moment the celibacy he had sworn himself to over a year earlier had not been an effort to maintain. He irritably pushed that realization aside. This is all nonsense, he told himself angrily. He had an aristo to deliver, and they were wasting precious time dallying here in the woods.

"Thank you for your warning, Mademoiselle," he said with a polite, slightly mocking bow of his head. "Rest assured, I will not touch you again, unless you force me to blister your tender little aristocratic backside by trying to escape me. Now, if you are quite finished with your wandering, I suggest we return to the cart." He gestured with his arm the direction back to the road, indicating that Jacqueline should walk ahead of him.

Neither of them spoke again for the remainder of the day. Frustrated by her failure to escape and the knowledge that with every turn of the wheels she was leaving her vengeance farther and farther behind, Jacqueline lapsed into a stony, sullen silence, refusing even to look at Citizen Julien. She fixed her gaze on the road ahead and the countryside around her, taking note of the dry, dead fields that were lightly powdered with frost, and the bleak, leaden sky that seemed an appropriate reflection of her mood. She drew in deep breaths of icy sharp air, so cold it hurt her lungs, and she was glad of the pain, because it reminded her that she was alive, and as long as she was alive, she would return. Until that moment she wanted to memorize every lifeless stalk of growth, to paint a picture in her mind of the sky, and the trees, and the rocks, and the tiny farmers' huts, as pitiful and wretched and dying as it all seemed, because this was France, and France was the country she loved, despite what those who had stolen its power and its glory had done to her, and to thousands like her. She wanted to remember, because remembering would bring her pain and grief, and as long as those feelings continued to torment her, she would never be able to put the past aside and begin a new life. The hours passed by and the road

continued to slowly unravel, until finally, exhausted beyond measure, Jacqueline closed her eyes and allowed herself to sleep.

It was the stillness that awoke her. The heavy clopping of
the horses' hooves and the incessant grinding of the cart
wheels had provided a rhythmic, soothing lullaby for her
as she slept, and when those sounds stopped and the cart
ceased its gentle swaying, Jacqueline wearily forced her
eyes to open. The night was as dark as pitch; not a single
star studded the velvety black sky that wrapped around
her like a great, somber cape. The smell of salt assailed
her nostrils, clean and sharp and vaguely fishy. She had
never inhaled that scent before, but she knew what it
meant. They had reached the coast.

She climbed out of the cart and looked around to see
where Citizen Julien had gone. He was standing some distance away with his back to her, gazing out at a seemingly
endless expanse of ink-stained ocean that was pitching
and roiling before him. She took a few steps toward him,
wanting to inquire about the time, and the turbulence of
the sea, and where was the ship that was to meet them?
But as she got closer something stopped her, and caused
her to put her questions aside and simply look at him
instead.

His legs were braced apart and his hands were
clenched into fists at his side, yet his stance spoke not so
much of anger as of power, power and utter, unwavering
determination. It was as if he was absorbing some of the
enormous, violent force of the sea, as if the sight and
sound and smell of that churning black mass was somehow fortifying him, penetrating his skin and muscle and
bone and soul, and filling him with irrevocable purpose.
She stared at him in silence, feeling all at once like she was
an intruder, secretly witnessing an interaction that was
private and personal. For some reason she could not bring
herself to make him aware of her presence. It was the first
time she had observed him during a moment in which he

was not aware of being watched, and therefore not actively playing a role for his audience.

The icy sea wind beat against his dark figure, causing his open coat to flap behind him and his gray-tinted hair to blow out over his collar. Who was this man, she wondered, who was able to transform himself from one identity to the next with such apparent ease, never raising the slightest doubt that he was anyone other than who he appeared to be at that moment? What could motivate a man like him to take such incredibly daring risks, slipping in and out of courtrooms and prisons, moving brazenly among his enemies, arrogantly defying the constant threat of capture and death? She reminded herself that this was his business, that he hired himself out to rescue wealthy aristocrats who were in danger of being murdered by the new Republic. But was it really the simple desire for money that drove him to constantly place his life in such grave danger? What kind of a man placed so little value on his life that he was willing to take such risks? Was there not someone who cared for him, who cried and desperately begged him not to go, and then anxiously marked off the days until his return with a mixture of terror and longing? He was an exceptionally handsome man, she allowed, when stripped of his makeup and wigs. Did the woman named Angélique know of his occupation, and wish with all her heart that he would give it up for her? These questions were unraveling and tangling themselves in her mind, when suddenly his massive figure twisted around and leveled a pistol directly at her chest.

She let out a frightened shriek as he did so, terrified that he was going to shoot her before realizing who she was. He stared at her blankly for a moment, allowing her appearance to register before slowly lowering his weapon.

"Never sneak up on me like that," he muttered irritably as he shoved the pistol back into the waistband of his trousers.

"I'm sorry," stammered Jacqueline, fighting to calm the frantic pounding in her chest. "I did not mean to startle you."

He turned and faced the sea again. Jacqueline took a few steps to stand beside him. Her eyes blinked in the cold, salt air as she searched the churning, inky black ocean for his ship. She saw nothing.

"Where is your ship?" she asked, thinking perhaps it had been delayed by the roughness of the sea. If so, she might have another opportunity to escape him before the ship arrived.

"*The Angélique* is hidden in a small cove on the other side of that point," he told her, lifting his arm to indicate where.

"And how are we to get to her?" she demanded, wondering if he thought they were going to swim to her.

"My men will be landing in a few minutes," he replied, pointing again into the darkness.

Jacqueline looked down, and after a moment she saw two men powerfully steering a small skiff through the waves and toward the beach that lay below.

Citizen Julien turned and extended his arm to her. "If you are ready, Mademoiselle, I shall assist you in the climb down," he offered politely.

"But what about the cart?" asked Jacqueline, suddenly gripped with a feeling of panic. The time had come. There was a ship waiting, and a skiff to take them to it, and she really was leaving France.

Citizen Julien looked at her with amusement. "Do not concern yourself, Mademoiselle. The cart will be taken away by one of my contacts within the next half hour."

Of course, she thought to herself sourly. It was not like him to leave any detail unresolved. "But is the ocean not too rough to attempt the crossing tonight?" she asked, still searching for some way to delay her departure.

"It is rough," he agreed. "But my men are experienced sailors who have navigated waters far more treacherous and violent than this. Come." Again he held his arm out to her.

"You forget, Citizen Poitier, that I do not require your assistance," she reminded him frostily, remembering that not once had he been willing to help her climb in and out of the cart. "I would prefer to keep it that way." She lifted her chin as she gathered up her coarse woolen skirts and swept by him with the majesty of a queen, and then awkwardly started to climb down the rocky bluff that led to the beach.

It was a difficult descent, to say the least, and by the time she stumbled down onto the beach, the skiff had landed.

"Evening, Captain," said one of the sailors as she and Citizen Julien approached. He was an older man and he seemed to have a kind face, although much of it was hidden behind a thick, graying beard.

"Good evening, Sidney," replied Citizen Julien with a nod. "John," he said, acknowledging the other sailor. He turned back to the older man. "Any problems?" he demanded.

"Nothing to speak of," replied Sidney with a shrug. "When you weren't here at the agreed time, we hid the ship around the point and sent some men into the village to see if there had been trouble. Everything was quiet and the jail was empty, so we figured you were just running late."

"Mademoiselle de Lambert and I were slightly detained," replied Citizen Julien. He turned to Jacqueline. "If you please, Mademoiselle," he said, indicating that she should climb into the skiff.

Reluctantly Jacqueline trudged across the wet sand over to the boat. The sailor named John held it steady, and Sidney offered her his arm as she stepped into it, which she made a great show of accepting.

"Oh, thank you, sir," she murmured prettily. "You are a true gentleman."

"Couldn't risk you harming the babe, now could we?" returned Sidney with a smile.

Citizen Julien let out a snort of laughter and Jacqueline sent him a look of disgust. She had totally forgotten about her filthy appearance and the fact that she looked about ready to give birth.

Citizen Julien waded waist-deep into the freezing water with the other men as they launched the skiff away from the beach. Then the three of them swung their sopping-wet legs over the edge and climbed in, splashing icy-cold water all over Jacqueline as they did so.

The skiff was tossed about on the surging black waves like an insignificant toy, but the two sailors pulled their oars through the water in a strong, steady rhythm, and finally they reached the ship. Jacqueline felt glad to be out of that tiny boat and on a good, firm deck, but found that her wet clothes and her uncontrollable shivering somewhat diminished the pleasure of being on board.

"Sidney, take Mademoiselle de Lambert below to my cabin and see that she is given everything she needs, including a hot bath," instructed Citizen Julien.

"Wait," cried Jacqueline.

Citizen Julien looked at her impatiently. He did not tolerate having his orders contradicted, especially on his ship and in front of his men, and the sooner the troublesome little aristo learned that, the better. "Do you wish to begin our voyage by defying me, Mademoiselle?" he demanded, his tone clearly indicating the folly of such a move.

"I would like to remain on deck a moment, to watch the coast as we leave," she explained.

"You are tired and you are freezing," argued Citizen Julien. "I'll not have you coming down with a fever while you are in my care." He motioned for Sidney to take her away.

"Please," whispered Jacqueline, taking a step closer to him so the men who were watching her curiously would not hear their conversation. "You are taking me away from my country, my home, from everything I have ever known. I implore you to allow me to take one last look."

He was surprised by the pain and sincerity in her voice. He looked down into her pleading eyes and could have sworn she was actually telling him the truth. But her past tricks and lies made him wary, wondering if this was simply one more attempt to escape him before they set sail. He would not put it past her to throw herself overboard, and he did not particularly feel like jumping in after her. He studied her hard, trying to decide whether or not he should trust her.

"Somebody bring a blanket," he called out finally. He continued to hold her with his gaze. "Sidney, you will stay with Mademoiselle de Lambert. Do not let her anywhere near the edge, and see to it that she is below in my cabin in exactly four minutes, or there will be hell to pay. Is that clear?" he demanded darkly, still staring at Jacqueline.

"Aye, Captain, clear as day," replied Sidney, obviously amused by the intensity with which the order had been given.

"Thank you," whispered Jacqueline.

Her eyes were shimmering with what might have been a mixture of sadness and gratitude. The pain in her gaze unsettled him. "Do not give Sidney any trouble," he ordered firmly, "or I will see to it that you cannot sit down for a month."

The pain in her eyes clouded over with irritation. "What is it you think I am going to do?" she demanded bitterly. "I can assure you I am not about to hurl myself from the ropes, since I do not know how to swim."

He was relieved to see some of the fire back in her manner. "I am glad to hear it, Mademoiselle," he told her pleasantly, "but since your tendency is to act first and think later, I would not put it past you to simply jump in and be forced to figure out the business of swimming while gagging and thrashing about in the water."

Her eyes flashed with indignation. "Has anyone ever told you how insufferably rude you are?" she asked haughtily, not caring if all the crew, who was staring at them, heard.

He restrained the urge to laugh. "Four minutes, Mademoiselle," he reminded her firmly. "After that, you had better be below in my cabin." He looked around impatiently. "Where the hell is that blanket?"

"Right here, Captain," called out a youth, who came rushing up to them and timidly offered Citizen Julien a blanket.

"About time," he grumbled as he took it from the nervous boy.

He opened the woolen cloth and carefully wrapped it around Jacqueline, arranging it so that only her face was left exposed. She held her breath as he performed this service, once again disconcerted by the closeness of him, by the touch of his powerful hands through the soft cloth, by the heat that seemed to emanate constantly from his massive frame when he was close to her. She shivered and took a step away from him.

"If you take a chill," he began, his voice oddly strained, "I will be bloody furious." He turned abruptly and walked away.

She clutched the blanket to her and focused her gaze on the black slice of land that was slowly receding as *The Angélique* got under way. The coast was dark except for an occasional faint spark of light—a house that was stirring early or a lantern left burning for someone who had not yet returned home. A feathery covering of trees stretched up into the night sky, becoming smaller and smaller as the ship slowly took her away from the place she loved.

"Farewell for now, my country, my home, my family, my life," she whispered softly into the cold, salt air. "I am not deserting you. You bleed, and so do I. But do not fear that I will forget. No matter what happens, I shall return. And Nicolas will be punished. I swear it."

"Captain said you were to go below now, Mademoiselle," said Sidney, interrupting her thoughts.

She sighed and followed him down to the captain's cabin.

It felt good to get out of the icy spray of the deck. The cabin was dry and warm, having been heated by a small black stove that stood in one corner. The room was quite small, to her way of thinking, especially considering it was the captain's room, but then she had never been on a ship before and really had nothing to compare it with. Its paneling was dark and richly oiled, its furnishings spare and clean-lined, including only a bed, a desk, a table with two chairs, a chest, and a cabinet. All the pieces were carved of glossy mahogany, and although elegant and gracefully executed, they were totally void of any fancy detail or gilt, and quite unlike the highly decorative furniture that had filled the rooms at the Château de Lambert. The effect was simple and masculine, giving the room a clean, airy feeling despite its relative lack of space.

Sidney invited her to make herself at home, telling her the clothes laid out on the bed were for her and her bath would be arriving directly. He informed her that the captain had said she could search his chest for soap and towels. Moments after Sidney left, there was a knock on the door, and two men entered carrying a heavy copper tub. They moved the table and chairs aside and positioned the tub in the center of the room. Then a procession of sailors marched into the cabin and emptied steaming buckets of hot water into the tub until it was full.

The minute the door was shut, Jacqueline raced over to the chest and carelessly rifled through its contents to find the precious soap and towels. That done, she stripped off her coarse, filthy peasant costume and pillow and abandoned the offending garments in a heap on the floor. With a sigh of utter pleasure she stepped into the tub and slid down until she felt the water close over her head.

Never in her life had a bath been so unbelievably wonderful. She lathered every inch of her skin with the fragrant bar of soap, and the moment she was rinsed off, she soaped herself up all over again. She washed her hair thoroughly, rinsing out every trace of the foul substance Citizen Julien had combed through it to make it dark. She scrubbed at her face with a cloth until her cheeks were stinging and pink, determined to remove the cosmetics Citizen Julien had used to make her appear ugly and old. Then, when the water began to cool and her fingers and toes were pale and wrinkled, she reluctantly stood and doused herself with the remaining bucket of clean water one of the sailors had thoughtfully left for her beside the tub.

She quickly dressed herself in the fine white linen

nightgown and wrapper laid out for her on the bed, idly wondering who they belonged to. If this woman Angélique was Citizen Julien's mistress, it was probable that she occasionally traveled with him on this ship that bore her name, and that they shared this cabin together. A hot blush crept into her cheeks as she stared at the bed and considered this. That is not my concern, she told herself firmly. She went over to the chest to look for a comb.

The fabrics she had so hastily cast aside in her search for a bar of soap were Citizen Julien's shirts, and as she set about straightening them and refolding them, she was surprised by their fine quality. The fabrics were costly and the workmanship impressive. Below his shirts lay several pairs of carefully tailored breeches and a splendidly cut charcoal jacket, simple of line and unadorned but, like the furniture he had chosen for his cabin, superbly crafted and elegant in its simplicity. It was obvious that despite his lack of aristocratic breeding, Citizen Julien was a man of taste, and his work obviously paid him enough to indulge in a high level of quality, if not flamboyance. She continued to casually explore the contents of the trunk, telling herself she was not really prying, but innocently looking for a comb or brush, and after all, Citizen Julien had sent her the message that she could search the trunk for whatever she needed. And so she felt only the least bit guilty when, long after she had found both a brush and comb, she discovered a small lacquer box nestled at the very bottom of the chest. Unable to control her curiosity, she picked up the box and lifted its lid to see what sort of treasures a man like Citizen Julien would keep hidden inside.

A small wreath of satiny ribbons, pink and cream and pale blue, lay coiled atop a snowy-white square of linen edged with lace. Jacqueline reached in and removed the tiny square. It was a ladies' handkerchief, with the initials *ASJ* intricately stitched in silver thread in one corner. Slowly she turned the delicate piece over in her hands, examining it as if it would reveal some of the secrets of Citizen Julien if she but gave it enough time. She surmised that the first initial stood for Angélique, and that the lacy square was given to him as a small memento of the woman's affections. She lifted the piece to her nose and inhaled, wondering if any trace of perfume clung to the fabric, but all she could smell was the spicy wood scent of the box. It seemed strange that a man like Citizen Julien would keep such a sentimental token, but then, there was much about him she did not know.

Not that there was anything about him she wanted to know, she reminded herself firmly as she carefully placed the handkerchief back in the box and nestled the ribbons on top of it. She laid everything back into the chest and closed the lid, then sat on the chair at the desk and proceeded to work at the tangles in her hair. Now that her hair was finally clean again, she experienced another stab of regret over its loss. All of her life her hair had been long, and now it barely brushed her shoulders. It could have been your head, she reminded herself impatiently. Sacrificing your hair was a small price to pay for the chance to go back and kill Nicolas. As she ran the comb through she noticed the loss of the extra weight was allowing her hair to spring into soft waves, and she took heart that while the look was short, it was perhaps not totally unattractive.

The sound of water sloshing over the sides of the tub interrupted her thoughts. For the first time she became aware that the cabin seemed to be moving up and down in a slow, rocking motion, making everything feel like it was all at once falling, and then just as suddenly swooping back up again. While the furniture in the cabin seemed to be well anchored to the floor and quite undisturbed by all this reeling to and fro, Jacqueline unfortunately found that she was not accustomed to such violent fluctuations. She tried to stand and the motion of the ship literally threw her back into the chair. Gritting her teeth, she stood again and headed for the door, determined to have a word with Citizen Julien and demand that he sail his ship in a more orderly manner. She had only taken a few steps when the floundering of the cabin made her dizzy and her knees gave way.

Slowly pulling herself up from the floor, she decided perhaps she was not quite up to having words with Citizen Julien at this particular moment. She thought she should sit down, but given her current state the bed looked much more inviting, and so she stumbled toward it, certain that after a few moments of quiet rest she would be fully recovered.

Within seconds she was overcome with the most violent nausea she had ever experienced, and she moaned in agony as the sensation flooded from the roots of her hair to the tips of her toes.

"She's all settled in, nice and comfy, just like you ordered," said Sidney in English as he joined the captain on the deck.

"Good," he remarked absently. He stared out into the darkness, evaluating the wind and the rough churning of the sea against the speed the ship was moving. "I had hoped we would have a calmer crossing than this."

Sidney looked at him in confusion. "We've sailed waters ten times worse than this," he scoffed with amusement. "So what if it takes us a little longer to cross?"

Armand scowled. "The faster we reach England, the faster I can be rid of her."

Sidney laughed and stroked his beard. "Gave you a bit of trouble, did she?"

"She was a thorn in my side from the moment I laid eyes on her," Armand grumbled irritably.

He clasped his hands behind his back and drank in a hearty draft of moist, salt-laden air. It felt good to be back on his ship, dressed in his own clothes, called by his own name and speaking English again. After giving the order to sail, he had gone below to remove the cosmetics and trappings of the farmer Jean Poitier. He had washed and shaved before dressing in a clean white shirt, fawn breeches, and a heavy black overcoat. He was tired, not having slept for more than two days, but the need to stand on the deck of *The Angélique* and absorb the reality that he had succeeded, that once again he had torn someone out from under the blade of the new Republic and not been killed in the process, superseded his need for sleep.

He had heard the rumors circulating about him when he was in Paris. The Black Prince, as he was now called, was considered a dangerous enemy to the Republic. Although he was clever, it was said, he was not clever enough to evade the justice of the guillotine forever. The theories about him were many and conflicting. It was said that he worked alone, and it was said that he worked with a whole network of counterrevolutionaries. It was rumored that he was a noble, and probably related to the royal family, and it was just as fiercely argued that he was nothing more than a greedy bourgeois whose only concern was money. It was generally agreed upon that he was French, for his speech reportedly never held the slightest trace of an accent, although he did have a definite ability with dialects, enabling him to speak equally well as a rough peasant from the north or a Paris-educated government official. Indeed, the only viewpoint never in dispute was that whoever this man was, he was exceptionally lucky, for no one but a man leading a charmed life could take the incredible risks the Black Prince took and not get caught. Luck, he thought to himself bitterly. I am an extremely lucky man.

"Why don't you go below and get some sleep, boy?" demanded Sidney, interrupting his thoughts. "There's nothing happening up here we can't handle. The crossing is going to take a few hours longer at the very least if this weather continues. You might as well get some rest."

He pulled his gaze from the sea and looked at his friend. Sidney had known him since he was a boy, when Sidney first signed on to work for his father's shipping line. Sidney had always been a first-rate sailor, and he knew he could trust him with his ship and his life. Despite the fact that he was now a grown man and the captain of *The Angélique,* Sidney still acted as if he was a boy who needed to be told what was best for him, although he was careful not to show this side of their friendship in front of the crew.

"Perhaps you are right," he agreed wearily. "I think I will lie down for a while."

He made his way below, thinking he would look in on her for a moment, just to make sure she had everything she needed and was finding his cabin comfortable. Not that anything could be considered uncomfortable after those weeks she spent locked in that hell hole of a cell in the Conciergerie, he reminded himself furiously. When he had first walked in under the guise of Citizen Julien and saw her there, brutally shoved against the wall with her skirts up to her waist and that animal in the process of raping her, he had very nearly lost his control and killed the bastard then and there. It would have meant the end of his charade and certain death, but in that moment of rage he had thought it would be worth it. The only thing that made him clench his jaw and force himself to continue with his masquerade was the sight of her, far more beautiful than her portrait had shown her to be, and achingly out of place among the filth and stench and corruption that surrounded her. But it was not her beauty that caused him to sheathe his overwhelming need to draw blood and continue with his performance, for he had been witness to that beauty earlier in the courtroom. No, it was something else, something in her manner, that made his desire to avenge her honor pale beside his sudden need to save her at any cost, to get her out of there and away from this country where madness reigned and everyone had become her enemy. And so he sputtered and apologized and coughed and wheezed, playing the role exactly as he had planned, but his watchful eye did not miss the fierce dignity with which she stepped away from her attacker and pulled together the shredded remnants of her torn bodice, or the icy contempt with which she treated all those around her, including himself. They had arrested her and terrorized her, they had killed her father and brother and taken away her home and all her belongings, and now they were going to take her life, yet they still had not been able to break her. She was strong. He admired that.

He knocked on her door. "It is me, Mademoiselle," he said in French. "I have come to see if there is anything you need."

There was no response. He thought perhaps she had fallen asleep, and wondered if maybe he should simply leave and check on her later. But light was spilling out from the crack under the door, and he realized if she slept then she had failed to extinguish the candles in the cabin, and that was extremely dangerous. A fire on a ship was no small concern. He lifted his fist and rapped on the door again.

"Mademoiselle, are you awake? You have left the candles burning in the cabin," he said sternly, his voice a little louder than before.

This time a faint moan answered him. He wrenched the door open and entered the cabin.

Icy-cold fear gripped him as he took in the sight of her lying on the floor, pale and weak and barely breathing, her face white and twisted in agony. Her eyes fluttered open to look at him, and she let out a pitiful sob.

"I am dying, Citizen," she whispered. Then, with what obviously took an incredible amount of effort, she lifted her head to the chamber pot on the floor beside her and retched into it violently.

He snatched up a towel that was draped over the bath and dipped a corner of it into the cool water before falling to his knees at her side. When she had finished her retching, he urgently took her head into his lap and wiped her face clean.

"What in God's name have you done to yourself?" he demanded, his voice low and trembling. Her eyes were closed and in his panic he started to shake her until she wearily lifted her lids and looked at him. She moaned in protest at his rough handling of her, but he was almost beside himself with concern and did not care to be gentle. "Tell me, Jacqueline, or with God as my witness, I will beat it out of you, sick or no. What have you poisoned yourself with?" he demanded, grasping her shoulders and forcing her to sit up.

She stared at him dully, confusion and nausea clouding her vision. At first she did not recognize him. He was not Citizen Julien, or the captain of the National Guard, or Jean Poitier, peasant farmer. No, he was stripped of his cosmetics, and he was back to being the man under the disguise, the man with whom she had shared a bed in a run-down inn in Paris. But who was he? And why was he so angry with her? She had not tried to escape. She was dying. Should he not treat a dying woman with a little more consideration? She lifted her hand and weakly tried to push him away.

"I am dying," she protested helplessly. "Why are you torturing me so?" She closed her eyes and sank back against his arm, not caring that he was still trying to make her sit. "Do you think I would bring this agony on myself?" she moaned.

He took a deep breath as her words reached him. She had not poisoned herself. Her anguish at leaving her country and giving up her fight was not that great. He did not know why he had rushed to that conclusion, but he did not pause to think on it. Now that he knew she was going to live, he was anxious to do something to relieve her considerable discomfort.

He placed his arms beneath her legs and shoulders and gently lifted her against his chest. She felt light, too light for a woman her height, he thought angrily. The weeks spent in that foul prison, coupled with months and months of deprivation living in a country that did not have nearly enough to feed its population, had obviously taken its toll on her slender frame. He stood and pulled back the covers on the bed before gently laying her on its clean sheets. Her face was as white as the linen of the pillowcase. He carefully drew the covers over her.

He went to the door to call for assistance and saw the boy who had brought a blanket for her on deck walking down the passageway.

"You there, bring me an empty bucket, a bucket of

clean, warm water, some cool drinking water, and some hard biscuits," he called out sharply. "And be quick about it."

"Yes sir, Cap'n, right away, sir," answered the boy excitedly as he bolted down the passageway.

Within minutes the boy returned with the required items. Armand took them and gave him the chamber pot in return, instructing him to empty it over the side and rinse it well before bringing it back. Then he closed the door and turned his attention to Jacqueline.

He removed his heavy overcoat and rolled up his sleeves before pulling a chair over to the side of the bed and seating himself on it. Then he dipped a clean cloth in the bucket of fresh water and gently washed her face, taking comfort in the fact that she did not feel the least bit feverish. After a few moments she opened her eyes and stared at him, her gaze distant and cloudy.

"I am dying, Citizen," she told him weakly.

He shook his head. "No, Jacqueline, I would never let you die while you were in my care. It would be bad for business." He gave her a smile and continued to gently sponge her face.

"Then what in the name of God is wrong with me?" she cried pitifully, before lurching up and retching horribly into the bucket he held for her.

He waited calmly until she had finished, then wiped her face and held a glass of water to her lips. "Take some to rinse your mouth and then spit it out," he instructed. "It will make you feel better."

She obeyed him, grateful for his assistance and at the same time mortified that he should see her in such an awful condition. It does not matter, she told herself weakly. I am dying, and only a fool would be concerned about appearances at a time like this. She felt him guide her back to lie against the pillow, and then the cloth was sponging her face again. The cabin was still swinging up and down in a dreadful, rocking motion, spinning her in circles and making her feel utterly miserable.

"Citizen Julien," she whispered feebly.

"My name is Armand," he told her. "Armand St. James."

She paused, letting that piece of information sink in. Of course. He had said he would not tell her who he was until they were beyond the danger of capture. And now they were safe, on his ship, heading toward England, and she was not going to make it after all because she was going to die. It seemed monstrously unfair that she should die before seeing her sisters, never mind the fact that she still wanted to kill Nicolas, but there it was. It did not matter anymore. Nothing mattered. All she wanted at this moment was for the ship to cease its rocking. Then she could die relatively peacefully.

"Monsieur St. James," she began again, her voice weak and quavering. "Could you please get your ship under control so it stops this torturous motion?" she pleaded.

He found he could not help but smile, so certain did she seem that he could accomplish such a feat. He realized she had never been on a ship before, and obviously knew nothing of how uncomfortable it could sometimes be. He was well used to the turbulence of a rough sea and was not bothered by the swaying and rocking that had reduced her to this pitiful state.

"Mademoiselle, were it within my power, I would stop heaven and earth to make you more comfortable, but unfortunately what you ask lies beyond my ability," he told her apologetically.

"But I am dying, and this constant movement is making it worse!" she protested, her voice filled with despair.

He smoothed her damp hair off her forehead and gently stroked her ashen cheek. "No, Jacqueline, I have already told you, I will not tolerate you dying while you are in my care," he quipped lightly. "It is merely the motion of the sea and the ship that has made you so ill, and believe it or not, it will pass."

She opened her eyes again and looked at him, her stomach threatening at any moment to lurch back up into her throat. "Are you sure?" she asked, quite torn between

her desire to live and, in that moment, her even stronger
desire to die.

"I am sure," he replied with a nod. "Once you are
finished with your retching, I will give you a little water to
drink, and then we shall see if we can get some of this
biscuit into you. It is thoroughly dry and tasteless, but it
will ease the turmoil in your stomach. Come morning you
will be feeling much better, I promise."

She lifted her lids once again to look at him. He
seemed sincere, with his blue-green eyes studying her intently and his large, strong hands lightly pressing a cool
cloth to her face. She was embarrassed that any man
should see her in such a profoundly humiliating condition,
yet somehow she took comfort in the fact that he was
there. He was gentle in his nursing of her, and his confident manner told her she really was going to live. At this
particular moment that was only a mixed blessing, but if
he said that come morning she would be feeling better,
then it must be so. She sighed and closed her eyes.

He watched her in silence for a few moments, and
then, thinking she had fallen sleep, he rinsed the cloth in
the pail of water and started to rise. He wanted to find
that boy and get him to bring back the clean chamber pot
in case she was sick again. The other bucket needed to be
emptied. The cabin seemed cold, more coal should be
added to the stove. Perhaps he should order some weak
tea for her. As he moved to see these things attended to,
her hand weakly fluttered up and grasped his, holding him
there.

"Do not leave me," she pleaded softly.

Her eyes were frightened, her grip on him feeble but
steadfast.

"I will be but a moment," he told her.

"Do not leave me," she repeated, shaking her head.

He felt her grip increase slightly, as if she would hold
him there by her own power, which of course she could
not.

Her request touched him. At this moment she wanted
him near, not because there was anything more he could

do for her, but because she took comfort in his presence. That realization pleased him, although he could not imagine why it should be so.

"Very well, Jacqueline," he said softly. Still holding her hand in his, he reached up with the other and lightly stroked her cool cheek with the back of his fingers. "I shall not leave you."

She sighed, a sound that was mixed with relief and exhaustion, and once again closed her eyes to sleep.

His promise made, he settled back in his chair and prepared to watch her for the remainder of the night.

Chapter 6

By the time they landed at Dover the following afternoon, Jacqueline was feeling somewhat better, although not entirely recovered. At Armand's insistence, or Monsieur St. James, as she preferred to call him, she managed to eat some plain biscuits and tea when she awoke. Satisfied that the worst of the seasickness had passed, Armand ordered her to spend the morning resting in his cabin while he left to tend to the duties of his ship. At first she was happy to obey these instructions. But by the time they were about to dock she had recovered enough to feel restless, and felt anxious to escape the confines of the cabin. She was gazing ruefully at her peasant's clothes, which lay discarded in a careless heap on the floor, when Armand returned carrying an armful of silk and lace.

The lavender gown he gave her to wear was trimmed with ruffles and puffed out generously over several layers of petticoats and an aqua-blue skirt. It would have been lovely on a woman who filled it properly, but on Jacqueline's thin frame the creation hung limp and shapeless. The extent of its poor fit was obscured somewhat by a filmy gauze scarf, which she crossed over the front and tied in a wide bow at the back of her waist. Once she had tucked the remains of her hair up into a blue satin hat with a fluffy gray plume and donned the matching blue cape trimmed in lavender, she decided that her appearance, although no longer beautiful, was at least presentable, and that was enough. Her days of fretting for hours in front of her mirror, wondering if her hairstyle was quite the latest rage, or if her gown needed more ribbons and lace, and did her tiny high-heeled shoes match her gown exactly, were gone forever. Her excessive preoccupation with her beauty and the latest trends in fashion was part of a Jacqueline who no longer existed. She had died, as surely as if she had mounted the steps to the guillotine and been extinguished beneath its heavy blade. She stared blankly at herself in the small shaving mirror she discovered in Armand's chest, feeling cold and distant toward the pale, thin reflection that gazed disinterestedly back at her.

When she stepped up onto the deck the crew members momentarily halted their activities to stare at her in amazement. As she walked by they seemed to regain their senses and politely bowed their heads to her. Although she realized that compared with her appearance when she boarded the ship anything would be an improvement, their reaction to her made her feel a little better. Perhaps she did not look quite as awful as she thought.

"Well, it's a vision you are and that's all there is to it," gushed Sidney enthusiastically in French. He bowed deeply before offering her his arm. "Come, I'll take you to the captain."

He led her to the bow of the ship, where Armand was supervising as men on the dock grabbed the heavy ropes that were being tossed to them by his crew and expertly tied them around huge iron posts. He turned as she approached and stared at her, critically eyeing her up and down as if he was trying to decide whether he liked what he saw.

"Are you feeling better?" he demanded, his tone brusque and impersonal.

"Much better, thank you," replied Jacqueline. She noticed he had changed into an immaculate pair of dove-gray breeches, a fitted charcoal frock coat, and a white shirt with a neatly tied cravat. A enormous open black overcoat further emphasized his unusual height and the wide breadth of his shoulders. His golden-brown hair was tied back with a length of black velvet ribbon, but several wisps at the front had worked their way loose and were blowing in the cold wind. As he stood there assessing her everything about him spoke of power, confidence, and control. There was an understated elegance to him, a bearing that could only be described as aristocratic, even though Jacqueline knew he was not. She suddenly felt uneasy in front of him, and acutely embarrassed by the memory of her illness the night before.

"Good." He turned abruptly to resume his supervision of the docking of his ship. Instead of being irritated by his brusqueness, Jacqueline was relieved his attention was no longer on her.

Sidney escorted her to a place by the railing where she could watch them dock and not be in the way. Once the ship was secured, a heavy plank was lowered to bridge the gap between the deck and this unknown place called England. It was then that Armand went to her.

"Come, Mademoiselle," he said, offering her his arm. "A carriage is waiting below to take you to your new home."

She looked at him and gravely shook her head. "It is not my home, Monsieur St. James, and it never will be. It is merely a place of refuge, for that is what I have become, have I not? A refugee?" She looked away. "I have deserted my country, which is crimson with the blood of injustice and persecution, for the peace and security of another," she stated bitterly, her voice heavy with self-contempt.

He stared at her thoughtfully a moment. "If it makes you feel any better, you did not exactly flee," he pointed out. "As you will recall, I had to practically drag you here against your will. But had I not intervened, Mademoiselle, you would have been executed, and I fail to see how death in France could possibly be preferable to life in England. You are not a deserter, Mademoiselle, you are a survivor, and by the very act of your survival you deal a blow to the new Republic."

She clenched her fists in frustration. "My survival is worthless, unless it is used to help bring about the end of the tyranny that is destroying France. Only that can give my life meaning. Can you understand that?"

His eyes narrowed and he took a step toward her. "If you think for one moment that I will permit you to involve yourself in counterrevolutionary activities here, you are very much mistaken," he told her in a warning tone.

Her eyes locked with his. "Forgive me, Monsieur St. James, but I was not aware I required your permission for anything I choose to do while I am here. Once you deliver me to Sir Edward I am no longer your responsibility, is that not so?" she demanded coldly.

He stared at her a moment, weighing the powerful sense of purpose that flashed in those silvery-gray eyes. She was right of course. Once he turned her over to Sir Edward, she was no longer any concern of his. She was just another rescued aristocrat. She owed him her life, but it was not his custom to demand payment of any kind from those whose lives he had saved. Nor was it usual for him to set parameters on the activities of his clients once they were safe in England and no longer under his protection. All he asked was that they not reveal his identity as their rescuer to anyone, ever. As long as they fulfilled that simple request, they could go about their new lives in England as they pleased. If they chose to assist the counterrevolution, that was their affair, not his. Why should this case be any different?

"You are right," he conceded brusquely. "Once you are with Sir Edward you become his problem, not mine." And what a relief it will be to be rid of you, he added silently. Once again he offered his arm.

She laid her hand stiffly on his arm and permitted him to escort her off the ship and into the fine black carriage that was waiting for them. The journey to Sir Edward's home was several hours, and for most of the trip they both remained silent. Armand settled back in his seat and closed his eyes, using the lengthy journey to finally catch up on some much needed sleep. Jacqueline stared out the window at the frozen countryside around her, thinking about the corruption and carnage she had left behind. But after a time she put those thoughts of death and injustice aside, and began to contemplate the reunion that lay ahead. She wondered if her sisters had changed during the five months since she had seen them. Monsieur St. James had told her Séraphine had not spoken since the news of her father's death. Perhaps the sight of Jacqueline would change that. Nervous excitement began to flow through her veins, filling her with a pleasant sensation of eager anticipation she had not experienced in many, many months.

"Do you know that is the first time I have seen you smile?"

Startled, she turned her gaze to him, and realized he did not sleep, but appeared to have been studying her for some time. "I was thinking of my sisters," she rushed out defensively, making it sound as if the act of smiling was a weakness on her part.

"It is no sin to smile, Mademoiselle," he remarked, his tone faintly teasing. "I have been known to do it on occasion myself."

Disconcerted, she turned her attention back to the window, even though it was now dark and she could see nothing.

"There is something I must ask of you, Mademoiselle."

"What is it?" she asked, still keeping her attention fixed on the blackness that stretched out forever beyond the windowpane.

He leaned forward in his seat, closing the distance between them, demanding her full attention. She shifted uneasily, feeling trapped by his proximity, by the strength and power he exuded even when he was simply sitting. She inhaled the scent of him, clean and masculine and vaguely spicy, and quite unlike the scent of any other man she had known. The memory of François-Louis flashed into her mind, and she was shocked by the realization that except for a brief moment of searching for him in the courtroom, the thought of her betrothed had not once crossed her mind during these past four days. Since she had not expected him to risk his life by coming to her defense at her trial, and it never occurred to her anyone would try the almost impossible feat of rescuing her, per-haps that was not so surprising. Their match was, after all, an arrangement worked out between her father and François-Louis, and neither really knew the other well enough to harbor any feelings of love. But thinking back to those occasions they had spent time together, and even stolen a few forbidden kisses, Jacqueline could recall the cloying scent of sweet perfume that pervaded everything about him, from his heavily powdered wig to the lacy handkerchief he kept tucked among the extravagant ruf-fles of his shirtsleeves. Not that the use of heavy scents by aristocratic gentlemen was in the least unusual in France. But Monsieur St. James did not smell like any gentleman Jacqueline had ever known. Stripped of his wigs and cos-metics and filthy disguises, he had a clean, crisp scent she found eminently preferable to the expensive perfumes the nobility of France regularly doused themselves with.

"I must ask you not to disclose that it was I who res-cued you from the Conciergerie," stated Armand seri-ously. "As far as Sir Edward and his family are concerned, I merely used my connections to get you to the coast, where I picked you up to take you safely to England. They know nothing of my activities within France, and it is es-sential that those details remain secret. Do you under-stand?" he demanded.

"But why?" asked Jacqueline in confusion. "Sir Ed-ward was a friend of my father's. He is as much against this revolution as I am. And England is at war with France. Why must your work be kept a secret here?"

"Because, Mademoiselle, there are spies everywhere," he explained. "If the revolutionary government learned it was I who was secreting condemned and suspected aristo-crats out of France, they would watch my movements closely and focus their efforts on trapping me. As soon as I was caught I would be executed. But as long as no one knows of my work, my actions are not watched and I can continue to cross the channel freely," he explained.

"How often do you go to France?" asked Jacqueline curiously.

He shifted back against his seat. "Often enough."

Jacqueline felt excitement rising within her. "When will you be going again?"

He regarded her suspiciously. "Why do you ask?"

Jacqueline hesitated. If she blurted out that she wanted to cross the channel with him the next time he went on one of his assignments, he would certainly say no. But if she could find out when he was going, she might be able to board his ship without his knowledge, and return to France secretly. It was a possibility that merited some consideration, but in the meantime she must be careful not to arouse any suspicion.

"No reason," she told him nonchalantly. "I was simply curious about how often you had to risk your life to earn your living." She idly ran her hand over the plush crimson velvet covering the seat. "If your ship and this carriage are any indication, you obviously have to risk it often enough to support a rather expensive style of living."

"Your concern for my welfare is truly touching," he remarked dryly. "But since your lying still needs practice, let me make something absolutely clear. Nothing you do or say could ever persuade me to take you back to France to have your vengeance on Nicolas Bourdon. You would never get out of there alive, and if you were captured they would not hesitate to use every painful, degrading means at their disposal to force from your lips the identity of the man who helped you escape in the first place. Therefore, Mademoiselle, you would not only be risking your own life, on which you obviously place little value, but also my own, and if I am to die, I would prefer that it be over a risk I have decided to take." He reached out and wrapped his hand firmly around her neck, pulling her closer and forcing her to meet his gaze. "Listen well, Jacqueline," he said softly. "You must abandon these fantasies of going back and concentrate on the new life you must build for yourself here. For I promise you, whether I have the authority or not, I will never permit you to return to France. Do you understand?" he demanded harshly.

She struggled to free herself from his grip, but he held her fast. "I understand perfectly," she bit out between clenched teeth.

He released her abruptly, causing her to fall back against her seat. "Good." Evidently thinking the matter settled, he closed his eyes and once again appeared to sleep.

It was very late by the time the carriage turned down the road that led to Sir Edward's home. Jacqueline peered out the window and saw an enormous, dark estate rising up into the moonlight, with only a few lights spilling through the windows on the main floor. When the carriage finally ground to a halt Armand swung the door open and climbed down, then turned and offered his hand to help her.

"Your new home, Mademoiselle," he said in a clipped voice that told her he did not want to hear any arguments to the contrary.

Jacqueline accepted his hand without comment. She was utterly exhausted from the difficult traveling of the past few days, and all she wanted was to be escorted to a bed where she could sleep undisturbed for at least a week. But there was excitement building within her as well. She was finally going to see Suzanne and Séraphine. As she mounted the steps that led to the front door, she found she could not restrain herself from squeezing Armand's arm with nervous anticipation. She felt his hand cover hers in a gesture of support, and for a brief moment the tension between them seemed to disappear.

The heavy oak door swung open and an elderly butler ushered them in.

"Good evening, Mr. St. James," he said stiffly in English.

"Good evening, Cranfield," returned Armand. "Are Sir Edward and Lady Harrington still up?"

"They had hoped you would be arriving tonight and await your presence in the drawing room," replied Cranfield. "If you will kindly follow me."

He led them to a massive room, heavily swathed with

ruby velvet draperies and dark oil paintings. A portly, smiling couple, whom Jacqueline assumed to be Sir Edward and Lady Harrington, were already rushing toward them as they entered.

"By Jove, Armand, you really did do it!" blurted out Sir Edward enthusiastically. He was a stout man in his late fifties, with a narrow fringe of gray hair circling a shiny bald spot at the top of his head. His nose and cheeks were rosy, indicating a love of good brandy, and his brown eyes were filled with genuine warmth and friendliness. He grabbed Jacqueline's hand and raised it to his lips. "Welcome, my dear Jacklyn, welcome," he said, beaming. "We have been waiting anxiously for your arrival, and of course Lady Harrington and I have been beside ourselves with worry these past few weeks that something might have gone wrong, or that those damned Frenchies had already harmed you and we would be too late. I tell you, when St. James did not appear at the door with you early this morning as promised, well, we just about went mad with anxiety—"

"You poor dear, you must be simply exhausted after such a long and dreadful experience," interrupted Lady Harrington. She moved up to Jacqueline and planted a warm kiss on her cheek. Like her husband, it was obvious she relished a good meal and did not care for too much physical activity. She carried her plump frame with elegance, and wore an exquisite gown of sapphire brocade that exactly matched the sapphires lying against her plump bosom. "Now you don't worry, you are safe now and you can forget all about those terrible things you have been through. Why, if you like, we will just not talk about them, we will simply wipe the slate clean and say that no one is to ask you about the horrors you have been forced to endure. Why, you poor child, you are as thin as a rail, and no wonder after being starved in that awful prison. Well, we'll soon fix that, we'll have the cook prepare all your favorite foods. Would you like something to eat now?"

Jacqueline stared at them blankly. She had not understood a single word they said. She turned and looked helplessly at Armand, who was watching her with an expression of concern. It was obvious he had not realized she did not speak any English whatsoever.

"*Pardonnez-moi,*" she began hesitantly, wondering if either of the Harringtons spoke any French. Surely if Sir Edward had been such a good friend to her father years ago, he must speak at least a little of her language? She turned her eyes to him. "*Je ne peux pas parler anglais. Parlez-vous français?*" she asked hopefully.

Sir Edward looked at her in surprise.

"Mademoiselle de Lambert does not speak any English," interjected Armand, silently cursing himself for not having realized that earlier. He should have prepared Jacqueline for the fact that the Harringtons spoke only a smattering of French.

"The poor dear, of course she doesn't." Lady Harrington clucked, making it sound as if her inability to speak English was due to some terrible form of neglect. "Let's see, er, Jacklyn, *avez-vous faim?*" she pronounced haltingly, asking if she was hungry.

Jacqueline shook her head as they stared at her expectantly. She was all at once feeling very isolated and out of place.

"Perhaps Mademoiselle de Lambert should be permitted to see her sisters," suggested Armand, sensing her distress and wanting to ease it.

"A splendid idea," agreed Lady Harrington. "Cranfield, have Miss Lindsey waken the girls and bring them down at once."

"As you wish, Lady Harrington," replied Cranfield. He bowed and left the room.

"Well now," said Sir Edward awkwardly, "I guess my old friend Charles-Alexander did not think it necessary for his daughters to learn English. Not to worry. We have engaged an excellent English tutor for Suzanne and Séraphine, and Suzanne's English is coming along splendidly. Séraphine sits in on the sessions of course, but as she is still not speaking, it is hard to say how much she has learned. You tell Jacklyn here that I wager within a month she will be speaking English like the rest of us," he asserted happily.

"Sir Edward, Mademoiselle de Lambert's name is pronounced *Jacqueline,* not Jacklyn," Armand pointed out, wondering as he did so why the anglicization of her name irritated him so much. Clumsy pronunciation of French names was common in England and generally accepted. It certainly happened with his own name. It was most unlike him to make an issue out of something so trivial.

Sir Edward looked at him in surprise. "Of course," he acknowledged. "Jack-el-een," he repeated slowly, thoroughly butchering her name once again, only this time in three painfully distinctive parts.

"Perhaps we should call her Jackie, to make it easier for everyone," suggested Lady Harrington brightly.

"A splendid idea, my dear," agreed Sir Edward. "Armand, ask Jacklyn if she would object if we all called her Jackie."

"No," replied Armand firmly. Sir Edward and Lady Harrington looked at him in shock, clearly taken aback by the intensity of his tone. He felt ridiculous. "What I mean is, I am sure if you practice, you will eventually get it," he explained apologetically.

Jacqueline stood silently and watched them have this discussion. She understood it had something to do with their inability to pronounce her name. Why had it not occurred to her that the Harringtons would not be able to speak French? Her father was a learned man who had traveled widely before he married, and was fluent in several languages. Obviously when he made friends with Sir Edward it was he who had transcended the language barrier. The Duc de Lambert had insisted that his son, the marquis, be educated in languages as well, a requirement that caused poor Antoine to complain bitterly, for he did not have a flair for accents. But the duc did not consider the ability to speak a foreign language necessary for his daughters, and therefore neither Jacqueline nor her sisters had been tutored in anything other than French. She wondered how Suzanne and Séraphine must have felt, being sent away to live in a strange house with people who could only communicate with them on the most basic of levels. Her heart bled for them.

"*Jacqueline!*"

She turned as the little voice gasped her name, just in time to kneel and be embraced by two small arms that wrapped fiercely around her neck and hugged her close to a blond cloud of curls.

"Suzanne, my pet, my dove, how wonderful it is to see you again!" she cried in French, kissing the little face that was pressed so close to hers. She looked up to see Séraphine, a smaller, blonder version of her sister, looking very pale and grave and uncertain, still standing in the doorway. "Séraphine, my little angel, come to me that I may kiss you, too!" Jacqueline called joyfully as she extended her arm to her.

The little girl stood rooted to the spot, staring at her with empty gray eyes as if she was a complete and total stranger.

"Séraphine, it is I, Jacqueline," she crooned, wondering if she could possibly look that much different from before. She reached up and pulled off her enormous blue satin hat so the little girl could see her better.

"Oh, Jacqueline," wailed Suzanne, "what happened to your beautiful hair?" She reached up to touch the short, ragged ends.

"Why, I cut it," stammered Jacqueline, realizing too late that the removal of her hat was not a good idea. Séraphine continued to gaze at her vacantly. "It was so much trouble, always having to wash it and brush it and pin it up, I decided I would be bold and start a new fashion," she rushed on desperately, hoping her voice sounded bright. "Isn't that right, Monsieur St. James?"

"Indeed it is," agreed Armand. "And now women all over France are picking up their scissors and cutting off their hair to achieve the De Lambert style."

Suzanne looked at Jacqueline skeptically.

"I thought I heard voices," breathed a soft, musical

voice in English. A pretty, auburn-haired young woman, dressed only in a pale blue nightdress covered with a filmy matching wrapper floated into the room. "Why, Armand, how wonderfully fit and well you look after your latest adventure crossing the channel," she gushed as she stepped closer to him. "I am simply dying to hear all about it." She gave him a lovely smile.

Jacqueline found she was momentarily distracted from Séraphine by the entrance of this girl. She could not understand a word she was saying, but it was obvious to her that the girl was flirting outrageously with Armand. A hot sense of irritation rushed through her.

"You must be Jacklyn," said the girl sweetly as she turned to acknowledge Jacqueline's presence.

"Jacklyn does not speak English, Laura, and you are not appropriately dressed to be down here in the company of men," said Sir Edward sternly.

"Oh Papa, it is so late, and besides, Armand is practically family," Laura protested, giving Armand a conspiratorial smile. With that dismissal of her father's comment she turned to Jacqueline. "Hello Jacklyn. My name is Laura and I can speak French," she said slowly in heavily accented French.

"A pleasure, Mademoiselle Laura," replied Jacqueline politely.

The formality of their introduction observed, Laura turned her attention back to Armand. "Now, Armand, I want to hear all about how you came to save this poor girl from those awful, murdering Frenchies. Were you in grave danger? Did they have ships watching the coast? Were any of your accomplices killed as they escaped with Jacklyn? Did you have to kill anyone?"

"That is quite enough, Laura," intervened Lady Harrington. "Why, our guests must be utterly exhausted after their ordeal, and I am certain poor Armand is in no mood to start recounting all the details of his journey to you now. Tomorrow morning will be soon enough. Right now I am sure our guests would like nothing more than to be taken to their rooms."

"Regrettably, Lady Harrington, I am not able to stay the night," apologized Armand.

"Oh, but you must," pleaded Laura, her lower lip jutting out into a pretty little pout. "Why, I shall simply die of curiosity if I don't hear all about your adventure, and you wouldn't want that, would you?"

Jacqueline noticed that the girl was standing very close to Armand, not quite touching him, but looking as if at any moment she might toss propriety to the winds and just throw her scantily clad self against him. She had to restrain the urge to take the silly girl aside and give her a good slap.

"You can hear about it from Mademoiselle de Lambert, and practice your French at the same time," suggested Armand smoothly. "I have been away from my home too long, and I must get back."

He turned to face Jacqueline, who still knelt with her arms wrapped around Suzanne.

"It seems, Mademoiselle de Lambert, the time has come for me to take my leave of you," he told her in a low voice in French.

She looked at him in surprise. "Tonight?" she whispered blankly, feeling as if he was abandoning her and at the same time wondering why that should be so. After all, he had completed his mission. He had saved her life and delivered her to Sir Edward, as he had been hired to do. He forced her to leave her country against her will, true, he had been overbearing and rude and totally uninterested in her wishes. But he had not let her come to harm along the way, and he had stayed by her side and nursed her when she had been so ill she wanted to die. They had been through much these past few days. She had told herself she would be glad to be finished with him, but now that the moment of separation had arrived, she found herself strangely reluctant to say good-bye.

"I thought perhaps you would be staying for a while. . . ." she began hesitantly.

He was surprised by the trace of vulnerability in her voice, but he was careful not to show it. He knew that at this moment she felt a little lost, but he also knew that she still hoped she would eventually be able to convince him to help her return to France. Well, he would not. His business with her was finished, and it was time he returned home. She was safe from her enemies and reunited with her sisters. Sir Edward and Lady Harrington would take good care of her. It would be difficult for her at first, but eventually she would learn English and start to fit in. Her dark fury and her consuming need for vengeance would gradually dissipate in the wake of frilly new gowns, gay parties and balls, and the stream of suitors who would undoubtedly soon ask permission to call on her. She was attractive enough, and her lineage as the daughter of the Duc de Lambert would make her a desirable match. True, she no longer had the great wealth she enjoyed before the revolution, but he was sure Sir Edward would set her up with an impressive dowry most bachelor aristocrats would find more than acceptable. He thought back to the moment in the woods when she smashed her fist into his jaw as he tried to kiss her, and he smiled. God help the poor fool who decided she was for him.

"Unfortunately, Mademoiselle, the extent of my time away makes it urgent that I return to my home," he told her. "I am sure you understand."

"Of course," she replied stiffly. His job was done, and even though he had been traveling for days at an exhausting pace and it was now the middle of the night, he was obviously anxious to return home, undoubtedly to the welcoming arms of a woman named Angélique. Her mind shot back to the tiny handkerchief carefully hidden in the bottom of the chest in his cabin. The silvery initials stitched into it were *ASJ*. Reluctantly her mind accepted the obvious. The initials stood for Angélique St. James. How utterly stupid of her not to realize it before. He was married.

"Pray, do not let me keep you from those who must anxiously await your return," she said coolly. "I thank you for your services, even though they were not in keeping with my wishes, and bid you a safe journey." Having dismissed him, she tightened her hold on Suzanne and lowered her gaze back to Séraphine, who had not taken her eyes off her.

He could not imagine what had provoked the sudden chill in her manner and tone, but he told himself it did not matter. He was finished here.

He bade the Harringtons good night, and even took a moment to say good-bye to Suzanne and Séraphine. Suzanne thanked him earnestly for bringing her sister to her, and Séraphine did not back away when he bent low and whispered a few words in her ear that Jacqueline could not hear.

And then he was gone.

She told herself she did not care, that she was glad to finally be released from his control and his constant company. She fixed her gaze on Séraphine, who remained standing in the doorway staring at her. She could not imagine what was going on in the little girl's mind to make her want to keep her distance. Patience, she thought. I must go slowly and not force her to accept me.

"Well now, I think it's time we all went to bed," suggested Lady Harrington.

Ignoring the suggestion, Suzanne loosened her arms around Jacqueline's neck and looked at her. "But where is Antoine?" she demanded with concern in French.

Surprised by the question, Jacqueline hesitated. She had not known that the girls were unaware of his death, and she was not sure this was the best moment to tell them. Since the death of their father had such a devastating effect on Séraphine, she did not think she should burden her sisters with even more grief at this time.

"Antoine was arrested and he remains in prison," Jacqueline lied.

Suzanne looked at her in confusion. "But why didn't someone rescue him so Monsieur St. James could bring him here with you?"

"Well, it is not so easy to rescue someone from prison," explained Jacqueline. "But I received a letter from him before I left, and he is perfectly well, in good spirits, and he sends you both his love," she continued seriously, hoping she was convincing.

"I think she is telling them that their brother is dead," said Laura to her parents, who could not understand the conversation.

"Well, I am not sure this was the time," fretted Lady Harrington, shaking her head. "But then, she is their sister, and if she decided this is the moment then she must know best."

Suzanne stared in shock at Lady Harrington, who was looking down at her sympathetically. Her blue eyes filled with a mixture of horror and tears.

"Liar!" she cried out accusingly at Jacqueline. "You lie!" Tears began to rush down her grief-stricken face, and without giving Jacqueline a chance to reply, she turned and fled the room, her cries echoing in the enormous hallway.

Uncertain what to do, Jacqueline turned her attention to Séraphine, to see if she had understood whatever Laura and Lady Harrington had said. Séraphine stared back at her, her gray eyes no longer vacant, but hard and cold and far, far too worldly for a mere child of six. Then she, too, turned and left the room, the chilling sound of her silence far more disturbing than the anguished cries of her sister.

Chapter 7

The next few weeks were miserable for Jacqueline.

Although she was grateful to be alive and reunited with her sisters, she knew her stay in England was only temporary, and therefore she had no desire to try to adapt to her new life. However, Sir Edward and Lady Harrington were anxious for her to put her past behind her and consider herself a member of their household, and that meant they wanted her to learn English as quickly as possible. Every morning she was privately tutored for three hours, but her lack of motivation made these sessions excruciatingly slow for both her and her teacher.

She spent her afternoons with Suzanne and Séraphine. Although Suzanne seemed to have come to terms with the news of Antoine's death, and had forgiven Jacqueline for not telling her the truth, Séraphine's feelings were a mystery, for the little girl remained distant and silent. Jacqueline decided it was best not to draw attention to Séraphine's silence, and so she ignored it. She passed the afternoons reading and talking to both girls in French, receiving responses only from Suzanne, but making sure to divide her attention equally between the two of them. She was amazed at how caring and patient Suzanne was with her younger sister. She was always talking to her and asking her what she wanted, as if the expression in Séraphine's eyes were answer enough. The separation from their home and the deaths they had endured had obviously bonded the two children, with Suzanne adopting the role of protective mother and Séraphine silently clinging to her wherever they went.

Lady Harrington and Laura had seen to it that Jacqueline was outfitted with a lavish new wardrobe. Jacqueline protested that the money she had sent with her sisters was not sufficient enough to be wasted on frivolous clothes, but Lady Harrington insisted on paying for the new wardrobe herself. She and Laura seemed to have a marvelous time with their project, cooing and smiling at Jacqueline's fittings as if they were dressing a new doll. They ignored Jacqueline's protests over all the evening gowns they ordered, even though Jacqueline tried to explain in her broken English that as she would not be attending any balls, she would have absolutely no use for the costly garments. They also largely ignored her preference for the color black, which Jacqueline wanted to wear to reflect her mood and her state of mourning. In the end Lady Harrington relented and allowed her to select two outfits in the somber color, a day dress and an evening dress, but only after insisting that the stomacher and hem of the evening gown be heavily encrusted with shimmering jet stones.

Lady Harrington was also thoughtful enough to engage a French maid for Jacqueline, a pretty girl named Charlotte. Charlotte had left France in the early stages of the revolution with a wealthy family who had decided to go to England until the situation in France calmed down. The family returned when the republican government began to threaten to confiscate the property and assets of émigrés, but Charlotte had been afraid of the turmoil raging in her birthplace and decided to remain in England.

On seeing Jacqueline's hair, Charlotte immediately fetched a pair of scissors and gave her a good trim, so all the ragged ends were gone. She then began experimenting with the wavy length that remained, and eventually came up with an easy, loose twist that softly framed Jacqueline's face, but did not require an hour to create or a massive quantity of pins and pomade to hold in place. Jacqueline found she was utterly uninterested in the matter of her appearance, and was quite happy to let Char-

lotte decide which outfit she would wear each day and
how her hair would be arranged. Fortunately Charlotte
took her work extremely seriously and had excellent taste,
the result being that, despite Jacqueline's utter indifference
on the matter, she always looked absolutely lovely.

Within a few days of her arrival at the Harrington
home, invitations to various social events began to arrive
for Jacqueline. It seemed everyone was most curious to
meet the young French aristocrat who had come so close
to death before her miraculous escape. From lavish balls
to intimate teas, Jacqueline declined every invitation extended to her. Although she explained to Lady Harrington
that it was too soon for her to go out after Antoine's
death, and that she did not feel her English was proficient
enough for her to enjoy herself, the real reason was simply
that she did not want to go. She had no interest in enjoying herself or making friends in this strange country.
All she wanted was to spend time with her sisters before
she returned to France. The knowledge that others like
her were still being murdered every day on the guillotine,
and the thought of Nicolas still alive, undoubtedly enjoying the rewards of having denounced her father and
brother, tore deeply into her every day.

She forced herself to think about him. She would
imagine him seated at the dining-room table of the Château de Lambert as her father's welcome guest. Nicolas
had played the role of eager bourgeois idealist well in
front of her father, denouncing the power of the monarchy, expounding on the rights of man, and offering the
duc advice on how to diversify his investments to increase
his wealth. From the beginning her father was totally
duped by his charm, his intelligence, and his idealistic enthusiasm for the new order. But something about Nicolas
had always disturbed Jacqueline. It was nothing that appeared on the surface, for he was handsome and charming, well-read and perfectly mannered. But sometimes,
when her father wasn't aware, she would look up from
her plate and see Nicolas staring at her from across the

table, his dark eyes burning into her with an intensity that was frightening.

When her father rejected his bold offer for Jacqueline's hand in marriage, much to Jacqueline's relief, and then almost immediately announced her betrothal to the Marquis de Biret, Jacqueline noticed a subtle change come over Nicolas. Although on the outside he still appeared friendly and charming, and assured her father that he understood his decision, there was a cold fury in his eye when he looked at her, a disturbing, brooding harshness that seemed to say he had not given up, that somehow she would be his, regardless of what her father thought. And he had very nearly succeeded. She constantly forced herself to remember every humiliating, degrading moment of his attempted rape that night in her cell, recalling how cruel he was, and how triumphant. She promised herself that when she finally killed him, she would be sure to make it as slow and painful as possible.

"Mother, do you think I should wear the peach silk or my dusty mauve satin to the Fleetwoods' ball tonight?" Laura's expression was grave, as if the entire future of England rested on this monumental decision.

Lady Harrington looked up from her embroidery. "I should think neither. It is, after all, a Christmas ball, and you should wear one of the deeper jewel tones of the season. One of your emerald or ruby velvets would be far more appropriate, and you will look lovely on the dance floor amongst all the red and green and gold Christmas decorations."

"But everyone will be wearing jewel tones," protested Laura. "And besides, the paler shades are ever so much more flattering against my skin tone." She turned and looked at Jacqueline. "What do you think Jacklyn?" she asked in English. "The peach silk gown is absolutely covered with an arbor of fluffy little silk flowers," she said enthusiastically, motioning with her hands as she envisioned it. "It is perfectly lovely and I have never even worn it. And the mauve gown has yards and yards of gathered lace at the wrists and the hem and in layers all over the bodice—why, it is absolutely delicious to look at. Which do you think I should wear?"

Pulled from her thoughts, Jacqueline closed the English grammar book she had been pretending to read and focused hard on the English words. Despite her relative lack of effort, over the weeks she had started to grasp enough of the language to comprehend some conversation, if it was spoken slowly, and make herself understood in return. She realized this apparently serious conversation had to do with the Christmas ball they were all invited to, and what Laura would wear. Jacqueline had already informed the Harringtons she would not be attending. Although at first they tried to convince her she would enjoy herself, in the end Lady Harrington had no choice but to accept her decision. Jacqueline studied Laura's face as the girl waited expectantly for her advice, and found she could not help but feel irritated. Was she ever as silly and frivolous and vain as this girl? she wondered. Did the question of which gown one wore really need to occupy so much of one's thoughts? How could they even think of going to a ball when England was at war and France was at this very moment slaughtering her own innocent subjects?

"I think . . . you must wear de peach gown," suggested Jacqueline haltingly in English. "You will be"—she hesitated a moment—"*comme une fleur du printemps*—a spring flower—at Christmas."

"Oh, what a perfectly lovely thought!" cooed Laura happily. "And doesn't it sound even lovelier the way Jacklyn says it with that darling accent?"

"Jacklyn, my dear, your English is coming along very well," commented Lady Harrington with approval. "I really think you ought to reconsider and come with us to the ball this evening. You need to get out and meet some people. Why, I am sure once you are there and dancing, you will find the evening will lift your spirits immensely."

"You are kind, Lady Harrington, but I stay in this

night," replied Jacqueline slowly. "My sisters and I are having a small supper, and go to bed."

"Well, that doesn't sound like much fun at all," declared Laura. "Honestly, Jacklyn, you cannot stay shut up in this house forever, you have to start going out and having some fun."

"Laura is right, my dear," agreed Lady Harrington. "I really think it is time for you to be introduced to society here. I realize you have suffered in ways that we can only imagine, but after all, life does have a way of going on, now doesn't it?"

Cranfield appeared at the drawing-room doors. "Excuse me, Lady Harrington, there is a messenger at the door bearing a letter for Lady Jacklyn."

"You see!" cried Laura triumphantly. "Another invitation! Why, people are just dying to meet you, Jacklyn. You really must say you will come out with us tonight just to appease their curiosities."

"Thank you, Cranfield, bring the letter here," instructed Lady Harrington.

Cranfield shook his head. "The gentleman says he has been instructed to deliver the envelope into Mademoiselle de Lambert's hands only," he explained stiffly, obviously insulted at not being trusted to deliver it himself.

They were speaking too quickly, and Jacqueline was only catching a few words here and there, but she understood that someone was there with something specifically for her, and since the only person she knew in England other than the Harringtons was Armand, her heart began to flutter with excitement.

She had not seen or heard from him since the night he delivered her here, and although she told herself she did not care, she often found herself wondering why he did not take the time at least to write a brief note and ask how she was. She had quickly learned he was not married, because after every party the Harringtons attended Laura would come in thoroughly disappointed that Armand had not been present. It was clear Laura had set her heart on him, and Jacqueline wondered if she knew about the mysterious Angélique, who she had decided was probably his mistress. The taking of a mistress was undoubtedly as common in England as it was in France, for one could not expect a man to control his desires and remain celibate before marriage. She thought back to the moment in the woods when Armand had tried to kiss her, and her cheeks began to burn. She was not sorry she had struck him with her fist, but sometimes as she lay in bed she found herself wondering what it would have been like had she allowed him to continue.

"Very well, Cranfield, send the gentleman in," instructed Lady Harrington.

A moment later a young man heavily dressed against the cold stepped into the drawing room, holding a snow-covered hat in his hand.

"I am Mademoiselle de Lambert," said Jacqueline, rising up from her chair. "You have something for me?"

The messenger reached into the layers of his woolen coat and produced a cream-colored envelope with a red seal. "I was hired in Dover to take this letter and see that it was delivered into your hands and no one else's," he explained seriously as he held it out to her. "The fellow who gave it to me was French, and he told me that a man's very life was at stake," he continued, obviously much impressed with the importance of his mission.

Jacqueline took the letter with a trembling hand, wondering who knew where to find her. Her name was penned in elegant script on the front. She turned the envelope over and examined the seal. She recognized it immediately. It was the seal of the Marquis de Biret. The letter was from François-Louis.

"Cranfield, please escort this young man to the kitchen where he can rest, and see that he is given something hot to eat," directed Lady Harrington.

Jacqueline broke the seal and tore the envelope open, her mind racing with the possibilities of its contents. Perhaps François-Louis had escaped and was writing to tell her he was safe and working for the counterrevolution.

Or perhaps he had news of her brother, who had not really died after all. Frantically her eyes scanned the page.

20 Frimaire, 1793

My beloved Jacqueline,

What torment it is to write you thus, secretly scratching away by the meager glow of the single candle I have been allowed to purchase to light my tiny cell. For, my dearest, shortly after your miraculous escape, I found myself arrested on charges of having conspired with you in that daring venture, which I trust has secured you a new life in a new land. Of course I am completely innocent of the charges against me, having no prior knowledge of your incredible rescue, which by now has become legend in the anguished corridors of the Conciergerie. It is widely speculated that the Black Prince himself came to your aid, for who else but he would have dared to orchestrate such an improbable flight?

Would that I were fortunate enough to have a guardian angel such as he, who could spring me from this iron cage and the evil nightmare I now must endure. But I do not write to seek your pity or your aid, only to inform you of my cruel fate, and to summon the last of my strength to bid you good-bye.

How bitter is this moment, to know that which should have been mine can never be! To hold only the tender memory of your beauty, your grace, your youthful sweetness, all of which was promised to me by your father, and which I looked forward to having as my most cherished possession forever. Sometimes, as I lie desolate in my cell, I imagine what our life together would have been like, how perfect. We, Jacqueline, are of the same world, and I would have cared for you and loved you with all the gentleness and devotion a rare and fragile flower like yourself deserves. You would have reigned as brilliantly as a queen in my château, slowly and carefully I would have introduced you to the delicate mysteries of love between a man and a woman—but there, I speak of what can never be, and my heart bleeds.

What remains, therefore, for me to do, but say good-bye? And yet this is the most vile, the most painful of acts I have ever known. I must admit my weakness and confess that tears flood my face as I leave you. Sweet Jacqueline, my dearest girl, my only heart, know that the love on which I planned my life and my future lies locked away within your breast. I am destroyed, not with the knowledge that I must face death, however premature, unjust, and cruel, but that I shall never again see your exquisite face, shall never lay my hand against the precious small of your back as we dance, shall never press another gentle kiss to your perfect lips, and shall never be able to look at you and feel my heart burst with joy at the knowledge that you are mine and only mine.

Farewell, my dearest love, farewell. You are the angel who has kept me from going mad during this insane ordeal, and I would gladly die a thousand deaths if I knew it would keep you safe from those who would harm you. How sad that we shall never be reunited, that the guardian angel who came to you has no plans to come for me. Each day I hope he will appear, I keep myself alert and ready to race away with him on a moment's notice, but he does not come, and I resign myself to the fact that it is my duty to die, for you and for France, and I do so willingly.

Live well, Jacqueline, my dearest love, the woman who I dreamed would be my wife. Harbor no anger toward the executioners who are extinguishing the noblesse of France. I pray that soon our great country will be delivered from the murderers who have taken control, and only wish I

*could live to rejoice with you at my side on that
glorious day.*

> *Your ever devoted servant,*
> *François-Louis*
> *from the prison of the Palais de Luxembourg*

"Jacklyn, dear, whatever is it?" demanded Lady Harrington with concern.

Pale and trembling, Jacqueline slowly lowered the letter. "It is my—betrothed," she replied slowly. "The Marquis de Biret. He is—arrested."

"Your betrothed!" gasped Laura. "Oh Jacklyn, how
perfectly awful. Were you to be married soon?"

Jacqueline shook her head, her mind still reeling from
the contents of the letter. François-Louis had been arrested, and would undoubtedly be executed, because she
had escaped. He was innocent of the charges against him,
but she knew that did not matter. The Republic was not
interested in finding its suspects innocent. They had lost
one aristo, and now they were determined to rectify that
loss with the wrongful arrest of another. She was certain
Nicolas had a hand in François-Louis's arrest, for he had
been outraged when her father turned down his marriage
proposal in favor of a marquis. She was responsible for
his arrest. François-Louis was a practical, careful man,
who would never have said or done anything that might
have cast a shadow of suspicion on him. That was why he
had not come to her trial, or even written or visited her
when she was imprisoned. The distance he had put between himself and her was not so awful. She had understood. He simply wanted to live. And now, because of his
association with her, he would die. His blood was on her
hands.

"We . . . stop our wedding date, when my father is
arrested," she explained slowly, struggling to piece together the English words and proper tenses. "After my
father is executed, I am too concerned about my family to
think about marriage. François-Louis understands, and he
agrees to wait."

"How utterly tragic," sighed Laura sympathetically. "The two of you, young and in love, but kept apart forever because of this horrid revolution."

Jacqueline looked at her in confusion. She had not said she was in love with François-Louis. The match had been arranged by her father, and Jacqueline had accepted it because it was a good match, and although she did not know François-Louis well, she did not have any reason to dislike him. After all, they shared the same life and background. They both came from the highest level of the nobility in France, the *noblesse d'epeé,* those families whose titles went back centuries, whose ancestors had fought in the Crusades. François-Louis had a lovely château not far from her home, so after she married she would have been able to see her family often. He was pleasant and well mannered. And he was young and fit, with good teeth, which was certainly a bonus when it came to arranged matches within the nobility. But other than a few meetings and several rather disappointing kisses, she did not know him very well. The passionate style of his letter was a little overwhelming, given the nature of their relationship, but François-Louis had always been dramatic in his speech, and flowery, impassioned letter writing was extremely popular between lovers in France. Also, although the Palais de Luxembourg was a far more comfortable prison than the Conciergerie, to have one's freedom stripped away and to be forced to stay in a room and await one's death was enough to make anyone reflect on that which might have been with a heightened level of emotion.

"Jacklyn, dear, I can see you are distraught," remarked Lady Harrington. "Why don't you go upstairs and lie down for a while?"

Jacqueline shook her head, barely listening. François-Louis was going to die, another successful denouncement for Nicolas. But if not for her escape, he might never have been arrested. His death was, at least in part, her responsibility. She could not bear the thought. Was she just to sit back and accept his execution? Or was there something she could do to help? The thought of Armand flashed into her mind. He had helped her. He had saved her from her executioners. Perhaps he could do the same for François-Louis. After all, saving endangered French aristocrats was his business. She had no idea what price he would put on such a mission, nor where she would get the money. But she had to at least ask him. Maybe she could convince him that it was necessary to take her with him. Perhaps she would make that a condition of their contract. The thought filled her with excitement. While he was saving François-Louis she would find Nicolas and plunge a knife deep into his chest.

"Will Monsieur St. James attend this ball?" she demanded suddenly.

"He is undoubtedly invited," replied Laura. "But he almost never goes to balls or parties." The frustration in her voice was obvious.

"He may attend this evening, however," interjected Lady Harrington. "It is, after all, a Christmas celebration, and it is possible he will not want to be alone this evening."

Jacqueline considered for a moment. If Armand did not attend the ball, then the whole evening would be a waste of her time, for she really did not want to go. However, if there was even the remotest possibility that he would be there, she had to take that chance. It was essential she speak to him right away. François-Louis could be brought before the Tribunal at any time, if he had not been called before them already. The letter was dated 20 Frimaire, which was the tenth of December. Today was the eighteenth. Already a week had been lost. She stood up quickly, filled with the need to take action.

"I believe, Lady Harrington, I go with you this evening," she announced.

The ballroom was beautifully decorated to reflect the gaiety of the season, which was entirely at odds with Jacqueline's mood. Miles of fragrant, thick garlands of pine and spruce were looped across the painted ceiling, with enormous bows of heavy, scarlet velvet tying them into place. Dozens of tall, full evergreens had been placed along the sides of the room and decorated with sparkling gold and silver baubles and massive quantities of shimmering ribbon. Each tree was topped with a magnificent jeweled star that captured and reflected light from thousands of candles softly flickering in the room. A small orchestra was playing lively waltzes from a gallery high above the spinning sea of graceful dancers, who were, as Lady Harrington had predicted, for the most part dressed in the deep jewel tones of the season. Once Jacqueline might have smiled with delight and appreciated the extraordinary amount of creativity and planning it had taken to transform the enormous hall into such a magical setting for a Christmas celebration. But tonight her mind was firmly focused on the plight of François-Louis and her need to return to France. For what seemed like the thousandth time she scanned the crush of dancers, searching for Armand among the hundreds of colorfully dressed men who were skillfully leading their partners around the dance floor.

"Jacklyn, dear, you simply cannot stand here all night. We must find someone for you to dance with," commented Lady Harrington. She had already managed to send Laura off with an awkward young man, who was, she informed Jacqueline conspiratorially, the only son of the Earl of Melfort. Jacqueline supposed that meant he was going to inherit a fortune, but after watching him turn beet red as he asked Laura to dance, and then observing the look of sheer gratitude and relief when Laura agreed, she could not help but think that this was not the man who was going to capture Laura's heart. She wondered if Lady Harrington was aware of Laura's obvious attraction to Armand. Perhaps she was aware of it, but given Armand's untitled status and the highly irregular way he earned his living, it was likely neither she nor Sir Edward would ever sanction such a match.

Lady Harrington gave up evaluating the room for a

moment and turned to her husband. "Edward, dance with Jacklyn while I see if I can find some nice young man to introduce her to."

Before Jacqueline could protest, Sir Edward had moved to stand in front of her and gave her a small bow. "My dear, if you don't mind being seen with an old man who still remembers at thing or two about moving around a dance floor, I would be honored," he said as he offered his arm to her.

Jacqueline wanted to say no, but to refuse her host's invitation to dance would be extremely rude. She smiled politely and laid her hand on the sleeve of his sapphire frock coat. "I am pleased to dance with you, Sir Edward," she replied graciously, the English words slow and heavily accented.

Sir Edward visibly puffed up with pride as he escorted Jacqueline onto the dance floor. Jacqueline found him to be a reasonably good dancer, and so she was able to relax in his arms as she gazed around at the other men on the dance floor, still searching for Armand. She noticed a few men and women discreetly turning their heads to look at her and then exchange a whisper. She supposed people had started to wonder about the escaped daughter of a duc who was now living with the Harringtons. She was glad she had decided to wear her black evening gown, despite Lady Harrington's protests. The somber garment made it clear she was a woman in mourning, and had been an effective deterrent to any man who might have wanted to ask her to dance.

"Jacklyn, my dear, you are a marvelous dancer, but then I expected no less of a daughter of Charles-Alexander," complimented Sir Edward enthusiastically. "In his younger days in London, your father certainly knew how to lead the ladies around the floor."

The mention of her father distracted Jacqueline from her search. "My father insisted I begin . . . lessons of dance with Antoine when I am six and Antoine is seven," she told him slowly, grateful for the concentration required to translate the words into English. Somehow the act of translation seemed to distance her from the subject, as if she was not talking about her life, but merely taking sentences and changing them into English. "Several years after my mother has died, my father begins to entertain again. I am now the . . . woman of the Château de Lambert. It is necessary I dance with guests," she finished, wondering if she had selected all the correct tenses.

"She was a beautiful woman, your mother," reflected Sir Edward, his voice gentle and sad.

"Yes," agreed Jacqueline. An overwhelming feeling of loss was beginning to grip her. Her mother had been very beautiful. And she had been a loving wife and devoted mother, but who was left who could remember that about her? Séraphine had never known her, and Suzanne, who was four when she died, was now a young lady of ten, and her memories of her mother were based more on stories Jacqueline had told her than actual recollections. Once Jacqueline was dead, which would probably be soon, there would be no one to remember what a fine and loving woman the Duchesse de Lambert had been. Her heart ached at the thought.

"Excuse me, Sir Edward, but Lady Harrington assured me you would not mind if I cut in," said a handsome young man with hair as blond as Jacqueline's and blue eyes that seemed to sparkle with amusement.

"Of course not," replied Sir Edward agreeably as he stopped and took a step back from Jacqueline. "Jacqueline, may I present Viscount Preston. Lord Preston, this lovely young lady is the daughter of a dear friend, and my honored house guest, Lady Jacklyn de Lambert."

"I am most humbly at your service, Lady Jacklyn," declared Viscount Preston as he swept into a courtly bow. He was colorfully dressed in a scarlet satin frock coat over an elaborately embroidered gold waistcoat, which on closer inspection depicted a crowded hunting scene. His blond hair had been set in two rows of neat curls at the sides of his head and very lightly dusted with powder, as had become fashionable in place of wigs in England. He stepped forward and boldly took Jacqueline into his arms. "Shall we?"

"Mais, oui," stammered Jacqueline, desperately wishing Sir Edward had not turned her over into the arms of a stranger.

"So you are the mysterious French aristocrat everyone is talking about," remarked her partner as he began to lead her gracefully around the floor. "Tell me, for I am most curious, however did you manage to escape France at such a frightfully dangerous time?"

"It was . . . *difficile,"* replied Jacqueline evasively, not particularly wanting to discuss the details of her escape with this stranger.

He smiled at her as if her response had been terribly clever. "I am sure it is a most exciting tale," he prodded.

"Non," she countered. "Not really."

"Come now, Lady Jacklyn," he persisted. "They say you were incarcerated in one of the foulest prisons of Paris, and that you were practically on your way to the scaffold when the Black Prince himself intervened, and stole you right out from under those murdering Frenchies' noses. Is that true?"

Jacqueline did not know which she found more upsetting, the treatment of her imprisonment and near death as idle ballroom chatter, or the fact that the gossipmongers of England seemed to have been entertaining each other with the story of her escape. What she did know was that any information she revealed, no matter how trivial, could potentially jeopardize Armand's future missions, and that was a risk she simply would not tolerate. She looked up at her handsome partner, knitted her eyebrows together, and shook her head in confusion.

"Je regrette, Monsieur, mais mon anglais n'est pas très bon, et je ne comprends pas ce que vous dites," she murmured apologetically, claiming that her English was poor and she did not understand him. She hoped he would cease his questioning.

Viscount Preston stared at her blankly. "I beg your pardon, I didn't quite catch that."

"She said she is terribly sorry, but she just remembered she promised this dance to me," said a low, firm voice.

Jacqueline looked up over Viscount Preston's shoulder to see Armand towering behind him, and her breath caught in her throat.

He seemed so much larger than she remembered. He was magnificently dressed in the simplest of costumes—a superbly tailored black frock coat over a white waistcoat and tightly fitted white breeches. No ruffles, no brocade, no fancy embroidery, just a crisply tied cravat and the unmistakable bearing of a man who wears elegant clothes with ease, as if it meant no more to him to be dressed for a ball than to be dressed in the rags of a peasant farmer. His hair was unpowdered and tied back with a length of black ribbon, and the soft, flickering light of the ballroom kept playing over the copper and gold highlights in it. His blue green eyes bore straight into hers, searching, demanding, assessing, ignoring Viscount Preston, ignoring everyone and everything around them, and for one brief moment everything stopped, and there was only the two of them, standing alone in an enormous ballroom amid the faint strains of some faraway music. She felt a wonderful sense of relief, as if for the first time in weeks some terrible burden had been lifted from her shoulders, yet at the same time she was overwhelmed with an inexplicable sensation of wariness and fear.

It was Armand who broke the spell. The corners of his mouth suddenly lifted into a faintly mocking smile, and he politely tilted his head toward her. "Forgive me for cutting in, Mademoiselle de Lambert," he apologized, his voice anything but apologetic, "but I do believe this is our dance."

Her heart was racing and she could not imagine why, but the velvety low sound of his voice reminded her they were not alone. She glanced over at Viscount Preston, who was glaring at Armand with barely disguised contempt.

"St. James, I must admit I never expected to see you here. Tell me, what is the occasion?" he drawled. "Too close to Christmas to sit at home alone? Or did your wine cellar run dry?" His voice was heavy with sarcasm.

Armand lifted his gaze from Jacqueline to look at him. "Strange, Preston, but I was not aware that my social life was any of your concern." His tone was pleasant, his expression utterly indifferent, but somehow Jacqueline could sense the fury awakening beneath his calm exterior. There was a barely controlled tension between the two men, a palpable dislike that went far deeper than the awkwardness of the present moment.

"*Pardonnez-moi, Monsieur,* but I did promise this particular dance to Monsieur St. James," Jacqueline burst out prettily, raising her hand to her throat and giving a light, silvery laugh. "I hope you do not mind?" She gazed up at Preston as if his feelings were the most important thing to her in the world, and was amazed at how easily she did so. It had been a long time since she had called upon her mannered feminine charm, but if that was what was required to calm the burning hostility between these two men, then so be it.

Viscount Preston pulled his eyes away from Armand and looked at Jacqueline in surprise, as if he was just noticing that she was there. The contempt in his expression instantly melted into a handsome smile, and he gallantly bowed and raised her hand to his lips.

"I am wounded, of course, Lady Jacklyn, but if you promise me another dance, I shall be sure to recover, just so I can feel you in my arms again." He pressed his lips to the back of her hand, lingering over the pale skin just a second longer than was appropriate.

"But of course," Jacqueline replied graciously, giggling at his outrageous remark. "I shall look forward to it." She lowered her lashes slightly.

Viscount Preston smiled at her and then turned to give Armand a curt nod before taking his leave.

"If you would prefer, I could forfeit our dance and bring him back to you," offered Armand with a scowl.

"Don't be absurd," snapped Jacqueline in French. "I would sooner dance 'La Marseillaise' stark naked in front of Robespierre than be forced to endure another moment with that ridiculous, prying peacock who is unsuccessfully masquerading as a man," she declared vehemently.

Armand stared at her a moment in surprise. And then he did something he had not done in a long time. He threw back his head and began to laugh.

He had not really expected to find her here. Although he did not generally attend these parties, he heard all about them when his sister, Madeleine, came to visit. She had told him the Harringtons were making all the usual rounds, but without their mysterious French guest in tow, which Madeleine found rather strange. Normally the French aristocrats who escaped to England were anxious to get out and begin a new social life. But Jacqueline's absence from parties did not surprise Armand in the least. He knew she did not want to make friends or create ties to this place. Even when she had finally accepted the fact that she could not escape him and that she would be going to England, he knew she had not completely abandoned her plan to return to France and have her revenge on Nicolas Bourdon.

"Monsieur St. James, I believe people are staring at us," remarked Jacqueline in exasperation.

Armand smiled. "I believe you are correct," he agreed, speaking to her in French. "But until your charade in front of Preston, Mademoiselle, I was not aware you were so skilled in the art of pretense. You know I have always thought you to be a perfectly dreadful liar. I can see now that my assessment was entirely inaccurate."

She looked at him in confusion for a moment, her brow creased in a delicate frown, as if she was trying to decide whether or not his remark should be taken as an insult or a compliment.

She was far, far more beautiful than he had remembered. Her honey-blond hair had been artfully arranged into a bouquet of soft curls that shimmered gold in the glow of the candlelight. The gown she wore was black silk, a stark contrast to the gay colors that filled the ballroom. If she had thought to avoid attracting attention by wearing such a somber color, then she had failed miserably, for the striking simplicity of her attire only served to accentuate her beauty. The gown was cut low, exposing the pale swell of her breasts and the graceful round of her shoulders. The fitted bodice emphasized her slender form, and he was relieved to see she had started to fill out a little in the weeks since he last saw her. She wore no jewelry, but the bodice and hem of the gown was studded with shimmering jet stones, which glittered and sparkled in the light of the ballroom like a symphony of brilliant black diamonds. She studied him with her huge gray eyes, and he was reminded of the color of the sea at dawn, deep and mysterious and unfathomable.

He reached out and wrapped his arm around her waist, pulling her close against him.

"Monsieur St. James, you are holding me entirely too close," protested Jacqueline.

"Perhaps," he agreed with a shrug. "But let us show them we can still enjoy ourselves, Mademoiselle, and really give them something to talk about."

Before Jacqueline could ask him what he meant by that, he began to move her in time to the music, effortlessly gliding her around as if they were the only couple on the crowded dance floor.

"Are you enjoying your stay with the Harringtons?" he asked.

"Sir Edward and Lady Harrington have been most kind," replied Jacqueline. "And of course, I am very grateful to be reunited with my sisters."

He nodded with satisfaction. Evidently she had started to settle in and accept her new life, as he had hoped she would. "Has Séraphine started to speak?"

"No," she answered unhappily. "I spend time with her each day, but she does not seem to want to talk. She lets Suzanne do her talking for her."

Armand considered this for a moment. "Perhaps you should separate them," he suggested. "Force her to speak for herself."

Jacqueline shook her head. "I have thought about

that, but I believe it would only make Séraphine withdraw even further. She is angry with me, angry for sending her away, angry for not being able to protect my father and Antoine. Separating her from Suzanne would do nothing to soothe that anger."

He looked at her in disbelief. "Why should she blame you for what happened to your father and brother?"

Jacqueline sighed. "When I sent Suzanne and Séraphine away, I promised them I would bring them back, that everything would be all right, and that we would all be together again. Obviously I did not keep that promise. First she learns her father has been executed, and then I return, but without Antoine. I think in her mind, she believes I betrayed her. Suzanne has been the one constant through all of this tragedy. If I take Suzanne away from her, it would only hurt her more, and I cannot bear to do that." Her voice was tight with guilt and despair.

"Give her time, Mademoiselle," suggested Armand gently. "She is only six. You both have many years ahead of you for healing and forgetting."

Jacqueline looked away. She did not have many years ahead of her. If Armand agreed to her request, she might not have more than a few weeks ahead of her. She swallowed. She had to speak to him alone before he returned her to Sir Edward and Lady Harrington.

"Monsieur St. James, I have a proposition to make to you," she began hesitantly.

He looked down at her, his curiosity evident. "Really?"

"But I do not wish to discuss it here in this crowded ballroom," she added quickly. "Do you think there is somewhere we can go where we might find a moment of privacy?"

His lips curved into a smile. He had no idea what she wanted to discuss with him, but the thought of being alone with her appealed to him immensely. "I think that can be arranged, Mademoiselle."

He pulled her even closer against him and began to dance with her toward the far corner of the ballroom, still moving in time with the music so it was not apparent to anyone that they were in fact leaving the floor. When they reached the corner he spun her behind an enormous Christmas tree, then took her arm and escorted her through a doorway that led off to a corridor.

They traveled down the hallway unnoticed, and Armand stopped when they reached the entrance to the library. He motioned for Jacqueline to go in ahead of him, then followed her and closed the door.

"So, Mademoiselle, what is this proposition you wish to put to me?" he asked, his voice slightly amused.

Jacqueline walked over to stand in front of the fireplace. "Is there something to drink in here?" She needed to fortify her nerves before she put her proposal to him.

Armand looked about and saw a silver tray filled with crystal decanters on a table against the wall. "Would you care for a glass of wine?" he offered as he walked over to it.

"Brandy," she replied quickly.

He looked at her with amusement. "This must be difficult for you." He lifted a decanter, splashed some of its amber liquid into a crystal glass, and walked over to her. "Here."

She gratefully accepted the glass. "Aren't you having some?"

"No."

She lifted the glass to her lips and took a hearty gulp. The liquid burned a path down her throat and warmed her chest, strengthening her sense of purpose. "Have you heard any news of the situation in France?" she asked suddenly.

He watched her as she clutched the glass to her bosom, wondering what it was she sought from him. Whatever it was, she obviously required more time to work up to asking him. He shrugged his shoulders and seated himself on the sofa in front of the fireplace, stretching his long legs out before him. He stared thoughtfully into the flames. "The revolutionary government has started to close the churches in and around Paris, in the name of the philosophy of Reason, which will soon be the only acceptable religion," he began, his voice low and serious. "Informing on one's fellowman continues to be a patriotic duty, and as a result the prisons of Paris are exploding with over seven thousand men, women, and children, who exist in nightmarish conditions as they await trial. The Tribunal and the guillotine cannot chop heads fast enough to keep up. Yet despite the arrests and executions of all these so-called enemies, the people continue to starve and inflation continues to soar."

"And this is what the people of France wanted," she whispered bitterly. She took another mouthful of brandy.

Armand shook his head. "No, Mademoiselle, this is not what the people of France wanted. Noblesse like your father dreamed of a new order in which the power of governing France would be more equitably shared between themselves and the monarchy. Perhaps he even shared the ideals of the philosophes and the bourgeois, in which the privileges and limitations of birth would be abandoned in favor of equality, where men would be judged by their character and abilities instead of their pedigree. It was a noble dream. But the peasants wanted something far simpler. They dreamed of bread on their tables and clothes on their backs, and an end to a system that stripped them of everything except their determination to survive. But the government in power today has little in common with the ideals that were expounded in 1789. The revolution has blown off course, and its original leaders have all been denounced and executed. Feudalism has been dismantled, the monarchy has been destroyed, the noblesse and bourgeois have been blamed for all the country's ills and are being exterminated. Yet the masses are still starving, and the new leaders are terrified."

Jacqueline tilted her head back and swallowed the rest of her drink. "They should be terrified," she stated bitterly.

He looked up at her, and once again was captivated by her beauty. She was standing before the fireplace staring intently into the flames, which were casting gold and peach light across the pale ivory of her skin. A wisp of her honey-colored hair had strayed down to her cheek, and he was filled with an overwhelming urge to touch those threads of silk, to lightly brush them off her face and at the same time to know the feel of her velvety skin against his fingers. He remembered the night he had painted her face to make her look old and filthy and haggard, and he wondered now how he had ever accomplished such a feat. With her high cheekbones, her delicately chiseled chin, her perfectly shaped nose, and those lusciously full lips stained the color of summer strawberries, it was impossible to imagine that any man could have looked at her and not wanted her there and then. The thought did not please him.

"Monsieur St. James, I wish to engage your services," she blurted out suddenly as she swung around to face him.

"Indeed?"

She set her glass down on the mantel and began to pace in front of the fireplace. "Today I received word that a friend of mine has been arrested and imprisoned in Paris. He has been falsely charged with assisting in my escape, but naturally his innocence will not spare him from the blade of the guillotine." She stopped her pacing and looked at him. "If he has not already been executed, I wish to hire you to rescue him."

A friend. He wondered exactly what that meant. "I see," he replied.

His expression was utterly neutral, so it was impossible for her to tell whether he was interested in the mission or not. He had not said no, but he was not asking any questions either, and she did not think that was a good sign. "Of course I will pay you for your services," she hastily assured him, lest he think she was asking him to return to France and risk his life simply as a favor to her.

He arched his brow skeptically. "And just how do you intend to pay me, Mademoiselle? Has Sir Edward placed a generous sum of money at your disposal? Or are we back to drawing on the fund you have set up for Suzanne and Séraphine?"

He was referring to her previous offer back in Paris, when she had asked him to help her kill Nicolas. He had refused her then. She did not want him to refuse her now. "Neither," she replied. "Although my financial resources are extremely limited here, I do have some wealth waiting for me in France."

He looked at her in disbelief. "Mademoiselle, you know all of the De Lambert holdings have been confiscated by the government, including the château and its contents."

"True," she admitted. "But since almost no one in France has any hard currency, and anyone who did would be afraid to spend it on something as grand and antirevolutionary as the Château de Lambert, it is unlikely the government has been able to find a buyer for it."

He still did not understand her reasoning. "What of it?"

She seated herself on the sofa beside him. "Do you remember at my trial, how the public prosecutor demanded to know where the De Lambert jewel collection was?"

He nodded.

Jacqueline smiled with satisfaction. "That was one prize they were not able to get their filthy, bloodstained hands on. They wanted it badly, for it is worth a fortune, and they knew they could easily sell it outside of France, for real currency that is worth more than the paper *assignats* the government continues to pour into circulation."

"As I recall, you told Fouquier-Tinville you had sold it."

"I lied."

He regarded her with interest. "Are you saying the jewels are here in England?"

"No," she replied. "I hid them at the château. But when we return I will fetch them."

His turquoise eyes clouded over with angry disbelief as understanding dawned on him. "So that is what this is all about," he began, his voice low and taut. "You still cannot forget this need for vengeance that poisons your every thought, preventing you from accepting your new life here." He stood and braced one hand against the mantel, staring hard into the flames as he fought to control the fury fast rising within him.

"This mission has nothing to do with vengeance," she burst out heatedly. "François-Louis has been arrested and he needs your help. Since I do not expect you to work for charity, it is necessary that I go with you so I can get the jewels. Once I have them I will wait for you wherever you tell me to. I have no intention of going anywhere near Nicolas." It was a complete lie of course, but she was certain her tone was sincere.

He turned around to face her, his expression harsh. "Do you take me for a fool, Mademoiselle? You know as well as I that you are obsessed with the thought of killing him. The very fact that you want to go with me clearly demonstrates how little regard you have for your own life, despite your responsibility toward your sisters." He turned away from her in disgust. "You are appallingly selfish." His voice was heavy with contempt.

"How dare you speak to me so!" she spat, rising from the sofa to stand beside him. "I am offering to pay you, Monsieur St. James, whatever price you ask, so François-Louis can be saved. I am willing to even risk my own life to secure his freedom, and you dare to call such an act selfish? You, a bourgeois merchant who deals in the movement of frightened, desperate human cargo as a way of making a living, and who would not even consider saving the life of another unless the price was agreeable to you? You dare to stand there and judge me selfish?" Her voice was shaking with anger.

He regarded her thoughtfully for a moment. "Tell me, Jacqueline, what is this man to you, that his survival is so important you are willing to risk your life for him?" he demanded.

"He is . . . a friend," she stammered, not certain why she chose to describe him as such. François-Louis was her betrothed, the man with whom she was supposed to have shared her life. Perhaps, since she would not live long enough to marry, such a description did not seem important.

"A friend," he repeated. Again he found himself wondering just exactly what that meant, and could not understand why it mattered to him. "And do you intend to return to France to rescue all your friends as they are arrested?" he demanded sarcastically.

"Of course not," she assured him. "But François-Louis has been falsely accused of assisting with my escape, and I feel honor bound to help him." She turned away from him, furious that he was questioning her motives. "Naturally I should not have expected you to understand, Monsieur," she declared sarcastically. "I had forgotten such a code of honor is not part of the history of your class."

It was as if she had slapped him. He reached out and clamped his hands on her shoulders, then spun her around so quickly she let out a gasp of outrage.

"Be warned, my haughty little aristo," he drawled softly as he held her in a painful grip. "I do not take such assaults on my character lightly. If you wish to criticize me, do so on the basis of my actions, not my birthright."

She glared up at him, her eyes the smoky gray of a summer storm that advances quickly across the ocean. Her breasts were rising and falling rapidly as indignation and anger stole her breath; they strained against the black jeweled silk of her bodice, barely touching him, and yet suddenly creating a desire within him that was appalling in its intensity. The honey-gold wisp of hair brushing against her cheek had been joined by another silky lock, that had tumbled away from its pins and come to rest against her collarbone. Her cheeks and throat were flushed from the heat of the fire, or perhaps from her fury. Her lips were moist and slightly parted, ready to demand he unhand her. She felt warm beneath his touch, warm and soft and filled with life, and despite every ounce of rational thought within him ordering him to let her go, he found he could not help himself. He bent his head and captured her lips with his.

Jacqueline's first thought was that she must fight, that this was another assault that she must fend off with every fiber of her being. Her entire body stiffened and she tried to pull away. But as Armand's lips began to move gently over hers, warm and firm and coaxing, she was overcome with a strange sensation that rendered her unable to fight. It was a feeling of warmth, and need, and curiosity, all melded together into one, making her dizzy and at the same time sharply aware of everything that was happening. In her mind she wanted to shove against him and push him away, she was certain of it, but her hands betrayed her, moving up to rest lightly against his chest, tingling at the feel of the hard, muscular wall that lay beneath the fine wool of his evening jacket. Armand's kiss grew more demanding and her lips parted, and then his tongue was gently sweeping into the wet heat of her mouth, startling her, confusing her, pleasing her.

He released her shoulders and lifted one hand to trace the delicate line of her jaw, while the other arm wrapped possessively around her waist, pulling her close. Her small, slender form sank against his enormous frame, molding herself to him until he was achingly aware of every soft curve. His tongue explored the sweet darkness of her mouth, and she began to respond with an urgency that matched his own, tasting, teasing, touching, wrapping her arms around his neck, and pressing into him until he was oblivious to everything except the need to be closer to her. His hand trailed down the ivory column of her throat and came to rest around the fullness of her breast. He stroked the soft mound and the nipple sprang to life beneath his palm, and Jacqueline moaned and clung to him even harder, as if she was desperate to be touched. Her need intoxicated him, it filled him with a passion he had long thought dead, and without pausing to question it, he tore his lips away from hers and began to kiss the fragrant skin of her neck, her collarbone, her breasts. Her scent was delicate and fresh; it reminded him of country air on a summer day, sweet and tangy and wonderfully clean. He wanted to touch and taste every part of her, to strip the black silk gown from her body and feel her naked beneath him, to pull the pins from her hair and plunge his hands deep into the blond thickness he knew barely touched her shoulders, knew because he had cut that hair with his own hands to save her life.

Until this moment he had not once thought of making her his. Now he could not imagine letting anyone else have her.

When he had left her that night with the Harringtons, his mission was completed, and yet he had felt as if he was abandoning her. She had seemed so lost and out of place, and for a brief moment he had actually wanted to lead her back to his carriage and take her home with him. He had tried not to think of her these past few weeks, and yet she had haunted him, interrupting his thoughts from morning until night. When he first saw her this evening, looking so pale and regal and beautiful, and in Preston's arms, he had been filled with a rage so intense it had shocked him. Now she was here in his arms, responding to his touch, and awakening things in him he had not experienced in years. It was wrong to touch her. He understood that. He had nothing to offer her. He was not titled. He would not marry her even if he were, for he knew with every trip he made back to France he might not return. It was his choice to constantly play this game with death. But he could not expect a woman to live with that kind of torment. He should stop, now, before they went any further. Yet he could not control himself. He crushed her against him and pressed his lips to hers, drinking in her sweet passion like a man dying of thirst who has suddenly been offered a cup of crystal cool water.

It was the soft creak of the door that alerted him. He released her instantly, taking care to shield her with his body while he steadied her. She looked up at him in confusion, her eyes troubled, her lips rosy and swollen from his kisses.

"There you are, Armand," sang out Laura's voice

prettily. "I have been looking for you all evening—whatever are you doing hiding in here?"

Armand took a deep breath and let an expression of absolute boredom cross his face. He turned and gifted Laura with a smile that seemed to say he was absolutely delighted by her interruption. "Mademoiselle de Lambert and I were just discussing the current situation in France," he drawled wearily in English, as if he found the subject utterly dull.

Laura looked at Jacqueline in surprise, obviously having thought that Armand was alone. Her glance swept over her, taking in her slightly disheveled look. "Why Jacklyn, we have been looking for you everywhere," she remarked stiffly. "Have you told Armand the perfectly awful news about your betrothed?"

Armand's expression darkened slightly. "I don't believe she has."

"Well, it is simply terrible," Laura assured him. "Jacklyn's betrothed, the Marquis de Biret, has been arrested and is awaiting execution in a prison in Paris. Jacklyn has been terribly upset about it all day, haven't you, Jacklyn?"

Jacqueline could sense Armand's anger, but she could do nothing to assuage it while Laura was here. She tried to think of something to say, but nothing came to her.

"That is distressing news indeed," agreed Armand sympathetically. "If you will excuse us for a moment, Laura, there is a small matter which I must discuss privately with Mademoiselle de Lambert."

Laura opened her mouth to protest, clearly not liking the idea of leaving the two of them alone.

"But do not stray too far, for I intend to claim you for a dance in ten minutes," he added quickly, his voice filled with promise. He took her hand and pressed a lingering kiss against it.

"Very well," sighed Laura, her mouth forming into a pretty little pout. "Ten minutes." She smiled at him and left the room.

As soon as the door was closed Armand turned to Jacqueline, his expression harsh. "As usual, Mademoiselle, I have underestimated you," he grated out in French. "Your highly enjoyable performance was worthy of the most seasoned courtesan. The marquis must be a very special man to have inspired such total, selfless devotion." His voice was heavy with sarcasm.

"How dare you speak to me so," she choked.

"Oh come now, Mademoiselle," returned Armand, irritated beyond measure at his own stupidity. How could he have been so foolish as to think she was actually responding to him honestly? Obviously his year of celibacy had clouded his perception where women were concerned. She had been using him, trying to seduce him into agreeing to help her. If he had not been so thoroughly taken in by her performance, he might have actually found it amusing. "You can abandon this show of false indignation. Tell me, for I am curious, just when exactly did you intend to tell me that this 'friend' of yours was in fact your betrothed?" he demanded.

Humiliation and anger swirled within her. By comparing her to a courtesan he had essentially called her a whore. Which was not true. She could not begin to understand why she had reacted to his touch the way she had, but it had nothing to do with her wanting him to rescue François-Louis. "I do not see how it is any of your affair what his relationship is to me," she informed him icily.

"But, Mademoiselle, you asked me to risk my life to save him," he reminded her. "That makes everything about him my affair. However, since I will not be saving him, I guess it does not matter. If you will excuse me." He gave her a curt nod and began to walk toward the door.

"Wait!"

He stopped and turned. "Forgive me. Is there something more we have to discuss?"

"Monsieur St. James, I proposed a business arrangement to you," she began, trying desperately to stay calm. If he did not agree to help her, François-Louis would die, and now more than ever his death would be her fault.

"So you did," he remarked agreeably. "And I have turned it down." He placed his hand on the door latch.

"Why?" she demanded in frustration. "Because I am asking you to rescue the man I was engaged to marry?"

He paused for a moment before answering. "No," he stated finally. "I am turning you down, Mademoiselle, because once again you have nothing with which to pay me."

"But I have offered you the De Lambert jewels," she reminded him.

He looked at her with amusement. "You forget, Mademoiselle, that in my business I find it necessary to require payment in advance. You are offering to pay me with something you do not have. Now, how could you reasonably expect me to accept such an offer?"

"I have offered to go and fetch the jewels myself," she told him in frustration, "but you will not let me. I have offered you money out of the fund I set up for Suzanne and Séraphine, but you will not accept it. What else do I have to offer you? What is it you want?"

He looked at her intently, sensing her desperation. "You," he stated flatly. He did not know why he said it, and he did not care.

She frowned in confusion. "What?"

"I want you," he repeated softly. "In my bed. For one night."

She paused and let his meaning sink in. "You must be mad!" she suddenly blazed in disbelief.

He shrugged his shoulders. "Perhaps," he agreed. "No sane man could possibly think a night with you was worth risking his life for. But that is my price, Mademoiselle. One night with you, before I leave to rescue your poor marquis. Take it or leave it."

Taut silence hung between them. He met the glittering gray fury of her eyes calmly, waiting for her to tell him to go straight to the devil.

"What you are proposing is out of the question," she informed him stiffly.

"Really?" he remarked with amusement, perversely pleased her devotion to her betrothed was not so great she was willing to sacrifice herself for him. "How unfortunate for your poor marquis." He began to move toward the door.

"Wait!" she cried, desperately trying to think of some way to negotiate with him.

He turned and regarded her questioningly. "Was there something else you wished to discuss, Mademoiselle?"

She hesitated. Perhaps if she agreed to spend the night with him, she could get him to accept the condition that it not be until after he had rescued François-Louis. By the time François-Louis was safe in England, Jacqueline would be on her way back to France. She realized it was extremely dishonorable to enter into an agreement one had no intention of fulfilling, but given the sordid, despicable nature of his proposal, somehow she did not feel overly guilty about lying to him. She closed her eyes and breathed a heavy sigh of defeat, as if she were struggling with a difficult decision.

"Very well, Monsieur St. James," she murmured wearily. "I accept your terms."

He could not believe he had heard her correctly. "I beg your pardon?" he managed, stunned.

"I said I accept your terms," she repeated. "I will give myself to you for one night, if you will return to France and rescue the Marquis de Biret."

He did not know which disgusted him more, the fact that he had been reduced to suggesting she prostitute herself, or the fact that she had accepted his offer so readily.

"However," she continued casually, "I do not believe I should have to fulfill my part of this arrangement until François-Louis has been removed from danger. After all, what if you are not successful?"

A curious mixture of relief and irritation flooded through him as he realized her game. She had no intention of sleeping with him. She was simply trying to manipulate him into rescuing her precious betrothed. Once this marquis was safely delivered, she would say thank you very much and that would be that. His mouth curved with amusement.

"I have already made it clear, Mademoiselle, that I require payment for my services in advance," he informed her. "If I do not succeed in a mission, it is because I am dead." He slowly moved his eyes up and down the length of her, hesitating at the creamy flesh that swelled above the black-jeweled bodice of her gown, then gave her a lazy smile. "And if I am to die on this particular mission, I would like to at least have the memory of what it was I risked my life for," he drawled silkily.

"That is not possible!" she burst out furiously, feeling strangely heated by his intense scrutiny of her.

He blinked his eyes with affected confusion. "But why not? What difference does it make whether you pay me now or later?" He paused and frowned. "Unless, of course, you have no intention of fulfilling your part of our agreement," he mused thoughtfully.

"Monsieur St. James, what you are asking is totally unreasonable," she blurted pleadingly, desperately trying to think of something else she could offer him.

"A pity," he remarked with an indifferent shrug of his shoulders. "Well then, Mademoiselle, if our business for this evening is finished, I hope you will forgive me if I take my leave of you."

She despised his flippant, cavalier manner. François-Louis was going to die, and because she would not agree to his price, Armand was utterly uninterested. Rescuing helpless prisoners from France was simply a matter of business to him and nothing more. "By all means," she replied tautly, feeling as if she was going to scream. "You must not keep Laura waiting for her dance."

He noted the angry brittleness in her voice, but he chose to ignore it. He gave her a small bow and left the room.

Jacqueline sank down onto the sofa and pressed her forehead against the heels of her hands. She had failed. She had not been able to get Armand to agree to help poor François-Louis, and now he would be executed. The horrendous burden of yet another death had been added to her shoulders. Her chastity for his life. She bit down hard on her lip as she wrestled with the terrible guilt swirling within her.

When the awful news of François-Louis's death finally reached her, she did not think she would be able to bear it.

Chapter 8

The rapping on the door was soft but insistent. "Jacklyn, dear, are you not going to join us for dinner?" called Lady Harrington from the hallway.

Jacqueline sighed and rose from her bed. "Forgive me, Lady Harrington," she apologized as she opened the door. "I am not feeling well. I should have sent Charlotte to you with this message."

Lady Harrington regarded her with concern. "Are you ill, my dear? Shall I send for a doctor?"

Jacqueline shook her head. "It·is nothing. But I do not desire to be dining this evening," she explained awkwardly, struggling to find the correct English tenses.

Lady Harrington appeared unconvinced. "You have barely eaten a thing for two days now. I think perhaps I should have our doctor look at you."

"*Non*," blurted out Jacqueline. "It is not necessary."

"You are worried about your betrothed, aren't you, my dear?" the older woman asked. Her voice was filled with sympathy.

Jacqueline nodded.

"You must try to put him from your mind. I know you think that is impossible, but you must try," she instructed. Her expression softened. "There is nothing any of us can do for him, Jacklyn," she added gently.

Wasn't there? wondered Jacqueline bitterly. Armand could save him. She knew he could. But unless she agreed to his odious proposal, he would not lift a finger to help poor François-Louis.

"I am going to have Charlotte bring you a tray," continued Lady Harrington. "And I want you to promise me you will try to eat something."

"I am not hungry," protested Jacqueline.

"Nevertheless, I want you to eat," she repeated firmly.

Jacqueline sighed. She knew Lady Harrington was acting the way any worried mother might. In a way she was touched by her concern. "Very well, Lady Harrington," she conceded wearily.

Lady Harrington gave her a smile of approval and then bustled down the hallway, her voluminous purple silk evening gown swishing noisily around her.

Jacqueline closed the door and leaned heavily against it. The excruciating headache that had started two days ago after her confrontation with Armand continued to pound mercilessly at her temples. She lifted her fingers and tried to massage the throbbing away, but she knew it was no use. Exhausted from the pain and the agonizing guilt she had been wrestling with these past two days, she staggered back to the bed and flung herself down on it. She did not know how much longer she could go on like this.

Because of her François-Louis was going to die. It was that simple. If not for her incredible escape from prison, he would never have been accused of conspiring to assist her. She was free and safe in England, and François-Louis was sitting in a miserable Paris prison awaiting execution for something he did not do. The cruel injustice of it was staggering.

She had tried to come up with another idea to help him escape, but the only person she knew who could help her was Armand. But how could she possibly agree to his terms? she wondered desperately. The idea of sleeping with a man as part of a business arrangement was utterly sordid and base. If she consented to it, her actions reduced her to the morals of a common whore. But what kind of morality would value her chastity over a man's life? When she received the news that the man she was pledged to marry had been executed, would she feel appropriately virtuous and pure because her virginity remained intact?

She knew without a doubt she would not. François-Louis's murder would cast a hideous black pall of unrelenting guilt over whatever little remained of her life. She squeezed her eyes shut and rolled onto her side.

Perhaps it was not such a terrible sin to barter with one's body, she reflected. Especially in such extraordinary circumstances, where the life of a friend was at stake. After all, she reminded herself, it was only one time. It would probably be over quickly, and no one other than Armand would ever know about it. Once she had completed her end of their agreement, he could leave immediately for Paris. François-Louis might be safe in England within a few weeks. Despite the extreme sordidness of his terms, Jacqueline had no doubt Armand would honor his end of their bargain. After all, he was a businessman who valued his reputation. He would do everything within his power to make sure the mission was a success. François-Louis would be alive and safe. And all this miraculous feat would have cost was her virginity.

She sat upright on the bed, her heart pounding as she struggled with her decision. Her virginity was a commodity that did not interest her at this point, she told herself fiercely. The only thing that mattered was that François-Louis be rescued.

She moved swiftly across the room to her writing table and began to pen a note to Armand, tersely informing him of her acceptance and asking him to make the necessary arrangements quickly. The sooner she fulfilled her end of their agreement, the sooner Armand could leave for France, she reflected as she waited impatiently for the ink to dry. As for the possibility Armand would fail and François-Louis would die anyway, she would not consider that.

Jacqueline stared out the carriage window at the enormous silvery-gray stone estate that stretched across the snow-covered grounds. The immense building was a glowing jewel against the blackness of the night, lit in every window as brilliantly as the Château de Lambert used to be when her father and mother gave one of their many lavish parties. At first she wondered if they had come to the right place, for Jacqueline did not believe Armand could possibly finance such a grand home merely by rescuing desperate aristocrats from France. His ship, she knew, must have been costly, but it was obviously essential to his line of business. To live in an estate as grand as this, which was far larger and much more magnificent than the home of the Harringtons, one would have to be enormously wealthy, and since Armand was not an aristocrat, with centuries of accumulated wealth and property behind him, she simply could not imagine how he could have accumulated such a vast fortune.

The carriage door swung open and the coachman offered her his arm as she descended the steps. She adjusted the collar of her cloak to protect herself from the icy December air as she stood and faced the enormous house. It did not have the graceful, ornate whimsy of the Château de Lambert, but there was an elegant simplicity to the structure that somehow made it just as beautiful. Three tiers of large windows graced the front of the building, and Jacqueline imagined that when the sun beat down on those windows, the interior of the house must be flooded with light, a feature she sorely missed at the oppressively dark Harrington estate. The grounds surrounding the house were extensive, and judging by the endless rows of carefully clipped evergreens and snow-covered stone sculptures, it was obvious the gardens were immense and well tended. It was a home that reflected wealth and power, but it also revealed something of the taste of its owner. That understated, streamlined simplicity Jacqueline had seen in the way Armand dressed and furnished his surroundings was evident here. There was nothing fanciful or decorative in the facade of his home, except for four magnificent Corinthian pillars that framed the massive oak front door. The structure was an architectural study of balance and order, of classical simplicity and timeless beauty. It was totally at odds with the highly ornamented architectural style Jacqueline had grown up with, but she did not find the building stark and unattractive. Instead she found there was a calmness to it, a quiet tranquillity that was restful and soothing. As she stood contemplating this the front door swung open, revealing a tall figure whose enormous physique practically blocked the light spilling into the darkness from the entrance hall.

"Good evening, Mademoiselle," said Armand pleasantly in French. "Are you going to come in, or would you like a few more minutes to reconsider our agreement? I can have Tom take you home if you have decided to change your mind."

She stiffened at his blatant reference to their arrangement in front of a servant. She turned to see the coachman dutifully standing by the carriage, obviously waiting to see if there were any further instructions before he returned to the stables. He nodded his head and smiled at her, which profoundly added to her embarrassment. Determined not to let a servant witness her humiliation, or give him anything to gossip with other servants about, she straightened her spine and proceeded regally up the steps.

"Ask your driver to keep the carriage ready," she instructed Armand icily. "I trust this matter will not take long." In actual fact she had absolutely no idea how long the act of lovemaking took, but she was not about to let him know that. She swept by him into the hallway, her manner very much that of a busy woman who has an insignificant errand to attend to and then must be on her way.

Armand gave a nod to the coachman and closed the door. He did not know whether to feel annoyed or relieved. He had told himself he would give her the opportunity to change her mind, right up until the moment she stepped into his house. He felt that was only fair. In truth, he had not really expected her to show up at all. When he received her note informing him that she accepted his terms, he had been totally shocked. He had written back to tell her how much he was looking forward to the prospect of her company. He said he would send a carriage for her the following night, and suggested she feign a head-ache and retire early, which would enable her to slip out unnoticed. He had assured himself that once she had more time to consider the crudeness of his proposal, she would come to her senses and realize she could not barter herself like a common whore. He had fully expected her to send his coachman home tonight with another note, either boldly telling him to go to hell, or imploring him to con-sider an alternate form of payment. Yet here she was, standing in his hallway, pulling off her hat and stripping off her gloves in a most businesslike manner, trying to hide her obvious nervousness behind a brisk, take-charge air. Part of him was utterly furious with her for being so foolish, and wanted to march her into the library and give her a two-hour lecture on propriety and what happened to women who bargained with their bodies, before send-ing her back to the Harringtons' in his carriage. But an-other part of him, a far deeper, less familiar part, was fascinated and intrigued by the fact that she was actually here, in his home, ready and willing to give herself to him. He could not forget the incredibly intense desire she had awakened in him when he had taken her in his arms the other night. Nor could he ignore the fact that she had responded to him with a passion and need that quite pos-sibly matched his own.

He knew she had not wanted to respond to him. She considered him beneath her. She was betrothed to a mar-quis from an ancient noble family, someone of impeccable breeding and great wealth, who undoubtedly never sullied his hands by engaging in commerce or working the land. How could he ever compete with that? She despised him for what she perceived to be his tainted source of income. She believed he made his living by trading in desperate human cargo, and he had said nothing to refute that erro-neous assumption. And beyond that, he knew she was fu-rious with him, for he had saved her life but at the same time he had stripped her of her choices, forcing her to flee the country she loved so dearly, and blocking her attempts to escape and seek her much-needed revenge. He understood her anger with him. He even understood the dictates of society that made her feel she was better than others, customs and rules that had evolved over the centuries, asserting that an untitled man like him was unfit for her to socialize with. Which made the fact that she was actually here all the more fascinating.

"Did you have to mention our arrangement in front of the driver?" Jacqueline snapped furiously as she wrenched at the buttons of her cloak. "Discretion may not be important to you, but I would prefer it if this sordid incident was kept strictly between us."

Her description of their meeting as sordid reminded him that he had forced her here, and once again he felt a wave of self-loathing. "Are you worried your precious marquis might not be understanding of the sacrifices you were willing to make to save him?" His voice was heavy with contempt, but not all of it was directed at her. Most of it was directed at himself.

She stared hard at him, her gray eyes glittering with barely suppressed fury. "I think there are very few people who would describe the price you have chosen to extract from me as either fair or honorable," she informed him tautly. "But since I have elected to accept your offer, I do not see any point in discussing it further. I do not, however, believe it is either wise or necessary to make our arrangement known to the entire world, do you?"

Armand sighed. He did not wish to begin their evening together with an argument. "You need not concern yourself, Mademoiselle," he assured her. "Tom has been in my employ for many years, and discretion has long been part of his job. You may trust me when I tell you no one will learn of our meeting through him."

She nodded with satisfaction and began to look around, uncertain what to do next. Armand walked over and assisted her with the removal of her cloak. Underneath it she was wearing a high-necked, long-sleeved gown of black silk, totally void of ornamentation. It was far less revealing than the gown she had worn the other night. It could not hide her beauty, but it was clearly meant to be as somber and unenticing as possible. He could not help but smile at her choice.

"I have had the servants prepare a small supper for us in the drawing room," he said as he led her down the hallway and threw open two enormous doors.

Jacqueline followed him into the room, where a huge fire had succeeded in warming the air to a point where it almost seemed cozy. A small oval table with two striped silk chairs was set in front of the fireplace, and the table had been laid with an exquisite selection of the finest china, crystal, and silver warming dishes. The delicious scent of roasted chicken and wine gravy filled her nose, and Jacqueline remembered that in her nervous anticipation of this evening she had not been able to eat all day.

"The meal is somewhat simple, but in the interests of privacy I thought it best to have the servants lay out the food in advance, and then I gave them the night off," Armand explained as he walked over to the table and pulled out a chair for her. "Mademoiselle?"

She stared at him in confusion, moved by his obvious thoughtfulness in ordering a meal but sparing her the need to face his staff and therefore run the risk of gossip. Despite his desire to have her, he did not seek to humiliate her. But to sit down and share a meal with him was not part of their arrangement, and somehow it made the meeting too intimate, too friendly, as if she was giving herself to him of her own choice, which she most certainly was not. Not that he was about to brutally force himself upon her, the way Nicolas had that terrible night in her cell. No, whatever one wished to call their encounter, it would certainly not be rape. But by giving her the ultimatum he had offered, trading her chastity for François-Louis's life, he had basically given her no choice, and in her mind that was almost the same as rape. She had had no other option but to accept. Hadn't she?

"Mademoiselle?"

He regarded her with one eyebrow raised questioningly. Despite her nervousness, she could not help but notice how devastatingly handsome he looked this evening.

His black fitted jacket clung to his broad shoulders like a second skin, and his tight, cream-colored breeches left no doubt that his legs were solidly sculpted from lean, hard muscle. His gold-and-copper hair had been neatly tied back with a length of black ribbon, and his ruggedly chiseled jaw was freshly shaven. He seemed perfectly at ease amid his elegant surroundings, as at home as he appeared when he was Citizen Julien and hunched over in the foul darkness of her cell, or when he was captain of *The Angélique* and standing with his legs braced apart on the deck, watching the pitching and rolling of the ocean. He really was an extraordinary man, she noted, taking no pleasure in the observation. He was able to change and adapt to his surroundings with the ease of a chameleon, switching languages, accents, and mannerisms as quickly and effortlessly as he changed costumes. It intrigued her, this ability to become what he was not, to act out a role and manage to convince everyone, including her, that he was what he appeared to be. There was so much about him she did not know. Not that she wanted to know, she reminded herself fiercely. Theirs was a business relationship and nothing more. He had rescued her from certain death on the guillotine, not because he cared in the least what happened to her, but simply because he had been hired to do so. And she was here now, not because she wanted to share an intimate dinner with him, but because she wanted to save François-Louis's life. And to do so she had agreed to sleep with him. The whole arrangement suddenly struck her as thoroughly base and common, and she shuddered.

"Mademoiselle," he repeated softly, somewhat disturbed by her obvious reluctance even to come near him, "come and sit down."

"I am not hungry," Jacqueline declared vehemently, as if he had just offered her a plate of poison. Then, as an afterthought, she added, "I ate before I came here."

As if in protest to that outrageous lie, her stomach selected that exact moment to growl a hopelessly loud and most undignified soliloquy, causing a scarlet blush to race to her cheeks. Armand looked at her with amusement.

"Perhaps you did not quite satisfy your appetite," he suggested pleasantly. He reached over and lifted one of the silver lids, pausing to inhale the savory aroma that wafted up from the oval dish. "I must admit, roasted chicken marinated in wine cream is a particular favorite of mine," he murmured appreciatively. "What else do we have here?" He began to lift the lids off other dishes, quickly taking stock of the small feast that had been prepared for them. "Veal roast in pastry, partridge, poached eggs in broth, vegetables in butter sauce, and to finish, a selection of pastries, cheeses, and fruit preserves." He raised his eyes to her. "It is perhaps a simple meal, but one which I think you will not find distasteful," he assured her.

Jacqueline was certain she would not find it distasteful at all, for it looked and smelled absolutely wonderful, but she reminded herself firmly that she was not here to eat, and she wanted this entire ordeal over and done with as quickly as possible. "Monsieur St. James, you are quite aware I did not come here to dine with you, I came here to—" At that point she suffered a sudden embarrassing loss of words. She paused and looked at him helplessly.

Armand resisted the urge to laugh. "Yes?" he prodded, as if he was sincerely trying to be helpful.

Sensing that he was enjoying her discomfort immensely, she sent him a withering look of irritation. She would not allow him to make her feel more nervous or uncomfortable than she already did. "What I mean to say," she began, her tone slow and dignified, "is that this evening is a business arrangement and nothing more. If it is agreeable to you, I would prefer to get the matter over and done with."

He regarded her with a look of surprise. "Mademoiselle, please forgive me for being so completely and utterly thoughtless," he apologized. He replaced the lid on the serving dish and hastily moved out from behind the chair. "I did not realize you were so anxious to lie naked in my arms. I am, of course, flattered and delighted by your enthusiasm, and since our agreement is that you will be mine for the night, the sooner we begin, the longer I will have to slowly search out the unexplored secrets of your enchanting body." He flashed her a dazzling smile and graciously offered her his arm. "Shall we adjourn upstairs to my bedroom?"

His words washed over her grim sense of purpose like an icy gush of water. The night. Dear God. She had agreed to share his bed for one night. How could she have been so stupid? Somehow when he had named his price she had thought it meant one quick encounter, which could probably be accomplished in a matter of minutes, or certainly no longer than an hour. She had not intended to cooperate with him any more than was absolutely necessary to get the act done, and even planned to keep as much of her clothes on as possible. But here he was, blithely talking about her lying naked in his arms and exploring the secrets of her body. She felt certain she was going to be sick. Or faint. Or both.

"Mademoiselle, are you all right? You look terribly pale. . . ." His voice filtered through her thoughts, low and slightly amused.

"I . . . I think perhaps I will have something to eat after all," stammered Jacqueline as she released herself from his arm and began to retreat hastily toward the table. "I just realized how absolutely famished I am."

Armand suppressed his urge to laugh and followed her back to the table. "As you wish," he replied as he seated her. "Perhaps a little wine will restore the color to your cheeks." He lifted the wine bottle and filled her glass with ruby liquid.

It suddenly occurred to her that if she could see to it he drank enough, he might pass out as soon as he lay down on his bed. Then all she would have to do was remove his clothes and cover him with some blankets. When he awoke he would not be able to remember what had happened, but she would leave him a note saying now that she had upheld her end of the bargain, she fully expected him to do the same. François-Louis would be saved, and her virtue would remain intact. It was a perfect plan. She smiled.

Armand placed the bottle back on the table and took his seat.

"Are you not having any wine?" Jacqueline asked sweetly.

"No," he replied. "I am not."

Her smile vanished. "Why not?"

He lifted the cover off a serving dish. "Because, Mademoiselle, I do not drink. Chicken?" he offered as he picked up her plate.

"What do you mean, you don't drink?" she demanded in confusion.

"Alcoholic beverages," he clarified. He served a portion of chicken onto her plate. "Veal?"

She nodded as she contemplated this information. Perhaps he was stricken with some physical ailment. Given his solid physique and general look of complete good health, she thought it unlikely he suffered from a stomach disorder, but if that was not the case, she simply could not imagine why he should not drink. She knew her curiosity was rude, but she could not restrain herself from asking. "Why don't you drink alcoholic beverages?"

Armand casually shrugged his shoulders and concentrated his attention on heaping more veal onto her plate. "Because I choose not to," he answered simply. "Partridge?"

It was clear this was an uncomfortable subject for him, which made her all the more curious. She thought back to their journey out of France, thinking surely there must have been at least one occasion when she had seen him take a glass of wine. She recalled that when he had his coughing fit in her cell, she asked the jailer to bring him some wine, but Armand had quickly interrupted and insisted upon water. During their long ride to the coast he had always drunk from a bottle of clear liquid, which she had assumed was a stronger form of alcohol than the wine she consumed. She realized now it must have been water. Even the other night at the Fleetwoods' ball, there had not been the faintest scent or taste of alcohol on him when he kissed her. In her experience, men like her father and François-Louis loved the taste of a fine wine or a good brandy. Even she preferred wine over water with her meals. To not drink alcohol was, quite simply, most unusual. She stared at him in amazement.

Armand looked up to see her staring at him and felt ridiculously self-conscious. "You needn't look at me as if I had just grown a second head," he snapped irritably as he handed her the plate.

"I am sorry," she apologized. "It is just that I have never met a man who did not drink alcohol." Embarrassed by her behavior, she lowered her gaze to her food.

He served his own plate and the two of them began to eat in awkward silence. Armand cursed himself for losing his temper. It was not her fault for being curious. It was only natural. But the reason he had decided never to drink again was still excruciatingly painful, and he did not like to be reminded of it. Yet how could he possibly expect Jacqueline to know something like that? He watched her from across the table as she picked nervously at her food.

There was no denying it. She was exceptionally, hauntingly beautiful. Although she had tried her best to present herself as unattractive by dressing in a matronly gown that might have been better suited to a funeral, the modest simplicity of the garment could not begin to play down her beauty. Her glossy blond hair had been swept up into a soft chignon that rested against the nape of her neck, but because it still lacked the required length to keep such a style firmly in place, small tendrils had worked their way loose and were falling in soft curls against her temples. Her skin was as luminous as white silk, giving her a pale, almost fragile quality, which he knew was totally at odds with the strength that dwelled within her. She continued to pick silently at the mountain of food he had inadvertently piled onto her plate, her smoky-gray eyes hidden below a dark sweep of lashes. He permitted himself the pleasure of just looking at her, drinking in her appearance and her delicate little mannerisms like a man who has never seen a beautiful woman before. It had been a long time since he had shared an intimate dinner with a woman. It had also been a long time since a woman had stirred the feelings of desire Jacqueline had awakened in him. He studied her as she continued to give all her attention to her plate, so obviously ill at ease. Suddenly he wanted very much to make her feel more relaxed. He knew she did not want to be here. He had not forced her, but he had used her betrothed's safety as a commodity, knowing full well she had nothing with which to barter except herself. But he had not expected her to accept his terms, and somehow the fact that she had infuriated him. It was clear she must care for her marquis a great deal, and this realization startled and annoyed him. He reminded himself that when she kissed him back the other night she had been using him, trying to seduce him into rescuing her so-called friend. Suggesting she sleep with him in return for his services was merely the logical conclusion of what she had already started. And although it was wrong, he wanted her. He was not so certain, however, that she wanted him. If in the end she decided she could not go through with it, he would not force her. Whatever was to happen between them this evening, he did not intend for it to be an unpleasant ordeal for her. She had been through enough ordeals to last a lifetime.

"I used to drink to excess," he began in a low voice, trying to break through the wall of silence that had risen between them. "I thought it was amusing. And since no one other than myself was lifting the glass to my lips, I assured myself I was in control."

His voice was taut, not apologetic, but not proud either. His willingness to talk about it seemed to be a kind of peace offering. Slowly Jacqueline lifted her gaze from her food to look at him.

"I felt as though I was invincible," he continued, meeting her gaze calmly. "After all, I had just about everything a young man could desire. My father had left me a considerable amount of money, and I made sure I was sober at least often enough to manage my investments. At first it was easy. Then, when I started to get drunk more often than I was sober, I made some extremely foolish business decisions and lost a lot of money. Rather than see it as a sign I was losing control of myself, somehow that struck me as funny."

"Why would you think losing money was funny?" asked Jacqueline, who could not imagine such a thing.

He shrugged his shoulders indifferently. "Because there was always so much more coming in from other sources," he explained. "I hold investments in sugar, to-bacco, tea, cotton, silk—anything the European market has a constant and insatiable demand for. When your in-vestments are extensive and diversified, it doesn't matter if some of them don't pay off in a given year. In fact, you expect it. So the fact that my work was suffering as a result of my drinking did not seem reason enough to stop." He paused.

Jacqueline waited for him to continue. It was obvious this was difficult for him to talk about, and undoubtedly not a subject that was broached often. She thought back to Viscount Preston, and his scathing remark when Ar-mand cut in on him the other night. *St. James, I must admit I never expected to see you here. Tell me, what is the occasion? Too close to Christmas to sit at home alone? Or did your wine cellar run dry?* Obviously his battle with alcohol was well-known, and had made him an ob-ject of contempt. She felt a rush of protective anger. If anyone ever chose to make such a foul comment in her presence again, she would lash into them with an intensity that would cut them to the bone.

"What made you finally stop?" she asked, sensing his reluctance to continue.

Armand struggled for a moment before giving her the answer. This was not a topic he had imagined they would discuss as they dined, but now that it was open, he had no choice but to tell her. He felt as if he was admitting some-thing to her that was intensely personal, and therefore not relevant to their relationship. But others knew, and it was only a matter of time before the gossip reached her ears. The only reason she had not yet heard about this sordid aspect of his personal life was because she had locked herself up in the Harringtons' home these past few weeks, and the Harringtons, he was certain, would never talk about it. Sir Edward had been a close personal friend of his father for years, and out of respect for that friendship, and a genuine affection for Armand, he had told Armand what was past was past, and not to be opened again.

"Because of me, several people were killed," he stated harshly, punishing himself with the words. "I was off on one of my many drunken binges, and unable to prevent it." He paused, as if to let the words sink in. "And that, Mademoiselle, is when I decided to give up drinking."

There was a finality to his tone that clearly said the subject was closed. His expression seemed calm and composed, except for a tightening of his jaw, so slight as to be almost imperceptible. It was that tightening Jacqueline focused on, for it told her how difficult this admission had been for him. She wished she had never brought the subject up. She felt as though she had been witness to something terribly personal and painful for him, and in her heart she felt a rush of compassion, which she most decidedly did not want to feel. She firmly reminded herself that her relationship with him was one of business, and nothing more. He was not her friend. He had saved her in exchange for money. And now he would save François-Louis in exchange for her body. Everything to him was a question of economics, of trading something in exchange for his remarkable ability to rescue people. It was coarse and base, which was what one must expect from a man who is not of noble birth, and therefore not raised with the ideals and principles of an aristocrat. And yet this glimpse into his past had moved her, had made her want to alleviate some of his pain by telling him those deaths could not possibly have been entirely his fault.

"How is your English coming?" he asked, interrupting her thoughts.

"Not so well," she admitted, grateful to have a new topic to discuss. "I don't believe I have a particular aptitude for languages."

He frowned. "You mean you are not trying," he said

accusingly. "You must work at it, Mademoiselle. You cannot live in England and not speak English."

Since she had absolutely no intention of remaining in England, that warning did not disturb her in the least. Armand might not take her with him when he went to rescue François-Louis, but as soon as her betrothed had been safely brought to England, Jacqueline was going to find a way to return to France. Nicolas had to be killed, and she would see that it was done. "How is it you speak French with no accent?" she asked, changing the subject.

"My mother was French," he explained, smiling as a look of surprise registered on her face. "Although she made England her home, she insisted from the moment my sister, Madeleine, and I were born that we have only French nannies. She believed French to be a far more beautiful language than English, and wanted to be sure that when we traveled to France we would not be regarded as foreigners. Eventually I was sent to France to study. I remained there for several years before the revolution began in 1789, and that is when I became aware of the innate problems eating away at the French monarchy and the seigneurial system."

"Why did your mother leave France?" asked Jacqueline, wondering how anyone could give up the beauty and elegance of France for England.

Armand smiled again, and Jacqueline was captivated by how terribly handsome he looked when he did so.

"She had fallen madly in love with my father, who was English, and could not imagine living without him. He was traveling in France when they met. When the time came for him to return to England, she agreed to marry him secretly and sail with him."

"Why did she have to marry him secretly?" Jacqueline asked. "Was it because your father was English and taking her away to another country?" She knew in her heart that her own father would never have agreed to a match where she would have had to live in another country. He had barely accepted the fact that once married to François-

Louis she would be moving into the Château de Biret, even though it was not far from the Château de Lambert.

"No, Mademoiselle, my father's nationality was not the issue. My mother was the eldest daughter of the Marquis des Valentes, and he did not believe his daughter should marry a lowly, untitled businessman, not when her own noble bloodlines ran back as far as the fourteenth century. After all, how could such a match be of any advantage to him? What sort of mongrel children would come from such an ungodly union?" His voice was heavy with sarcasm and contempt.

Jacqueline shifted uneasily in her chair, sensing that some of his hostility was directed at her. What he was describing was, she realized, the attitude of almost every noble father toward his daughter, including her own. Love, or even mutual affection and respect, was rarely a factor in these unions. If two people from noble backgrounds fell in love and wanted to marry, that was purely a matter of luck, and most people simply were not that lucky. The nobility felt it was important to perpetuate itself, and to keep its bloodlines strong and pure. Everyone understood that, including the wealthy bourgeois who railed against the injustice of the system while at the same time desperately trying to marry into even an impoverished noble family so they could elevate their own social status.

"When my father went to the marquis to ask for my mother's hand in marriage, my grandfather went into a rage. He ordered my father out of his home and forbade him to ever lay eyes on her again. Then he told my mother if she ever attempted to see my father again she would be cast out of the family, stripped of her title, and left destitute." He paused and looked at her, as if he was condemning her for being a part of a class that could be so rigid.

"Obviously your mother did not think much of his threat," commented Jacqueline.

"She ran away from home that same night. She and

my father married, and left for England almost immediately."

"And what of her father?" asked Jacqueline curiously.
"Did he carry out his threat?"

"He decided the marriage could not possibly last, and
so he offered my mother another chance. After waiting
three months, during which he convinced himself that she
was undoubtedly living in absolute misery and had likely
learned her lesson, he wrote and told her if she came back
immediately, he would arrange to have the marriage quietly annulled and all would be forgiven. He even had a
young comte selected for her to marry, one who would be
most understanding about the fact that she was no longer
a virgin."

The mention of virginity caused Jacqueline a moment
of discomfort, not because of the delicacy of the topic, but
because it reminded her that it was a state she would no
longer find herself in by tomorrow. She firmly pushed that
thought aside as something she would worry about later,
if at all. Still engrossed in the story of Armand's parents,
she asked, "What did your mother do then?"

Armand shifted back in his chair and smiled. "She sent
a letter to my grandfather, informing him she had no intention of leaving my father, that she was happier than
she had ever been in her life, and that if he could not bring
himself to accept their marriage, then she would simply
renounce her title and her ties to the Valentes family."

"And did your grandfather accept that?" demanded
Jacqueline.

"No. He was a determined old bastard. A few weeks
later he sent word to my mother that he was dying, and
asked her to come home so he could see her before he
died. He was most specific, however, that he did not wish
my father to accompany her. My father did not want her
to go, and they fought, but ultimately my mother defied
him and went home to her father's side, only to discover
he was as healthy as a horse. He locked her up and tried
to quickly have the marriage annulled, thinking to force

her to marry the comte before my father became suspicious and came for her.

"But my father only waited a day before setting out after her. When he arrived at their château he was refused entry, and told by my grandfather that my mother had changed her mind about the marriage and never wished to see him again."

Jacqueline looked at him in shock. "Did he believe him?"

"No. He pulled out a gun and calmly told the old man if he didn't hand his wife over to him then and there, he would do him the service of putting a hole in his chest. But my grandfather didn't believe for a moment he would carry out his threat, and so he just laughed." Armand paused and thoughtfully took a drink of water.

"Well?" demanded Jacqueline. "What happened?"

He sighed. "I am afraid my grandfather was right. My father might have been an enraged, determined husband, but he was not a murderer. Since he could not exactly rush into the château, grab my mother, and run out amidst all the servants who were ordered to stop him, he calmly put his gun back into his waistband and left."

"He left?" sputtered Jacqueline in disbelief. "Just like that?"

Armand smiled. "He did not go very far. He went to the stables and found the marquis's favorite horse, which he led onto the lawns in front of the château. Then he called to my grandfather, telling him if he did not want to see his horse's brains splattered all across the lawn, he had better produce my mother by the time he counted to ten."

Jacqueline nodded with approval, thinking his actions very clever. "What did your grandfather do?"

"Well, my grandfather was exceptionally fond of his horse. And while he was fairly certain my father was not insane enough to shoot him, he was not nearly so certain he would not shoot his horse. To hear my father tell it, he did make rather a grand show of holding the beautiful animal steady as he held his pistol at its head and slowly counted. And finally, out of sheer terror for the well-being of his horse, my grandfather relented and allowed my mother to go down to him. After that my mother renounced all ties to her family, and vowed never to set foot in France again."

Jacqueline looked at him incredulously. "Do you mean to say after all that trouble of luring her back, locking her up, finding her another husband, and risking having a gun pointed at his chest, he traded his daughter for a horse?"

"It makes one wonder where his priorities were, doesn't it?" remarked Armand.

"Would your father have shot the horse?" she asked curiously.

Armand looked at her with amusement. "Never. He later teased my mother that if she had not come down, he simply would have taken the horse to England instead. He said it was a damn fine animal."

Jacqueline began to laugh, a light, silvery sound that surprised and pleased him. It was the first time he had heard her laugh with sincere pleasure, and the sound was so sweet and musical he leaned back in his chair and drank in the feeling of her bringing the room to life with her presence.

When her laughter was finally spent she leaned forward to take a hearty drink of her wine. "It would seem rescuing people from France is a family tradition," she mused as she twirled the stem of her glass in her fingertips. She took another swallow of wine, enjoying the easy rapport that had fallen between them. It had been a long time since she had laughed, and the sensation made her feel light and free, as if nothing else in the world mattered except this moment and the fact that she had started to enjoy herself. She took another sip, and to her surprise found her glass was already empty.

"More wine?" suggested Armand.

"Thank you," she replied. She really ought to try not to drink too much, but the wine was excellent, and if it helped to relax her a little, that was probably a good thing. "Tell me," she began conversationally, "how do you plan to rescue François-Louis?"

His look instantly became shuttered. "I never discuss my plans with anyone," he stated flatly. "It is too dangerous, both for the person I am rescuing, and for me."

"Of course," stammered Jacqueline.

There was awkward silence for a moment before Armand casually asked, "What is he like?"

She looked at him curiously. "Why do you want to know?"

He shrugged his shoulders. "Call it professional curiosity. I like to know something about the people I am saving. Let's start with his looks."

"He is quite tall," she began.

"Taller than me?" he demanded. For some reason he hoped he wasn't, which was, of course, utterly absurd.

"No—not quite as tall as you," she replied. She thought for a moment. "And he is not as heavyset as you are—but that is not to say he is not strong," she quickly added, lest he think she was betrothed to a weakling.

Armand appeared to consider that piece of information before asking, "What color is his hair?"

"Why—I am not certain," she stammered. "I mean, he is always wearing a wig—he has several very beautiful ones," she added, as if in his defense. "I have not had the occasion of seeing him without one."

The idea that she had never seen him without his wig pleased Armand immensely.

"He has rather lovely eyes," began Jacqueline again.

"What color are they?"

"They are blue," she answered, this time with only the slightest hesitation. At least she was fairly certain they were blue.

"Pale blue or deep blue?" Armand prodded, sensing her uncertainty and taking satisfaction from it.

Jacqueline thought for a moment. "His eyes are a strikingly deep blue," she finally announced with conviction.

"Unlikely," he informed her. "If they were that striking, you would have remembered immediately."

She gave him a disgruntled look. "Monsieur St. James,

do you presume to tell me what my betrothed looks like when you have never met the man?" she demanded irritably.

"My apologies," he said, his voice only slightly contrite. "Please go on. What more can you tell me of him?"

Jacqueline considered for a moment, astounded at her own lack of memory for François-Louis. It had been so long since she had given him any real thought, she was having trouble forming a picture of him in her mind. "Well, unlike you, he absolutely loves beautiful clothes—"

"I beg your pardon?" He looked at her with one eyebrow raised.

Jacqueline felt herself color slightly with embarrassment. "What I mean is that he loves clothes that are, well, colorful and highly decorated—"

"The dress code of the French aristocracy," Armand interrupted, his voice heavily sarcastic.

"Well, yes," admitted Jacqueline, "although since the revolution the fashions have changed. Nobles have generally been dressing in more simple fashions for fear of being harassed, but François-Louis loves fashion and simply could not bring himself to dress without ruffles."

"It is good to live by certain principles," remarked Armand dryly. "Strange," he mused, "but I don't remember seeing him in the courtroom. Did he decide to sacrifice his ideals and dress down for the occasion?"

"No," she replied. "He was not there."

Armand stared at her in disbelief. "His betrothed was about to be sentenced to death and he was not there? Why the hell not?"

Jacqueline sighed. "Other than in matters of dress, François-Louis has always erred on the side of caution. That is why he never wrote or came to see me after my arrest, and that is why he was not in the courtroom the day of my trial. He would have seen it as too risky."

"I see," said Armand, disliking the man more by the minute. "He did nothing to help you when you were in trouble, yet he expects you to save him now that he is in exactly the same position."

"He expects nothing of the kind!" protested Jacqueline. "He merely sent me a letter informing me of his arrest and bidding me good-bye, which is entirely appropriate when one's betrothed is about to be executed."

"Really?" he drawled out. "How touching. Tell me, Mademoiselle, did you send him a letter from your cell saying good-bye?"

"No," she admitted.

"Why not?"

Jacqueline hesitated. She was not sure why she had not written François-Louis from her cell. Perhaps because there were too many other things on her mind at the time. After all, she had been concerned about her brother. And her sisters. And furious about how the revolution had destroyed her family and her life. Quite simply, François-Louis had not been at the forefront of her thoughts. But she did not want to give that reason to Armand. To do so would be to suggest that his life was not important to her, and that might make him reconsider their agreement. "I did not write him because I thought to do so might make him suspect," she lied.

"Where is the letter he wrote to you?" he demanded.

"It is in my cloak—I brought it in case you wanted to see it."

"Later." He regarded her thoughtfully for a moment. "Tell me, Mademoiselle, was the marquis your choice, or your father's?"

"He was my father's choice," admitted Jacqueline.

"And were you happy with his choice?"

She hesitated for only the barest of seconds. "Of course I was."

The pause had been slight, but he noticed it all the same. He leaned back in his chair and tried to make his voice sound casual. "So you are in love with this man?"

Jacqueline sighed. "In January of this year, Nicolas Bourdon went to my father and asked for my hand in marriage. Louis the Sixteenth had just been guillotined, the monarchy was abolished, and the old order that went with it seemed to have been virtually destroyed. After several years of acting as my father's friend and financial adviser, I suppose Nicolas felt that he was finally on equal ground with him, and therefore had the right to make an offer for his daughter."

"But your father did not see it that way," interjected Armand.

"No. And neither did I. Nicolas had been a friend of my father's since 1788, the year before the revolution began. I was only fifteen when he began to visit us, and I always felt uncomfortable around him. I don't know why, exactly. It was just a feeling I had, a feeling that somehow he was not what he appeared to be. He was always extremely polite, and my father enjoyed his company because he was well-read and had challenging ideas about liberty and the rights of man, and what the new social order would bring. He was also a successful investor, and my father was most anxious to learn how to manage his money, especially after feudalism was abolished and we were no longer permitted to collect taxes, which for centuries had been our sole source of income. Like many nobles, my father was not in agreement with that decree, but he could see the ideals of the time were riding on a crest of enthusiasm, and he had no choice but to accept it. He was, however, concerned about how our family wealth was to survive, and realized he had to act quickly to get his money working for him.

"Nicolas came to the château often to advise my father, not as an employee, but as a friend. He would stay for days at a time, but I only saw him during meals, or if he was out walking in the grounds. Somehow I always felt he was watching me, looking at me as if I was something he wanted. I tried to tell myself it was ridiculous, but at the same time I was careful to avoid being alone with him. Sometimes I would accidentally meet his gaze from across the table, and the intensity of his eyes would send chills down my spine. He looked as if"—she shuddered—"as if he wanted to *devour* me."

Armand watched her in silence for a moment as she

idly picked at her food. He could well understand how a man like Bourdon could want her with such overwhelming intensity. "And finally he decided to ask your father for your hand in marriage."

She nodded. "I suppose he felt the timing was right, and there was no need to wait any longer. I had just turned nineteen, and my father had not yet arranged a husband for me, because I was needed at home to look after Suzanne and Séraphine. Nicolas thought he was the perfect choice. He considered himself a family friend, my father liked him, and since he did not have a château of his own, he was more than willing to move in and live at the Château de Lambert."

"But your father turned him down, because he was untitled and therefore common."

"No doubt that was part of it," Jacqueline admitted. "Like most nobles, my father felt the philosophy of equality among men was an ideal, a utopia to be strived for over the next hundred years, not an instant reality to be rammed down our throats and forced into our lives. Although we had given up our titles and our coats of arms, you cannot erase centuries of tradition and a deep-rooted way of life with one simple decree. My father liked Nicolas and respected his abilities, but he did not feel he was an appropriate choice for me. And I was perfectly happy with his decision, because I did not like Nicolas."

"What did Nicolas do when your father rejected him?"

"At first he seemed to take it very well," Jacqueline reflected. "He remained financial adviser to my father, and continued to visit the château. But his bold offer had startled my father, who suddenly realized I was no longer a child, and that other men might soon start to offer for me. And so he quickly negotiated a match with François-Louis, who was the Marquis de Biret. François-Louis was from an excellent family, he was relatively young and healthy, and most important to my father, his estate was not far from the Château de Lambert, so I would be able to visit often."

"Did you know him very well?"

"No," admitted Jacqueline. "I had met him a few times at various balls, but there was nothing between us other than friendship."

Despite his conviction that he did not care, he had to ask the next question. "Tell me, Mademoiselle," he began slowly, "if I save him and bring him back to England, will you honor your betrothal to him?"

His question took her by surprise. In truth, she had not really thought about her betrothal to François-Louis. The only thing she knew for certain was that she was going to return to France and kill Nicolas. Since she did not think she would be able to escape after that and return to England, her betrothal to François-Louis was not really an issue. But she did not want Armand to suspect her intentions. If he did, she knew he would do everything in his power to stop her, which might mean warning Sir Edward, who could easily arrange to have her watched constantly. It was best Armand think she was starting to accept her new life here.

"He is my father's choice," she began hesitantly. "He is French, and Catholic, and titled. He is from my world. If we married we would undoubtedly get along well. Besides, how could I not respect my father's wishes?" It was not an outright yes, but it was very close.

"Indeed." It was the answer he had expected, yet it annoyed him all the same. What the hell had he hoped she would say? And what the hell did it matter whether she married this fop or not? It was not his affair. The only thing that mattered at this moment, he reminded himself firmly, was that she was his for the night. He abruptly rose from his chair. "I believe it is time we retired upstairs."

His change of manner was sudden and disturbing. She felt the blood drain from her cheeks. "So soon?" she asked, her voice thin and strained. "I thought I might have another glass of wine." She was stalling, but she needed more time to prepare herself.

"I have wine upstairs," he informed her brusquely. He

could see she was reluctant to go with him, and that made him feel even more loathsome. After more than a year of celibacy, he was practically forcing a nervous, inexperienced virgin into his bed. What the hell was the matter with him? "Mademoiselle, do you wish to change your mind?" he demanded abruptly. If she did, he would permit it. He was not at all sure he wanted to save this man anyway. He sounded like a spineless fop, and Armand was not convinced he wanted to risk his life to bring him back for Jacqueline to marry.

She looked at him, her gray eyes wide with hope. "If I do not go to bed with you, will you save François-Louis anyway?" she asked, her voice soft and imploring.

"No," he answered curtly. He felt like a bastard for saying it. "I will not."

She hesitated. He was offering her one last chance to back out of their agreement. She could simply thank him for dinner, get her cloak, and leave. Since everyone in the Harrington household believed she had gone to bed early, she could easily sneak back into the house and no one other than the carriage driver would ever know she had been here. She would wake up tomorrow as untouched as when she had awakened today.

With the knowledge that because she had failed to uphold her part of the bargain, François-Louis was going to die.

She bit her lip in confusion. It was probably not so terrible to make love with a man. From her rather limited understanding, Armand would use her body to gain pleasure for himself. She thought back to Nicolas roughly forcing her against the wall of her cell and she shuddered. Once it was over she would never have to do it again. And since she had no intention of marrying François-Louis before she returned to France to kill Nicolas, the loss of her virginity was really not an issue. She lifted her gaze to Armand. His expression was perfectly neutral, as if it was of no interest to him whether she decided to go through with it or not. Whatever his reason for proposing this sordid agreement, it was obviously not out of some uncontrollable need to have her. That suited her fine. Perhaps that meant the entire ordeal would be over that much faster.

She lifted her chin and willed her voice to be steady. "Let us go upstairs."

Armand released the breath he had been holding and went around to pull out her chair. He offered her his arm and together they silently walked out of the drawing room. His heart was hammering against his chest as they slowly mounted the stairs to the second floor. By the time they stood in front of the door to his bedroom, he felt as awkward and nervous as a schoolboy. This is ridiculous, he told himself firmly. Get hold of yourself. He opened the door.

Jacqueline stepped into the room, which was warm and lit by the soft glow of a dying fire. She stood in the center of the room and nervously clasped her hands, quickly taking in the dark, masculine furnishings that were so reflective of Armand's taste. A thick, intricately woven Persian carpet of dark burgundy stretched warmly across the floor. In one corner stood a heavy chest of drawers, in another a desk, both simply carved and without a single ornament or paper cluttering their polished surfaces. She was vaguely aware that Armand had gone over to the fire and was adding more wood. She lifted her eyes to the bed. It was magnificently carved from the darkest, glossiest mahogany. She thought it must have been made for Armand, for it was longer and wider than any bed she had ever seen. She swallowed.

"Would you care for some brandy?"

She tore her gaze from the bed to nod vaguely and watch Armand fill a glass with amber liquid.

He poured her drink slowly, trying to think of some way to calm her. He wished he could have a drink also. He quickly shoved that thought aside and took the glass to her.

Numbly she accepted it and took a hearty gulp. The liquid burned a path of fire down her throat and spread into her chest, instantly filling her with a delicious sensation of warmth. She sighed and took another swallow, determined to take all the strength she could from it.

"Feel better?" Armand asked casually. He was slowly lighting candles around the room, acting as if he were in no hurry whatsoever to get her into his bed.

"Yes." Jacqueline clutched the glass to her chest and watched as Armand performed his task. With his back to her, absorbed in the act of lighting the room, he seemed far less predatory and threatening than she had imagined he would be. She had no idea what he would do once he decided the room was lit to his satisfaction. She decided to use this moment of reprieve to make her position clear. "Monsieur St. James, there is something I think you should know. . . ." she began, surprised that her voice sounded so strained and hollow. She hesitated, thinking he would say something to encourage her to continue. He did not. She took another sip of her drink and decided to try again. "I am afraid I have never done this before," she blurted out nervously.

"I know." Having lit the room to a soft glow, he walked back to the fire and added another log. He could see she was terrified, and he cursed himself for it. No doubt her only previous experience with lovemaking was when that bastard tried to rape her in her cell. God knows what she thought he was about to do to her. It would be different for her this time, he promised himself. But he had to go slowly. He lifted the poker and began to adjust the logs, which were already blazing and did not require attention in the least.

She waited for him to do something. Or was she supposed to do something? She was not certain. She decided he had not understood her meaning. Swallowing every ounce of her pride, she timidly confessed, "Monsieur St. James, I am afraid I do not know what it is you wish me to do."

He did not turn, so she could not see him smile. "Jacqueline," he began, his voice low and gentle, "it would please me a great deal if you would call me Armand."

And then he turned to her. His face was lit by gold and

apricot light from the flames of the fire and in that instant all she could focus on was how utterly, unbelievably handsome he was. His rugged features could not have been more perfect had they been sculpted from marble. His hair was the color of copper, and gold, and every imaginable variation in between. His eyes were dark, more emerald tonight than blue, and glittering with an intensity that burned right through her, revealing something of himself that she had never seen before. Desire. Hunger. Need. For her. So powerful it wrapped itself around her from across the room and flooded her with a thousand sensations, suddenly stripping her of her ability to think clearly.

"Jacqueline," Armand called, his voice low and soothing, "come here."

Hypnotized by the velvety sound of his voice, she obediently crossed the room to him, her breath coming in little shallow puffs, her body awakening with prickles of anticipation and fear. She stopped and stood in front of him, her eyes locked with his, her blood racing through her veins. She stared into the hard glitter of his eyes and waited, waited for him to wrap his arms around her and crush her against him, or to push her against the wall and wrench her skirts up to her waist, or perhaps to lift her high into the air and carry her over to his bed, claiming her as if she was something that was to be conquered, a trophy that he had long wanted and was finally his.

"It would please me if you would remove my jacket," he said simply.

She looked at him in surprise, utterly confused by his request. His expression was calm, still intense, but rigidly under control. Too grateful to question his tactics, she lowered her gaze to his chest and slipped her fingers beneath the lapels of his evening jacket. She slowly eased the garment over his enormous shoulders and down his arms, allowing it to drop carelessly on the floor. That task done, she looked up at him for further instructions.

"And now my waistcoat."

Her fingers obediently reached out and set to work on

the shiny gold buttons that held his waistcoat closed. Once they were freed from their holes, she opened the garment and deftly slipped it over his shoulders and down his arms, permitting it to fall on the floor.

"And my shirt."

This, Jacqueline realized, was going to require a little more work. She studied his cravat for a moment before deciding which end to pull. Having selected one, she gave it a firm tug, and was delighted when the snowy linen fabric easily unraveled. She then removed the studs from his cuffs and left him for a moment to place them carefully on his desk before continuing. It was only when she began to unfasten the buttons of his shirt that her fingers began to tremble and became clumsy. One by one the buttons were slowly released, and the shirt began to open and reveal the powerful wall of muscle that lay beneath it. Reminding herself firmly that she had seen his chest before, that night in Paris when they had shared that tiny room and that even tinier bed at the inn, she yanked up his shirtfront to release the fabric that was tucked into his breeches and undid the last button. She could feel the heat of him emanating across the few inches that separated them. Her own curiosity began to mix with a strange desire to reach out and lay her fingers across the hard muscles of his chest. When she suddenly realized that something within her *wanted* to touch him, she stopped.

Armand felt as if he was going lose the thin thread of control he had managed to carefully maintain as she undressed him. He wanted to wrap his arms around her and cover her with kisses, to strip off her clothes and touch her and taste her and worship her until she was hot and moaning and senseless with pleasure. Just the slightest touch of her delicate hands as she eased him out of his clothes, the faint scent of her shimmering hair as she bowed her head to her task, the soft, silky rustle of her dress as she walked away from him to place his shirt studs on his desk, everything about her was making him insane with the need to have her. But he knew she was afraid, and he was determined to ease her fear. By allowing her to go slowly, by giving her a measure of control, he was empowering her, making her an equal partner in this voyage of discovery. He believed this would lessen her fear while giving her own desire a chance to awaken. He only hoped he could maintain his control a little longer.

"Jacqueline," he whispered hoarsely, "it would please me if you would remove my shirt."

His voice seemed strained, shaken, as if he was not feeling well. She raised her eyes to his in confusion. And saw the raw, barely leashed need that filled his gaze with fire as he stared down at her. His body was rigid with tension, his eyes were clear and focused, yet he did not reach out for her, he did not move toward her, he did nothing that might frighten her or pressure her. And suddenly she understood. He did not want to simply use her for his pleasure, the way Nicolas had that night in her cell. He did not want to force her to give in to him. He did not want her to give in to him at all. No, he wanted something much, much more than that.

He wanted her to want him.

"Why?" she asked, her voice barely a whisper.

Armand looked into her eyes, smoky gray, reminding him of the clouds that roll across the ocean before a summer storm. He saw her lips, trembling slightly, like the soft petals of a poppy quivering in a warm breeze. He knew she was not asking why he wanted her to remove his shirt. She was asking why he wanted her and, more importantly, why he wanted her to want him. They had an agreement. He knew she would honor it. Her wanting him was not part of that bargain, nor was it necessary to see the act completed. But for him it had become essential. He knew he could sweep her into his arms and kiss her and touch her until her body released her mind and her resistance passed. He had started to do that the other night, and God only knew how far he would have gone if Laura Harrington had not walked in. But it was not enough to simply seduce her. He wanted to know, right from the start, that some part of her wanted him, needed him, the way he needed her.

"I do not know why," he admitted quietly. "Does it matter?"

She studied him a moment, her mind swirling with conflict. She had agreed to give him her body. For one night. She had not agreed to enjoy it. She still was not convinced she was going to. But something between them had changed, although she was not sure when or how it had happened. She was attracted to him. She could not deny it. He was handsome. Confident. Clever. He had saved her life. Just for the money, of course, but the act had required an enormous amount of daring all the same. He was common. He was beneath her. He despised her class and her world. But he had protected her when she was in danger, and he had cared for her when she was sick. He had forced her into this bargain. Hadn't he? She was not so sure anymore. He wanted her to want him. Why? What did it matter to him? A tempest of feelings were rioting within her. His shirt. He wanted her to remove his shirt. And more than that, she wanted to remove it, and to lay her hands upon the warmth of his skin. Beyond that, she was not going to think.

She reached out, her hands trembling, and laid her palms against the solid muscles of his chest. He felt warm against the coolness of her fingers, warm and smooth and hard, as hard as steel. Hesitantly she began to trace the contours of his chest, fascinated by the tawny hair that grew there. Her fingers brushed lightly against his nipple and it immediately tightened in response. Intrigued, she gently caressed the other one, and this time she heard Armand inhale a quick breath. She looked up in confusion and saw him staring down at her, his eyes glittering with need, his mouth drawn in a tight line. Encouraged by the effect she was having on him, she boldly reached up and slowly slipped his shirt over his shoulders and down his arms, letting the linen drop to a heap on the floor.

His skin was golden bronze in the light of the fire; it looked as warm as it felt. His chest and shoulders and arms were solidly layered with muscle. She let her fingers trail over him, around his enormous shoulders, across his massive chest, down the flat length of his stomach, allowing herself to become familiar with the rigid patterns the muscles formed beneath the velvety surface of his skin. All the while Armand simply stood there, allowing her to explore his body, which did not seem nearly as terrifying as she had thought it would be, but instead was sleek and powerful and exciting. Her touch grew more confident, firmer, seeking to elicit some response from him. But his arms remained anchored at his sides and he did not reach out to her. Torn between the need to feel that this was not her choice, that she was doing this only because she had to, and the even greater need to feel Armand's arms wrapped tightly around her, she hesitated. She looked up at him, her lip trembling slightly, her eyes filled with uncertainty.

Armand looked down into the magnificent depths of her silvery eyes. He could see she was unsure, that she wanted something more to happen, but she did not want to be the one to initiate it. And so he began to lower his lips to hers, slowly, seeking not to frighten her, trying to remain in control, wondering how he would keep from crushing her against him the minute he tasted the sweetness of her mouth. And suddenly she lifted her arms up and looped them around his neck, pulling him down to her mouth and pressing her slender body against his bare skin with an intensity of desire that left no doubt that she wanted him, that she was not simply doing this because of a bargain they had struck. She let out a little moan as she opened her lips to his, and in that instant reason abandoned him, and nothing mattered except that she was here, offering herself to him, and everything else, past and future, could damn well go to hell.

He wrapped his arms around her and pulled her tight against him as his mouth took possession of her lips. His tongue slid into the sweet heat of her, and she responded with a little sigh, instinctively arching her soft body against his as her own tongue awakened and began to tentatively explore his mouth. Her scent intoxicated him; she smelled of citrus and roses, fresh and light, like a garden that was just beginning to bloom. His hand reached up to touch the softness of her skin, tracing a path along her satiny cheek, up the fragile line of her jaw, and around the perfect shell of her ear, and then it plunged deeply into the silk of her blond hair, shaking loose the pins that held it in place. It was not long, but it was gloriously thick and full, and he ran his fingers reverently through it, remembering the moment she had shaken it loose for him in her cell, and how it had pained him to cut it. He had risked his life to save her, and he would do it again in a second, for he could not bear the thought of her ever coming to harm. She was his, if not for him she would not be alive, and the thought filled him with a fierce wave of possessiveness as his hand released her hair and he began to explore the soft curves of her body.

Jacqueline pressed herself against Armand as he touched her all over, tasting him, clinging to him, rubbing her fingers against the sandy surface of his jaw, and moving her mouth over his again and again. She threaded her hands into his hair and pulled the ribbon loose, releasing the coppery locks onto his shoulders, taking pleasure in the fact that she could explore him in the same way he was exploring her. His hand cupped her breast through the fabric of her dress while the other grasped her hip and pulled her against his hardness, and to her surprise she was not shocked or frightened, but instead she found pleasure, and instinctively she began to rub herself against him to increase the sensation. In reaction to her boldness he moaned and began to swiftly attack the fastenings of her dress, deftly unhooking them with the speed of a man who is extremely familiar with the intricacies of a woman's gown. If that should have bothered her she did not care, because all she knew was that she wanted to be closer to him, she wanted to feel her skin against his, she wanted his fingers to caress her without any barriers in between. And so when the gown was lying limp about her shoulders and the ties of her petticoats had been released, she stepped back and allowed him to ease the garments down, listening to the swishing sound they made as they collapsed into a pool of black and cream silk at her feet.

She stood before him in her chemise and stockings, her pale skin faintly peach-colored against the fine white linen, her golden hair tumbling wildly onto her shoulders. She lifted her arms to cover herself, suddenly uncertain, and he took a step forward and grasped her wrists, unwilling to let her.

"My God," he breathed hoarsely, "you are exquisite."

He bent his head and took possession of her lips once more, drinking in the sweet taste of her. She trembled slightly, and he thought she might be cold, so he lifted her into his arms and cuddled her against the warmth of his chest. Her shoes fell to the floor as he carried her to the bed, not once releasing her lips from his. With one swift motion he pulled down the covers, and then he lay her against the cool sheets, pausing only to remove his shoes before stretching out beside her and pulling the covers over them both.

He lowered himself against her, sharing his warmth, and began to kiss her once more, tenderly at first, and then with a renewed passion as he felt her begin to respond. His hand moved down the thin fabric of her chemise until it found the bottom of it, and then it began to move up inside the garment, ascending slowly, across the silky flat of her stomach, along the delicate ridges of her rib cage, and finally stopping at the mound of her breast, which was cool and full and lush. He caressed the petal-soft peak until he felt it tighten, and then, unable to restrain himself any longer, he tore his lips from hers and lowered his head to take the sweet bud into his mouth. Jacqueline moaned and arched herself against him, and then threaded her fingers into his hair, holding him at her breast, encouraging him to suckle, and letting out a little cry of disappointment when he lifted his head briefly to seek out the other breast and give it equal attention. He pulled away again to remove her chemise entirely, and instead of resisting she helped him take it off, as if she was just as anxious to be rid of it as he. He pressed himself against her to feel the cool softness of her skin against the warmth of his, and began to kiss her hungrily as his hand reached down to take off her stockings. Her thighs were soft, her legs long and firm, and once her stockings were removed he quickly peeled off his breeches and tossed them to the floor, then stretched out beside the glory of her beautiful body.

Jacqueline ran her hands across the taut heat of Armand's skin, learning the muscular surface of his back, his shoulders, his arms, his chest, unable to touch him enough, longing to know everything about his body. She tilted her head back so he could press hungry kisses against her throat, behind her ear, across her collarbone, and then she pulled his head up so she could claim his mouth again, exploring it with a new boldness as her hands roamed up and down the length of him. She was vaguely aware that his hand was moving down again, brushing against her breasts, across the valley of her stomach, and around the swell of her hip before stopping to caress the inside of her thigh, startling her. Gently his fingers moved up and down, encouraging her legs to relax, skimming lightly over the sensitive skin. Her body became languid, enjoying the sensation of being touched. His fingers slowly moved up, gently caressing that mysterious place that had begun to ache with a need Jacqueline did not understand. Before she could think to resist, his fingers had slipped inside the tender folds of skin, moving leisurely, lightly, in and out, up and down, slowly, then faster, caressing, exploring, filling her with a pleasure so sweet and intense she felt sure she would lose her mind from it. She kissed him hungrily as she writhed against the rhythm of his fingers, pressing herself against him, feeling an unfamiliar need burst into flames within her. His mouth left hers to trail kisses down her breasts, across her stomach, and onto the silky triangle where his hand was working its magic, and then his tongue flickered lightly inside her, and she could not keep from crying out.

"Please, Monsieur St.—"

"My name is Armand," he told her, his voice raw and adamant.

"Please, Armand, I do not think I can bear it," she whispered.

He hesitated, and then he moved back up to claim her lips with his. He wanted to pleasure her, he wanted to gradually take her to the stars and bring her back again, he wanted to fill her with a need so intense and then a fulfillment so glorious that she would always be his, even if they never touched each other again after tonight. She was so achingly beautiful, so devastatingly sensual, he was not at all certain how much longer he could control himself. It had been a long time since he had been with a woman. *Slowly,* he reminded himself. She was a virgin, and she would need the utmost care.

He lowered himself on top of her, easing her down into the softness of the mattress. His hardness pressed against her and her eyes grew wide, shimmering with uncertainty. He kissed her tenderly, seeking to relax her as his knee moved between her legs and encouraged them to open. His hand slid down and gently stroked her, and she sighed and closed her eyes, giving in once again to his teasing exploration. And when she was moaning and writhing against him he positioned himself against her slick heat, filled with a desire to bury himself inside her so intense he felt certain he could not stand it a moment longer, and yet he did, because above all else he did not want to hurt her. *Slowly,* he reminded himself, his jaw tense with effort. *Slowly.*

Jacqueline could feel the velvet tip of him against her heated flesh, and she wondered why he hesitated. There was an ache inside her, a deep, painful, exquisite ache that she felt sure would be relieved if only he would enter her. She raised her hips slightly to encourage him, and he began to fill her, slowly, gradually, and then he withdrew, only to slide in again, a little more this time, stretching her, filling her, and just when she thought she could not take any more of him, he withdrew again. And then he glided into her once more, a little farther this time, and waited, allowing her to get used to the feel of him, giving her body time to adjust.

"Look at me, Jacqueline," he whispered hoarsely.

She opened her eyes to look at him, and saw that he was controlling himself, that he was going slowly for her benefit, for it was going to hurt her, she understood that now. And so touched was she by his concern for her, by his reluctance to do something he knew was going to cause her pain, that suddenly she did not care if it hurt, she only knew that she wanted him inside her, now. She reached up and grasped the back of his neck, pulling him down to her, and she laid her hand against his cheek and whispered his name. "Armand."

It was all the invitation he needed. Lost in the shimmering pools of her eyes, which were brilliant with a mixture of trust and desire, he found he could not hold back any longer. He whispered, "Jacqueline," and in one blinding thrust of ecstasy he drove himself into her.

He felt her body tense and tighten around him, and he thought surely he must die from the torture of it. He held himself steady and closed his eyes, fighting for control. And then he opened his eyes and looked at her. She was watching him, her face drawn and pale, her lashes sparkling with tears. And his heart constricted with the need to ease her discomfort, and so he bent his head and kissed her eyelids. "Easy, my love," he whispered gently. "The pain will not last. I promise."

Jacqueline released the breath she had been holding, and with it the tension that had momentarily gripped her began to dissipate, like sand spilling out of a sack. And then Armand began to move within her, gently, slowly, stoking the flames of need that were still burning inside her. He moved his hand down to stroke her where their bodies were joined, and he kissed her, tenderly at first, and then hard and hot and demanding, overwhelming her with sensations that were dark and wonderful and frightening. An urgency possessed her, a need to feel more, taste more, touch more, and she kissed him wildly as she pulsed against him, matching his rhythm, taking him deeper and deeper inside her. She knew that she was pleasing him, she could sense it in the strained hardness of his body, the clenching of his jaw, the powerful way in which he drove into her again and again, and the idea that they were sharing this incredible pleasure together made her even more abandoned. She began to let out little soft, panting moans, and the fire inside her began to grow, hotter, hungrier, more intense, until it was consuming her with a need that was strange, incomprehensible, frightening. Still Armand stroked her and filled her and kissed her, whispering husky words of praise and encouragement she could not understand, could barely even hear because her breath was coming in raspy, shallow little gasps. Her entire being was tight and tense and focused, she could not think about anything except that she wanted more, needed more, and so she thrust herself against him and held him close, and the sensations came faster and faster and faster, until suddenly she was exploding through the air like a shooting star, soaring into the darkness and away from everything she had ever known. For one brief, magnificent moment the world was flooded with light and joy, and she cried out, a cry of wonder, and pleasure, and happiness.

Armand covered her mouth with his and her cry rang into him as he thrust into her, again and again and again, his body straining and swollen, drinking in the pleasure of her ecstasy. He wanted to lose himself inside her. He wanted to always feel the heat of her silky skin against his, to inhale the delicate fragrance of her hair and taste the sweetness of her mouth and feel the wonder of her passion and know that she was his, forever. He wanted her to the point where he thought he would lose his mind. And the realization was agony, because she was not his, except for this one, bittersweet moment, and he wanted it to last longer, but his control had deserted him. He called her name, a cry of desire and despair, and then he kissed her deeply and drove into her, a long, powerful, agonizing thrust, and spilled himself into her as she wrapped her arms around him and held him close.

They lay together for a while, their hearts pounding,

their breathing shallow and rapid. Jacqueline clutched him tightly, confused by what had just happened between them, and unwilling to surface and admit that it was over. Nothing had prepared her for such a glorious union, or for the unbelievable way she had responded to him. Nothing.

Armand was the first to stir. Concerned that he was crushing her with his weight, he gathered her into his arms and rolled onto his side, taking her with him. Then he pulled her close and wrapped his arms around her, inhaling the sweetness of her hair.

Lying next to him, feeling the steady rise and fall of his chest against her bare skin, his warm, powerful body pressed intimately against hers, she felt shy suddenly, shy and awkward and uncertain. Her mind was a riot of conflicting emotions, confusing and disturbing her.

"I should be going," she whispered hesitantly.

Her words cut into the peaceful serenity that had descended upon him. She wanted to leave. But he did not want her to go. He wanted to lie there and hold her in his arms and pretend, just for a moment, that she was his. He wanted to fall asleep feeling as though he still had something left in this world to live for. For the first time in over a year he wanted to dream, not the painful, guilt-ridden dreams that haunted him night after night, but that there was a future waiting for him, a future filled with something other than the terrible need to punish himself for the past. Jacqueline had the power to make him forget. And perhaps, given time, he might have had the power to make her forget. But there was no time. The man she wanted was in prison, and he was going to return to France and risk his life so that someone named François-Louis could escape to England and marry her.

"I must return before the servants are up," persisted Jacqueline, feeling shy and awkward, and wondering why he did not release her.

Armand's response was to pull her even closer, so her face was pressed against the warmth of his neck. He lifted one hand and brushed a silky wisp of hair off her cheek, taking pleasure in the fact that she did not resist, but allowed him to touch her as if it was his right to do so. No matter what the future held, for this moment she was his, and he was not ready to let the moment end.

"Rest awhile, Jacqueline," he murmured, his voice low and persuasive. "It is not so late. I will see that you are awakened in good time to make the journey back to the Harrington estate."

Jacqueline hesitated. She was so comfortable and warm in Armand's arms. And she was a little sleepy. The idea of getting up and crawling into an icy-cold carriage was not the least bit enticing. And he wanted her to stay. A delicious sense of complacency enveloped her, and she yawned.

"You are sure I will get back in good time?" she managed, already closing her eyes and instinctively nestling against him.

Armand smiled and caressed her satiny cheek with the back of his fingers. "I promise."

She awoke with a start to the sound of light tapping on the door. She was alone in the bed. She sat bolt upright, trying to remember where she was, and to her horror discovered that she was naked. She yanked the covers up against her chest as her eyes swept the room, which was dark and cold, looking for some sign of Armand, but there was none. The tapping continued.

"Mademoiselle de Lambert, are you awake?" called a woman's voice softly in French.

The door slowly creaked open, letting in a yellow shaft of light from the hallway. A middle-aged woman dressed in a white night wrapper stood before her, carrying a candelabra. "Monsieur St. James asked that you be wakened at two o'clock," she explained in a hushed voice as she closed the door. "Your carriage is being prepared, and I have come to help you dress." She walked over to the fire and began to stir the glowing embers and add more wood to it.

Jacqueline pulled a cover around her as she rose from the bed, trying to shield herself from the chill that had fallen on the room. She was grateful to Armand for sending a maid to waken her and help her dress, for it saved her from the embarrassment of having to face him. If she did encounter him on the way out, she knew she would not have the faintest idea of what to say.

"Come over to the fire where it is warm," instructed the maid as she began to gather up Jacqueline's clothes from the floor.

Jacqueline obediently went to the fire, which was now crackling brightly. She waited there until the woman returned with her clothes, and then she dropped her blanket and began to dress.

"There now," declared the maid as she fastened the last hook. She was an older woman, with a kind, mothering manner that Jacqueline found comforting. "Now, sit yourself here and we will see what can be done with your hair."

Jacqueline sat down in the chair and waited while the woman quickly worked a brush through her hair and then pinned it in a loose chignon. There was no mirror in the room for her to see herself, but the maid worked with such speed and proficiency Jacqueline felt confident her appearance was more than acceptable. If anyone did see her before she made it back into her room at the Harringtons', at least she would not look like a woman who has been out making love half the night.

"Thank you for your help," murmured Jacqueline as the maid adjusted the last pin. "Tell me, what is your name?"

The woman smiled. "I am Madame Bonnard," she informed her.

Jacqueline looked up at her, taking in her delicate features, her warm, green eyes, and her wavy blond hair, which was slightly streaked with gray and worn in a loose braid down her back. She felt there was something vaguely familiar about her, but she was not sure why. She was certain she had never met her before.

"Come, Mademoiselle," said Madame Bonnard as she opened the door. "Your carriage is waiting."

Jacqueline followed her down the stairs to the front hallway. Madame Bonnard left her there a moment while she went to fetch her cloak. Nervously Jacqueline looked about, wondering where Armand was, dreading the possibility that he might appear at any moment to say good night. If he did appear, she would have utterly no idea what to do or say. She wrung her hands together and paced down the hall, wishing Madame Bonnard would return quickly so she could leave.

And then she saw it.

The envelope was propped against a slender crystal vase, in which a single crimson rose had been placed. Her name was scripted across the paper in bold, fluid strokes, leaving no doubt in her mind it was Armand's handwriting. Confused as to why he would write her a note instead of bidding her good night personally, she picked up the creamy envelope and broke the seal.

Jacqueline,
 I shall do everything within my power to see he is delivered to you safely.
 If I do not return, remember, my rescue of you is one of my greatest achievements. Do not throw it away on something as meaningless as vengeance.
                                                                Armand

Black, cold fear began to grip her as the meaning of his words sank in. He had gone to rescue François-Louis. But how could he have left so quickly? It was the middle of the night. Surely he was still there, somewhere. She looked up from the note as Madame Bonnard returned with her cloak.

"Where is Monsieur St. James?" she demanded, her voice trembling slightly.

"Why, he is gone, Mademoiselle."

"Gone?" repeated Jacqueline in disbelief. "Gone where?"

"He had some business to attend to at one of his estates in the north," Madame Bonnard informed her. "He said he would be back in about two weeks."

Numbly Jacqueline stood and allowed the woman to help her with her cloak as she absorbed that piece of information, Armand's note still clutched in her hand. An icy blast of air slapped her in the face as Madame Bonnard opened the door for her. Tom was outside waiting with the carriage. She accepted his help as she climbed up into it. The air in the carriage was warm, having been heated by hot bricks wrapped in blankets, but Jacqueline was chilled to the bone. The carriage jerked into motion. Her mind reeling, she shivered with fear as she stared into the blackness of the countryside.

He was on his way to France. She had fulfilled her part of the bargain, and now he was about to fulfill his.

Chapter 9

The city of Paris lay blanketed under a white shroud of fluffy snow. The flakes were piling up everywhere, topping the magnificent steeples, cupolas, slate roofs, and balconies like a glorious, feathery frosting. It had accumulated in the intricate niches of Notre Dame, that imposing structure that dominated the very heart of the city. The building was no longer a Christian cathedral as it had been since 1163, when Bishop Maurice de Sully ordered it built on a site that had been a place of worship from ancient times. Under the republican government's new policy of dechristianization, the majestic edifice had been stripped of its sacred objects and rebaptized the Temple of Reason. Sacred or not, the snow continued to fall on it, as it had for hundreds of winters. It piled up on the thick balustrades of the arched bridges that joined the left and right banks of the city across the Seine. It covered the streets, temporarily masking the filth and garbage that were testimony to the miserable, crowded living conditions and the lack of sanitation. It fell on citizens and citizenesses as they went about their lives, indiscriminately covering red wool caps, stiff military hats, elaborate bonnets, and bare heads. It sifted its way down onto the Place de la Revolution, slowly floating over the steamy work of the guillotine before it landed on the blood-soaked ground. Some of the flakes melted immediately in the hot red liquid, while others piled onto the ground and absorbed the scarlet flow that gushed out of silent, mutilated bodies, which only moments earlier had been men and

women who stood and watched the delicate wisps of frozen lace dance against the ashen sky.

Armand adjusted the rough wool collar of his coat and blew warm air on his fingers, which were aching and stiff from the cold. He gazed idly at the facade of the Luxembourg prison, assessing the size of its windows and their distance to the ground. No one thought it strange that he was doing so. To anyone who passed by he was just another bored, frozen street vendor, desperately trying to earn a few *livres* by selling his bottles of thin, homemade wine. If one could not afford the inflated prices set by the wine merchants who sold from their shops, then one could take a chance on the cheap wines that were sold in the streets, providing you did not mind the acidic taste or the terrible headache that was almost certain to accompany each bottle. For six days Armand had been selling wine from this spot, attracting no more attention than any other filthy, aged, desperate street vendor. It was a disguise that left him freezing most of the time, his back aching from standing bent over for hours, but it had enabled him to study the exterior of the prison in which François-Louis was incarcerated, and more importantly, to establish himself as a regular fixture outside that prison.

The Palais de Luxembourg was built by Marie de Medici, the wife and queen of Henry IV, who on the death of her husband decided she no longer wished to live in the Louvre. In 1615 she commissioned Salomon de Brosse to create a palace for her that would be reminiscent of the Florentine palaces she had been accustomed to before she left Italy to live in France. And so the Palais de Luxembourg was built, an elegant structure of large windows and rusticated stonework, consisting of a main pavilion covered by a cupola and framed by two tiers of ringed columns, with two other pavilions at the sides, joined to the central unit by galleries. The building had been taken over by the revolutionary government and was now a state prison, but its ugly new purpose could not destroy its architectural beauty, its spacious, light-filled interior, or the lovely gardens that surrounded it. It was considered by far the most pleasant prison in all of Paris. The prisoners incarcerated there were largely former nobles, men and women who were quite familiar with the gilded, ornate surroundings in which they were now held captive.

Armand could not help but be irritated that François-Louis was in such a comfortable prison, when Jacqueline and Antoine had been sent to that hellhole Conciergerie. It was well-known that the nobility imprisoned at the Luxembourg made every effort to carry on as if they were simply reluctant guests at someone else's home, filling their days with salons and little gatherings in which they played cards, recited verse, played music, gossiped, and even put on little plays. Although the living conditions were not sumptuous, and occasionally one of the prisoners was taken away to appear before the Tribunal and then executed, the inmates at the Luxembourg were sheltered from the filth, sickness, squalor, and terror that was part of daily life in most of the other prisons of Paris.

The prison was quiet most of the time. A few new prisoners had been ushered through its doors at the beginning of the week, but Armand noticed that the only people who regularly came and went from the Luxembourg were the guards reporting for duty, and the people who delivered food, letters, and personal articles to the prison staff and inmates. In the few words he exchanged each day with the guards he noted that they were bored and cold, an attitude he would be counting on when he tried to get through the doors. With the calculated patience of a man who knows he must not make a move until exactly the right moment, he blew on his hands and stamped his feet, waiting for the light to fade and the day to grow even more frigid.

Although he fought against it, his mind drifted to Jacqueline. She had invaded his thoughts often this past week, despite his determination to keep his attention sharply focused on the task that lay before him. At night he found he could not sleep, and so he would finally relent and permit himself to lie awake and think of her. He tried to picture her in all the different ways he had seen her; a ragged yet defiant prisoner, a filthy, street wise sansculotte, an awkward, pregnant peasant wife, a pale and shivering patient, and finally, playing the role she had been born to, that of a gloriously regal and haughty aristocrat, who did not for a moment accept the idea that all men were created equal. But the image of her that kept returning the most was that of an achingly beautiful woman standing before the fire, clad only in her chemise, looking at him with a mixture of desire and uncertainty while apricot firelight danced against her creamy skin.

He had wanted her that night as he had never wanted any other woman, and the magnitude of his desire appalled him. He had thought to have her once, to show her for one night that he was more than an equal match for her, and to briefly block out the pain and guilt of his own past. He had also thought he would assuage the need that had been growing within him from the moment he first laid eyes on her. But far from satisfying his thirst, his night with her had increased it a thousandfold, leaving him bitter, restless, and unfulfilled. He knew she had agreed to sleep with him because it was the price he demanded to rescue her François-Louis, but something within him did not accept that was the only reason. Perhaps it was intuition, or perhaps it was just male vanity, but he could not believe she could have responded with such glorious passion had she not felt at least some attraction for him.

It does not matter, he reminded himself impatiently. She was not his and she never would be. She was betrothed to another, and she had made it clear she considered him beneath her. Her conviction that she was somehow his superior by right of birth infuriated him, but even if it were not so, there was no room in his life for a woman. With his frequent missions to France, his life was not his own. And France grew more dangerous by the hour. Of course he was always careful, but he knew it was only a matter of time before his luck ran out. He had understood that from the beginning, when the constant risk of discovery and death had been such a large part of the appeal for him. He did not care if he died. He had succeeded in saving dozens of lives, but all of them put together could not begin to make up for the three deaths he had been unable to prevent. The pain and guilt of it still tormented him, day after day, invading his thoughts and slashing into his soul until he wondered how he could bear it another moment. But he did bear it, and he went on, because to simply withdraw from the world in a drunken stupor and let himself rot would have been far, far too easy, and he had no desire to go easy on himself.

A robust, sour-faced woman came by and began to argue with him over the cost of his wine, interrupting his thoughts and forcing him to focus on the present. After a satisfactory period of loud and determined bartering on both sides, the woman bought two bottles. Once she was gone, Armand decided the day had advanced sufficiently for the guards on duty outside to be adequately bored, freezing, and ready for some diversion. Experiencing the familiar quickening sensation that coursed through his veins whenever he started to put a plan into action, he rubbed his hands together, picked up the wooden handles of his cart, and began to roll it slowly through the snow toward the entrance of the Luxembourg.

"Good day to you, Citizens," he called out in a thin, raspy voice as he approached the two young guards who stood by the door.

"A slow day for you, eh, old man?" commented one of the guards.

Armand set down his cart and shrugged his shoulders. "Not so good," he replied easily. "The snow does not help. Most people do not want to be out longer than is necessary, so they do not stop to buy. Which leaves me with all this wine and a very big problem," he pronounced as he drew back the coarse brown blanket covering the dark bottles.

"What's the problem?" demanded the other guard as he stared with interest at the wine.

Armand cocked his head to one side and scowled. "My wife," he admitted in exasperation.

The two guards snorted with appreciative laughter, exposing dark, gap-filled smiles. "I know what you mean, old man," declared one jokingly. "My wife could nag a man straight into his grave. At least there he would have some peace." He laughed again.

Armand joined in the laughter, and then doubled over in a severe coughing fit, which sounded as if every breath he took might be his last. Finally he spat in the snow and looked up at them, shaking his head in apparent misery. "I am old, Citizens. I have been on the streets since dawn, and I am chilled to the bone. Yet if I return home now with so much wine unsold, my wife will make sure all of Paris hears her shrewish bellowing until morning." He reached into his cart and pulled out one of the bottles. "Since I do not think I am up to it, I wish to make a proposition to you. If you find it agreeable, I believe we will all find the evening much more enjoyable."

The two men looked at him with guarded interest. "What proposition?" one of them demanded.

"It is almost dinnertime for the prisoners, is it not?" Armand asked, raising the bottle to his mouth. He clamped his teeth on the cork and pulled it out.

"It is," agreed the guard. "What of it?"

"Perhaps some of the former aristos in there would like to purchase a few bottles of wine to take them through dinner and into the night," Armand suggested casually as he passed the bottle to the guard closest to him. "If you let me go in and do some business, for every bottle I sell I will donate a bottle to the guards. That way I can go home with my purse heavy and my cart light, and my wife will have nothing to complain about. Try it," he insisted brightly to the guard who held the bottle. "I make it myself. I think you will find it is better than the piss others are passing for wine these days."

The guard lifted the bottle to his lips and tilted his head back, drinking until the wine ran in two scarlet rivers down the sides of his mouth. Then he wiped his mouth on his filthy sleeve and passed the bottle to his friend.

"Well?" prodded Armand. "What do you think?"

"It's good," admitted the guard.

Armand nodded his head at the compliment. "I told you so."

"So good I think we will need two bottles given to the guards for every one sold," finished the guard.

Armand's smile vanished. "But, good citizen, I cannot afford to give so much away," he protested. "At that rate I will lose money."

"Then raise the price of the bottles you sell to the prisoners." The guard shrugged indifferently.

"The prisoners are not fools," pointed out Armand. "They know the value of a bottle of wine. If I price it too high, they may not want it."

"Then price it accordingly," snapped the guard impatiently. "Or leave now and make no sales at all. It is up to you."

Armand pretended to consider this for a moment, wringing together his hands in indecision. "Very well," he said finally. "Two bottles to the guards for every one sold."

"Good," grunted the guard with satisfaction. "I will have to clear this with Citizen Benoît, the prison keeper. Give me your papers and wait here."

Armand reached into his coat and produced the forged papers that identified him as Citizen Laurent, a Paris winemaker. The guard accepted them and disappeared through the huge doors, leaving Armand to wait outside in the cold. About fifteen minutes passed, during which Armand tried to keep a conversation going with the remaining guard. Just when he was thinking the other guard must be having trouble convincing the keeper to let him in, and that perhaps he would have to come up with an alternate plan, the guard returned wearing a satisfied smile.

"Very well, Citizen Laurent," said the guard, handing him back his papers. "To help with your sales we have informed the prisoners that we ran out of wine this morning. Anyone who wishes to have wine with their meal must purchase it from you. Just be sure you hold back enough of your stock for the guards," he warned.

"Excellent, Citizen," rasped Armand as he began to eagerly gather a number of bottles into his arms.

The guard opened the door for him and Armand stepped inside, where another guard was waiting to escort him to the prisoners. Armand clutched his armful of bottles against his chest and followed him down the enormous hall, suppressing the urge to smile. So far the plan was working perfectly.

He was led to what was once the drawing room, which now served as a common room for the prisoners. The sight he took in had such an aura of unreality to it, he wondered for a moment if he was indeed inside a prison. The room was crowded with aristocratic men and women, elegantly dressed in their finest costumes, with their wigs and hair artfully arranged, looking very much like guests at a party who were having a splendid time. It was not a scene he had come upon in any of the other prisons he had visited, and once again he experienced an irrational surge of irritation. Jacqueline and Antoine had been placed in a damp, foul, rat-infested nightmare, in which Antoine had died, while François-Louis had been sent to an exclusive club for aristocrats. A closer inspection revealed that the fine gowns the women wore were wrinkled and soiled, while the expensive shirts and jackets of the men had long since lost the crisp, spotless appearance that was expected of such attire. At first the hairstyles looked impressive, but if one cast a second glance one could see the wigs were sorely in need of a professional dressing, while those who wore their own hair would probably have given almost anything for the opportunity to wash it. There was an odor to the room as well, the heavy, sour smell of too many people crowded into the same space, of bodies that were not bathed sufficiently, and of linens that were worn day after day without washing.

Yet the prisoners before him seemed cheerful, as if they were unaware of the fact that they had been stripped of their freedom and their lives now hung on the whim of the republican government. A cluster of women were seated together in a corner, laughing and chatting amiably as they worked on their embroidery, while at the other end of the room a group of men who had obviously been senior officers in the army were loudly recounting tales of their victories. There was a merry gathering seated around a small table playing cards, while others at another table were busy writing letters. High-pitched, feminine laughter was coming from a group of attractive young women gathered around a fellow lounging idly in a window seat. He was amusing them with bawdy verses and bits of song, and the women were almost beside themselves, feigning horrified shock and then shrieking with laughter. The entire scene was terribly noisy and gay, but there was an overwhelming sense of desperation to the laughter and the chatter, as if everyone knew they were only pretending to enjoy themselves, but the charade was so comforting that no one wanted to see it end. They addressed each other by their former titles, and they were a privileged group indeed, for the addresses Monsieur le Duc, Madame la Comtesse, Monsieur le Prince and Madame la Marquise flew about the room constantly.

The little elite society these people had created was, Armand realized, a way of fighting back. These people were not blithely living in a fool's dream. They knew exactly what was going to happen to them. But in accordance with every strict rule of etiquette that had been drummed into them over the course of their lives, they were refusing to stoop to the level of their captors. Clearly they must have been appalled by what was happening to them and their loved ones. Yet somehow they were managing to maintain the only thing they had left, which was their dignity. Perhaps that was what enabled them to keep their sanity in a situation that was so clearly insane. Armand wondered how he would react were he faced with the same fate. Somehow he did not think he would be able to accept it with such docility and grace.

"Listen here now, all of you," bellowed the guard who

had escorted him to the room. A hush fell over the gathering as everyone looked up. "As you know," continued the guard, "there is no wine left for dinner tonight. But this good citizen of the Republic here has agreed to come in and sell you some of his wine. Those of you who are interested step forward now."

The silence that had fallen over the room immediately disintegrated into chatter and the sound of chairs scraping back as people rushed forward to take advantage of this unexpected piece of luck. Armand was quickly mobbed by men and women who were only barely interested in the price of the wine as they thrust money at him and collected their bottles. Within a few moments every bottle he had carried in was gone, and he was forced to make two more trips back to his cart, making sure to leave enough to pay off the guards.

"Enjoy it, Citizen," he rasped as he collected money from a young man and handed him a bottle. He made a quick study of each of the young men who came forward, trying to determine which one was François-Louis. He did not have much of a description to go on, other than the fact that he was tall with blue eyes and a fondness for frilly clothes. Since all the men had dressed for dinner, their outfits were generally ruffled and colorful, as if in open contempt of the darker, more sober fashions dictated by the revolution, so that piece of information was not much help. He was able to eliminate a number of men as either too old, or too short, or with the wrong eye color, and of course he did not consider those few who did not wear wigs. But when he had sold bottles to almost every man and woman who had come forward and still had not found him, he began to quickly scan the room, worrying that perhaps the Marquis de Biret was not there. If he had been moved to another prison, with prison records as disorganized and inaccurate as they were known to be, it could take weeks to find him. And if after all that it turned out he was already dead—

"What do you say, good citizen, is the wine really worth your price?" asked a voice with amusement, interrupting his thoughts. "The lady and I wish to celebrate, and are in the mood for a particularly fine vintage."

The fellow who had been entertaining the group of women with his verses and song had come over to him. He had a pretty, dark-haired girl hanging on to his arm, but Armand was barely aware of her, so focused was he on the man. His eyes were blue, far too pale to be called striking, in Armand's opinion, but blue nonetheless. He was tall as well. Certainly not as tall as Armand when he was not hunched over in disguise, but tall relative to the other men in the room. He wore a silvery wig, which was carefully groomed and well powdered. But what struck Armand most was the immaculate state of his clothes. He wore an elegant frock coat of emerald satin, which was intricately embroidered with silver and gold thread, and there was not one wrinkle or spot on the fragile garment. His shirt was the snowiest white, as if it had just been freshly laundered, with a lacy jabot that spilled down over his chest, and no less than three layers of ruffles bloomed from his wrists. He wore mustard-colored culottes, although the tight-fitting breeches had been abandoned by most French nobles because they were part of the dress code that had been exclusive to the aristocracy, and beneath them he sported silk stockings that were striped emerald and white. In that instant Jacqueline's words struck him. *What I mean to say is that he loves clothes that are, well, colorful and highly decorated.*

"The wine is good," remarked Armand simply, almost positive he had found him. "If you have something to celebrate, it would be a pity not to raise a glass or two, especially on a night as cold as this."

The man turned his attention to the girl who clung on his arm. "What do you think, my pretty Lucile? Shall we buy a bottle and drink to the gods who have kept us together another day?" He gave her a long, intimate look, and then added in a playful whisper, "And night?"

The girl colored prettily and gazed back at him with obvious infatuation. "Oh, François-Louis, you mustn't say such things in front of others," she scolded him in a high, appropriately shocked voice.

Armand was careful to hide the emotions that coursed through him as he heard the girl utter his name. The first was simply satisfaction. He had found the subject of his rescue and could proceed with his plans as scheduled. But the other emotions were more complicated. One of them was perhaps jealousy, although the feeling was so unfamiliar to him he could not be sure. Standing before him was the man Jacqueline was going to marry. The man who would share her world, her mind, and her body. Who would build a new life with her and spend long, passion-filled nights slowly making love to her and creating children with her. He was obviously found attractive by women. He was handsome enough, Armand supposed. He was entertaining. Charming. And he was also, without a doubt, sleeping with the girl who clung so possessively to his emerald satin sleeve. Armand did not know how or when they managed to arrange it, but he supposed no guard was immune to bribery. He also knew that many imprisoned women who realized they were probably going to be executed were eager to make up for all the years of abstinence society demanded of unmarried women, if the opportunity presented itself. He was not in a position to condemn François-Louis for indulging in a few carnal pleasures with an attractive woman before he left this world. Certainly Armand had indulged in more than his share when he was drinking. But when he thought of this man's passion-filled letter to Jacqueline, which complained of his painful separation from her, of the cruel conditions of his incarceration, and practically begged Jacqueline to do something to save him, he was so disgusted by the hypocrisy he was tempted to abandon his plans and leave François-Louis there to rot.

"Very well then, Citizen, let us have a bottle of your precious drink," said François-Louis enthusiastically as he reached inside his frock coat and produced a purse.

Armand looked down at the bottles that remained and selected the one he had held back specifically for François-

Louis. "Here you go, Citizen," he said as he passed him the bottle and took the money. "Enjoy."

"Thank you, good citizen," replied François-Louis. "We shall." He turned, the bottle tucked under one arm and the girl clinging to the other, and made his way back to his post in front of the window.

Only a few others remained to purchase wine. Almost everyone had bought a bottle, and Armand felt confident that those who had not were simply relying on the generosity of their dinner partners. Once he completed his last sale, the guard who had escorted him to the room took him back to the main doors where his cart was waiting.

"How did it go?" demanded one of the guards at the door.

"My wife will have nothing to complain about tonight," rasped Armand with satisfaction. "And now, good citizen, we come to your payment." He lifted the blanket covering the cart and counted out the bottles he owed the guards, handing them over until he was left with only one.

"My friend, this is an extra gift for you," he said as he handed it to the guard who had checked with the prison keeper and gained him entrance. "I shall not soon forget your willingness to help an old man make a few *livres* on a cold winter night."

"Glad to do business with you, Citizen Laurent," said the guard. "Maybe we can work out something again in the future."

"Enjoy the wine, Citizen," returned Armand. He paused to rub his hands together before lifting the handles of his cart. Then he slowly began to trudge through the blanket of fresh snow, down the path, and into the darkness. Behind him he could hear the sounds of the guards laughing and joking over their good fortune, and then silence as they started to drink.

So far, so good, he thought to himself with satisfaction.

· · ·

It was almost three o'clock in the morning when Armand returned to the Luxembourg. The snow had finally stopped, and the sky was like a velvety black cape studded with diamonds. A slender arc of moonlight spilled down onto the city and reflected off the billions of crystals of snow, creating more light than Armand would have liked. Other than that, the night was perfect. A good night for an escape.

The elderly disguise of Citizen Laurent was gone. For tonight he had decided on the disguise of a guard, and in his bag he carried an extra outfit for François-Louis. A National Guard uniform was excellent protection when one was moving quickly through the streets in the middle of the night. If anyone inside the Luxembourg was awake enough to stop him, he would say that he was new that evening and had not yet met all the other guards. And just to be sure no one would have an accurate description of him once he was gone, he had colored his hair black, dirtied his face, and left his teeth with the brown smile of Citizen Laurent, except for one tooth that now appeared to be missing from the front.

From what Armand could see, the Luxembourg was almost completely dark. That was a good sign. He had been by several times earlier this week at the same hour, and usually there were candles burning in the hallways where the guards were posted. The fact that some of those lights had been allowed to go out was promising indeed.

He approached the palace slowly, from the side, using the cover of the trees and statuary in the gardens to shelter him from view. Although he was fairly certain that the guards at the front entrance had passed out by now, he decided he would use a servants' entrance. One of the back doors was sure to be unlocked, and the fewer guards he encountered, sleeping or not, so much the better. When he got to the building he crept along the side until he came to the back. He found a door and paused to listen for a moment before trying it. Locked. He moved along to the next door. It was also locked. Undaunted, he moved along quickly, trying doors until finally there was one that groaned slightly before giving way. He opened it slowly, every sense alert, his ears straining to hear something, his eyes searching through the faint light of the room before him. He took in the sight of two bodies collapsed where they sat at a large oak table, and a third body comfortably stretched out on the kitchen floor. Slowly he expelled the breath he had been holding. It had worked. The guards and prison staff had drunk the wine he had given to them, which was heavily laced with laudanum. Depending on how much they had imbibed, they would sleep at least until the next morning, and possibly longer. Since all the prisoners except for François-Louis had also been given drugged wine, the Luxembourg would be a virtual tomb hours after he and the Marquis de Biret were gone.

He swiftly made his way through the kitchen and into the hallway. A sleeping guard sat on the floor propped against the wall with his head lolling to one side, snoring loudly. Armand stepped around him and continued toward the stairs. A few candles in sconces on the wall had not quite burned out, so he had some light to guide him. When he reached the second level, he found another guard stretched out on the floor and sleeping soundly. Armand walked softly past him and made his way to the end of the hall, where he began opening doors and looking inside.

The first three rooms he looked in each had about ten women sleeping in them, huddled on narrow trestle beds and covered with thin blankets. They were, he realized, but a few of the thousands of women lying in Paris prisons tonight, most of them falsely accused or denounced on the basis of a statement, letter, or association that someone had decided was antirevolutionary and therefore sufficient cause for arrest and execution. Separated from their husbands, lovers, parents, and children, these women undoubtedly had to fight each day just to keep their spirits up, to accept their situation and face their fate with the calm and grace that was expected of them. As Armand looked in on their sleeping forms he was overcome with a familiar rage that tore into his soul. The ladies who slept so peacefully before him had been raised to marry and bear children, to entertain and embroider and be charming and look beautiful. They had not been raised to change the world, or question their station, or fight a revolution. Yet here they were, labeled dangerous criminals and enemies of the Republic, and doomed to pay the price of their previously noble status with their blood. He wanted to save them all, to rouse them from their drug-induced sleep and march them out of this prison and away from this country that had taken its newfound idealism to such vicious and murderous extremes. Over the past year he had saved literally dozens of men and women from the cruel slice of the guillotine. Yet none of those successes could begin to make up for the three important lives he had lost, or for the thousands of others he could not save. And he knew he could not save all the prisoners at the Luxembourg. He was here only to save one. For Jacqueline. Reminding himself of his purpose, he closed the door on the sleeping women and went on to the next room.

Silently he pushed the door open and saw that the ten beds in this room held men. Moving through the darkness with the silent grace of a cat, he went to each of the beds to determine by the pale glow from the candles in the hallway if one of these men was François-Louis. It was not an easy task. Some of the men slept with their faces half-buried beneath the covers, and he found he had to either wait for them to move or try to pull the covers back slightly to see if he had found the right man. After inspecting the faces of four men and deciding that they were not François-Louis, he moved on to the next bed.

"Who might you be looking for, Citizen?" called a casual whisper from across the room.

Armand spun around to see one of the prisoners sitting up in his bed, watching Armand intently. Without responding, he moved closer toward him, quickly trying to determine if this was the Marquis de Biret. Although it was too dark to see his eye color, his features were identical to those he had seen earlier that day. Except for one thing.

He was almost entirely bald.

Armand knew the pleasure he felt as he took in that fact was petty and unworthy, but he allowed himself to indulge in it anyway. No wonder Jacqueline's betrothed always wore a wig. He would probably even wear it to bed if he could. He wondered if François-Louis took it off when he bedded his women, or if he kept it on and simply took the chance that it might fall off at an inopportune moment. If it did fall off, he imagined his women must have been understandably shocked and disappointed. Unbelievably, these were the thoughts that were going through his head as he stared at the man he was risking his life to save.

François-Louis stared back at him curiously. "You're not one of the regular guards—who are you?"

Armand ignored his question and tossed the bag of clothes he was carrying onto the bed. "Put those on," he ordered brusquely. "We're leaving."

François-Louis's pale eyes grew wide as understanding began to dawn on him. "My God," he breathed in apparent disbelief, "you're the Black Prince."

"I am afraid not," replied Armand impatiently. "But I will have to do. Get dressed."

"Did Jacqueline send you?" demanded François-Louis as he hastily threw back the covers and began to put on the guard's uniform Armand had provided. "Are you the same man who helped her escape?"

Armand did not like all these questions, especially when they had not even left the prison yet. "Monsieur le Marquis, save your questions for another time. Hurry up."

"Of course," stammered François-Louis as he fumbled with the buttons on his jacket. He bent down to reach under his bed and pulled out his wig.

"No wig," stated Armand flatly. "It is too fine a piece. Besides, the description they send out of you when they realize you are gone will undoubtedly include your wig."

"But I must have my wig," protested François-Louis indignantly. "I shall not leave without it."

It was ridiculous to argue over such a thing at this moment, Armand realized, and so he relented. "Very well. Put it in the bag and let's go."

He led François-Louis out of the room and down the dimly lit hallway, moving quickly but silently. François-Louis froze when he saw the sleeping guard on the floor.

"It is all right," Armand assured him. "He is dead to the world. Just move quietly around him."

Armand skirted around the body and François-Louis followed, staring at the guard as he did so. "What is the matter with him?" he whispered curiously.

"Perhaps he drank too much," replied Armand with a shrug as he began to descend the stairs.

They moved along the main level of the palace, carefully avoiding the unconscious bodies of two more guards. Armand headed toward the kitchen, thinking to leave by the same door he had come in. "There are identification papers in your jacket," he told François-Louis as they hurried along. "If we are stopped on the street, you are Citizen Claude Roucher. You are from Reims, and you have only been a member of the National Guard for two months. I am Citizen Michel Belanger. We have been out drinking at a friend's. I will do the talking, but if by chance you do have to say something, for God's sake keep it short and simple. Do you understand?"

"Yes," replied François-Louis, "I understand."

Armand led him through the kitchen to the back, making sure to point out the body of the man on the floor. The men seated around the table were snoring deeply and had not moved. *I must remember this trick with the wine,* Armand thought to himself with satisfaction. *It has worked exceptionally well.* He squeezed down on the latch of the door and swung it open, letting in a blast of cold air as he stepped out into the night with François-Louis following behind him.

"Well, well," mocked a low, satisfied voice from the icy shadows. "What do we have here?"

Armand paused for a second, his adrenaline racing through his blood, his hand firmly clamped on the handle of his pistol. He could not see the man who had discovered them clearly, and until he could determine if they were being detained by a guard from the prison or simply a curious passerby, he would not shoot. Besides, it was always preferable to talk one's way out of a situation like this. Adopting a tone of impatient authority, he stared into the shadows and snapped, "Who goes there? Come out at once!"

"Very good," murmured the voice sarcastically. "Were I just some poor, ignorant lout from the streets, I might actually believe you were a guard. Unfortunately for you, however, I am not that stupid." As the voice spoke a dozen armed guards suddenly appeared from behind trees, statues, and doorways. They formed a circle around Armand and François-Louis, making escape utterly impossible. Armand scanned their faces and recognized among them the guards from the front door with whom he had bargained earlier that day.

A trap. The whole thing had been a trap, and he had walked into it like a blind, bungling fool. He cursed himself for his stupidity.

The man from the shadows stepped forward and entered the circle of guards. His dark features were illuminated by the pale wash of moonlight, and he glared at Armand with a hatred and malevolence that sliced through the air between them.

Armand clenched his jaw and stared back with an expression of complete and total indifference, giving absolutely no indication that he recognized him. But all he could think of was Jacqueline, and how if he were simply to raise his gun and shoot, her need for vengeance would be assuaged, and she could get on with the rest of her life. For the man who had laid the trap he had so stupidly walked into was none other than Nicolas Bourdon.

"A pleasure to finally see you again," remarked Nicolas bitterly, his narrow gaze focused on Armand.

Armand looked at him blankly. He was not sure how

much Nicolas actually knew and how much he merely suspected. The less he told him, the better. He raised his eyebrows in confusion and said politely, "I fear you have me at a disadvantage, Citizen. Have we met before?"

Nicolas did not respond, but signaled to one of the guards to step forward and disarm him. Realizing he could not fight all of them, Armand calmly handed the guard his gun, and did not protest as the guard searched him and found the other gun in the back of his waistband, and the knife hidden in his boot.

Once he was weaponless, Nicolas stepped forward and smiled. Then he drove his fist straight into Armand's jaw, causing his head to snap back with dizzying force. Armand shook his head to clear it and gently moved his jaw to see if it was broken. It was not. Pleased with that discovery, he looked at Nicolas and smiled back. "Have I done something to upset you, Citizen?" he asked pleasantly.

Nicolas scowled and moved away from him, obviously irritated by Armand's calm reaction. He went over to François-Louis. "What did you find out?" he demanded sharply. "Is she here? Did she send him?"

"He would not say," replied François-Louis. "Although I cannot imagine who else would have sent him. He denies he is the Black Prince, but even if he is not, he is still a worthy catch, don't you think?" There was an edge to his voice, as if it was imperative Nicolas agree with him.

Nicolas turned and studied Armand a moment, evidently weighing a decision. After a moment he turned back to François-Louis. "Did he give you false identification papers?"

"Yes," replied François-Louis. He hastily fumbled in his jacket to produce them.

Nicolas scowled as he looked them over. "These are excellent counterfeits," he remarked irritably. He handed them back to him. "Very well then, Citizen Roucher. You are free to go. I do not anticipate you will have any trouble getting out of Paris. The rest is up to you."

Relief flooded François-Louis's features as he shoved the papers back into his jacket. He looked at Armand. "I am sorry," he apologized. "You must understand, I really had no choice. You see, they told me that your capture, or Jacqueline's capture, was my only hope of getting out of here alive. I simply did what I had to do."

So that was it, thought Armand. Nicolas had used François-Louis to trick Jacqueline into returning, but failing that, he would make do with getting the man who had helped her escape. And François-Louis, ever the spineless, self-preservationist that Jacqueline had unwittingly described him to be, had gone along with it. Contempt for the man he had risked his life to save flooded through him. "Not very noble of you, was it, Monsieur le Marquis?" he observed with disgust.

François-Louis returned his glare calmly. "These are difficult times," he declared with a shrug. "If one wishes to survive them, one must be prepared to do what is necessary."

"Thank you for the advice," drawled Armand. "I shall bear it in mind."

"Get going," ordered Nicolas sharply to François-Louis, "before I have reason to reconsider our agreement."

The Marquis de Biret needed no further encouragement. He immediately turned and hurriedly moved down the path that led away from the Luxembourg.

"And as for you, my friend," continued Nicolas, "we shall see how much you have to tell us about your most interesting habit of rescuing dangerous enemies of the Republic. No doubt there are many fascinating escapades you would like to share with me before your execution."

"Actually this was my first time," said Armand innocently.

Nicolas looked unconvinced. "Really? Then perhaps we will have to find a nice dark cell for you to rot in until your memory returns."

"As you wish." Armand shrugged. "I believe the Luxembourg has a vacancy."

"Oh no, my friend," ground out Nicolas. "I do not believe the likes of you belongs in a gilded cage like this. But do not concern yourself. I am sure we can find something more appropriate." He nodded to the guards and two of them stepped forward and grabbed Armand from each side. "Take him to La Force," he ordered brusquely. "All of you act as escort. I will follow in my carriage."

The guards permitted Nicolas to get through before closing in around Armand. They walked him to their horses, where they bound his hands behind his back before helping him to mount. Then they mounted their own horses and slowly started out for the prison La Force.

Momentarily putting aside the issue of how he could have been so stupid as to walk into a trap, Armand tried to focus on his situation. It was obvious Nicolas believed he had captured quite a prize. If Nicolas could show that he had finally caught the Black Prince, the public humiliation Armand had caused him by snatching Jacqueline right out from under him at the Conciergerie would be forgotten. Nicolas would be heralded a hero. But Armand sensed that would not satisfy Nicolas's personal disappointment that he had not managed to catch Jacqueline as well. It was possible Nicolas might try another tactic to lure Jacqueline back to France. Armand realized he would have to be careful not to do or say anything that might make Nicolas believe he could use him as bait.

Whatever was to happen to him, he was ready for it. He had always known he would eventually get caught. If he was to die under the blade of the guillotine, then so be it. He stared calmly into the black night of Paris, resigned to his fate, and eminently grateful that despite his mistakes, he had not been foolish enough to let Jacqueline go with him.

Chapter 10

The city of London lay blanketed under the same snow that covered the streets of Paris, although Londoners would have been loath to accept the idea that they shared anything in common with "those murdering Frenchies" across the channel, including the weather. Sir Edward and Lady Harrington had moved their extended family into the city after Christmas, because Laura had complained that there was absolutely nothing to do in the country. In London, she argued, she and Jacqueline could go shopping, visit friends, and attend the theater. The fact that Jacqueline had not the slightest inclination to do any of these things seemed to give merit to Laura's argument, and did not diminish Laura's enthusiasm for London in the least.

After considerable pressure had been put on Jacqueline to get out and enjoy herself, she finally relented one night and went with the Harringtons to the theater. But the play was a fast-paced English comedy, and after about five minutes she gave up trying to understand the words. For the rest of the evening she stared at the stage and pretended to listen attentively, but her thoughts were firmly centered on Armand, as they so often were since he had left. She wondered where he was, what plan he had devised to rescue François-Louis, if he had started to put that plan into action, and if in fact he had already successfully completed his mission and was on his way back. During intermission she found herself searching through the crowd in the theater, as if she expected him to appear at any moment, and had to mask her disappointment when he did not. After the theater the Harringtons joined a group of friends for a late supper in an elegant restaurant, and Jacqueline was seated beside Viscount Preston, who seemed determined to fawn over her all evening. Jacqueline remained polite but cool with him, pretending not to understand when at the end of the dinner he kissed her hand and said that he would like to call upon her. His smitten behavior did not escape Laura's watchful eye, and she gave Jacqueline an enthusiastic lecture in the carriage afterward on all the things that made Viscount Preston an excellent catch. Jacqueline thanked Laura for her advice, but politely reminded her that she was still betrothed to a man who was awaiting trial in a Paris prison, and informed her she was not looking for a "catch," excellent or otherwise. She hoped that put Laura's mind at ease, for she was certain Laura's sudden interest in her romantic life was in reaction to the night she had walked into the library at the Fleetwoods' ball and seen Jacqueline and Armand together.

Madame Bonnard had told Jacqueline he would return in about two weeks, and as the second week dragged to a close Jacqueline grew more and more anxious as she anticipated his return. She never wanted to leave the house, just so she could be there when he and François-Louis arrived. Every time the butler appeared to announce a visitor she went rigid with tension, waiting for him to say Armand's name. But the butler never did announce his name. The second week ended and the third week began, and still there was no word from him. Jacqueline assured herself that this was no cause for alarm, that sometimes his missions probably took longer than he anticipated. Had he not told her it had taken him a while to locate her and Antoine? A few days more meant nothing. He was probably setting sail on *The Angélique* this very moment and would be here by tomorrow. And so she waited, day after day, hour after hour, until finally the third week was over and the fourth had begun. And still she kept telling herself, He is all right, he has done this many times before, he is just waiting for the right time to strike, he will be here any moment and he will look at me and say in that arrogant way of his, "Did you think I would leave you, Mademoiselle?" And one night as she lay in bed silently repeating these assurances to herself, she suddenly realized that not once had she thought about the safety of François-Louis, who was her betrothed and the reason she had pleaded with Armand to return to France in the first place. And that realization so stunned and confused her she curled up into a tight little ball, buried her face in her pillow, and fought to stifle a sob. Once the sob was controlled, she lay there, silently, clutching her pillow and thinking that if she allowed herself to shed a single tear she might never stop. First she would weep for her father, and for Antoine, and for the girl she had once been, a girl who was now a distant and unfamiliar shadow from a life that was over. And then she would weep for her sisters, who were trying so hard to fit into the new life they had been thrust into, and who would eventually forget their father and brother, in the same way that Jacqueline was having trouble remembering things about her mother. And finally she would weep because she was afraid, because somehow she knew that Armand should have returned by now, and if something had happened to him she would never, ever forgive herself for sending him to France.

She did not go down for breakfast the next morning, so exhausted was she from her sleepless night. When she finally did appear the butler informed her that Suzanne and Séraphine were upstairs having their lessons, Sir Edward had gone to his club, and Lady Harrington and Miss Laura were out shopping. Grateful beyond measure at not having to face anyone for the next few hours, Jacqueline ordered coffee and a roll to be brought to her in the small salon off the music room, where the bright winter sun was streaming through the windows. She had not been settled in there more than five minutes when the butler appeared and told her a Lady Charles Fairfax was there and wished to see her.

"But . . . I do not know a Lady Fairfax," protested

Jacqueline slowly in English, not particularly wanting to endure the ritual of visiting with someone who had heard she was an escaped French aristocrat and was eager to ask her a lot of questions. "Perhaps she would come back . . . when Lady Harrington and Miss Laura are in," she suggested hopefully.

Cranfield shook his head. "She did not ask to see Lady Harrington or Miss Laura, she asked to see you, your ladyship. She said to tell you she is the sister of Mr. Armand St. James."

Jacqueline practically leapt out of her chair. Armand's sister? Here? No doubt she had been sent to give her a message from Armand. "Send her in *immédiatement,*" burst out Jacqueline, positive that this meant Armand had returned safely.

The woman who stepped into the salon a few minutes later bore such a strong resemblance to Armand that for the first moment all Jacqueline could do was stand and stare at her. She was very pretty, and Jacqueline guessed her to be in her late twenties. Her hair was the same coppery gold as Armand's, not quite blond, and not quite brown, but a magnificent mixture of light and dark, swept back into a thick cluster of curls that cascaded down from an elegant emerald velvet hat. She wore a matching emerald velvet coat, which at first made her eyes look quite green, but on closer inspection Jacqueline realized that Lady Fairfax's eyes were also flecked with blues and grays, making them change color from one moment to the next. It was a family trait that had constantly worked to Armand's advantage when he was in disguise, she reflected. In stature Lady Fairfax was as petite and dainty as Armand was large and powerful, but she shared the same, unmistakable confidence and sense of purpose that always came through in every movement Armand made.

"I hope I am not disturbing you, Mademoiselle de Lambert, but I must speak with you on a most urgent matter," explained Lady Fairfax in French. Her voice was high and musical, but it also sounded troubled.

"Please sit down, Lady Fairfax," invited Jacqueline in French. "Would you care for some tea?"

"No, thank you," she replied as she seated herself on the small sofa across from Jacqueline.

"Do you have a message for me from Armand?" asked Jacqueline hopefully.

Lady Fairfax shook her head. "I am afraid I have come to seek information rather than to give it," she replied. "I am most concerned, you see, because my brother has disappeared, and I fear that something terrible may have happened to him."

Jacqueline struggled to keep her expression calm and composed. She did not know how much Lady Fairfax knew about Armand's activities in France. Armand had asked her not to disclose to anyone that it was he who had rescued her from the Conciergerie, because that information could find its way to the wrong person and pose a threat to him. Even Sir Edward, who had hired him to rescue Jacqueline, believed that Armand merely used his connections in France to get Jacqueline to the coast, where he picked her up and sailed her across the channel. Although Lady Fairfax was his sister, it was possible his work was kept secret even from her. She must be careful not to reveal too much.

"What makes you think something has happened to Armand?" she asked casually.

"Mademoiselle de Lambert, I know you are aware of the work my brother does in France," began Lady Fairfax, "just as I know it was he who rescued you from some terrible prison there and brought you here to safety. You must believe me when I say you can trust me, for my sole concern is the welfare of my brother. What I must ask is, can I trust you?" She looked at her pointedly, as if trying to decide whether or not she had made a mistake in coming here.

"Yes," replied Jacqueline quickly, her concern for Armand growing by the minute.

Lady Fairfax considered a moment, and then, evidently feeling she had little choice but to trust her, continued. "Yesterday the first officer of my brother's ship, Mr. Sidney Langdon, came to see me. He informed me that Armand sailed to France some four weeks ago, but did not return to *The Angélique* on the day he said he would. At first Mr. Langdon was not overly alarmed, because my brother often must alter his plans to compensate for unforeseeable circumstances. His men know that twenty-four hours is an acceptable period of time for him to be delayed. But after two days without a message from him they sent three men ashore to see if they could find out what happened to him. This was nearly impossible, since Armand never informs anyone of his plans, out of concern for their safety as well as his. The only thing they could determine with certainty was that he had not made any of his connections outside of Paris, which led them to believe he never left the city. Since they did not know who his target was, and there were no public announcements concerning his capture, they had very little to go on. After waiting several days in Paris and learning nothing, they followed the orders Armand has given them if he does not show up within a week. They returned to *The Angélique* and sailed home."

"They left him there?" gasped Jacqueline in disbelief. "Without knowing if he is alive or dead?"

"They followed his instructions," repeated Lady Fairfax. "Armand has always been very concerned about the safety of his ship and crew. He would not want them to remain on the French coast any longer than necessary. And Sidney felt that if he could speak to me, he might learn more about Armand's mission in France, which would enable him to go back and find him. Unfortunately, Armand does not keep me informed of his plans because he knows how much I worry, so I could not be of much help. We went to his home last night to see if we could find a note or anything which might shed some light on his latest mission. Of course we did not. Armand would never be so careless as to leave something in writing which might endanger his operations. We then decided to question the servants. Which led me to you."

Jacqueline colored slightly.

If Lady Fairfax noticed Jacqueline's embarrassment, she gave no sign of it. "Armand's servants are very devoted to him, and at first refused to say anything about your visit, which of course was in accordance with his instructions. But once I explained to Madame Bonnard our urgent need to know anything that might explain why he went to France, she finally admitted that Armand had dined with a Frenchwoman at his home the night he left. Sidney was convinced by her description it had to be you, but it was the carriage driver who confirmed it and told us where you were staying. And so here I am, and now I must beg of you to share with me any information you have that could help us find my brother." She looked at her intently, her blue-green eyes filled with hope. "Do you have any idea who Armand was trying to save in France?"

Jacqueline heard the question, but the voice sounded far away because of the roaring in her ears. The room was beginning to spin, and she closed her eyes, trying to make it stop, and trying to come to grips with what Lady Fairfax was telling her. Armand was missing. Something had gone wrong. Maybe he had been captured. Or killed. The thought caused a tightening sensation around her chest, making it difficult for her to breathe.

"Mademoiselle de Lambert, are you all right?" asked a voice from far away, a voice that seemed to be filled with concern.

It was her fault. He had risked his life to save her, and in return she had pleaded and bargained him into going back to save her betrothed. It had seemed so important at the time. She had thought she could not live with the guilt of François-Louis's death. That guilt was nothing compared with the panic and terror that was gripping her now.

"I sent him to France," she whispered, wondering how she could not have considered the danger involved.

Lady Fairfax looked at her in confusion. "What do you mean, you sent him?"

Jacqueline raised her eyes to her. "I hired Armand to

rescue someone for me," she explained, her voice heavy with guilt.

Lady Fairfax appeared dumbfounded. "You *hired* him?"

Jacqueline nodded miserably. "At first he did not want to take the job. I am afraid I did not have enough money to cover his fee. But we worked out an agreement that was acceptable to both of us." She should never have agreed to his terms. At the time his price had seemed inordinately high. But now she could see that the exchange had been far from even. Her virginity in return for his life. What on earth had she been thinking of?

Lady Fairfax frowned in confusion. "That is completely unlike Armand," she remarked, shaking her head. "He has always performed these rescues because he wanted to help people. It was his own personal war with the revolutionary government of France. I have never known him to charge anyone."

"But he was hired by Sir Edward to go to France and rescue me," protested Jacqueline.

Lady Fairfax looked shocked. "Did Sir Edward tell you that?" she demanded.

"No," admitted Jacqueline. Suddenly she was not quite sure when she first knew that Armand had been hired to save her. She thought back to the first night she met him, when they shared a room and a bed in that small Paris inn. "After Armand rescued me from the Conciergerie, I asked him if he was the one they call the Black Prince," she recalled, "and he told me he was merely a man of business and that I was a package he had agreed to deliver. He was quite open about it," she finished matter-of-factly.

Lady Fairfax smiled, apparently relieved by her explanation. "And do you think, Mademoiselle de Lambert, that if the man who had just saved your life was indeed the Black Prince, he would be foolish enough to admit such a thing to a young, terrified stranger, when you were both on the run and in such grave danger of being captured?"

Jacqueline stared at her in disbelief. Was she saying Armand was the legendary Black Prince? Impossible. From the moment he met her, he made it clear she was a parcel to be delivered, and nothing more. And he certainly was not any great admirer of the French aristocracy. If anything, he was infuriatingly sympathetic to the cause of those bloodthirsty revolutionaries. He had argued their side to her many times. Why then would he risk his life to go to France and save members of the French nobility, if not for the money?

"He made it quite clear that he did not want to go to France and rescue my betrothed, the Marquis de Biret, who was falsely accused and imprisoned," pointed out Jacqueline. "The Black Prince has saved scores of men, women, and children from imprisonment and death in France, and not once has there been the slightest suggestion that he was doing it for monetary reward. Many of the people he has saved have no money left, and could not possibly pay him even if they wanted to. Armand not only demanded payment from me, but he wanted it in advance, in case anything happened to him and he was not able to complete his mission. Now, does that sound like the conduct of the Black Prince?"

"I cannot imagine why he would have wanted payment," commented Lady Fairfax. "Armand is an exceptionally clever investor, and as you undoubtedly realized when you went to his home, he is extremely wealthy. I can, however, understand why he might have been reluctant to go to France and rescue the man you plan to marry," she murmured thoughtfully as she studied Jacqueline.

"Why?" demanded Jacqueline.

Lady Fairfax smiled. "I think perhaps you know the answer to that better than I."

A warm blush swept across Jacqueline's cheeks. "I am afraid I don't know what you mean, Lady Fairfax," she stammered, feeling enormously uncomfortable with the direction the conversation had taken. "My relationship with your brother is one of business, nothing more."

"It would please me a great deal if you would call me Madeleine," Armand's sister returned gently, obviously not convinced. "And I should be very honored to call you Jacqueline."

Jacqueline nodded silently. Madeleine took almost the same care with her name as Armand did when he said it, stretching out the sounds as if they were a lush piece of music, and Jacqueline was filled with a painful longing. Until this moment she had not realized how much she missed hearing Armand say her name.

"So you believe my brother risks his life to save people he does not know for money," summarized Madeleine, her tone clearly indicating how ludicrous she thought this idea was. "I take it then that Armand has not told you about his past?"

"He has told me about your parents, and how your grandfather refused to accept your father because he was untitled, forcing your mother to renounce her title and her ties to her family in France," returned Jacqueline. "I suppose that explains his contempt for the French aristocracy and his sympathy for the ideals of the new Republic," she finished thoughtfully, surprised that she had not pieced this together earlier.

"But has he told you anything about himself?" persisted Madeleine.

"He told me about how he used to drink to excess," Jacqueline replied matter-of-factly, unwilling to let Armand's sister think that this mattered in the least to her, "and now he will not touch a single drop."

"Did he tell you why he does not drink anymore?"

"Yes," answered Jacqueline. "He stopped because some people were killed and Armand blames himself, but I simply cannot believe that he ever would have done anything to bring harm to anyone."

Madeleine smiled sadly before asking, "Jacqueline, do you have any idea who those people were?"

"No," she admitted. "But it does not matter. Whatever happened, I cannot believe Armand was responsible."

"Armand was married," began Madeleine in a quiet voice, "and his wife was killed."

"Married?" gasped Jacqueline in disbelief.

Madeleine nodded.

There was silence between the two of them as Jacqueline struggled to absorb this piece of information. Armand had been married. Of course. It made sense. After all, Armand was a handsome, wealthy man, and many beautiful women had undoubtedly chased after him, Laura Harrington included. Obviously one had captured his heart, and he married her. "He must have loved her very much," she reflected in a small, hollow voice, "to have named his ship after her."

"I believe he did love Lucette very much," remarked Madeleine.

"Lucette?" repeated Jacqueline blankly. "But who is Angélique?" She wondered if Armand had named his ship after a mistress.

"Angélique was his daughter," replied Madeleine softly. "And she was also killed."

"His daughter?" whispered Jacqueline, her voice thin and small. Her mind swirled back to the night she spent on *The Angélique*. She remembered going through Armand's chest, ostensibly looking for a comb, but in reality searching for clues that might reveal something about the man who had risked his life to rush in and snatch her away from death. And suddenly she remembered the lacquer box hidden at the very bottom of the chest, which held a pastel wreath of satiny ribbons and a tiny white handkerchief embroidered with the initials *ASJ*. At the time she had assumed the box held tokens given to him by a mistress, and found the sweet sentimentality of the articles incongruous with the unyielding, impatient, methodical man she knew as Citizen Julien. She realized the blue and cream and pink lengths of satin were for a little girl's hair, and the tiny square of linen and lace was meant for the sleeve of an elegant little dress. Those dainty scraps of fabric had belonged to Angélique St. James. Armand had named his ship after his daughter. And he held himself responsible for her death.

"What happened to them?" whispered Jacqueline.

"They were arrested in France, along with my mother, and charged with being émigrés, spies, and enemies of the Republic," replied Madeleine, her voice strained. "And they were guillotined."

"Oh my God," breathed Jacqueline, unable to contain her horror. And then, before she realized how accusing her words sounded, she demanded, "How could Armand have possibly let that happen?"

"It is strange," remarked Madeleine tautly, "but that is the same question all of London society asked, and continues to ask, as if they somehow believe that Armand had it in his power to race in and stop the proceedings of the French justice system. And that is the question he constantly demands of himself, to the point where the need to avenge their deaths and show that he would have died to save them if he could has completely taken over his life."

"I am sorry," apologized Jacqueline, realizing how insensitive her question had been. "I did not mean to insinuate that Armand was responsible for their deaths." She thought back to Viscount Preston's open contempt toward Armand at the Fleetwoods' ball. Obviously there were those who did believe he was responsible and did not hesitate to let him know it.

Madeleine sighed. "The problem is, Armand believes he is responsible for their deaths. That is why he sends himself on these dangerous missions. Part of him is extracting vengeance from the government that murdered his family, by snatching away other helpless victims right out from under their noses. But another part of him is taunting death, running just one step ahead of it and daring it to try to take him as well. He feels that if he could not have saved his family, then he should have gone to France and died with them. Quite simply, he no longer cares if he lives or dies. I suppose for a long time that attitude has helped him, because it enables him to take

outrageous chances that fortunately have been successful."

"Why did he not go to France and try to help them?"
asked Jacqueline.

"Because," said Madeleine slowly, "he did not know
they were there."

Jacqueline looked at her in confusion. "But how could
he not know where his wife and child were?"

Madeleine sighed. "Although Armand loved Lucette, I
am afraid that for her, it was not the happiest of marriages. You see, Armand was something of a rake as a
young man. All he wanted to do was enjoy himself. He
was hopelessly irresponsible and a heavy drinker, which
infuriated my father and worried my mother. It was as if
he simply did not want to grow up and settle down. Even
after father died, and the business of managing the St.
James investments fell to him, Armand refused to take it
seriously. He loved traveling, drinking, gambling, and
women, and nothing anyone could say or do made him
want to change."

Jacqueline listened to this incredulously. The irresponsible, carefree man Armand's sister was describing bore
no resemblance to the man she knew.

"Armand met Lucette on a trip to France when he was
in his late twenties," continued Madeleine. "She was the
daughter of a silk merchant who did a lot of business with
the royal household at Versailles. Her family was untitled
but quite wealthy. Lucette was very pretty and charming,
and Armand loved to make conquests of pretty girls. After
a few months they married and Armand brought her back
to England and presented her to our mother, informing
her that he and Lucette were going to have a child. My
mother was pleased that Armand had married a French
girl and was apparently going to settle down and be a
proper husband and father."

"What happened?"

Madeleine sighed. "At first, Armand tried to be a loving and devoted husband. Lucette told me that in the beginning he was very good to her, and loved to be at home

with her. But after Angélique was born, Armand began to grow restless. He loved to be out with his friends, gambling and drinking until all hours of the morning. As a young mother, Lucette was often tired, and more importantly, she felt she should be home with her baby. Armand accepted this, but he did not believe such a sedate life applied to him. He quickly fell back into his old ways, drinking and womanizing, and disappearing for days at a time. Lucette was left on her own, to run the house, entertain, and raise their daughter."

Jacqueline sadly shook her head. The marriage Madeleine was describing was not uncommon among the aristocracy. The men often believed that one married to secure heirs and have a gracious hostess to run the household. Fidelity was not an issue. "Why did Lucette return to France?"

"Like many wealthy members of the bourgeoisie who had provided services and luxuries to the now imprisoned royal family, Lucette's father was denounced and arrested in the late autumn of 1792," explained Madeleine. "Despite his bourgeois status he was accused of being a royalist, and a traitor to his country, because his daughter was an émigré. Lucette received word of this while Armand was away on one of his drinking and gambling binges. She had no idea where he was or whom he was with, since Armand never felt the need to tell her and she never asked. But the thought of her father in prison both frightened and infuriated her, and she decided not to wait until Armand's return before taking action. She contacted my mother and informed her that she was going to France to try to help her father. My mother, erroneously believing that she could be of some assistance because of her former noble status, offered to travel with her. And at the last minute Lucette decided to take Angélique, who was only four and pleaded with her not to be left alone with the servants."

"Oh my God," whispered Jacqueline in horror. "How could they have been so foolish?"

"Neither Lucette nor my mother had any idea of how

dangerous France had become," replied Madeleine. "My mother had not set foot in France for years, and Lucette had left with Armand before the revolution. The information coming to England from France was often sketchy and confusing, so it is not entirely surprising that they did not anticipate they would come to any harm. If anything, Lucette believed that the revolution was being fought on behalf of men like her father, which of course in its early stages it was. All she could think was that her father needed her, and that he might be cheered by the sight of his only grandchild. I imagine they believed that two women traveling with a little girl would never be seen as a threat to the security of the new Republic."

Of course not, thought Jacqueline. If they believed the world was fair and just, that there were laws to protect them, and that God was watching over them, then why wouldn't they return to the land of their birth? Her heart was sickened by it. "When were they arrested?"

"On the day of their arrival," Madeleine told her. "Their carriage was stopped by a rough group of men and they were ordered to show their papers. Since both women were émigrés, and obviously wealthy, they were detained for questioning. Lucette grew angry and informed them that her mother-in-law was the daughter of the deceased Marquis des Valentes, that she herself was married to the marquis's grandson, and that her child was his great-granddaughter, which of course was exactly the wrong thing to tell them. You see, my grandfather had been a staunch royalist in his day, and to admit that they were his émigré relatives was equivalent to admitting they were counterrevolutionaries and enemies of the Republic. They were immediately charged and imprisoned, and with remarkable efficiency they were tried the next day and sent to the guillotine. It was all over before Armand returned home to find that they were gone."

Jacqueline gripped the arms of her chair with such intensity she felt as though her fingers would break. It was too appalling. The idea that a man could go away for a few days and return to find his family had been executed

—the shock and the horror must have been absolutely unbearable.

Her father and brother had been killed, so she understood the agony of losing those you love. But her father had been in prison for months before he was finally brought to trial, and although Jacqueline had not wanted to believe it, she had always known that his execution was a possibility. As for Antoine, she had understood the danger they both faced after her father was executed with complete clarity. That was why she sent Suzanne and Séraphine to England. France had gone mad, and in a world gone mad she and Antoine had no protection except each other. When the guards forced their way into her home to arrest him, she had fought them with every ounce of her strength, knowing Antoine was too ill to withstand being in prison, and that even if he had been able to endure it, they were going to execute him anyway.

But Armand had been away, gambling and drinking and probably savoring the delights of some woman, totally oblivious of the dangers his mother and wife and child were in. And when he returned home, expecting to find his pretty Lucette and his little Angélique waiting for him as usual, he instead learned that they had gone to France with his mother and been guillotined. How did one deal with a tragedy so overwhelmingly brutal and unexpected?

"What did Armand do?" she whispered.

"He went insane with rage," replied Madeleine. "At first he simply would not believe it. We had received a letter from my mother which she wrote hurriedly before they took her to be executed, explaining what had happened and begging us not to set foot in France until stability had returned. Of course Armand wanted to go to France and find them, thinking there had been a mistake and that they were alive. My husband and I practically had to stand guard at his house to prevent him from leaving, so terrified was I that he would go to France and get himself killed as well."

Jacqueline could well imagine that Armand would not

be one to sit idly by and do nothing. And if he went to France and discovered they were dead, he would not simply turn around and go home. He would want revenge.

"At first he fought with us terribly, so determined was he to rush to France and find them," continued Madeleine. "And then, when we finally were able to make him see that such an act would merely give the republican government another victim, he withdrew completely. He locked himself up in his study and began to drink himself into a state of complete and utter oblivion. For three weeks he refused to see anyone. I begged him to at least let me in, but the door was only opened for his butler, who brought him trays of food and endless bottles of liquor. I fought terribly with the man over it. I ordered him not to take in any more liquor, but Armand's servants are unfailingly loyal to him, and the man refused to heed my instructions. I realize now he was probably acting out of compassion. I am sure he thought that Armand was better off in a drunken stupor than sober and facing the reality around him."

"What made him come out of it?"

Madeleine drew her delicate eyebrows together in a frown. "I don't know exactly. All I know is one day he appeared at my door, bathed and shaved and utterly sober. He told me that he was all right, and that I was not to worry about him. He was going to visit one of his properties in the north for a few weeks. He was obviously still in great pain, but he seemed calm and rational, and I remember feeling terribly relieved. When he returned from his trip four weeks later he seemed revitalized, as if he had discovered a new purpose. At first I thought perhaps he had met a woman, someone who was helping him to heal. I later discovered that was when he performed his first rescue mission to France."

Jacqueline silently absorbed this information. So that was it. Armand was not some opportunistic merchant, risking his life to save endangered French aristocrats in exchange for an enormous fee. Nor was he a bored, eccentric adventurer, traveling to France for sport, abducting the condemned for the sheer thrill of it. He was a man in agony, a man tormented by the terrible black guilt of his past, who was waging his own personal war on the country that brutally murdered his family. And because of that pain, and that hatred, and the need to inflict revenge, he had started saving people who were beyond the hope that anyone or anything could possibly save them. People like his wife, mother, and daughter, who had undoubtedly been terrified as they awaited their fate, and would have done almost anything to survive. And people like Jacqueline, who were so bitter and angry with the world they were past caring whether they lived or not.

"I sent him there," she breathed, more horrified than ever by her actions. He had not wanted to go. Perhaps he had been tired, and wanted a rest, a break from the danger. Perhaps he had sensed there was something amiss, had known somehow that the mission would not be successful. But she had forced the issue by agreeing to terms she now realized he never expected her to accept. He had gone because she met his challenge. She had given herself to him for one night. And in return he went to France to save a man who had not lifted a finger to help Jacqueline when she had been in prison, had not even come to visit her out of fear that his name might be tainted by his association with her. And in trying to free this man, Armand had been caught.

"Why in God's name did I ask him to go back?" she cried, hating herself at that moment more than she knew possible.

"You must not blame yourself, Jacqueline," soothed Madeleine gently. "No one could ever make Armand do anything he did not want to do. If he has been caught and is still alive, his men will come up with some way to help him. At least now we know what his objective was. Surely that will help us in securing more information. If we only knew where he is being held, we could arrange to get him out."

Jacqueline rose from her chair and went to the window, suddenly restless with the need to move, to think, to do something. Armand had once told her that if he did not return, it was because he was dead. Jacqueline could not accept that possibility. Armand was too clever, to adept at thinking quickly, at changing his character, his accent, and his story. No, he could not be dead. Trapped, perhaps, maybe even arrested and imprisoned, but not dead. It was not possible. "There are over fifty prisons in Paris alone," she said vacantly as she watched the snow beginning to fall again. "Armand has never found it difficult getting into them. The question is, which one do we want to get into?"

Madeleine rose from her chair. "I shall suggest to Mr. Langdon that he and his men begin by investigating the Luxembourg," she declared. "Even if he is not being held there, if he was caught while rescuing your betrothed, someone at the prison will know about it."

Jacqueline nodded. "The prisoners at the Luxembourg are not held in solitary," she recalled, thinking back to when her father was incarcerated there. "There is a lively gossip mill, and an escape attempt would provide entertaining conversation for weeks afterward. If one of his men could get in there and talk to either a prisoner or a guard, he is certain to learn something of Armand's arrest."

After another sleepless night Jacqueline rose and listlessly went through the motions of daily life in the Harrington household. She took breakfast at eight, met with her tutor for English lessons at nine, had lunch at one, and then went to the music room with Suzanne and Séraphine in the afternoon to listen to Suzanne try her hand at the pianoforte. She and Madeleine had agreed not to inform Sir Edward or Lady Harrington of Armand's disappearance, since there was nothing either of them could do to help anyway, and when Armand returned he would doubtless expect that his exploits to France had remained confidential. It was also possible that whoever was detaining him in France had absolutely no idea of whom they had captured, since Armand had probably been in disguise at the time, and therefore it was more essential than ever to keep his identity a secret. Madeleine would instruct Sidney to investigate the Luxembourg, and Jacqueline would be informed the minute they had any new information. Beyond that, there was nothing she could do except wait, and pretend that everything was fine.

It was almost impossible.

To sit there calmly, and say yes, I will have tea, and no, I do not wish to go shopping, and that is very good Suzanne, when inside she was screaming *Where are you? What have they done to you?* and *Please, please forgive me for putting you in this awful situation,* was almost more than she could bear. By midafternoon her head was throbbing with an excruciatingly painful headache, so she sent the girls off to their governess and retired upstairs to her chamber, unable to carry on the charade any longer. She drew the curtains and the room was plunged into a heavy, gray darkness, which served to accentuate her desolation. When she lay back on the bed she noticed a tiny shaft of light piercing through a crack in the drapes with fierce determination, illuminating the slowly spinning dust motes and reminding her that there was a world outside, despite her effort to block it out temporarily. As she watched the dust float and twirl lazily in the warm ray, she recalled another moment, weeks ago, in a bare, cold little room in a cheap Paris inn, where she had awakened to see shafts of sunlight streaming through the cracks of the shutters. For a brief instant she had felt safe, and peaceful, and then she had realized that she was alone, and that Armand, or Citizen Julien as she had known him then, had deserted her. And she had been filled with panic, had been convinced that he had betrayed her. But he had returned, dark, scowling, enormous, filling the room with his presence, and demanded, *Did you think I would leave you, Mademoiselle?* as if the very idea was insulting, ludicrous, unfathomable. And when he saw that she truly had believed he had abandoned her, he made a solemn promise. *I will always come back for you, Made-*

moiselle. So simple, those words. So reassuring. And so
easy to say. He had saved her from being raped in her cell.
He had stolen her from her executioners. He had pulled
her from the clutches of a bloodthirsty mob and smuggled
her through the gates of Paris. He had gone after her
when she tried to escape him and torn her away from the
country she loved. He had nursed her when she had been
so ill with seasickness she wanted to die, and not left her
side once during the night. He had kept his word. He had
stayed with her until she was safely delivered. But he had
not done it for money, as she had believed. He had done it
because he wanted her to live, because by living she was a
slash across the face of the republican government, and
because her life was a spark of light against the darkness
that enveloped him every day of his life.

She never should have asked him to go back. But she
had thought she was hiring him, a simple business trans-
action, nothing more. She should have known better.
What kind of businessman would ask a woman to sleep
with him in exchange for risking his life? And when she
thought back to how it had been between them that night,
all apricot light and liquid fire and achingly sweet tenderness, how he had held her against the sleek, hard warmth
of his body, filling her with his strength, his life, his need,
and his pain, her eyes began to fill with unshed tears, and
in that moment she knew that he had changed her, had
reached out and touched her soul and made her feel things
she had never thought to feel, had not wanted to feel, not
now, not ever. "Damn you," she whispered into the darkness as the tears began to spill from her eyes and slowly
trickle down the sides of her cheeks and into her hair.
"Damn you."

She awoke to the sound of knocking at her door. "Jacklyn," cried an excited voice, "are you awake?"

Slowly she opened her eyes. The room was completely
black, so she knew it was night, but she had no idea how
many hours she had slept. Her eyelids felt sore and puffy,

and her head still ached, the dull, muffled ache that follows a restless, tormented sleep. She sat up and saw that she was still in her clothes, lying atop the counterpane. Stiffly she pushed herself up until she was sitting.

The door swung open, letting in a bright shaft of light and the shadowy figure of Laura, dressed in an enormous lemon-yellow gown, her dark hair a mass of buoyant curls decorated with matching yellow ribbons. She held a three-tiered candelabra, which cast a yellow glow on her.

"Oh Jacklyn, you will never guess," she squeaked with excitement, "he is back, safe and sound, and he is here, right now, downstairs in the library with my father."

"He is—here?" Jacqueline repeated vacantly, unable to believe that Laura could be telling her the truth.

"Yes!" shrieked Laura, almost beside herself with enthusiasm.

Jacqueline blinked and took a deep breath, trying to absorb what Laura was telling her. Armand was here? Now? It was incredible. It was wonderful. "But, how—"

"Come downstairs and he can tell you all about it himself," interrupted Laura, her curls bouncing as she shook her head impatiently. Her expression grew dreamy. "He has been through the most terrible ordeal, and then made a wonderfully daring escape, and he said that all through it, only the thought of you kept him going. Isn't that positively romantic?"

Jacqueline looked at Laura as if she had lost her mind. "He said he thought of me?" she repeated stupidly.

"Yes!" shrieked Laura again, piercing Jacqueline's ears with the high-pitched sound. "Come downstairs and hear it for yourself!"

Jacqueline needed no further encouragement. Now fully awake and shaking with excitement, she bolted from the bed and practically flew along the corridor and down the stairs ahead of Laura, her black wool skirts flapping and bobbing behind her, without shoes, her hair almost totally free from the pins that had been holding it earlier that day, tumbling down onto her shoulders in a tangle of disarray. Armand was back. It was too wonderful to be believed, but there it was. He was alive, he was safe, and he was back. And he had come to her. She raced down the hallway that led to the library, her breath coming in short, shallow gasps, desperate to see him, to touch him, to hear the warm, deep, velvety sound of his voice. She threw the door to the library open with a bang and burst into the room, panting from the exertion and her excitement, her eyes hungry for the sight of the man who stood with his back to her beside Sir Edward, politely laughing over some pleasant joke.

Icy-cold disappointment washed over her in a giant, suffocating wave, robbing her of the ability to speak. She stared blankly at the figure who stood before her, resplendent in a turquoise velvet frock coat shimmering with elaborate silver embroidery, with splendid lace cuffs blooming out from the sleeves, breeches of the snowiest satin over white stockings, and delicate black shoes with diamond buckles, his head capped with a magnificent silvery white wig, his slender hand idly holding a crystal glass half-filled with brandy. The Marquis de Biret turned slowly to face her. Using every shred of the self-discipline that had been instilled into her since she was a child, she bit down on her trembling lip and managed to meet his gaze calmly, instead of screaming *Where is Armand? Why is he not with you?* at the top of her lungs.

François-Louis stared at her. For the briefest of moments he looked stunned, as if she was not at all what he had expected. His eyes swept over her critically, and Jacqueline realized he was taking in her short, tangled hair, her wrinkled black gown, her pale, drawn skin, and puffy, red-rimmed eyes. A far cry from the sight she had been when he had last seen her, she recalled bitterly, over six months ago now, shortly before her father went to trial. She had received him in the garden at the Château de Lambert, dressed in a gown of fern green and pale yellow stripes, with an elegant matching ruched silk bonnet to protect her head from the sun as she worked clipping roses to fill an enormous basket. They had already decided to postpone their marriage until her father was released, but François-Louis had come to inform her that he was going to be extremely busy over the next few months and would not be able to see her as much as he would like. Jacqueline had understood, in fact not really minded, for she was far too preoccupied with her father's welfare and the running of the Château de Lambert. After her father was executed François-Louis had not come rushing to her side as he should have, but instead had sent her a note, scented and beautifully scripted, filled with words of sorrow for her loss, encouraging her to be strong, and apologizing for his inability to be with her due to a troublesome illness that necessitated that he remain in bed.

"Jacqueline, mon amour," he murmured, sweeping into a low bow before her and pressing her hand to his lips. He raised his eyes to hers, which were not deep blue at all, but a pale, watery blue, and frowned with apparent concern. *"Etes-vous malade?"* he demanded, asking if she was ill.

"Non," replied Jacqueline, desperately trying to control the maelstrom of emotions that were surging through her. Calm yourself, she told herself slowly. He may have decided they should travel separately. He might be on his way to her at this very moment. Anything was possible.

"I am relieved to hear it," François-Louis returned in heavily accented English. "Sir Edward and Lady Harrington have been telling me that you are faring well, except for your concern for my welfare these past few weeks. I hope now that I am here, all your concerns may be put to rest." He gave her a satisfied smile, evidently confident that the mere fact of his presence was enough to make her world right again.

"I am pleased to see that you are safe," returned Jacqueline honestly in English. *But where is Armand?*

"Well now," boomed Sir Edward, "let us all sit down while the marquis continues his story of how he managed to escape those murdering revolutionaries. Jacklyn, you sit over there," he instructed, pointing to a low chair next to Lady Harrington.

François-Louis positioned himself in front of the fireplace and leaned casually against the mantel, totally at ease before his small, attentive audience. "As you all know, I was arrested shortly after Jacqueline escaped, and falsely charged with conspiracy. I was imprisoned at the Luxembourg. It was, of course, horrendous beyond imagination, to be stripped of my rights and held against my will, but I was comforted by the knowledge that Jacqueline and her sisters were safe. I knew it was simply a matter of time before they called me before the Tribunal and sentenced me to death, but I had made peace with God and with myself, and was resigned to my fate." He paused to take a sip of his drink.

"How brave you were," sighed Laura, entranced.

Jacqueline turned her head to see Laura perched like a little yellow bird on the edge of her seat, gazing adoringly at François-Louis. She is attracted to him, she thought to herself, with more amazement than irritation.

The marquis gifted Laura with an indulgent smile. "It was the middle of the night," he continued in a low, hushed voice. "I was lying on my bed, or rather the small, hard frame that passes for a bed in prison, when I became aware of a dark figure prowling about in my room. I immediately sat up and demanded to know who the devil he was and what was he doing, skulking about in the middle of the night. I thought perhaps he was one of the guards, looking to see what he could steal from the prisoners while they slept. Such thievery is common in prison, but I was not about to let it happen to me or any of my fellow prisoners.

"Well, although the fellow is dressed in a guard's uniform, he is not someone that I have ever seen in the prison before. He looks a bit shocked when he realizes I am awake, but then regains his composure and asks if I know which of the prisoners is the Marquis de Biret. 'I am he,' I told him without hesitation. 'What is it you want of me?'"

Jacqueline thought it strange that Armand would be so careless as to ask a prisoner to identify the man he was looking for, but she said nothing.

" 'I am here to rescue you, Monsieur le Marquis,' the man replies gravely," continued François-Louis. " 'Are you indeed?' I asked, more than a little amused. 'And just how do you propose to do that, good citizen?' 'The guards are drugged,' the fellow assures me. 'Dress yourself in this uniform and we will simply walk out of here.' "

"As easy as that?" gasped Laura.

François-Louis smiled at her. "That is what the poor fellow thought, anyway. In truth, it was not such a bad plan, if not for one major flaw." He paused again and thoughtfully swirled the amber liquid in his glass around and around, teasing his audience, holding their attention taut.

Jacqueline bit down hard on her lip and resisted the urge to beg him to continue, which she knew was exactly what he wanted. It was all a game to him, she realized bitterly. He was talking about a man's life, about events that could shed light on what had happened to Armand, but to the Marquis de Biret, who was standing safe and sound in a warm English library sipping brandy before the fire, it was simply a performance, an interesting story he would tell again and again before he had exhausted its entertainment value in the privileged circles of English society.

"Come now, man, do not leave us hanging, what was the flaw?" demanded Sir Edward jovially.

"I am afraid not quite all the guards were drugged," replied François-Louis. "We made it out of my cell and through the corridors of the prison, but when we stepped outside there were a half-dozen armed guards waiting there to greet us."

"Oh my," breathed Laura with a mixture of excitement and horror. "Whatever did you do then?"

"We had to fight them," François-Louis told her casually, as if such activities were a normal part of his everyday life. "I myself managed to incapacitate four of them, and was working on a fifth when I noticed that my accomplice was not faring nearly so well."

"What do you mean?" demanded Jacqueline sharply.

François-Louis peered at her over the crystal rim of his glass. "I mean he was being badly beaten," he clarified.

Jacqueline paled.

"De Biret, perhaps such details are not entirely appropriate in the company of ladies," suggested Sir Edward.

"My apologies," returned François-Louis with a small bow to Jacqueline. "I forget that I am no longer in France, where violence and bloodshed is a part of everyday life, even for ladies."

Jacqueline returned his apology with an icy stare. No one needed to tell her what life in France was like. Dear God, why had she ever asked Armand to go there?

"Naturally I went to the man's assistance, and succeeded in making the odds a bit more even, at which point he was able to break free and we both started to run," continued François-Louis. "We actually put some distance between ourselves and the guards, but the Luxembourg grounds are extensive and there was little to offer us cover. The guards began to fire upon us. I was fortunate enough to escape being hit, but my accomplice was not so lucky."

Jacqueline bit down viciously on her lip to keep from crying out. The warm, metallic taste of blood seeped onto her tongue.

"Of course I stopped and tried to help him up, but his injury was in the leg, and severe enough that he was no longer able to run. 'Go on without me,' he pleaded, 'that at least one of us might live.' And so, although it went against the most basic code of honor by which I have always led my life, I made the decision that it was better for me to live and see that his life was not wasted for naught. 'God be with you, friend,' I said. And then I ran, as hard and as fast as I could, until I was sure the devil himself could not have kept up with me had he wanted to. And then—"

"You left him there?" interrupted Jacqueline suddenly in French, unable to control herself any longer. It could not be true. He was mistaken. "You left him injured and bleeding in the snow, for the National Guard to arrest?"

"There was nothing I could do for him," returned François-Louis flatly, speaking to her in French. "I thought it best that at least one of us get away."

"You could have tried to help him," insisted Jacqueline, her voice beginning to shake with emotion. "You could have helped him up and dragged him with you. You could have fought the guards and tried to secure a weapon. You could have held one of the guards hostage. You could have allowed yourself to be arrested with him and looked for another opportunity to escape—" She was babbling on in French, listing off all the alternatives she would have tried before abandoning the man who had tried to save her life. "You could have done something, *anything,* besides leaving him there—"

"Jacqueline," interrupted François-Louis firmly, visibly puffing up with indignation, "you speak of things you know nothing about. You yourself tried to take on the National Guard when they went to arrest your brother, and where did it get you? Antoine was still arrested, and you were sentenced to death by the Tribunal—"

"At least I tried to help him," countered Jacqueline, her voice breaking. "At least I did not simply stand back and let those murderers take him—"

"Jacklyn, my dear, I believe you are overwrought," broke in Lady Harrington, who had been trying without success to follow their argument. She rose from her chair and went to her. "I think you should come upstairs with me now," she said gently, holding out her hand. "The marquis is spending the night here. You may see him again tomorrow, when you are feeling better."

Jacqueline looked up at Lady Harrington through blurred eyes. Numbly she reached out and took her hand, taking comfort from the strength of the older woman's firm, motherly grip.

"If you will excuse us," said Lady Harrington as she steered Jacqueline toward the door. "We bid you good night."

Jacqueline did not turn, could not bring herself even to look at François-Louis. Blindly she allowed herself to be led out of the room, wishing to the very depths of her soul that she had never asked for the safe return of the Marquis de Biret.

Chapter 11

Crying, soft, feminine and persistent, filled the frozen morning stillness of the prison called La Force.

Armand did not try to block it out as he used to when he first arrived. Instead he forced himself to listen, using the pitiful whimpering to intensify his fury as he slowly pushed himself up and down against the frigid stone floor of his cell. The muscles of his arms and chest were rigid and swollen from the effort. He knew they would ache by tonight, but he bit down hard on his teeth and forced himself to do five more, and then five again, enjoying the utter concentration that the task demanded, the single-mindedness of purpose that temporarily relieved him from thinking of anything but pushing his body to its absolute limits. His arms quivered and shook in protest at their treatment, and with a grunt of satisfaction he released them and fell against the floor, breathing heavily, his hot cheek resting against the filthy, cold stones. He turned over onto his back and stretched his arms out above him, then slowly began to lower and raise them in a smooth arc over his chest, flexing his wrists, then bending his elbows, easing away the rigid tension in his muscles, stretching them to minimize the pain he knew he would feel later. After a minute he stood and gave equal attention to stretching out the muscles in his back, his sides, and his legs, rewarding them for the exercises he had put them through these past two hours. He breathed slowly and deeply, wondering at his ability to inhale air that on his arrival had seemed so thick and foul he had thought he would probably choke on it. The realization that he had finally grown accustomed to it revolted him.

His exercises done, he walked over to the wall on the far side of his cell and studied the neat row of pale nicks carved into it. There were twenty-one of them, each one representing another endless day spent in this godforsaken hole. He bent down, picked up a small, sharp stone that lay in the corner, and patiently added another one. He took his time with the task, taking care that the mark he made was even with the others, and wondering absently if he should go back to the beginning and make all the nicks a little deeper so they would be sure to last once he was gone from this place. He ultimately decided against it, feeling it did not matter whether the nicks lasted or not, as long as they were there to help him keep track right now. He knew he had only considered it because the day stretched out emptily in front of him and he wanted something to do, and that realization seemed so grossly pathetic he was infuriated with himself. He heaved the stone against the wall with such force it burst into three small, uneven shards, and he refused to acknowledge his regret at destroying his writing instrument by going over to pick up the pieces. Instead he threw himself down against the hardness of his trestle bed, which was far too short to accommodate his height, and attempted to focus on something other than this place. He closed his eyes and tried to free his mind so pleasant images would appear, but for some reason nothing would come, not even a mental picture of Angélique, and he was filled with a crushing sense of despair.

He wanted a drink badly. It was unlike him to give in to self-pity, but at the moment he felt that if he could just down a bottle or two, things might start to look up. It was ridiculous, of course, it went against everything he had taught himself about survival, but he did not care. He wanted a drink, almost as much as he wanted to see Jacqueline, to hold her in his arms and feel the creamy slim softness of her crushed against him, just once more before they executed him, and that also seemed so pitiful and ridiculous he began to laugh, a harsh, mocking sound that was certain to confuse the guards and his fellow inmates. No doubt they would think he was starting to become unbalanced. He wondered grimly if perhaps he was.

He was going to die. He was quite sure of it, having considered all the possible alternatives. He had no doubt that Sidney and his men had looked for him, but without knowing who he had gone to France to save, the chances of them tracking him down in this prison were minimal. He had been arrested under the identity of Citizen Michel Belanger, so a check of prison records would lend no clue as to where he was incarcerated. In accordance with his instructions, the crew of *The Angélique* would have returned to England after he missed meeting them by a week. He knew Sidney would not leave it at that, that he would desperately try to dig up information on who had been Armand's target in France. But Armand never made any notes about whom he was going to rescue, so there would be no written clues waiting for Sidney at his home. The only person who could offer any information was Jacqueline, and Sidney would have no reason to think to question her.

He wondered if her precious marquis had arrived in England yet. He probably had, given that Bourdon had agreed to honor his safe passage out of France in exchange for Armand. The papers Armand had provided him with were good. As long as De Biret kept his head there would be no reason for him to be detained while he traveled to the coast. Once he got there, Armand had no doubt that Monsieur le Marquis was resourceful enough to get himself onto a ship to England. The counterrevolutionary network ran deep, and the profits of illicit trade meant there were usually British smuggling ships to be found looming off the coast. For many, the immediate profits of war were far sweeter and certainly more tangible than the bloated ideals the revolutionary government had promised but not managed to deliver.

What kind of welcome would Jacqueline give her long-lost betrothed? he wondered with contempt. Would she run to him and shower him with tears, her beautifully aristocratic face pale and drawn with worry? Unlikely, he decided. Quite frankly, he could not imagine Jacqueline showering anyone with tears. She had never wept in his presence, not when she had been sentenced to death, nor when he had told her of Antoine's death, nor even when she had stood alone on the deck of *The Angélique* and watched the lights of her beloved France flicker and fade into the darkness. Jacqueline, he sensed, carried far too much pain, and death, and hatred, to let anything make her cry.

But she was nothing if not practical, his Jacqueline. After all, had she not agreed to sleep with him, an untitled, dishonorable merchant of human cargo, simply to see her far more noble betrothed safely delivered to her? And with that same practicality in mind, she had ultimately decided to permit herself to enjoy it. After all, why not? She was only sampling a taste of what De Biret would be giving her every night of her married life, if the man had either the brains or the balls to realize what a brilliantly erotic jewel he had stumbled upon. He clenched his fists in fury at the thought of De Biret laying his hands upon her. It was not right that he should be permitted to do so. The man was a spineless fop who had left her to rot and die in the Conciergerie without so much as paying a visit to see how she was faring. And then, when he was threatened with his own execution, he agreed to a vile, cowardly plan in which the life of the man who sought to save him was traded for his own. His actions filled Armand with loathing. The man was not fit to be in the same room with Jacqueline, never mind touch her and taste her and call her his wife. He shifted restlessly on the bed and stared up at the ceiling.

Jacqueline would never know the true circumstances of her betrothed's escape, he reflected bitterly. De Biret would undoubtedly describe it to her as if he had performed some great act of daring and heroism, and she would have no reason not to believe him. She would probably be dismayed that Armand had not returned, perhaps even experience some needling twinge of guilt, but in time she would get over it. The revolution had forced Mademoiselle Jacqueline de Lambert to contend with tragedies and losses far greater than his death. He wondered if she would marry her marquis right away. She probably would. After all, there was no reason to wait.

He let out a bitter sigh and closed his eyes.

She would be forced to wear a gown other than black for the occasion. He smiled. If he were to pick a gown for her, it would be of the iciest gray silk, shot throughout with shimmering strands of silver, to match the sparkling brilliance of her silvery eyes. Her honey-colored hair would be piled high in loose curls, with a few wayward tendrils cascading down the length of her neck, idly grazing the silken skin across her collarbone. If she were his, he would see to it that she had diamonds to wear, for only the rarest and most brilliant of diamonds could lie against her skin and not be dulled by the magnificence of her own beauty. And when they were finally alone, he would slowly remove the pins from her hair until it poured over her shoulders like liquid gold, and then he would reach out and gently take her face in his hands and claim her lips with his, tasting her and touching her and coaxing her until she was clinging to him and pressing against him with all the need and hunger that he knew she held locked within her. He let out a groan of frustration and angrily flung his arm over his eyes, blocking out the image.

A new thought occurred to him. What if, during their one incredible night of lovemaking, they had managed to create a child? It was unlikely, but possible nonetheless. Strangely enough, the thought of leaving behind a child with Jacqueline did not displease him in the least. But the realization that their child would be raised as the son or daughter of the Marquis de Biret filled him with a dark and painful rage. The man was weak, vain, selfish, and cowardly. What the hell kind of father would he make? Not that he himself had been much of a father to Angélique, or husband to Lucette, he reminded himself with disgust. He had loved them more than anything in the world, but that had not stopped him from spending most of his time chasing his own pleasure rather than taking care of them. He had not been able to protect them, had not been there when they needed him most. He had failed them, just as he had failed his mother. And if, by some twisted jest of fate, he had managed to create a child with Jacqueline, he was failing that child, too, by dying and abandoning it to be raised by a lily-livered coward who cared more about his own preservation than the principles by which he lived his life.

Voices were filtering down the corridor, interrupting his thoughts. One was the coarse, guttural sound of his jailer, a nasty, hulking brute by the name of Pinard, who never missed an opportunity to make it clear to his prisoners that he enjoyed his work immensely. The other voice was clipped, tense, and filled with impatient authority. Armand's lips curved into a smile. Nicolas Bourdon had finally come to pay him another visit. The day was going to have some diversion after all.

The jangling of heavy keys sounded outside his door. He stood up so he could meet his guest on his feet and waited with eager anticipation as the door creaked and then swung open, revealing the filthy Pinard and the immaculately dressed Nicolas Bourdon.

"Inspector Bourdon, it is my pleasure to welcome you once again to my humble quarters," Armand murmured as he made a small bow. "You will, I hope, forgive the condition of my suite, but the staff here is not overly preoccupied with matters of cleanliness." He shook his head and sighed dramatically.

"Leave us," snapped Nicolas to the jailer as he stripped off his heavy leather gloves. He waited until the door had closed before turning his attention to Armand.

"Perhaps you would like to sit," suggested Armand graciously, indicating a hard wooden chair.

"No," replied Nicolas, his voice cold and adamant, as if accepting Armand's invitation to sit would be equivalent to accepting a bribe.

"Then you will not mind if I do?" returned Armand,

already pulling out the chair and stretching his long legs in front of him as he seated himself. He lazily folded his arms across his chest and regarded Nicolas with amusement. "Tell me, Inspector Bourdon, to what do I owe the honor of your visit?"

Nicolas scowled. It was clear he did not think Armand should be so relaxed in his presence. "I thought perhaps you might have tired of your accommodations," he began, his voice sarcastic and slightly taunting.

"You have come to offer decorating suggestions?" asked Armand pleasantly, as if the idea appealed to him immensely.

Nicolas ignored the remark. "I have been authorized by the Committee of Public Safety to make you an offer which I think you will find most interesting." He paused, waiting for some expression of curiosity from his audience. Armand eyed him calmly and said nothing.

Nicolas began to slap his gloves rhythmically against his thigh. "If you are ready to confess, we could see about having you moved to a place considerably more comfortable."

Armand looked at him in confusion. "Confess?" he repeated blankly.

"I could not get you a full pardon, of course," qualified Nicolas. "The Committee of Public Safety does not take kindly to those who plot against the Republic of France. But I can see to it your life is spared, and that you are sentenced only to serving time. In exchange for saving the Tribunal the costly business of another trial, they have agreed to be lenient. I am willing to suggest to them that you be deported. Of course there would be forced labor involved," he acknowledged, "but that would not last forever. Perhaps ten years, say fifteen at the very most. I am told the climate in the tropical colonies is actually quite pleasant. I think you would find such an arrangement preferable to the chill of this cell, or the blade of the guillotine."

Armand thoughtfully drew his eyebrows together, pretending to contemplate Nicolas's offer. "That's it?" he asked after a moment's silence, his voice tinged with suspicion. "You simply want me to confess?"

"In writing, of course," qualified Nicolas. "I need you to produce a signed statement outlining your crimes against the Republic of France. Once you have done that, I will present it to the Committee of Public Safety. In exchange for your cooperation you will be spared execution."

"Why would they be interested in sparing me?" demanded Armand, obviously still not convinced.

Nicolas casually slapped his gloves against his thigh. "France's prisons are exploding. Paris alone is holding over seven thousand people who are awaiting trial and vehemently protesting their innocence. The guillotine, as impressive an instrument as it is, simply cannot chop heads fast enough. So you see, any confessions that reduce the work of the Tribunal are welcome. Especially," he emphasized, "if they include the names of your connections and accomplices."

Armand looked at him blankly. "Accomplices?"

"Those who have aided you in securing false documents, transportation, information, and so on," explained Nicolas.

"Oh," replied Armand stupidly. "Those accomplices."

"Well, what do you say?" demanded Nicolas. "Do you wish to accept my offer?"

Armand hesitated a moment, enjoying the act of keeping Nicolas in suspense. Then he looked at him brightly. "Absolutely," he exclaimed. "I would be a fool not to."

"I have quill and paper with me," offered Nicolas as he produced them from a pocket inside his heavy overcoat.

"How fortuitous," observed Armand. "Bring them here and I shall write out my confession immediately."

Armand pulled his chair over to a small table and waited for Nicolas to lay out paper, a quill, and a small pot of ink. He took up the pen, dipped it in the ink, and began to scratch it quickly across the page, writing in bold, sweeping strokes. Nicolas stood by and watched him with satisfaction, obviously pleased with himself at having been able to secure a confession. After a moment Armand paused, scanned what he had written, and signed it.

"Here you go," he said brightly, holding the paper out to Nicolas.

"So fast?" asked Nicolas in confusion as he took the document. He quickly read through what Armand had written, which was a brief confession of impersonating a member of the National Guard and unsuccessfully attempting to rescue the Marquis de Biret from the Luxembourg prison, for which he was extremely repentant. The confession was signed by Citizen Michel Belanger.

"You know this is not what I want," grated out Nicolas, his face reddening with fury.

Armand looked at him with feigned confusion. "No?" he returned innocently.

"Do not play games with me," Nicolas warned, his voice soft and threatening. "You know as well as I that you are not Citizen Michel Belanger."

"Is that so?" asked Armand with amusement. "How interesting. Pray, do not keep me in suspense, Inspector. Who am I?"

Nicolas smiled darkly. "You, my friend, are the one they call the Black Prince."

"Am I indeed?" returned Armand, his tone patronizing and slightly mocking.

Nicolas nodded. "You are the same man who sold drugged wine to the guards in the disguise of Citizen Laurent, winemaker."

"You don't say?" said Armand. He leaned back in his chair and laced his fingers behind his head. "How intriguing. Tell me, have the guards attested to this?"

"No," admitted Nicolas, his irritation apparent. "Evidently your disguise was good, because those fools say they do not believe you could be the same one." He stepped in closer to Armand and began to circle him slowly, like an animal closing in on its prey. "But then, they are not aware of your remarkable ability to play any role you please," he conceded darkly. "They have not made a point of studying your career." He stopped and stared hard at him. "And they have not had the opportunity to see you in disguise before." He bent his head so that it was level with Armand's. "Have they—Citizen Julien?"

Armand met his gaze calmly, looking more amused than interested. He was not about to give Nicolas any indication that he was correct in his assumptions.

From the moment of his arrest Nicolas had been intent on proving he had successfully snared the Black Prince, and was furious when François-Louis was unable to confirm this. Armand suspected Nicolas's need to trap him was partly for his own personal satisfaction. The idea that he had caught the man who had stolen Jacqueline from him was sweet vengeance indeed. Such a remarkable achievement was also certain to impress the Committee of Public Safety, and would undoubtedly be generously rewarded. But at the moment Nicolas lacked proof. The Marquis de Biret had written a letter to his betrothed asking for help, but there was nothing to suggest that Citizen Michel Belanger had been acting on behalf of Jacqueline de Lambert, or that he was the one known as the Black Prince. Knowing that Nicolas was desperate to prove he had caught an important enemy and make himself a hero to the Republic gave Armand a perverse satisfaction in denying him that proof. And whether they ultimately decided he was the Black Prince or not, he would die before he revealed the names of those who helped him with information, false documents, and transportation.

"I am afraid you are mistaken, Inspector," he declared nonchalantly.

Nicolas ignored his denial. "You have plagued the Republic in many forms this past year," he continued as he began to circle again. "Young and old. Male and female. Constantly changing your face, your hair, your character, and your accents. You have been a formidable enemy, always managing to stay just one step ahead of revolutionary justice." He stopped circling and stood in front of him. "But your days as a counterrevolutionary and royalist sympathizer are over, my friend." He smiled, an expression of victory stained with bitterness. "You sealed your fate the day you stopped me from taking what was rightfully mine. You remember the moment, don't you?" he demanded softly. He leaned in close to him. "I always meant to have the little bitch, one way or another. But you interrupted us. And then you took her away." He straightened up again and began to pace the confines of the cell. "I paid for that, I can tell you. The chief inspector lets the Black Prince take a condemned prisoner right out from under his nose. They threatened to arrest me. They said I must have been an accessory, because of my prior personal relationship with the former Mademoiselle de Lambert and her family." He shook his head in disbelief. "I was the one who arranged for her father and brother's arrest, and there they are saying I must have helped her. Ironic, don't you think?"

Armand politely tried to stifle an enormous yawn and stretched his arms high above his head. "Forgive me, Inspector Bourdon, I am sure this story of yours really is fascinating, but as I do not know the people of whom you speak, I am afraid I can only offer limited interest."

Nicolas's face hardened into a mask of hatred and contempt. "Well, Monsieur le Prince, perhaps this will hold your interest a little better," he snarled. He began to pace again. "I know you are the Black Prince, and I intend to see to it that you are tried and convicted as such. I don't give a damn if it takes months, years, or the rest of your worthless, miserable life, do you understand? You can sit and rot in this stinking cess pit until you confess, or until I have the necessary proof to see you executed as such. But think carefully about the cost of remaining silent," he warned. "First, you will lose your health. Bad food, stale air, cold, damp, cramped quarters—these things will quickly take their toll on your body. And of course, as the months and years go by, your youth will fade into the past. All you will have will be your memories, which will become distant and cloudy. Finally you will start to lose your mind, as your life becomes a chain of endless, empty, meaningless days and hours and minutes, with no beginning and no end. So let me know when you are ready to confess, Monsieur le Prince," he stated triumphantly. "You can either have a speedy trial and be executed with dignity, or you can exist in these subhuman conditions and die an appallingly slow, lingering, filthy, humiliating death."

Loud, deep, even snoring filled the confines of the tiny cell. Nicolas turned to see the subject of his discourse sound asleep, with his head resting on one shoulder and his long legs comfortably stretched out in front of him. His expression seemed serene, as though he were blissfully unaware of the horrors Nicolas had just described to him. Nicolas ground his teeth together in frustration.

"Guard!" he barked through the small grille in the heavy wooden door. He turned to look at Armand as he waited for the guard to let him out. "As you wish, my friend," he spat between clenched teeth. "Stay here and rot for as long as you like."

Jacqueline spent the morning in her room, seeking to isolate herself from the rest of the world. She knew eventually she would have to go downstairs and face François-Louis, but first she needed time to herself.

Armand had been captured. Her worst fears had been confirmed. Somehow, something had gone terribly wrong. The National Guard had been there waiting for him. Perhaps there had been an error in his plan. Or perhaps his luck had simply run out. Either way, he had been shot, possibly even injured fatally, and François-Louis had left him there.

It was not unforgivable that he had done so, she realized. After all, Armand had insisted that he go on. She knew if Armand felt he was going to die, he would not want it to be for nothing. But somehow the idea that Armand was dead was inconceivable, unacceptable, impossible. After all, François-Louis had seen him captured, but he had not seen him die. Jacqueline knew if Armand's injuries were severe he would not last long in the harsh, septic conditions of a Paris prison. But somewhere between logic and likelihood was a small, radiant spark of hope, a slim chance that he had survived his injury and had not yet been executed. It seemed so unlikely she almost brushed it aside, but the alternative was accepting the fact that she was responsible for Armand's death, and that was so devastating she decided to cling to the fragile possibility that he was alive. Which left her with two choices. She could either remain in England and pray for the improbable chance that somehow Armand could escape on his own. Or she could go to France and try to help him.

By the time her maid came knocking at her door to announce that Monsieur le Marquis was waiting to see her in the music room, she had made up her mind. She went down the stairs with a sense of purpose she had not felt in weeks, and she drew comfort and strength from it. There was no more time to wallow in a sense of helplessness, feeling sorry for herself and angry at God for destroying her life. Everything had suddenly become incredibly simple. Armand was in danger and he needed someone to help him. Jacqueline would go to France and try to get him out of there. She had no idea how she would do it, and she knew the chances of her being successful were almost nonexistent. It did not matter. All that mattered was Armand needed her. She would try her best not to fail him.

Lively music was filtering down the hallway from the music room. When Jacqueline reached the doorway she saw François-Louis seated at the pianoforte merrily playing a gavotte while Laura sat in a chair and gazed at him, her eyes bright and round with admiration. She looked quite pretty in a low-cut gown of white satin striped with pink and decorated with small clusters of pink satin flowers. François-Louis was almost as pretty as she was, in his silvery white wig and an apple-green frock coat over a silk waistcoat of buttery yellow with green embroidery. Great quantities of lace puffed out from his sleeves, flouncing up and down as his pale hands danced effortlessly over the ivory keys. This is my betrothed, she thought to herself, and she was stunned at how strange that seemed. François-Louis had come from her world. He shared her history and her convictions, he understood the beliefs she had been raised with and knew firsthand what the revolution had cost her. In another time, in a different music room, that would have been her seated before him in a pretty day gown, watching him with open pleasure as he entertained her with his musical proficiency and his easy manner.

The piece ended, and Laura began to clap enthusiastically. "That was wonderful," she exclaimed, her voice high and sweet, like the chirping of a bird. "Simply wonderful. Oh, but you cannot stop now, François-Louis, surely there is something else you have not yet played for me."

François-Louis stood up from the piano and dramatically laid his hand over his heart. "Mademoiselle Laura, for the sunshine you bring when you enter a room with that beautiful smile of yours, I would play until I had exhausted my entire repertoire, and then, just to keep you near me, I would start at the beginning of your father's musical library and not stop until I had played every last note." He stepped away from the piano, bowed low before her, and then took her hand from her lap and pressed a gallant kiss against it, causing Laura to sigh prettily and beam with pleasure.

"Perhaps I must—come back later," stammered Jacqueline awkwardly in English, feeling like an intruder. She vaguely wondered why the flirtatious little scene she just witnessed did not annoy her for any reason other than that it seemed so contrived and silly.

François-Louis straightened up and smiled, obviously not disturbed in the least that Jacqueline was there. Laura seemed a little more startled, but she did not appear to be uncomfortable with the fact that the man Jacqueline was engaged to marry had just been fawning over her. If anything, the look she gave Jacqueline was strangely triumphant, as if she had set out to prove something and had been successful.

"Jacqueline, we are pleased to see you," said François-Louis pleasantly. "Are you feeling better today?" He was smiling but his eyes were slightly wary, as if she was a stranger to him and he was not quite certain how to deal with her.

"I am fine," replied Jacqueline, disliking immensely the insinuation that her behavior last night was due to the fact that she was unwell. "You wished to speak to me?" she demanded stiffly. Now that she had made the decision to help Armand, every moment was precious. She was not about to waste time sitting here listening to François-Louis play the pianoforte.

"Yes." He turned to Laura. "Mademoiselle Laura, it is necessary that I speak to Jacqueline in French, as both of us are more at ease in that language. Since we have no wish to appear impolite, perhaps you will excuse us?"

Laura smiled prettily. "Of course," she answered sweetly. She rose from her chair and floated across the room, leaving the scent of rose water behind her.

François-Louis waited until she was gone, and then he walked over and closed the door. "So, Jacqueline," he said in French as he turned to face her, "it has been a long time."

"You look well, François-Louis," commented Jacqueline. "Obviously prison life did not overly disagree with you."

He shrugged his shoulders. "I adapted to the conditions," he replied nonchalantly. "Also, I am the Marquis de Biret. They knew better than to throw me into a prison with the scum off the streets." He pulled a scented lace handkerchief out from his sleeve and dabbed his forehead.

"Like the Conciergerie?" retorted Jacqueline sarcastically.

"It was most unfortunate that they took you and Antoine there," he observed. "It must have been terrible for both of you." He looked at her sympathetically.

"Antoine died there," she whispered. She wanted to say it in anger, but the words were too painful to say in a harsh voice.

He stepped toward her and took her hand between his. "If I could bring him back for you, my sweet Jacqueline, I would, even if it meant I had to sacrifice my own life." His voice was gentle and kind, and for a moment Jacqueline allowed herself to draw comfort from it. "However," he continued, "we must honor his memory, and your father's, and that of every member of the noblesse who has fallen victim to this blood-soaked revolution, by carrying on with our own lives. We must show those filthy peasants that we cannot be destroyed, and that we will not tolerate their stealing what is rightfully ours."

Those filthy peasants. That was how François-Louis dismissed most of the population of France. At one time she would have agreed with such a statement and not thought anything of it. But something bothered her now about such a sweeping denunciation of her fellow countrymen. She found herself thinking back to her argument with Armand, who told her that the peasants were people who starved as they struggled to grow food out of land that belonged to the nobility. Food that would be served on tables groaning under the weight of different dishes, served on elegant china and gleaming silver, while the men, women, and children who had plowed and planted and harvested and hauled it to market went to bed cold, dirty, and hungry. Surely there was something wrong with a system that propagated such misery?

"I will be leaving the hospitality of the Harringtons today to stay with an old friend," continued François-Louis, interrupting her thoughts. "I only accepted Lady Harrington's kind invitation to remain last night so I could see you. However, before I go, I am afraid I find myself in a rather embarrassing predicament, and am forced to ask a favor of you."

"Yes?"

He released her hand and coughed slightly. "I find myself temporarily short of funds," he began awkwardly. "Unfortunately I did not have the foresight to funnel money out of France when such activities were possible. Hence I must ask if there is any way you could lend me some money until I find a way to resolve this most distressing situation."

"Of course," replied Jacqueline hesitantly. "I regret it cannot be much, however, as I am also rather short of funds," she apologized. "At the moment my sisters and I are living on the generosity of the Harringtons." Although she had set up a fund with Sir Edward the previous year to pay for the expenses of Suzanne and Séraphine, she knew Sir Edward had been most reluctant to draw upon it. The amount was small, and was all the equity she and the girls had.

"I shall be most grateful for whatever assistance you can offer," stated François-Louis politely.

"Let Sir Edward know what your banking arrangements are, and I will ask him to transfer five hundred pounds into your account."

"Five hundred pounds?" repeated François-Louis, as if he had not heard correctly.

Jacqueline felt herself torn between embarrassment and irritation. She knew that with François-Louis's customary lavish style, five hundred pounds was nothing. "It is all I can afford," she informed him tautly. She was sure the outfit he wore had cost more than that and wondered how he had managed to pay for it.

"I appreciate your generosity," he returned stiffly. He made a great show of tucking his handkerchief back into his sleeve. "There is one more matter I think we should discuss before I go."

She regarded him curiously. "What is that?"

"The matter of our betrothal." He stepped over to look out the window. "I wish to know your feelings on the subject. It goes without saying that our circumstances have changed considerably since your father and I first worked out the terms of our betrothal." He coughed slightly. "Other than my title, I have far less to offer you here than I did in France. My financial future is, shall we say, somewhat uncertain. Since you are also without funds, I would understand if you told me that you wished to marry some English noble who could comfortably provide for you and your sisters." He turned to face her. "In short, I would like you to know that I will not hold you to our betrothal if you do not wish it."

She was silent for a moment. He was offering her a way out, releasing her from an agreement she was not at all sure she wanted to honor. On the one hand, he was her father's choice. The esteemed Marquis de Biret, a man of honor, character, and wealth, whose noble lineage went back over three centuries. In France he had been an immensely desirable match. Beyond his wealth and his pedigree, women had always found François-Louis handsome, charming, and an amusing companion. Certainly Jacqueline used to think so. If she had to marry, he would have made an excellent choice, even now. He was titled. He was from her world. He spoke her language. He had known her father and brother, and spent time at the Château de Lambert. He understood completely what she had lost. And when things finally returned to normal in France, he would undoubtedly want to move back.

But marriage and her future were not at the forefront of her mind just now. All she could think about was returning immediately to France to help Armand. If by some miracle she was successful at that, she would stay to kill Nicolas. Beyond that she would not think. But since she could not inform François-Louis of her plans, how could she possibly break off their betrothal without causing him insult? It would simply look like she did not want him because he did not have any money. Such a gesture would be callous and humiliating. He deserved better than that.

"François-Louis, there is no need to make such a decision now," she pointed out reasonably. "We have both been thrust into a new country, and we need time to adjust. There is no great urgency to this matter. If it is acceptable to you, I think we should discuss it again sometime in the future."

He gave her a little bow, the picture of elegant formality. "As you wish, Jacqueline," he declared solemnly. "We shall speak of this again at a later date."

He stepped toward her, rested his hands lightly on her shoulders, and lowered his head to press a kiss against her lips. The kiss surprised her, not because it was not his right to give her one, but because it was so restrained, so formal, so utterly proper. So utterly unlike the kisses Armand gave her, which caused restless heat to blaze through her entire being like a streak of lightning. Was it always like this? she wondered as she stared up into his pale blue eyes, acutely aware of the sickly-sweet scent of his cologne.

"I will be leaving for my friend's home this afternoon," he informed her. "But I shall call upon you once a week, to see that you are faring well. I will also leave my address with Sir Edward, so if you need to contact me you will know how to do so."

I will be gone within a day or two, she thought to herself. I may never see you again, François-Louis. "Thank you," she murmured softly.

He bowed and began to move toward the door.

"François-Louis," she called out, suddenly not quite ready to let him go. Perhaps he could tell her something else about Armand. Perhaps he could assure her that he was not dead. Perhaps he would help her.

He turned and looked at her questioningly. "Yes?"

She stared at him, a frothy vision of apple and butter silk and snowy-white curls. Here was the man she had once thought she would marry. He was the reason she had sent Armand to France. The man who had abandoned him, leaving him injured and bleeding on the ground so he could escape. "Nothing," she stammered.

He regarded her curiously, then bowed again and left the room.

She turned to stare out the window, feeling only a small amount of grief that yet another part of the life that had been so comfortable and familiar had come to a sudden end.

Chapter 12

Icy-cold sea air blasted against the ashen skin of her face as Jacqueline leaned over the rail of *The Angélique* and fervently prayed for death. The seasickness would eventually pass, she knew, but that seemed like small consolation as her body gave another violent heave and a terrible retching sound tore from her throat. There was nothing left in her stomach to bring up, she was certain of it, but her body continued to heave and so she remained where she was. She stared bleakly at the hull of the ship as it rose and then crashed against the frigid, black seawater, trying to focus on the movement. Somehow that was more comforting than sitting in Armand's cabin watching the room lurch up and down.

She pressed her forehead against the freezing cold wood of the railing and drew a shaky breath. The air was salty but clean, and she felt a little better. She had forgotten how terrible seasickness was. Not that it would have made any difference in her decision to make this journey. Armand was in France; to get to him she had to cross the channel. It was that simple. Other than the seasickness, the most difficult part of it so far had been getting Sidney Langdon to see just how simple it was.

After François-Louis left, Jacqueline penned a note to Armand's sister, Madeleine, asking her to come for a visit. When she arrived later that afternoon, Jacqueline informed her that she had new information about Armand's capture and needed to see Monsieur Langdon immediately. Under the pretext of going out for a drive, the two women went to his home, where Jacqueline announced that she was going to France to find Armand, and if Sidney and Armand's men wanted to help, they could take her as far as Calais. At first he refused, informing her that he was not about to take responsibility for her death, and that if she knew something about Armand then she should just tell him and let the crew of *The Angélique* take it from there. Jacqueline assured him as politely as possible that she was going to France whether Sidney took her there or not, and that she would not reveal one detail of Armand's capture until she had been set ashore in Calais.

The ensuing argument had been long and loud, but Jacqueline remained adamant and in the end Sidney had relented. It was obvious that his loyalty to Armand and his desire to see him rescued outweighed the responsibility he felt for Jacqueline's safety. Within twenty-four hours the crew had been assembled, the ship made ready, and Jacqueline had stolen out of the Harrington home and was on her way to Dover with Sidney, having left behind a brief note in which she explained to Sir Edward and Lady Harrington that there was something she simply had to do and she trusted them to care for Suzanne and Séraphine until her return.

And so here she was, so ill she barely could stand, wondering how she was going to make it down the steps to her cabin, never mind how she was going to travel to Paris and find Armand and save him. Her body heaved again and she was forced to hang over the rail and retch into the frigid salt spray of the ocean. She wanted to weep, she wanted to collapse in a pool on the deck and die, and more than anything she wanted Armand to lift her in his arms and put her to bed, telling her in no uncertain terms as he did so that she was not to die because it would be bad for business if she did.

She did not notice when Sidney walked up to her, only felt someone placing a thick woolen blanket around her shoulders, then turn her away from the railing and begin to guide her across the slippery deck to the stairs that led to the cabins below.

"You need to rest awhile," he told her in French as he

escorted her to Armand's cabin and opened the door. "We won't be reaching the coast for a few hours yet. I want you to change out of these wet things, and then you should lie down and try to get some sleep. I'll call you when the coast is in sight."

"*Merci, Monsieur Langdon,*" she managed between chattering teeth as she clutched the blanket close to her.

He nodded briefly and closed the door. It was clear he was not overjoyed at having her on board.

Jacqueline stripped out of her wet clothes and hung them on a chair before the stove to dry. Although she had packed a plain linen nightgown for sleeping in, she went to Armand's chest in the corner and searched through it until she found a soft cotton shirt, which she slid over her head. The warm shirt reached below her knees, and the sleeves completely covered her hands. Best of all, the faint, spicy scent of Armand clung to the fabric, making her feel cozy and protected. She crawled into his bed and drew her knees up to her chest, feeling weak but no longer ill. She wrapped her arms around Armand's pillow and told herself for the thousandth time that he was alive. All she had to do was find him.

When Sidney knocked on her door several hours later, Jacqueline was already up and dressed in her plain black traveling costume. She put the last of her things in her bag and once again examined the false papers Sidney had quickly managed to secure for her from one of Armand's contacts in London. During her trip to Paris she would be Citizeness Pauline Duport, a recent widow from Blois, whose husband had been a cabinetmaker by trade. If anyone was to ask, her husband had died from an infected leg caused by a deep gash when a heavy plank of wood had fallen on him. She was now on her way to Paris to live with her aunt, who ran a small fabric shop and needed someone to help her. It was a simple enough story, which she hoped would satisfy any curious traveling companions who might be sharing the coach she would be taking to Paris. It also enabled her to wear a plain black bonnet with a sheer veil, which would offer her privacy and prevent anyone from getting too close a look at her. Although she doubted that Paris was still actively searching for the escaped Citizeness Jacqueline Doucette, formerly Mademoiselle Jacqueline de Lambert, convicted criminal and traitor to the Republic of France, she knew that a young woman traveling alone often attracted unwanted attention from men who fancied themselves as desirable and wanted to see what might come of it.

She went up to the deck to watch as the coast of France began to appear through the early-morning darkness. Strangely enough, it looked much the same as it had when she left, nearly three months ago. The feathery pines were now heavy with snow, and there were more lights burning through the windows of the tiny, weathered houses dotted along the coastline, because it was not yet dawn and people were beginning to rise from their beds. But the land was still dark and rugged and beautiful. Jacqueline was overwhelmed by the bitter stab of relief that shot through her as she watched her homeland slowly appear. It had not been burned by the mobs or cast into the sea by an angry God. It was still there, waiting for her to return, patiently enduring the cruelty and madness that was raging upon it, languidly stretched out against the sea and saying *In one hundred years they will all be gone and I will still be here.*

The Angélique kept her distance from the shore, slipping quietly along the water, escaping notice under the velvety black shroud of the night sky. She pulled in behind a craggy point of land and stopped, a skiff was lowered into rough, cold waves, and before Jacqueline knew it Sidney was carrying her bag and leading her to the rope ladder that had been flung over the side. It was time.

"Well, Mademoiselle de Lambert, I have done as you asked. I have brought you to Calais." He set down her bag on the deck and turned to face her. "Now it's your turn. Where is he?"

"He has been arrested," began Jacqueline, trying not to look down at the little bobbing skiff in which two men were tightly gripping the ladder to keep the boat from being carried away by the waves.

"I guessed as much as that," replied Sidney impatiently. "What else do you know?"

"He was arrested trying to rescue the Marquis de Biret from the Luxembourg prison. There were members of the National Guard waiting for them on the prison grounds, and Armand was taken prisoner."

"How do you know this?" demanded Sidney.

"The marquis managed to escape. I heard it from him."

Sidney looked unconvinced. "You're telling me that this marquis got away but Armand did not? How is that?"

"He was shot," explained Jacqueline. "He was unable to run. The marquis was forced to go on without him."

"How bad?" demanded Sidney, his voice taut.

"I don't know," admitted Jacqueline. "But I am hoping that it was not too bad, and that the wound is healing."

He was silent a moment, obviously considering what she had told him. "He could be dead," he said finally.

"No," replied Jacqueline firmly. "He could not."

He looked unconvinced. "How do you know?"

How could she explain it to him? *Because I feel him, somehow. Because if he were dead I would sense it. Because somewhere in my ravaged heart and soul there is a tiny shred of light, so small and faint as to be almost imperceptible, which was not there until Armand came into my life. Because if he lives, I know there is some justice in this world after all, and that maybe, just maybe, this life that God has given to me is still worth living. But if he is dead, then I am dead, too, an empty shell of pain and hatred and guilt that can never be healed, and does not wish to try.*

"I know," she said simply.

He studied her a moment, trying to understand. "Do you know where he is?"

"No," she admitted. "But I will find him." She raised

her chin and stared at him with absolute, unwavering conviction, daring him to contradict her.

"I will go with you," he announced suddenly.

"No," stated Jacqueline emphatically. "You would be more hindrance than help. A citizeness traveling alone, a young widow going to Paris to find work, is apt to arouse a modicum of sympathy and respect, and has a good chance of being left alone. But a woman traveling with a big, burly man such as yourself can only arouse questions and suspicions. What do you do for a living? How is it that you can take time to make a trip to Paris? What is your relationship to me? What of your accent? Where are you from? Where are your traveling documents?" She shook her head. "I am much safer on my own, Monsieur Langdon. Surely you can see that."

He looked unconvinced. "Armand wouldn't like it," he argued.

"Monsieur St. James will not like the fact that I am here at all, escorted or not," she pointed out.

"That's true enough," admitted Sidney. He sighed. "Very well. My men will see you safely to the shore. After that you are on your own—"

"*Merci,*" breathed Jacqueline.

"On the condition that you meet us in Boulogne in exactly eight days," he finished.

"Eight days!" gasped Jacqueline.

Sidney nodded. "That gives you two days to take the coach to Paris. Four days to find Armand and get him the hell out of there. And two days to make it back to Boulogne. That should give you lots of time."

"Eight days," repeated Jacqueline in disbelief.

"The longer you are there, the greater your chances of being captured," he pointed out. "And when you find him, you must act quickly to get him out of there, before those bloody bastards have a chance to send him to the guillotine."

"But what if I cannot find him in four days?" she protested.

Sidney pinned her with his gaze. "Then you get yourself on a coach and travel to Boulogne without him. Is that clear?"

Never. She would never leave France without him. But rather than admitting that to Sidney, she regarded him seriously and nodded. "I understand."

He looked at her with satisfaction. "Good. We will begin to send men out to watch the beach where we picked you and Armand up the first time after seven days, in case by some miracle you are early. Do you think you can find it?"

"Yes," lied Jacqueline. She had been asleep when they approached it last time. It did not matter. If Armand was with her, he would know how to find it. If he was not, she would not be going there anyway.

"I am giving you eight days, Mademoiselle de Lambert," Sidney reminded her firmly. "Do not be late." He lifted her bag and tossed it down to one of the men in the skiff below.

"I won't," promised Jacqueline solemnly. She turned around, took a deep swallow, and slowly began to climb down the ladder.

The coach trip to Paris was long and tiring, and Jacqueline's nerves churned her stomach into a tempest of nausea the entire time. After landing on the shore she trudged over four miles along the snowy road that led to the village of Calais, where a local fisherman told her where she could find the coach bound for Paris. She was able to secure a seat on the coach without any trouble. Thinking the coachman might find it strange that a young woman was there alone without anyone to see her off, she explained to him that a neighbor had been kind enough to drive her to Calais, but could not stay to watch her depart. The coachman shrugged his shoulders and rudely informed her that as long as she paid her fare he didn't give a damn how or why she came to be there.

During the two days it took to reach Paris they were stopped several times by rough-looking detachments of the Revolutionary Guard and asked to produce their traveling documents. Jacqueline struggled each time to remain calm and composed, obediently showing her papers and answering their questions without the slightest hesitation. Each time she felt certain that the guard who asked the questions was suspicious of her, but after the third interrogation she realized the guards were equally suspicious of everyone. Her traveling companions all visibly relaxed once their papers had been returned and the coach began to move slowly down the road again. Evidently the paranoia of the government had managed to strike an element of fear into all the citizens of France, regardless of whether they were guilty of a crime or not.

It was late afternoon of the second day when the coach finally ground to a halt. Slowly Jacqueline stepped out onto the street, her back stiff, her joints aching, her legs weak from sitting in such cramped conditions for so long. The other passengers quickly murmured their good-byes and were on their way, none hesitating to see if the imaginary aunt Jacqueline had mentioned to them had indeed come to meet her at the coach stop. It was not their business, so they did not care, she realized with a mixture of relief and surprise. These days no one looked out for the other.

Clutching her bag tightly, she began to walk. The first part of her plan was to find Armand's friend Justin. She recalled that he lived in the faubourg Montmartre, which was in the northern part of Paris, on a street called rue de Vent. If she could find that street, she knew she would be able to recall which house belonged to Justin. Once she found him, she would ask for his help in finding Armand. Thinking back to the intense loyalty the two men obviously shared, she did not doubt that if Justin knew Armand had been captured, he would be willing to offer assistance.

She walked along for perhaps a half hour, hoping she was headed in the right direction, but the streets were narrow and twisting and the cold, gray light of day was fading fast. She began to worry that she would have to stop and ask someone the way, which she did not want to do. Any interaction with a stranger could potentially lead to disaster. The citizens of the Republic were always anxious to demonstrate their loyalty to the new order, and therefore eager to denounce anyone whose dress seemed a bit too fine, whose speech was a touch too aristocratic, or whose attitude seemed incompatible with the murderous, self-righteous fury of a devout revolutionary. A wayward look, a casual comment or complaint that could be construed as critical of the government or sympathetic to the thousands who had suffered since the revolution began, and that was sufficient grounds for a denunciation and arrest. So she hurried along, hoping that eventually something familiar would appear.

She turned down a street that was crowded with vendors' stalls, and thick with people arguing furiously over prices. She moved with haste, realizing this was not the street she wanted. Her body twisted and turned as she tried to avoid being shoved and jostled by the crowd. Just as she managed to steer clear of an enormous woman who was thrashing her way through the street without any regard for her fellow citizens, she was struck in the ribs and stomach by a small boy who had appeared out of nowhere and seemed desperate to get through the crowd. The sudden impact knocked her off balance and down she went, causing the boy to trip over her and drop whatever it was he held cradled in his arms.

"There he is!" bellowed a man's furious voice. "Stop him!"

Before Jacqueline could draw a breath and sit up, a wall of people had suddenly formed around the two of them, effectively blocking any exit. The boy scrambled to his feet and balled his hands into fists, which he held out threateningly as he turned around and glared at his captors, daring one of them to try to lay a hand on him.

Since no one made a move to help Jacqueline up, she pulled herself to her feet and quickly took in the ragged appearance of the boy. He looked to be about eleven, certainly not more than twelve, but he was so thin and malnourished it was possible he was older. His angry, defiant face was filthy, his hair long, dark, and matted. The clothes he wore were threadbare, torn and dirty, and totally insubstantial for the middle of winter. His greasy jacket was held closed by an old piece of frayed rope that had been knotted in several places, and his pants, which might have fit him at an earlier age, were tight and ended at midcalf, leaving his red, rawboned legs and ankles bare to the bitter cold. His shoes were badly cracked, and through the slits Jacqueline could see that they had been stuffed with scraps of newspaper in a pathetic effort to keep out the freezing wet snow. Abandoned at his feet lay a loaf of black bread, the object he had been holding in his arms as he ran.

"Let me through," bellowed a furious voice as a burly man shoved his way through the excited crowd.

He saw the boy trapped and he smiled, a twisted, malicious smile that caused the breath to freeze in Jacqueline's throat. It was a smile she recognized, cruel and vicious, the smile of one who loves to brutalize and coerce, to punish with an iron fist in order to terrify and dominate.

"So," he began menacingly as he slowly advanced toward the boy, "you think you can steal from me, do you, you filthy little pig?"

The boy trembled slightly as the man moved toward him, but he held his place and kept his fists high in the air.

"If you please, Citizen," began Jacqueline, thinking she would simply offer to pay for the bread and the incident would be resolved.

"I will show you what happens to thieves who try to steal from me," continued the man, ignoring Jacqueline and moving closer to the boy. "First, I am going to break every bone in your miserable little body. And when I am finished, I will let the National Guard cart away whatever mangled pieces remain. What do you think of that, you little son of a whore?"

The boy let out a screech of fury and lunged at his tormentor, fists swinging, legs kicking, teeth biting. The man swore in surprise as he tried to push him away, and then let out a grunt of pain as the boy's teeth sank into his wrist.

"Goddamn little bastard—" He clenched his other hand into a heavy fist and smashed it full force into the boy's face, knocking him back a few steps and stunning him in the process. Jacqueline screamed, but the sound was muffled among the cheers of the crowd. The boy stood frozen for a moment, and then shook his head to clear it, which caused the blood that had started to stream from his nose to spurt across his face. He eyed his opponent warily, and then suddenly leapt at the man with a snarl, realizing his only choice was to either fight or stand there and be beaten. He battered his fists against the man's chest and stomach, his height preventing him from landing any blows against his face, and for a moment the man simply stood there and endured it, as if he was amused by the pathetic effort of the child to fight him. When he decided he had had enough he reached down, grabbed the boy by the scruff of the neck, and began to smash him across the face with his enormous fist. The crowd whooped and hollered and cheered, obviously thinking that the beating of a young thief was fine entertainment.

Jacqueline screamed again, but even she could not hear the sound among the enthusiastic cries of the crowd. The boy continued to struggle, but he was no match for the massive brute who held him prisoner as he bashed him in the face and head. His lip began to bleed, as did a cut under his eye, and the blood spread with every blow until his face was a smear of red.

With a primitive cry of rage Jacqueline hurled herself against the massive form of the brute who seemed intent on killing the lad, and began to tear frantically at his hair and claw at his face.

"Let him go, you bloodthirsty bastard!" she screeched wildly as she grabbed a fistful of his hair and yanked down on it with all her might.

The man roared as he felt the roots of his hair leave his scalp. He released the boy and put his hands to his head in disbelief. As he did so Jacqueline pulled her arms together and drove her elbow into his exposed ribs as hard as she could. The man let out another bellow of rage and turned around to face her, momentarily forgetting the boy, who instead of using the opportunity to run simply stood there and watched, as if confused by this turn of events.

"Evil, loathsome son of a bitch," raged Jacqueline as she reached out and slapped the man soundly across the face.

"The boy stole from me," sputtered the man, obviously stunned by Jacqueline's attack. "It is my right to protect what is mine."

"And so you have the right to beat a starving child to death?" demanded Jacqueline furiously. "Is that what this new Republic has done—given filthy peasant scum like you the right to bash a defenseless boy in the face until he collapses in a mangled, broken heap at your feet?"

The man's eyes narrowed. "And just who might you be, Citizeness, that you would call a man filthy peasant scum?"

Instantly Jacqueline recognized her mistake. Once again she had spoken in a manner that betrayed her aristocratic background. Her mind began to race as she tried to correct her error. "I beg your pardon, Citizen, I meant no insult, I simply wish to pay for the bread—"

"Looks like we got ourselves a little aristo here," boomed the man triumphantly as he stared hard at Jacqueline.

The crowd began to murmur in surprise and agreement.

"No, you are mistaken," protested Jacqueline, suddenly gripped with panic.

"She's an aristo all right," called out a woman in the crowd.

"Knew it from the moment I saw her," affirmed another.

"But I have done nothing wrong," rushed out Jacqueline defensively.

"You complained about our government," insisted the

man. "That would make you suspect, now wouldn't it?"
He smiled at her, clearly pleased that he had found a legal
way to have his revenge on her for interfering.

The boy, who had been watching this exchange without making any attempt to flee, suddenly dropped his
mouth open in horror. "Oh my God," he breathed as a
look of recognition crossed his blood smeared face. "She
ain't no bloody aristo, that's Camille Dubé, whose husband just died of the plague not ten days ago."

The crowd let out a gasp of fearful uncertainty.

Jacqueline stared at the boy in confusion.

"Get her away from here," he shrieked in terror as he
began to back away from her. "Take her away—lock her
up—she shouldn't be allowed to wander the streets so,
spreading her poison everywhere—oh my God, *she
touched you!*" he screamed at the man who had beaten
him before suddenly turning and starting to run.

The crowd immediately began to break away, leaving
Jacqueline alone with the man, who had by now taken a
step back.

"Here now, what's he talking about?" he demanded
suspiciously as he took in her black mourning costume.
"Did your husband really die from the plague?"

"Well—yes," stammered Jacqueline, quickly gathering
her wits enough to play along with the boy's ruse. "But it
was over two weeks ago now—his body was covered in
festering sores—well, in some places he was totally blackened by the disease and that's the truth of it—but I've got
no sign of it at all, none, other than this one small sore
that came up not three days ago, on my arm—" She began
to roll up the sleeve of her coat to show him.

"Get away from me!" roared the man, his eyes bulging
in horror. He began to rub his hands frantically on his
jacket, trying to cleanse himself of her. "Get off this street
—we don't want your kind here, spreading your poison
everywhere—be off with you!" He took another few steps
away from her, clearly terrified.

Jacqueline slowly looked around at the crowd. People
were staring at her with a mixture of fear and morbid

curiosity, waiting to see what she would do next. The boy's trick had been unbelievably effective. She had to keep herself from smiling. "Very well," she sighed meekly. She went to pick up her bag, which she had dropped when the boy ran into her. The crowd crushed itself against the sides of the street, giving her as much room as possible. Jacqueline gave them a mournful look and then began to slowly walk down the narrow street, trying her best to appear dejected and miserable.

She wandered the streets of the faubourg Montmartre, determined to find Justin's home without any assistance. After her latest encounter she decided it was safest not to interact with anyone unless it was absolutely necessary. The paranoia of the times made it dangerous even to open one's mouth, with everyone so anxious to prove themselves a loyal citizen by turning in another. But after two hours of walking in the cold, it became painfully clear she had absolutely no idea where she was going. She was freezing, she was exhausted, and the light of the afternoon was quickly disappearing. She stood on a corner, dropped her bag, and rubbed her hands together, wondering bleakly what she should do next.

"Do you know you are walking in circles?"

Startled, she spun around. The boy was standing behind her, casually leaning against the brick wall of a building.

"Are you following me?" Jacqueline demanded.

The boy shrugged his thin shoulders. "I wanted to make sure you got away all right."

His answer only partly appeased her. She did not want anyone following her, regardless of their motives. "Thank you for your concern," she said stiffly. She noticed the blood had been wiped from his face, but the damage the man had done was substantial. His left eye was puffy and turning black, his lip was swollen and cut, and purple bruises were starting to show beneath the pale skin of his cheeks. "I should have killed the bastard," she swore softly.

"You were stupid to interfere," the boy remarked. "You almost got yourself arrested."

"You were stupid to steal," countered Jacqueline angrily. "You almost got yourself killed."

"It's not the first time I've taken a beating," he informed her, casually shrugging his shoulders. "If I don't steal, I don't eat."

The stark reality of that statement defused the harsh lecture she had been about to give him on taking things that were not his. "Do your parents know you steal?" she demanded instead.

"They're dead," he replied. His voice was flat and emotionless.

"Oh." So much for ordering him home to his father. "Whom do you live with?"

"No one," he returned irritably. "I'm on my own." He straightened up and stared at her defiantly.

"I see." She did not think he could be more than twelve years old. The idea that a child so young was trying to survive on his own, having to steal when he wanted to eat, was appalling. "What is your name?"

"Philippe Mercier," he told her. "And yours?"

"Pauline Duport," she answered without hesitation.

The boy studied her a moment. "You're not from Paris, are you?"

"No."

"I didn't think so," he remarked with satisfaction. "Where are you going, walking in circles?"

Jacqueline hesitated. It was possible this boy could help her find Justin's address, but she was not certain it was wise to let anyone know her destination. On the other hand, she had absolutely no idea where she was, or how she would find Justin's house on her own. It was also growing dark, and she could not spend the night on the street. Every hour that passed was another hour in which Armand's life was in danger. She had to get to Justin as quickly as possible so they could develop a plan to rescue him.

"I am trying to find my aunt's home, which is on the

rue de Vent. Do you know where that is?" she asked hopefully.

"Of course—it is back that way, about a half hour's walk."

"Do you think you could tell me how to find it?"

"I'll take you," he announced. He turned and began to walk in the direction from which she had just come.

Again Jacqueline hesitated. "I don't really need you to take me," she protested, reluctant to have anyone know where she was going. "If you could just explain to me how I can get there—"

"You will never find it on your own, Citizeness," he informed her flatly. "Besides, you might need me in case you have any more trouble." He continued walking.

Jacqueline did not want to point out that the reason she had trouble in the first place was because he had come crashing into her. She stood for a moment, debating whether or not to follow him.

He stopped and turned to look at her. "Are you coming?" he demanded impatiently.

She realized it would be foolish not to accept his offer. "Yes," she replied. She snatched up her bag and began to hurry after him.

"Where are you from?" asked Philippe as they trudged along through the snowy streets.

"From Blois," lied Jacqueline. "My husband died recently and I am going to live with my aunt."

"I'm sorry."

"What of your parents?" she asked. "How did they die?"

"My mother died in prison last year," he told her matter-of-factly. "Never knew my father. As far as I'm concerned, he is dead."

"Have you no other family?" demanded Jacqueline. It was upsetting to think he was all alone.

"No."

"But where do you live?"

He shrugged his shoulders. "Wherever," he replied, as if the subject was not one of great concern to him. "After my mother was arrested, I lived in the room we rented for a while, waiting to see if she would come back. Then the lady that owns the place tells me she's got to throw me out, because I'm not paying my rent. She says I can sleep in her kitchen, though, and get food, too, if I bring in some money, or stuff that's worth money. So I start stealing, and give whatever I get to her. It worked out all right for a while. But then she took up with this mean bastard, who moved in and started ordering me around, like I was his bloody slave. He drank and liked to use his fists on me, and when I told the lady about it she said he was just trying to be like a father. Well, the hell with that, I said, I don't need to pay to sleep on the floor and have someone smack me around. So I left, and I've been on my own ever since."

"But how do you survive?" asked Jacqueline incredulously. "Where do you sleep?"

"Anywhere." He shrugged. " 'Course, it's easier when the weather is warm. Churches used to be good, until they started closing them down these past few months. I know a couple of café owners who don't mind letting me use their floor after they close, if I help them clean up. And there are a few ladies I do errands for who will let me stay the night if they aren't busy."

Jacqueline gasped. "Do you mean prostitutes?"

He gave her an amused look. "No, Citizeness, I mean nuns." He laughed, a knowing, brazen laugh that told her he was worldly beyond his years.

"Exactly how old are you, anyway?" demanded Jacqueline suspiciously.

"Thirteen," he informed her. "Fourteen this summer."

He was small for his age, she realized, undoubtedly because of insufficient food and poor living conditions.

"Well," she huffed, only partly mollified by the fact that he was not quite as young as she had originally believed, "thirteen is rather young to be spending the night with a prostitute."

He shrugged his shoulders. "At least it's warm."

She had nothing to say in reply to that.

They trudged along in silence for a while. Darkness was spreading steely-gray shadows across the snow-covered city, turning the narrow streets into dark, forbidding tunnels, and Jacqueline realized that without Philippe's help she never would have been able to find Justin's house. No one seemed to take any note of them as they walked by, even though she supposed they must have made quite a pair, her in her black mourning costume and him in his ragged beggar's clothes, his face swollen and bruised. But Philippe moved with confidence and purpose, as if he owned the streets he walked on, and Jacqueline drew comfort from his easy manner. It was obvious to anyone that he was totally familiar with his surroundings and knew exactly where he was going. It was an attitude Jacqueline would have to learn to feign if she wanted to move about Paris without attracting attention.

"This is it," he said finally as they turned down a narrow street.

Jacqueline gazed at the row of crumbling houses stretched out before her, trying to decide if anything looked familiar. She thought back to the day Armand had brought her here, after having rescued her from that terrifying mob. She had ridden in front of him on his horse. He had ordered her not to speak, and so they had come here in icy silence, with Jacqueline mentally rehearsing all the things she was going to say to him once they were alone. Slowly she began to walk down the street, trying to recall that day, trying to remember how far along the street they had traveled before Armand turned their horse down a lane that led to a coach house.

"Didn't your aunt tell you the number of her house?" asked Philippe quizzically.

"She did," stammered Jacqueline, "but I lost the paper it was written on." She continued to walk along, staring at the buildings.

"Why not just knock on one of the neighbors' doors and ask which house is hers?" he suggested.

"No," blurted out Jacqueline. To do so would be to

draw attention to Justin and herself, and that might arouse suspicion.

"Why not?" demanded Philippe. He looked at her as if he thought she was acting strangely.

"It is late," explained Jacqueline, "and I have no wish to disturb anyone. I am sure I can find it on my own." She continued to study the houses.

"Citizeness Duport—"

"I think this is it!" exclaimed Jacqueline, standing in front of a house that looked familiar. "In fact I am certain of it." She turned to him. "Thank you, Philippe, for your assistance in bringing me here. If you will allow me to pay you something for your trouble—"

"Do you think I could come inside and get warm?" he asked.

Jacqueline hesitated. It seemed cruel to send him off into the night, cold and hungry, after he had gone so much out of his way to bring her here. But she did not want to involve him with counterrevolutionary activities, or place Justin in any danger by bringing an outsider to his home. She bit her lip. "I am really sorry, Philippe, but I do not think—"

"I'm not leaving until I am sure this is the place and you are safe," he stated emphatically. "A cup of something hot to drink wouldn't hurt either," he muttered irritably under his breath. He began to march up to the front door.

"Wait!" cried Jacqueline, hurrying up behind him.

He folded his arms across his chest and looked at her defiantly.

Jacqueline sighed. "Very well," she conceded. She lifted her hand and rapped on the door, three rapid knocks followed by two long ones, the same code Armand had used when they were here before.

After a moment the door swung open. Justin stood before her, holding a candle and looking at them warily.

"Citizen Justin, perhaps you will remember me," began Jacqueline as she pulled the veil of her hat off her face so he could see her better.

His expression was blank. "Have we met before, Citizeness?"

Jacqueline stared at him in confusion. "Yes," she stammered, wondering why he did not immediately recognize her. And then it suddenly occurred to her that she had been disguised as a boy when she arrived, and as a pregnant farmer's wife with dark hair and yellow teeth when she left. "I stayed here one day a few months ago," she hastily explained, "and when I left I was pregnant and married to a—"

"Cousin Delphine!" he cried out suddenly as he stepped forward and wrapped his free arm around her. "And little Cousin Henri," he added, smiling down at Philippe. "Come in, come in, you must be exhausted after your long journey," he pronounced as he ushered them through the entrance and closed the door.

"What's the matter with him?" asked Philippe as he stared at Justin and frowned.

"Did Armand send you?" demanded Justin urgently, his pretense at being Jacqueline's cousin dropped now that he was certain no one could see them.

"Not exactly . . ." replied Jacqueline, "but I am here because of Armand—"

Justin turned his attention to Philippe. "Who is the boy?"

"He is a friend—"

"I am Philippe Mercier. Who are you and where is Pauline's aunt?" demanded Philippe.

"What?" asked Justin, confused.

"Justin, if I might have a word with you, *alone*—" said Jacqueline, giving a meaningful look toward Philippe.

Justin looked at Philippe and smiled. "You must be hungry, my friend. Let us go into the kitchen and find you something to eat."

Philippe needed no further invitation. Justin began to walk down the hall toward the kitchen and Philippe immediately turned and followed him.

A lamp was burning in the small sitting room off the

hall, and Jacqueline went in there to wait for Justin. After a few minutes he returned, frowning.

"His face is badly battered. It will have to be cleaned soon." He sat down in a chair opposite Jacqueline. "How can I help you, Citizeness?"

Jacqueline took a deep breath. "Armand has been arrested."

His expression grew taut. "So the rumors are true after all," he said quietly.

She looked at him in confusion. "What rumors?"

"All of Paris is celebrating that the Black Prince has finally been caught," he explained. "They say he was trapped in a clever plan laid for him by an Inspector Bourdon, who works for the Committee of Public Safety."

Jacqueline felt the blood drain from her face. "A trap?" she repeated in disbelief.

Justin nodded. "Apparently a man was caught trying to assist the Marquis de Biret in his escape from the Luxembourg prison. Somehow this Inspector Bourdon knew about the escape attempt and managed to thwart it, capturing the Black Prince in the process."

"But the marquis escaped," protested Jacqueline.

Justin shook his head. "According to the official reports, the marquis was shot and killed as he tried to get away."

"But that is not true," protested Jacqueline as she tried to sort out what Justin was telling her. "He escaped and made it to England."

Justin frowned. "How do you know?"

"Because I have seen him there." She looked at him miserably. "The marquis was my betrothed. I am the one who asked Armand to rescue him. I guess the Committee of Public Safety does not want to admit that they let a prisoner escape."

Justin pondered this for a moment. "Perhaps," he allowed. "At any rate, when I heard these rumors I was naturally concerned that they might have captured Armand. I had not heard he was in France, but he only informs those who will be directly involved with his plans.

So I made some discreet enquiries. The man imprisoned in La Force says he is Citizen Michel Belanger, a deserter from the National Guard. This was on the papers he carried, but evidently they were forged. He insists he was acting alone. Of course they could execute him just for trying to help the marquis escape, but he is being held until his real identity can be determined. No doubt the committee feels there are others who could be arrested if they can get him to confess."

"Armand will never confess," said Jacqueline with certainty. "He would never endanger the lives of his contacts."

"That is true," agreed Justin. "Just as none of us would ever endanger him."

But I did, thought Jacqueline miserably. I knew it was dangerous for him to try to save François-Louis, but I asked him to go anyway. A suffocating wave of guilt assaulted her.

Justin rose from his chair. "Now that you have confirmed this man is Armand, we must develop a plan, and get someone to go in there and get him out," he announced.

"I will go," stated Jacqueline.

He stopped and looked at her in disbelief. "Don't be ridiculous," he scoffed. "You know nothing of these matters. You will simply endanger Armand and probably get yourself killed in the process."

His rejection of her offer did not faze her in the least. "I know about the inside of a prison," she pointed out calmly. "After all, I have spent a considerable amount of time in them, as both a visitor *and* an inmate."

"Forgive me, Citizeness, familiarity with prisons is useful, but it is not enough," argued Justin. "We need someone who is not afraid, who can maintain his composure whatever happens, and who is enough of an actor to fool everyone he comes in contact with."

"I can do all that," Jacqueline assured him.

He looked at her skeptically.

"Do not forget, I have been with Armand on one of

his escape missions, from start to finish," she pointed out. "I have seen him at work. I have watched him react to the unexpected. I have studied his disguises, his accents, his mannerisms—"

"Could you kill someone if you had to?" he demanded curtly.

"Yes," she answered without hesitation. "Absolutely."

He considered this for a moment. It was obvious he was not convinced.

"If you don't use me, who else will you get?" demanded Jacqueline. "The men from Armand's ship are currently sailing along the coast of France. It is impossible to get a message to them. His contacts in Paris are established here, and might be recognized, regardless of how effective their disguises are. If one of them is caught, their loss will be a serious blow to the counterrevolutionary network. But I am not known here, and if I am caught, your organization will not suffer."

"You speak of your life as if it were a commodity of little value," he observed.

She looked away, staring into the flames of the little fire burning in the hearth. "Before Monsieur St. James rescued me, I had resigned myself to the fact that I was going to die," she told him quietly. "I felt my life had been destroyed, and I had ceased to care what became of me. But Armand insisted that I live, regardless of whether I wanted to or not. If not for his determination to save me, he would not be in La Force right now, and you and I would not be having this conversation." She pulled her gaze away from the fire to look at him. "If I sound casual where my life is concerned, please do not misunderstand. It is not that I wish to die. It is simply that if Armand is executed because I unwittingly led him into a trap, I do not wish to live."

He stared at her in silence a moment. "He has made a great impact on many lives," he finally murmured softly.

Jacqueline regarded him curiously. "Did he rescue you as well?"

He nodded. "My mother, sister, and I were about to

be arrested," he told her. "Armand learned of it, and got us out of our house before the National Guard arrived. He put my mother and sister in plain caskets and got them beyond the barricades by telling the guards he had rotting corpses in his cart."

Jacqueline looked at him in amazement. "Didn't the guards demand he open one of the caskets so they could see?"

Justin smiled. "It was summer, and the day was stiflingly hot. Armand placed another casket on top of theirs, and filled it with rancid meat and rotting vegetables. The stench was so bad, when the guards neared the cart they simply held their breath and waved him on. Not one of them was brave enough to risk a look inside."

Jacqueline looked at him with amusement. It was obvious Armand never ran out of creative ideas. "Where is your family now?"

"They both went to England with Armand. Within six weeks my sister fell madly in love with a composer and married. She is now expecting their first child."

"And your mother?"

"My mother grew very fond of Armand, and decided to accept his offer to stay and work for him."

Jacqueline looked at him incredulously. "Your mother works for Armand?"

He nodded. "As his housekeeper."

Jacqueline stared at him, taking in his wavy blond hair and his emerald-green eyes. "Your mother is Madame Bonnard," she exclaimed suddenly, recognizing the similarity between the two.

"Yes."

"I knew when I met her she looked familiar, but I could not imagine why," she recalled.

"My family had known Armand for many years, from when he was a young man and used to visit France for months at a time," explained Justin. "Since my father was dead, and my sister and her husband only had a small apartment, my mother had no where to go. And so Armand offered her work, knowing that pride would keep her from simply moving in and living off his charity."

Jacqueline was silent as she absorbed this information. Justin had known Armand for years. Which meant he probably knew his wife. She was unable to control her curiosity. "Did you know Lucette?"

"I met her a few times," he admitted, "but I did not really know her."

"What was she like?" she asked, trying to sound casual.

"She was very beautiful," he recalled. "And very amusing. She loved to make people laugh."

"I see," murmured Jacqueline vacantly. She did not know what else to say.

He looked at her curiously for a moment. "He means a great deal to you, doesn't he?" he demanded finally.

She looked away, unable to face his searching gaze. "He gave me back my life," she replied simply. "I want to do the same for him."

He was silent for a while. Finally he sighed. "Do you have any valuables?"

"I brought some money," she replied. "In French *livres*, not *assignats*," she clarified, referring to the government-issued banknotes that by now were virtually worthless.

He shook his head. "The help we will need is expensive," he told her. "Information, forged documents, transportation. Armand always paid in either silver or gold. That way you can be assured of quality and discretion."

Jacqueline thought back to the jewels hidden in the Château de Lambert. The château would have been confiscated and undoubtedly stripped of its furnishings, but it was possible no one had discovered her hiding place. It would be extremely risky to go back there. If she was caught at the château, she would never get the opportunity to free Armand. She tried not to think about that.

"I know where I can get some," she informed him.

"Good." He rose from his chair. "For now, you will

eat something. Then you must get some rest. We will begin planning in the morning."

Jacqueline would have liked to start planning immediately, but she meekly rose and followed Justin to the
kitchen, where Philippe was devouring a loaf of bread and
a bowl of stew. Justin fixed her a plate, and after she had
eaten he led her and Philippe upstairs. Jacqueline was
given the same room in which Armand had transformed
her from a revolutionary youth to a farmer's wife, which
was across from Justin's own room. Philippe was given a
room down the hall. Exhausted from her long journey,
Jacqueline quickly washed and changed into her nightdress, then wearily climbed into bed. She was about to put
out her candle when she heard the sound of someone
moving outside her door. Thinking that Justin wished to
speak to her again, she rose from the bed and went to see
what he wanted.

Curled up on the bare floor in front of her doorway
lay Philippe, still fully dressed and with only one thin
blanket draped over him to protect him from the cold.

"Philippe, what on earth are you doing?" she demanded in a whisper.

He raised himself up on one elbow and looked at her.
"I thought I would sleep here by your door, just in case
you needed me," he informed her simply.

"Don't be ridiculous," she chided. "Why ever would I
need you in the middle of the night? Go back to your own
room at once."

Philippe did not move, but instead looked meaningfully at the door to Justin's room across the hall. "I think
I'll just sleep here, if it's all the same to you," he replied.
He lowered himself back down to the floor and closed his
eyes.

Jacqueline stared at him in exasperation. And then
suddenly it dawned on her why he wanted to stay so
close. Philippe was worried about her safety where Justin
was concerned. Although touched by his concern, she certainly did not want him sleeping in the hallway all night.

Nor did she wish to argue with him about it when Justin might hear the two of them and possibly be insulted.

"Philippe, please come in here for a moment so we can discuss this," she whispered softly as she held the door open for him.

He looked at her suspiciously a moment before gathering himself up off the floor and following her into her room.

Jacqueline closed the door behind him and then regarded him with just a hint of amusement. "Philippe, I am most touched by your concern for me, but I can assure you it is not necessary. Nothing untoward is going to happen this evening, and I would like it very much if you would go back to your room and go to bed."

He shrugged his shoulders, obviously unconvinced. "A lady like you doesn't know about men," he said with grave authority. "Since I do, I know that I would rather sleep in front of your door. I don't mind the floor. I'm used to it." He moved to open the door.

"You cannot sleep in the hallway," announced Jacqueline firmly.

He shrugged his shoulders again. "You can't stop me," he told her.

Jacqueline sighed. She was touched by his concern, however unwarranted she felt it to be. She did not believe Justin posed any threat to her, but how could she make this boy, who lived on the streets among drunks and thieves and whores, see that? And she did not want to be having this conversation anyway. All she wanted to do was crawl into bed and get some much-needed sleep.

"Very well," she relented. "If you are that worried about my virtue, then you do not have to go to your room."

"Good," he replied as he reached for the door handle.

"You may stay in here with me."

He turned and looked at her in disbelief. "What?"

"I will not have you sleeping on the floor when there is a perfectly fine bed in here that can easily accommodate both of us," she informed him as she went to turn down the covers.

"Citizeness Duport, or whatever your name is, there is no way I am going to get into that bed with you," he informed her flatly.

Jacqueline fought to restrain a smile. Only three months earlier she had told the same thing to Armand, then known to her as Citizen Julien. Propriety had seemed so important then, regardless of practicality or discomfort. "I believe logic dictates that since the bed is large enough, we share it," she stated, recalling Armand's words to her.

"Absolutely not," said Philippe, clearly astounded by her suggestion. "It isn't proper."

Jacqueline sighed. It was obvious this boy saw himself not as a child, as she did, but as a man, and there was no way she could change that without causing him insult. She decided to compromise.

"Take these pillows and this blanket and arrange them on the floor so you can lie on them," she instructed as she tossed down the pillows from the bed.

Evidently that request seemed reasonable to him. He quickly made up a bed for himself on the floor. He was just lowering himself down onto it when a new thought occurred to her.

"Philippe, did you wash?" she asked.

He looked at her in confusion. "Wash what?"

"Yourself," she clarified. "Your face, your hands, your teeth—was there not soap and water laid out in your room?"

He shrugged his shoulders.

"Don't shrug your shoulders, Philippe, it isn't polite. Was there soap and water?"

"I guess," he replied disinterestedly.

"Well, that was for washing. Since you are here now, however, you may use mine. There is fresh water in that jug. Get up and scrub your face and hands thoroughly, and rinse your teeth."

He gave her a mutinous look. "If you want I can sleep in the hall—" he offered threateningly.

"No, that won't be necessary," she informed him. "It will, however, be necessary for you to wash, if you want me to ask Justin to make you a nice, big breakfast tomorrow morning. If you are content with cold tea and gruel, that is fine, too. The choice is yours." She smiled at him sweetly.

He gave her a dark scowl and got up. For the next few minutes she heard the splashing of water and what was possibly cursing, but she tried not to notice. Finally he stomped back across the floor, his bruised and cut face now relatively clean. With a huff of annoyance he threw himself against his makeshift bed and drew the blanket up over his shoulder.

Jacqueline blew out the candle and lay in silence, waiting for sleep to claim her. But after a while she realized she could not sleep, and so she stared into the darkness, lost in contemplation of how she might gain entrance to La Force.

"I am going to go with you," stated Philippe suddenly, piercing the silence with his unexpected declaration.

"What are you talking about?" demanded Jacqueline.

He lifted himself up on one elbow and looked at her. "I am going to go with you, to help you get this man out of La Force," he informed her gravely.

"You were eavesdropping!"

"The walls in this house are thin," he protested innocently.

"Liar—you were trying to hear," accused Jacqueline.

"What does it matter? What is important is that I am going with you," he pointed out.

"No, you most certainly are not," countered Jacqueline.

"I could help you," he insisted. "I look younger than my age. I have lived my life on the streets. I have no reason to love the aristocracy. Therefore I will not be suspect. But you will. As soon as you open your mouth you show everyone that you are an aristo. Look what happened to-day."

"Today was an accident," retorted Jacqueline defensively. "I was not expecting you to come crashing into me, and having to watch some filthy pig beat you to a bloody pulp over a loaf of bread."

"That is exactly what I mean," argued Philippe. "No one else in that crowd cared whether I got killed or not. You did. Things happen and you are quick to react, but you react as *you,* not as the person you are pretending to be."

"I won't make that mistake again," asserted Jacqueline solemnly. "I will be more careful."

"You need me," insisted Philippe. "And I want to help."

Jacqueline rolled over to the side of her bed and looked down at him. "Why?" she demanded. "Why do you want to help?"

She could not make him out very well in the darkness, but she knew he shrugged his shoulders.

"Because you risked yourself to help me," he said simply. "No one has ever done that before."

"And then when it looked like I was going to be arrested, you helped me by saying I had the plague. I got away because of you, so I would say we are even."

"I am not offering to help because I feel I am in your debt," retorted Philippe. "I will help you because I want to."

Jacqueline sighed. She had no intention of using this boy to assist her with her mission. But she was far too tired to argue about it anymore. All she wanted to do was sleep. "We'll see," she said evasively as she turned over and closed her eyes.

That seemed to satisfy him. He settled back down on his pillows, and for the next few minutes neither of them spoke.

"What is your real name?" asked Philippe suddenly.

"What do you mean?" she muttered, her voice thick with sleep. "I told you, my name is Pauline Duport."

"No," he replied, obviously quite certain that she was lying. "I want to know your real name."

She yawned. There was probably no harm in telling him. Was there? "Jacqueline."

He was silent for a few moments, and Jacqueline supposed that he had finally fallen asleep. She snuggled into the blankets and prepared to let the same happen to her.

"Good night, Jacqueline."

She awoke with a start. He had said her name slowly, with a languor and care that was achingly familiar. She blinked and looked around the room in confusion. When she realized that Armand was of course not there, she settled back, her fragile heart now trembling and filled with longing.

Chapter 13

The Château de Lambert was seven hours from Paris by coach.

In the past Jacqueline had always traveled in one of her father's many private carriages, which were large and sumptuous, and therefore the trip had not seemed overly tiresome. But a private coach would attract attention, so she was forced to take the crowded public coach, which only went as far as the town of Orléans. Justin had quickly arranged new traveling papers for her in the name of Jeanne Vacquerie. In her new identity she was a maid who worked in a small Paris household. Her father had just died, and she was returning home to comfort her grieving mother. If anyone asked where she was going when she left Orléans and headed toward the Château de Lambert, she was to explain that the Vacquerie cottage was on land that had once belonged to that traitorous aristo the Duc de Lambert. At first she objected strongly to using such an insult, feeling it was unnecessary to betray her father's name, but Justin finally convinced her that the more revolutionary she could appear, the less apt people would be to question her.

Early that morning Philippe again insisted he wanted to help Jacqueline free Armand from prison. Jacqueline had great difficulty convincing him it was impossible, and that under no circumstances would she permit him to become involved. Their argument was loud and long, and Justin finally had to order them to lower their voices, fearing that the neighbors might hear them and wonder at their argument. Finally Philippe relented, although it was clear he was not happy. He ate the enormous breakfast Justin prepared for him in stony silence, pausing every now and then to glare at Jacqueline. He then accepted a bag from Justin filled with food and warm clothes, bade the two of them a curt good-bye, and left. As Jacqueline watched him go out the door she felt a sudden painful stab of regret. What would become of him? she wondered miserably. The bag of food he carried would run out quickly, and once again he would be forced to steal. The next time he was caught, he might not be fortunate enough to have someone intervene on his behalf.

If her life had been as it was a few years ago, she would have kept him with her and seen to it that he had a warm place to sleep and decent food to eat. She would have brought him to the Château de Lambert to live, perhaps on the pretense of hiring him, just so she knew he was safe. But she did not have the power to protect him now. She was here to risk her life to save Armand, and no matter how much Philippe wanted to help her, she could not allow him to become involved in something so dangerous.

It was late afternoon when she finally arrived at Orléans. Jacqueline stepped down from the coach slowly, her back stiff and her legs aching from sitting in such a cramped position for so long. She adjusted her bonnet, clutched her traveling bag close, and began to walk toward the road that would take her to the château. She hoped she would be able to get a ride with someone for at least part of the way. Although her bag held only a few garments and was therefore not heavy, the day was cold and a light snow was falling, making walking difficult.

"How much farther is it?" asked a curious voice.

She whirled around in surprise, only to find Philippe casually gazing back at her.

"What on earth are you doing here?" she managed, stunned.

He shrugged his shoulders. "I felt like getting out of Paris for a while," he told her innocently.

"How did you get here?" she demanded, her shock quickly being replaced with anger.

"Same way you did," he replied, tilting his head back toward the coach. "Except I rode on the back, of course."

She noticed he was bundled in the new clothes Justin had given him, including a warm-looking red wool cap and sturdy leather boots. At least he had had some protection from the cold during the long trip, she reflected. "Well, you just turn around and get yourself right back on a coach to Paris," she ordered firmly. "I'll pay the fare so you can ride on the inside."

"No," he replied, shaking his head. "I don't think I'll be leaving just yet."

She sighed in exasperation. She had no way of forcing him to go back. "Fine then," she snapped. "Do what you like. But you are not to follow me, is that clear?"

He seemed unfazed by her irritation. "Like it or not, Citizeness, you need me. And I know I can help. So why don't you just accept it so we can get on with this?"

He spoke with quiet insistence, as if he were much older than his years. She stared at him, slightly torn. It was possible he could be of assistance to her. A woman with a young boy who was so obviously a child of the streets was far less likely to be considered suspicious. A second pair of eyes could keep watch while she got the jewels. And ridiculous as it was, somehow she drew comfort from his presence. He always seemed so calm, so sure of himself. The fact that he was here actually made her feel better, although she could not imagine why. Besides, she did not like the idea of him traveling all the way back to Paris alone. Perhaps it would be better if they stayed together.

"Very well," she sighed. "You may come with me."

"I knew you'd see it my way," he told her cheerfully.

She began to walk briskly. "Do you know why we are here?" she asked, careful to keep her voice low.

"To get money," he replied. "But I don't know where we are getting it from."

"We are going to my home," she informed him. "For now, that is all you need to know."

It was almost dark when they finally stood in front of the shadowed facade of the Château de Lambert. At first glance the castle looked much as it had when Jacqueline last saw it, a sparkling jewel of cream-colored towers, huge, shimmering windows, and a gleaming, icy-blue slate roof. The château had been built in the early 1500s, not as a fortress, but as a home, and a fine example of Renaissance architecture. The result was a celebration of balance, harmony, and grace, with turrets and machicolations used for decorative whimsy rather than with any defense purposes in mind. One could imagine that on a sunny day the interior of the château would be flooded with light, for there seemed to be windows everywhere, across the front, around the towers, and along the sides. Many of them were now broken and had rough boards nailed against them, giving the château a forlorn, unloved look. As Jacqueline and Philippe walked up the driveway to the entrance, they passed two rows of classical statues, Greek gods and goddesses who once welcomed visitors with their elegant forms and serene expressions. Some had been wrenched from their pedestals and lay in broken heaps upon the ground, while others had had their heads hacked off, a grim reminder of the violent rage felt toward those who dared to live their lives surrounded by such peaceful splendor and opulence. Dozens of trees and shrubs in the surrounding park had been cut down, undoubtedly for firewood, destroying the carefully planned symmetry of the gardens, which had taken more than a hundred years to achieve maturity. Enormous peach-colored marble urns from Italy, which had overflowed with a riot of flowers every summer, now lay smashed to pieces on the ground. The magnificent dove rising out of the fountain in the front garden, the De Lambert symbol of peace, had also been destroyed, its broken wings and head abandoned in the cracked base of the fountain.

"Goddamn—you live here?" whispered Philippe, clearly in awe.

Jacqueline nodded silently as she took in the pitiful sight of her home. She wanted to cry, but of course she could not. It was just one more thing, one more reason to hate the revolution and what it had done to her and her family. She was returning home, but not to stay, so what did it matter if her chateau had been vandalized? At least it is still here, she told herself firmly. It is still standing, and that is all that matters. They have done their damage, but they have not destroyed it, just as they have not destroyed me. I will never live here again, but one day Suzanne and Séraphine will return, and they will restore it to its former grandeur. Comforted by that thought, she forced herself to walk on, steeling herself for the damage that awaited her inside.

They continued up to the front door, where a sign had been crudely nailed into the heavy polished oak. Jacqueline bit down hard on her lip as she read: NATIONAL PROPERTY. REPUBLIC ONE AND INDIVISIBLE. LIBERTY, EQUALITY, FRATERNITY, OR DEATH!

"What's it say?" demanded Philippe, looking at it suspiciously.

"It says it is national property," replied Jacqueline in a tight voice.

"Really?" remarked Philippe with interest. "Does that mean I own part of it?"

"Not exactly," answered Jacqueline. "The government owns it."

He shrugged his shoulders in disgust. "Can't see how that does me any good."

"It doesn't. Come on, we'll get in through the back." She turned away from the hateful sign, resisting the impulse to tear it from the door.

They trudged through the snow around to the back of the château. Jacqueline tried several of the doors, but all of them were locked. Philippe suggested that they simply smash the glass of one of the doors leading onto the terrace so he could crawl in and unlock it from the inside. Although Jacqueline was reluctant to inflict any further damage on her beloved home, she could see this was the only way they were going to get in. Philippe scanned the back garden for something heavy and finally settled on the smiling head of a broken statue. With a small grunt he lifted it up in his skinny arms and heaved it through a glass door. He then climbed through the jagged hole he had created and quickly undid the latch, throwing the door open for Jacqueline to enter.

She stepped into the cold gray shadows of the library and looked around in horror. The outside of the château was nothing compared with the level of ransacking that had occurred inside. Paintings, furniture, and carpets were either missing or completely destroyed. An avalanche of expensive leatherbound books lay mangled and torn on the floor, making it almost impossible to walk from one side of the room to the other. More books had been stuffed into the enormous fireplace in the middle of the library and burned, a vile display of contempt for those who had time to enjoy the luxury of reading. What few pieces of furniture remained had been viciously attacked; a large sofa had had its legs chopped off, possibly for firewood, while the delicate upholstery of several matching chairs had been slashed for no apparent reason, other than to cause their stuffing to spill forth wildly. Jacqueline picked up her skirts and trekked across the sea of books, trying her best to ignore the destruction. But when she got into the corridor and saw three exquisite oil paintings slashed to ribbons, her resolve not to care wavered. She continued down the hall in silence, pausing to glance into the rooms she passed, taking in the wanton destruction, too appalled to speak. Philippe trudged along behind her, glancing into the rooms with more curiosity than dismay, yet sensitive enough of Jacqueline's state not to say anything.

She intended simply to go upstairs to her room and find the jewels. After all, that was the only reason they were here. But the door to her father's study was closed, which normally would not have seemed strange, except that the doors to all the other rooms were open. This small incongruity caused her to stop and push down on the latch. The door swung open with a heavy groan.

Jacqueline stepped inside and looked around in disbelief. Unlike the rest of the château, the Duc de Lambert's study was perfectly neat and in order, as if the destructive fury of the revolution had simply bypassed it. All the furnishings were there, from the beautifully intricate ruby and charcoal Persian carpet to the duc's exquisitely carved mahogany desk, which was inlaid with mother-of-pearl and gilded with gold leaf. Although Jacqueline had not been here to see that the room was cleaned for months, there was not the slightest trace of dust anywhere. The duc's books and papers were neatly laid out upon his desk, and his silver ink set was polished and gleaming. Everything in the room had been carefully tended and preserved, in eerie contrast to the pillaging that had occurred in the rest of the château. Disconcerted by the orderly state of the room, Jacqueline turned to leave.

A startled cry escaped her lips as her eyes fell upon the enormous painting on the wall facing her father's desk. It was a portrait of her family that her father had commissioned in the summer of 1789, just before the fall of the Bastille. The painting depicted the duc seated on a chair beneath an ancient oak tree, with his four loving children positioned around him. Antoine, tall and proud even at sixteen, stood behind his father, while Jacqueline stood beside him, leaning on his massive shoulder with one hand and gently clasping Suzanne's delicate little hand with the other. Séraphine, who was only two at the time, played on the grass by her father's feet. The painting was utterly tranquil and idyllic, a handsome, devoted duc with his beautiful children, a scene perfect in every way except for the obvious absence of the children's mother, and the trace of sadness Jacqueline had always felt was evident in all their eyes.

But the serenity and innocence of the painting was at

odds with the vicious mutilation that had been performed on it. The painting had been assaulted, but not in the random, frenzied manner that other paintings in the château had fallen victim to. The portrait of the De Lambert family had been very carefully slashed, right across the throat of each family member, including little Séraphine. Scarlet paint trickled down their necks and over their fine clothes, until it welled into a deep pool of blood at their feet. The effect was so deliberately horrific that Jacqueline could not take her eyes from it, and so she stood, transfixed, frozen by the awesome hatred that seemed to radiate from the canvas.

"Is that supposed to be you?" asked Philippe as he pointed to Jacqueline's likeness.

She nodded.

He studied her for a moment. "You don't look like that anymore," he said finally.

Jacqueline looked at the fifteen-year-old girl in the portrait, who had been painfully scarred by the death of her mother, but was still totally sheltered from the cruelties of the world beyond the Château de Lambert. She was smiling as she gripped her father's shoulder, so strong and solid and comforting. And she held Suzanne's little hand firmly, fully at ease with her new role as mother to her young sisters. Life had seemed so simple then. Her responsibilities had been clear, her future set. She had thought herself mature and worldly, because she had endured the agony of her mother's death. But now she realized what an innocent she had been. She had known nothing of hunger, or poverty, or misery. She had been innocent of rage and hatred, other than hating God for a time when he took her mother from her. She had not yet understood what it was to hate with a passion that never abated, that grew and darkened and festered until it consumed her every breath.

"I am not like that anymore," she stated bitterly. "That girl is gone."

She turned abruptly and left the room, leaving Philippe staring at the painting.

She mounted the stairs and moved quickly down the hallway that led to her room, trying to ignore the destruction around her. The light was quickly fading, there was no time for her to indulge in anger or self-pity. When she reached her room she found it had not been spared; if anything it had been more thoroughly ransacked than any of the other rooms. Her mattress and pillows had been sliced open and the stuffing torn out, paintings had been wrenched from the walls and cut to pieces, her wardrobe had been emptied of its gowns and chopped into firewood. Even the walls had been attacked; the delicate yellow paper on them had been torn off in many places, and huge holes had been gouged into them every few feet. It was obvious to Jacqueline that whoever attacked this room was not merely venting their rage at a way of life they found abhorrent. The person who so deliberately swept through this room had been on a far greater mission. They had been searching for the missing De Lambert jewels.

She moved quickly across the room to the fireplace. Kneeling down, she ran her hand along the right interior wall, examining the bricks with her fingertips. She traced the edges of the center brick, then grabbed the poker beside her and used it to carve a groove around it. She worked fast, rooting out the sand and ash she had carefully packed around the stone over a year earlier. When she had created a deep ridge around the brick, she inserted the tip of the poker and began to pry, slowly at first, alternating from one side to the other. She jiggled the poker until finally the brick began to move, bit by bit, until it was out just far enough for her to grasp it by the edges and pull it out the rest of the way. She lowered it onto the hearth and reached deep into the black hole she had created. Her hands came to rest on a cool, square object. With a sigh of relief she pulled out an intricately carved wooden box. Sitting back on her heels, she paused to wipe her blackened hands on her skirts before slowly lifting the lid.

Nestled against the black satin lining of the box was a

sparkling collection of priceless jewelry, including elaborate necklaces, earrings, bracelets, rings, brooches, and hair ornaments, all heavily studded with icy diamonds, midnight sapphires, sea-green emeralds, and blood rubies. Ropes of luminous pearls were mixed in with the brilliant pieces, as well as several exquisite gold watches. Jacqueline plunged her hand in among the jewels and rooted around to find a tiny blue velvet bag. She held it upside down over the palm of her hand and an enormous diamond ring spilled out. With a soft sigh she placed the ring on her finger and held it up to the fading light filtering through the windows. It was her mother's favorite piece, a magnificent, utterly colorless diamond surrounded by a shimmering halo of smaller diamonds. Her father had given it to her mother in celebration of the birth of Antoine, their first child and the future Duc de Lambert. She watched with pleasure as the ring sparkled with fire and light, like a tiny, perfect star bound to her finger with gold.

"I knew you would return."

She let out a startled gasp and sprang to her feet, dropping the box of jewels onto the floor. Her heart pounding with fear, she slowly turned around.

Nicolas was blocking the doorway with his huge frame, making a sudden dash to safety impossible. His heavy winter coat was flecked with snow and his boots were wet; it was obvious he had just arrived. He stared at her and smiled, a hard, bitter smile that spoke more of triumph than pleasure.

"What is the matter, Jacqueline?" he demanded mockingly. "Did you honestly believe we would never meet again?"

"No," she answered, her voice low and filled with loathing. "In fact, I always hoped we would."

Her answer seemed to surprise him, and that pleased her. He studied her a moment, taking in her simple attire, her filthy skirts and her blackened hands.

"By what guise are we here today?" he asked curiously. "Scullery maid?"

She did not answer.

"It is not terribly becoming on you, whatever it is," he mocked. "Although, I must admit, it is probably more becoming than the outfit you wore to sneak your way out of the Conciergerie. Every guard you passed swore to me on their mother's grave that it was an old man and a filthy boy who walked out of the prison that night. None would believe it could possibly have been the beautiful daughter of the Duc de Lambert. You and all your traitorous accomplices are to be commended on carrying off so convincing a charade."

She stared at him calmly, unwilling to confirm or deny his accusations, desperately trying to think of some way to get past him.

"I paid for your little escape, I can tell you," he continued bitterly as he stepped into the room and began to strip off his gloves. "The Committee of Public Safety does not take kindly to condemned prisoners slipping through the walls of justice. And since I was the last person with you, and I foolishly agreed to leave you with that Citizen Julien, there was even some suspicion that I might have been involved in your sudden disappearance." He tossed his gloves onto the floor and began to undo the buttons on his coat.

"How unfortunate for you," commented Jacqueline sarcastically. She glanced casually around the room, searching for something to use as a weapon. She cursed herself for not at least having thought to hide a knife in her boot.

"But then I almost found you, didn't I?" he went on, ignoring her comment. "Once the word was out that we were looking for a young boy and an old man, we were of course flooded with dozens of reports. One of them came from that innkeeper, Dufresne. He said he was not sure, but he did not think that the old man's grandson was very enthusiastic when he talked about the executions of the day. I got there as quickly as I could, but you were just one step ahead of me, weren't you?"

"I don't know what you are talking about," Jacqueline

declared. She had no idea how much he knew about Armand and his involvement with her escape. The less she said, the better.

"Of course you do," Nicolas assured her. "When we got into your room, we saw that he had purchased women's clothes for you. That was enough, but it was the bar of perfumed soap that really convinced me. Poor Jacqueline, did those long weeks in prison leave you needing a bath?" he taunted.

She met his gaze calmly. In her mind she was still searching the room for something to kill him with, but she tried to appear docile and resigned to the fact that he had found her.

"Your friend was lucky to get you away from that mob," Nicolas commented as he dropped his coat to the floor. "And, I must admit, it was a nice touch to send that boy to me inquiring about his reward. That was when I realized I was not dealing with someone who merely wanted to see that Mademoiselle Jacqueline de Lambert did not have her pretty neck severed by the guillotine." He smiled. "That was when it became clear I was dealing with the Black Prince. Only he would be arrogant enough to snatch an escaped aristo from a hostile Parisian mob, and stupid enough to then flaunt his arrogance in my face."

Jacqueline continued to stare at him blankly, trying to look as if she hadn't the faintest idea what he was talking about. She had decided the best weapon available to her was the brass poker lying on the hearth. The question was, how would she snatch it up without Nicolas getting to her first?

"The challenge, of course, became not just to get you back, but to capture the Black Prince as well," Nicolas continued. "After a few weeks had passed without an arrest, I felt sure you had left the country. Recalling your great fondness for your sisters, I realized you must have gone to England. Knowing where you were made trapping both of you incredibly easy."

"Really?" said Jacqueline, slowly moving closer to the

poker, pretending she was simply inspecting the destruction inflicted upon her room. "How is that?"

"I used your precious betrothed, of course," he replied. "You remember, that idiotic fop your father thought was good enough for you, when I was not? I had him arrested, on charges of conspiring in your escape. I must tell you, he required little coaxing," he sneered. "He was more than willing to tell me where your sisters were in England. I then had him write to you there and plead for help. I was not sure if you would come, or if you would send your infamous new friend, but either way I would be rewarded for trapping one of you."

Jacqueline still managed to look at him calmly, but fury and regret were churning within her. Justin was right, the whole thing had been a trap. And Jacqueline had stupidly sent Armand into it.

"When your friend appeared out of nowhere to rescue Monsieur le Marquis, I was right there to catch him," Nicolas boasted. "But alas, you did not appear to be with him. So I let your precious marquis go, in the hopes that he would tell you what had happened. I suspected your inbred sense of noble duty would lead you back to France to try to help the Black Prince."

He was clever, she had to give him that. He had planned the whole thing, sensing Jacqueline would be unable to ignore François-Louis's or Armand's plight. The revelation that François-Louis had agreed to help Nicolas in exchange for his freedom was a shock, but at this moment it did not matter. What mattered was killing Nicolas for his crimes against her and her family. Then she would rescue Armand.

"I come here often, you know," continued Nicolas, looking about her room as he began to unbutton his jacket. "Whenever I can get away from my work for a day or two. I tore this room apart myself looking for those jewels. I must admit, it did not occur to me to look in the fireplace. Somehow I could not imagine the pristine Mademoiselle de Lambert dirtying her hands, not even to hide something so incredibly valuable."

"I am surprised you did not tear apart my father's study," commented Jacqueline acidly, trying to keep him preoccupied with his talking as she casually took another step toward the hearth.

"I did have it searched," Nicolas admitted, "but very carefully. After all, I did not want the room destroyed. I wanted the room where your father rejected my offer for you preserved for my own use. As you may have noticed, I have kept it exactly the way it was when your father was alive and I used to come here as a welcome guest and friend. You remember those days, don't you, Jacqueline? I was invited here because of my superior knowledge of finance and investment, which your father sorely lacked. With the abolition of feudalism, pious aristocrats like your father, who once thought business was common and therefore beneath them, suddenly had no means of income. If not for my advice that your father invest his money in industries like sugar, tea, and silk, your brother would have inherited nothing but this old château and the mountain of debt that goes with it. I saved your family from financial ruin, do you realize that?" he demanded furiously. "Your father owed me. It was therefore a great shock when he refused my offer for you. That, of course, was when I realized what a hypocrite he was. Him and all his noble friends, who spouted liberal ideals over their fine dinners, accepting men like me as equals in theory, but not in fact."

"Do not delude yourself, Nicolas," interjected Jacqueline. "I never thought you were an equal in theory either."

The insult found its mark. With two strides he had closed the distance between them and slapped her hard across her face.

"Think carefully before you make such a regrettable comment again," he warned menacingly as he gripped her by her shoulders. "I would hate to have to send you to the guillotine with your lovely face bruised and battered like some common peasant wife."

She wanted to spit in his face, but if she hoped to reach the poker she would need him to release her, and so she held her tongue and simply glared at him, her loathing and hatred so intense it nearly sickened her.

"But here we are, fighting again," he said mournfully as he lightly stroked her cheek where he had struck her. "This is not how I imagined our reconciliation. Let us agree to put aside our differences, just for tonight. After all, tomorrow will come soon enough."

"Tomorrow?" repeated Jacqueline warily.

"I have dreamed of having you for years," continued Nicolas, slowly pulling on the ribbon that held her hat in place. "First as my wife, and then, when your father refused me, as my mistress." He lifted the hat from her head and tossed it onto the floor. "But you continued to spurn me, didn't you?"

He lifted his hand to trace the contour of her jaw. Jacqueline instinctively flinched and tried to move away from him, and he responded by snaking his fingers around the back of her neck to hold her still.

"It was most regrettable that you were arrested with your brother," he commented. "As I tried to explain to you before, that was not the way it was supposed to happen. Antoine was to have been imprisoned, leaving you all alone here, except for a few servants. Then you would have seen how I could have helped you. Providing, of course, you were willing to make me welcome."

"You are a fool if you believe I would have asked for your help," Jacqueline assured him. "No matter how desperate I was, I never would have gone to you for help, Nicolas. Never."

"It does not matter." He sighed, sadly shaking his head. "We are far beyond my being able to protect you. You have escaped republican justice, and now you have been caught. It is my duty to turn you over so you can be questioned and executed. Regrettably, that is what lies before us."

"And you will be commended not only for capturing me, but for finding the De Lambert jewels as well," added Jacqueline bitterly, trying to think of a way to escape his grip without arousing any suspicion.

"Capturing you will definitely repair the damage your escape did to my career," admitted Nicolas. "The jewels, however, are another matter entirely."

"Do you mean to say you are going to keep them?" she demanded in disbelief.

He shrugged his shoulders and released his hands from her. "The small fortune spilled across this floor cannot begin to pull the government out of the enormous debt it has amassed with the war effort. I, on the other hand, could profit greatly from the investments these jewels represent."

"So you are a traitor and a thief, even to the government you claim to support?" she taunted, backing away from him a step.

"This discussion is fascinating, but I believe we have talked enough," remarked Nicolas irritably as he started to move toward her.

"I agree," replied Jacqueline. She swooped down to snatch up the poker from the floor and brandished it threateningly at him. "Take one more step, and I will bash your brains in," she warned.

Nicolas looked at her in amusement and laughed. "You do not disappoint me, Jacqueline," he told her. "I have always known you would fight me right to the very end." He took another step toward her, utterly unimpressed by her weapon. "Which makes the anticipation of finally having you all the more pleasurable."

She swung wildly at him, but he grabbed her arm and easily knocked the poker from her hand. With a cry of rage she smashed at his face with her fist, but she had barely made contact before he had secured her wrist and wrenched her arms down to her sides.

"Now what, Jacqueline?" he demanded mockingly. "Would you like to give up?"

"Never!" she hissed. She pulled back her knee and drove it hard into his crotch.

Sensing what she was about to do, he turned himself slightly. Her knee landed hard against his thigh, causing him to wince in pain. "You little bitch," he growled, releasing one of her arms to slap her hard against her face.

Her head snapped to one side from the impact of his blow, and she momentarily lost her balance. Nicolas used this opportunity to trip her leg out from under her and send her sprawling across the floor. Jacqueline immediately struggled to get up, but Nicolas was already lowering himself down onto her, pinning her against the carpet with his weight.

"Take your hands off me, you loathsome son of a bitch!" she swore as she fought to get him off her.

"Shut up!" he snapped, cracking her hard across the face again with the back of his hand.

Tears of frustration and pain sprang to her eyes as she felt him wedge his knee between her legs and force them apart. She fought to keep her thighs closed, she struggled to move out from under him, she beat his back and shoulders with her fists, but she was no match for his superior strength and weight. He pinned her down by squeezing cruelly against her breast while his other hand yanked up her skirts. Blindly she reached around on the floor for something to use as a weapon, but her fingers felt only carpet and fabric and stuffing. Her stockinged legs were exposed to the cold air, she was aware of him fumbling to release himself from his trousers, and then suddenly her fingers closed around something cold and smooth and jagged. Without pausing to see what she had found, she reached up and raked it against his face.

Nicolas let out a howl of pain. He looked at her in confusion. A brilliant ruby arc of blood was slowly seeping down his face. Somehow she had managed to carve a deep gash from his temple down to his chin. She raised her hand to slice at him again, but he was too quick for her. He grabbed her wrist and smashed it against the floor until her fingers opened and she dropped the broken piece of porcelain she held. He knocked it so it was out of her reach, then lifted his fingers to his cheek and drew them away, studying the warm blood that stained his fingers in horror.

"Goddamn whore—" he snarled viciously. He lowered his bloodstained hand to her neck and tightened his fingers around her throat.

Jacqueline clutched his fingers and tried to pry them off her neck. Nicolas tightened his grip and began to squeeze slowly. She gasped for air, but found she could draw none. She coughed and thrashed her head from side to side, but he held fast. She stared at him, her eyes caught between fury and pleading, and he smiled, a dark, savage, evil smile. She could feel him pressing his hardness between her legs, brutally forcing his way into the dry, delicate flesh, and she wanted to scream but she could not, and so she closed her eyes and sobbed inwardly, torn between wanting to kill him and wanting to die.

There was a sudden, sickening thud, and Nicolas's entire body relaxed against her, releasing her throat and ceasing its brutal invasion of her. She choked and gasped for air before opening her eyes to see what had happened.

Philippe stood trembling above her, his bruised face contorted with rage. In his hands he held a heavy silver mantel clock, dripping with blood, and poised to strike again if Nicolas made the slightest movement.

"Are you all right?" he demanded, his voice taut and shaking.

"Get him off me," she pleaded, her own voice thin and wispy.

Philippe threw down the clock, grabbed Nicolas by one arm, and roughly dragged him off Jacqueline. She pushed down her skirts and allowed Philippe to slowly help her stand.

"Jesus Christ, you're bleeding!" he cried in horror.

She gingerly touched her fingers to the corner of her mouth and felt the warm seep of blood where Nicolas had struck her. "It's nothing," she assured him.

"Not there—your neck," he qualified. "He cut you somewhere."

She laid her fingers on her neck and then pulled them away. A smear of blood stained the skin. "That's not my blood," she said stiffly. "That's his."

They both looked at Nicolas, who was lying motionless facedown on the floor. Blood was seeping from a wound in his head and forming a huge wine-colored stain on the carpet.

"I—I think I killed him," stammered Philippe.

"Good," replied Jacqueline curtly. She felt like she was going to be sick. She turned away and quickly began to collect the scattered jewels on the floor and stuff them back into the box. Her hands were trembling, making her slow and awkward at the task. Philippe did not offer to help, but simply stood where he was, staring at Nicolas.

"Let's get out of here," she said urgently as she buried the box of jewels underneath the garments in her traveling bag. She moved toward the door and then turned. "Philippe?"

He tore his gaze from Nicolas's body and looked at her. His eyes were huge, haunted, the eyes of a child who is suddenly uncertain and afraid. "I think I killed him," he repeated hoarsely.

She put down her bag, walked over to him, and wrapped her arms around him in a fierce embrace. "You saved my life," she whispered as she held him tightly against her. "Thank you."

Philippe stood there stiffly, his arms rooted down at his sides, as if he did not know how to return a hug. But he did not move away, and so they stayed together like that for a moment, giving and drawing comfort from each other. And then Jacqueline felt his arms relax and gradually move up to wrap around her waist.

"Let's get out of here," he said quietly.

She nodded, and slowly the two of them began to walk toward the door, leaving the motionless body of Nicolas bleeding into the carpet behind them.

Chapter 14

The warden of La Force planted his elbows on top of the mountain of papers cluttering his desk and wearily rubbed his temples. He had not had a good day, and it looked like once again he would be here well into the night. His prison was already filled far beyond capacity, yet here was another stack of documents that had to be processed without delay. They were ordering the admittance of yet another fifteen prisoners, who had just arrived and were currently sitting outside his office crying and shouting and noisily protesting their innocence. Where in the name of God was he going to put them? he wondered in frustration. The cells and common rooms were overcrowded, despite the fact that there was a constant flow of inmates leaving each day to go before the Revolutionary Tribunal. Thanks to the services of several spies planted within the prison, the evidence against these former aristos was more than enough to send them directly to the guillotine. Yet a bed was not empty more than an hour before someone new had arrived and been assigned to it. How on earth did they expect him to keep up?

Running La Force was an ongoing struggle to feed and oversee hundreds of prisoners, all of whom were constantly demanding better food, clean linen, more blankets, letters that had to be sent, personal artifacts that were supposed to be documented and distributed, not to mention the continual parade of visitors, including husbands, wives, children, servants, mistresses, business associates, doctors, lawyers, and officials of the Committee of Public Safety. The sheer volume of human traffic that passed within these walls each day was astounding. How could they expect him to manage the daily activities of running the prison effectively, and see to all the paperwork that was required of him as well? Beyond the documents issued every time an inmate was admitted to the prison, there was the daily authorization of the roll call, which invariably did not match the names and numbers on the prison registers, the investigations into prisoners who claimed to be someone else, the reports on prisoners who required further evidence against them, the reports on prisoners thought to be actively plotting in counterrevolutionary activities, the reports on prisoners whose files had somehow gotten lost, the reports on the daily costs of the prison, including itemized accounts of how much food and wine was consumed at each meal, the daily ordering of food, wine, candles, oil, and straw, the records of payment to the guards and prison staff, the documents required to transfer an inmate to another prison—the list went on and on. He was always at his desk before daybreak, and never left until well into the night. And yet he could not seem to get caught up in his work. His wife had been complaining of his hours for months now, but what was a man to do? The number of arrests was accelerating all over France, and the Tribunal seemed unable to cope with the numbers awaiting trial. Somehow, somewhere, he would have to find room for the fifteen traitorous wretches who were waiting outside.

The sound of a child wailing interrupted his thoughts. He frowned. He did not believe in arresting children with their parents. Children had a tendency to grow sickly and die in prison, and that always looked bad in a report. Besides, there was no mention in any of these documents of a child being arrested. The wailing grew louder and more piercing, until it felt like each cry was a knife slowly carving its way through his brain. How the hell was he supposed to concentrate with that racket going on? He irritably shoved his chair away from his desk and went to see what was happening.

"I just want my mother's things—you can't keep them

from me," cried a small, thin boy who was struggling to free himself from the grip of one of the guards.

"What seems to be the problem here?" demanded the warden.

The guard looked at him apologetically. "Sorry to have disturbed you, warden, but the boy here says his mother was executed this morning, and he has come to collect her things."

"Then why the devil don't you give them to him and get him out of here?" he snapped.

The guard looked sheepish. "Truth is, we can't seem to find any record of his mother being here," he explained.

So what else is new? thought the warden irritably. "What was your mother's name, boy?"

The boy looked at him with tear-filled eyes. His face was badly bruised, to a degree even the warden found shocking. He had two boys of his own, and although he was not averse to giving them a good smack every now and then, he did not approve of beating a child to a pulp.

"Her name is Claire Blanchard," said the boy in a quivering voice. "Was, I mean," he corrected himself. He dissolved into another loud wail.

The sound sliced like a hatchet through the warden's head. "Are you sure she was a prisoner here?" he demanded, his voice tight with strain.

"Yes," answered the boy shakily. "She was only here three days."

Three days. It was possible her papers lay buried somewhere on his desk. She could have been admitted and discharged without him even knowing about it. Now she was dead, and this boy was entitled to whatever notes or locks of hair or other personal effects she may have left in the care of her guard. He sighed.

"Stop your sniveling and come in here," he ordered brusquely.

The boy wiped his nose on his filthy sleeve, picked up the bag he had dropped on the floor, and followed him into his office.

The warden began to rifle through the mountain of

papers on his desk. After a few minutes he realized it was hopeless. There were scores of documents here that he had not even seen, obviously added to the pile on those rare occasions when he was out of his office.

"Why don't you go home, boy, while I look into this matter? If you come back tomorrow, I am certain we will have found your mother's effects by then," he suggested.

The boy gave him a wild, frightened look. "My father said if I come home without her things, he'll beat me worse than he did the last time," he told him, clearly terrified. "Please, Citizen, he's awful mean when he's mad. Couldn't you try to find out where her things are?"

Judging from the boy's face, if he were beaten worse than the last time, his father intended to kill him. He did not relish the idea of sending the boy home to that. Not when his mother had just been executed. He sighed.

"What did your mother look like?" he demanded.

The boy thought for a moment. "She was pretty," he told him softly. "Her hair was brown, and her eyes were brown. She was not too tall, but then, she was not exactly short either. Her height was sort of medium. Do you know who I mean?" he asked hopefully.

Yes, thought the warden. You mean like over half the women incarcerated here. "Was there anything about her that was a little unusual?" he asked, trying hard to be patient.

The boy knit his brows together. "She liked to sing," he said finally, as if he felt certain that would set her apart from everyone else.

She probably didn't do much singing here, thought the warden acidly, but he refrained from pointing that out to the boy. This whole thing was impossible. "Look, lad, I really think if you can just wait until tomorrow we will be able to—"

The boy's temporary composure dissolved and he began to wail louder than ever. The pain in the warden's head immediately doubled, no longer like a knife, but like someone was using a heavy mallet to slowly bash his brains in.

"Stay here and don't touch anything," he snapped as he stomped out of his office and closed the door. He would look into this matter himself, even if it was just to get away from all this crying and screaming.

He returned about twenty minutes later. He had not been able to find a guard who recognized the name Claire Blanchard, but many of the guards didn't bother to learn the names of inmates who were here less than a week. At any rate, his head was feeling somewhat better. That was something. He opened the door to his office, bracing himself for the wailing that would start when he told the boy he had been unsuccessful.

The boy was not there.

"Guard!" he barked. "What happened to the boy who was waiting in my office?"

The guard came running and looked around the empty room in confusion. "I thought he was in here," he said blankly.

"He was," snapped the warden. His head was beginning to throb again. "And now he clearly is not. Didn't you see him leave?"

"No," replied the guard. "Maybe he decided to come back tomorrow."

The warden wearily closed his eyes. "Get out," he ordered.

He shut the door and walked over to his desk. He quickly scanned it, and then went through all the drawers to see if anything was missing. Nothing appeared to be out of order. He sighed.

Maybe the boy had simply grown tired of waiting and decided to go home. He would probably be back tomorrow. At any rate, he had already wasted enough of his precious time. He still had a roomful of new prisoners sitting outside his door, and it was clear he was going to be here late. Dismissing the incident as unimportant, he picked up his pen and went back to work.

•　　•　　•

Armand lay on his trestle bed with his eyes closed, imagining he was sailing on *The Angélique*.

He had been in La Force for twenty-eight days. During that time he had been refused even the simplest requests, such as the luxury of a book to read, or a walk outside in the fresh air. Nicolas had promised him an existence that was cramped, monotonous, filthy, and humiliating, and he had been true to his word. In a bid to keep himself from going mad, Armand had taken to meditating on a restful and pleasant image for at least an hour every morning, afternoon, and evening. This ritual, in addition to his two hours of daily exercise and his constant thoughts of Jacqueline, which had evolved into what he realized by now probably amounted to an obsession, helped to get him through the empty, miserable hours that now made up his life.

He hoped they would execute him soon.

In his mind he was no longer a prisoner confined day and night to a tiny, dark, frigid cell, surrounded by the stench and sound of human misery. For him the day was sunny and warm, the wind strong and steady, filling *The Angélique*'s enormous white sails and sending her flying across the water like a graceful, low-flying gull. The ocean was liquid sapphire, sparkling in the white glare of the sun and rhythmically crashing against the hull of his ship, surrounding him with color and light, movement and music. He leaned against the rail and breathed in the sharp, clean scent of the sea, filling his lungs with its crystal-clear purity. The cool salt spray brushed against his skin, his hair, his clothes, invigorating him, freeing him from the dank confines of reality as he sailed into an endless expanse of sapphire and light. He turned to see Jacqueline standing behind him, dressed in the silvery gown he had designed for her. The wind blew the gown against her body, revealing the lush swell of her breasts, the graceful tapering of her waist, the firm length of her legs. Her hair was tumbling wildly about her shoulders, dancing in the sea wind, brilliant in the sun, the color of champagne and firelight. She stepped toward him, slowly, gracefully, a faint smile on her lips, her silvery-gray eyes shimmering with desire. She stood in front of him, her exquisite body barely touching his, and languidly reached up to loop her arms around his neck and pull him down close to her, her lips soft and parted and trembling as she sighed and whispered, "So I've finally found you, you goddamn, good-for-nothing, son-of-a-bitch traitor!"

His eyes flew open.

A woman was standing before him, her face obscured by an enormous hat and the dark shadows of the cell. She wore a filthy brown coat, which had been tied around the excessive girth of her waist with a ragged length of rope. At first glance he thought she was simply fat, but a second look made it clear that her horribly swollen form was in fact very much with child. Her clothes were thin and poor, a faded yellow cotton blouse tightly pulled down over the waistband of a much-mended gray skirt, covered with mud stains. She wore a battered gray hat with a cockade pinned to it, over a badly arranged pile of greasy red hair. He was certain he had never seen her before in his life. He could not imagine why his jailer had allowed her into his cell.

"So this is where you've been hiding your good-for-nothing ass, is it?" she demanded furiously. "Lying on a bed all day having your meals brought to you like royalty while I'm out in the pissin' cold freezin' my butt off to earn money so this brat of yours will have a roof over its head. Well, if you think you can just dump your responsibilities by going and getting yourself arrested you can just think again, you good-for-nothing, lazy bastard, I know you've money put away and I intend to see that me and your brat gets our share, do you hear? What kind of man are you that you could leave a woman with a babe on the way and no food on the table? And if you think you can get away with leaving us high and dry just because of your criminal ways, well, let me tell you just how mistaken you are, you filthy traitor. . . ."

Armand blinked as he watched her continue her hysterical tirade. He knew he must be losing his mind. For underneath her greasy, ragged exterior, her pregnant shape, and her gutter language, he felt almost certain he was looking at Jacqueline.

It was utterly, hopelessly impossible, of course. He realized that he must be suffering from some sort of temporary insanity, brought on by the endless minutes and hours and days and nights spent locked in this grotesquely small, dark cell, left alone with nothing but thoughts of her to occupy his mind, the thought of her and the hope that soon he would be executed and this ungodly confinement would be brought to an end. And so he stared at the woman in fascination, somewhat horrified by the trick his mind was playing on him, and yet mesmerized by the shape of her chin, the curve of her mouth, the slant of her smudged little nose. She was pacing now, moving awkwardly, gesturing wildly with her arms as she asked him how he could have betrayed her and his child and France with such a despicable act? She turned to pace to the other side of the cell and the light from the hallway spilled through the open doorway where his jailer was standing, sending a faint splash of light across her face as she looked at him and told him what a low, deceiving son of a bitch he was. And he saw her eyes, silvery gray, burning in their intensity. Enraged. Determined.

And terrified.

His heart leapt into his throat. It was Jacqueline, here, in his cell, acting out some crazy plan, and in that moment he felt such a rush of fury and horror that he could not trust himself to speak. What in God's name was she doing here? Did she think she was going to sneak him out underneath her skirts?

"She's got spirit to her, don't she?" quipped his jailer, who was watching Jacqueline's performance with great amusement. "If she was mine, I'd have beaten that out of her. Since you're stuck in here and she's not, I guess she'll be havin' the last word, won't she?" He laughed, a guttural, sneering sound that made Armand want to grab him by the throat and choke the laughter right out of him.

He had to get her out of here, now, immediately, before she put herself into any further danger. Obviously she was hoping he would play along with her act, acknowledging that she was his mistress. He would do no such thing.

"Citizen Pinard, I do not know this woman," he stated flatly. "Please remove her from my cell."

Jacqueline stopped her rambling and stared at him in surprise. What on earth was he trying to do? she wondered frantically. Was it possible that he really did not recognize her yet?

"Ooooh, you're a low-down bugger not to even admit what you've done to me," she screeched. She turned her attention to the jailer. "I was a good girl before I met him. Now here I am, all alone and about to bring a new citizen of the Republic into the world, not asking for much, just that he give me enough so I can care for the babe and get my strength back, and then hire a wet nurse so I can go out and find some work. He's got money—where he's going he won't be needing it—yet he won't even own up to the fact that it's his. What kind of a man would do that to a girl, I ask you?" She began to cry pathetically.

Armand was impressed by her acting. She had certainly improved since he had first met her. "Citizen Pinard, I would like this crazy woman removed from my cell," he repeated firmly.

"Well now, I'm sure you would," snorted his jailer, his voice heavy with contempt. "After all, it's much easier not to have to face one's responsibilities, isn't it? Well, you won't be getting any help from me, you spineless dog. You set things straight with this girl, do you hear?" With that pronouncement he slammed the cell door shut and twisted the lock.

Armand turned to face her, his mind reeling. What the hell was happening? Jacqueline was here, standing before him, locked in his cell, in grave danger, and goddamn it if she wasn't actually *smiling* at him.

"What in the name of all that's holy are you doing here?" he ground out in a soft, savage voice.

She did not answer him. She simply stood there, fro-

zen, staring at him, her expression caught somewhere between laughter and tears. And then her lower lip began to
tremble, and suddenly he could see just how terrified she
was, and all the anger he felt immediately evaporated. He
held his arms out to her.

With a muffled cry she threw herself against him. He
wrapped his arms tightly around her and ground his lips
against hers, roughly, desperately, starving for the taste
and touch and scent of her, unable to believe she was real,
unwilling to believe she was not. She clung to him as
closely as her expanded stomach would allow, making
soft little whimpering sounds as she kissed him back with
a passion that astounded him. It was insane, he knew
that, but in that moment he was prepared to accept the
fact that he had absolutely lost his mind, as long as that
meant he could keep on holding her.

It was Jacqueline who finally broke the kiss, pushing
him to arm's length so she could think straight.

"You must do as I say," she whispered urgently as she
glanced at the door. She looked down at his leg, wondering which one had been injured. "Can you walk?"

"Of course I can walk," he snapped softly. What on
earth was she talking about?

She pulled up the bottom of her skirts to reveal a large
bundle tied around her waist. With fumbling fingers she
managed to loosen the rope that held it secure, until it
dropped to the floor by her feet.

"We must keep arguing," she whispered as she began
to untie the bundle. She took a deep breath to steady her
nerves. "How dare you pretend not to know me, you vile,
rotten bastard!" she shrieked.

Armand watched in amazement as she quickly undid
the bundle, revealing a gun, a dagger, and a warder's uniform. How had she managed to get her hands on all that?

"You'll have to take care of the jailer," she whispered,
handing him the gun, the dagger, and the rope. She
quickly shoved the uniform back up her skirt, let out a cry
of pain, and collapsed to the floor. "Oh my God, now
look what you've done, it's time, it's time!" she wailed.

Stunned, Armand stared at her as she curled up on the filthy floor in apparent agony.

"Call the jailer!" she hissed. "Oh my God, how could this be happening now?" she cried dramatically.

Gathering his wits, he stuck the dagger in his boot and shoved the pistol in the waistband of his trousers. "Guard!" he yelled, running to the cell door. "Citizen Pinard! Come quickly, there is an emergency!"

"What's all the noise about?" grumbled Pinard as he peered through the grille.

"I think she's having the baby," replied Armand anxiously.

Jacqueline let out a terrible, ear-piercing scream of pain.

"Here now, you can't be having any brats in here, you've got to go," gasped Pinard as he fumbled for his key.

"Ohhhhh," moaned Jacqueline, writhing on the floor.

The cell door swung open and Pinard stepped inside. "Listen to me, Citizeness, I am telling you, you cannot have your baby here." He walked over to where she lay. "Get up and get out now, do you hear me? You cannot—"

Jacqueline let out another scream of pain as Armand brought his pistol crashing down onto the jailer's head. He grabbed him as he fell so he would not collapse on Jacqueline.

"Take his keys and put him in the bed," she instructed as she stood up and began to pull the prison uniform out from under her skirts once more.

Armand removed the enormous key ring that was tied to Pinard's waist and dragged him over to the bed.

"Give me your jacket, and put this uniform on— hurry!" ordered Jacqueline.

He quickly tore off his jacket and handed it to her. She then labored to get it on the unconscious jailer, which was no easy task. Once she had finished she rolled him onto his stomach and tied his hands behind his back. Then she stuffed a kerchief into his mouth and drew the blanket

over him, making sure his face was turned toward the
wall. If one only took a quick look, and as long as he
remained still, it would appear that Citizen Michel Belanger was sleeping in the bed.

She turned to look at Armand, who was almost finished donning the warder's uniform. It was far too small
for him. Jacqueline scooped up the shirt and trousers he
had removed and quickly stuffed them under her skirts,
making her appear pregnant again.

"You will have to hunch over as we move down the
halls," she told him, taking in his short coat sleeves and
the buttons straining across his chest. "You are obviously
much bigger than the man who usually wears that uniform."

He obediently adjusted his stance. "Ready?"

She nodded.

"Then start moaning," he whispered, opening the
door.

Jacqueline began to whimper in pain as she staggered
out with him. Armand locked the cell door behind them
and they began to hurry down the hallway. Jacqueline
sobbed and groaned as she waddled along, clutching her
enormous stomach, while Armand hunched over her, sup-
porting her with his arm and keeping his face turned in
toward hers, all the while impatiently scolding her for being so foolish as to go out when she was so near her time.

They cleared one hallway without meeting any guards
and started down the next. At the far end a warder sitting
on a stool watched them approach.

"What's this then?" he asked with interest.

"The babe has decided it's time to join us," snapped
Armand irritably, not slowing his pace.

"In here?" returned the guard with disbelief.

"I'll see how she feels when we get to the front," he
replied. "If the pain is past, she can bloody well go home
to have it." He moved past him.

Down a dark flight of stairs, along another dank hall,
passing the miserable, stinking cells Jacqueline had
walked by on her way up to visit Armand. Many of the

guards they encountered had seen her go in not a half
hour earlier and did not seem to be concerned that she
was an escaping prisoner. Some of them made crude jokes
about her condition. Armand was intimidating as he
spoke to Jacqueline, acting like a man who had greater
things to worry about than some stupid girl who had
come to visit a prisoner and gone into labor in the process. Once again Jacqueline was amazed by his ability to
slip into a character so effortlessly. Armand's act of impatient authority, combined with his uniform and the darkness of the corridors, seemed to be convincing enough for
everyone.

"Keep moving—we can't take responsibility for you—
we don't have the room or the means to birth your child,
do you understand?" he snapped as he pushed Jacqueline
along.

"Yes," gasped Jacqueline weakly as she pretended to
be enduring a great stab of pain.

"Is there a problem?" called out a voice from behind
them.

Armand did not stop. "The citizeness has decided it is
time to have her baby," he replied over his shoulder. "I
am taking her to the front gate."

"Let me help you," offered the guard, hurrying up behind them. "You should not be—" He stopped in mid-
sentence and stared in confusion at Armand. His
expression grew hard. "Who the hell are you?"

"Actually, I'm new here," explained Armand calmly as
he released his grip on Jacqueline. "I was just transferred
from the Abbaye."

The guard looked at him suspiciously. "Then you
won't mind coming with me so the warden can confirm
that, will you?"

"Not at all," replied Armand pleasantly. "I'll just see
this girl to the front gate and—"

"Now," interrupted the guard. "The girl can wait."

Armand sighed and stepped over to the guard. As he
did so Jacqueline clutched her stomach and let out a terrible shriek of pain. The guard took his eyes off Armand to

look at her, and Armand grabbed him and smashed him hard against the stone wall. His eyes rolled back into his head as he slumped down against Armand.

"What's all the racket?" complained a disgruntled prisoner. He pressed his face agaist the grille of his cell door.

"Drunk again," snapped Armand in exasperation as he dragged the guard over to an alcove and lay him down on the floor. He turned to look at the prisoner. "Go back to bed, Citizen."

He walked over to Jacqueline and they began to make their way down the hallway once more.

"Not too much further, Citizeness," he said as they approached the front doorway.

Jacqueline wondered if he was saying it as part of his performance, or if he was actually trying to reassure her.

There were two guards posted at the front doorway. They were great, burly fellows, whose job it was to make certain that no one left the prison without clearance. Armand kept up his irritated tirade as they approached, ordering Jacqueline to go home to have her baby, that they had enough to worry about without women like her coming in to visit prisoners and then suddenly deciding it was time to give birth, and that if she set her mind to it he was sure she would get home in plenty of time to have the child. He huddled over her as if he was trying to support her as she walked, effectively shielding his face from view until they had reached the guards.

"Leaving so soon, Citizeness?" quipped one of the guards as she and Armand approached.

"Ohhhhh," moaned Jacqueline, pretending to be in too much pain to answer him.

"Looks like her visit gave her more than she bargained for," joked the other guard as he opened the door for her.

"Come on now, you can make it," snapped Armand impatiently as he walked with her through the door.

"Where do you think you're going?" demanded one of the guards.

"I am just going to help her to the street," Armand replied. "From there she is on her own."

"That isn't necessary," the guard informed him. "Get back inside."

Jacqueline grabbed her stomach and let out a terrible cry of pain. Armand did not let go of her. "She needs my assistance," he pointed out reasonably. "At the street she will be able to hire a carriage. It will not take more than a minute."

"She is not your responsibility, Citizen," the guard informed him. "You have other duties to attend to. Get back inside."

Armand stood there, glaring at the guard, still not relinquishing his hold on Jacqueline.

They were so close. A half hour ago he had been resigned to the fact that he was going to die here. But from the moment he stepped out of his cell he started to believe escape really was possible. He could almost feel the deck of *The Angélique* swaying and rolling beneath him. But he could not allow Jacqueline to come to any harm in her bid to save him. He knew he could not risk a confrontation at the front of the prison with these guards, or they would both end up being arrested. He looked down at her, deep into the clear, silvery pools of her eyes, which were shimmering with fear and hope. *Do something,* she seemed to be saying to him. So full of trust, as if at that moment she truly believed he could do absolutely anything.

There was so much he wanted to say to her, and now he never would. How cruel fate was, to tear away his wife, daughter, and mother, shattering his life, making him hate himself with a passion so strong it nearly destroyed him. And then to send Jacqueline to him, like a glorious, rescuing angel, tantalizing him with feelings that for one magnificent moment had seemed so very real. And then, just as he started to believe that maybe he was getting a second chance, that maybe God was giving him something to make life worth living again, that chance was snatched away from him. He was going to spend the rest of his days rotting in this hellhole after all, alone, filled with bitterness and guilt, knowing that somewhere out there, the only person who had the power to save him was living her life without him. A sickening mixture of panic and acceptance churned violently within him as he forced himself to release his hold on her.

"Very well, Citizen," he said. He stepped through the open doorway without looking back.

Jacqueline stood there, watching him go through the doors, wondering what his plan was, anxiously waiting for him to make his move. And just as the two guards began to close the doors he turned and looked at her, his expression filled with aching tenderness and bitter regret. And suddenly she understood. He was going back. He was sacrificing his chance at freedom so she could get away.

"No!" she screamed, unable to control herself. "You cannot leave me! You cannot!"

She lunged through the doorway after him, grabbing onto his arm as if she thought she could drag him with her to safety.

"What the hell is going on here?" snapped one of the guards.

Armand looked down at Jacqueline. Her eyes were wild and filled with tears.

"You cannot leave me," she repeated softly, her voice breaking. She pressed his hand against her heart.

"Arrest both of them!" ordered the guard to the other as he grabbed hold of Armand from behind.

Armand immediately straightened up, lifting the guard right off his feet. He then drove himself backward into the wall, smashing the guard against the stone until he felt him relax his hold and fall to the ground. Jacqueline meanwhile was doing her best to keep the second guard occupied, by jumping on his back and clawing at his eyes with her fingernails. The guard was stumbling about blindly, trying to dislodge her, and barely knew what hit him when Armand brought his heavy pistol crashing down on the back of his head.

"Move!" he thundered, grabbing her and pulling her through the doors with him.

They raced down the walkway that led from the prison to the street. They could hear shouts coming from the prison.

"This way!" commanded Jacqueline as she pulled him with her into the crowd that congested the busy rue Saint-Antoine.

They moved quickly through the crowd, being careful not to run, which would, of course, attract attention. Armand noticed that Jacqueline had lost her pregnant shape; probably his shirt and trousers had fallen out from under her skirts when she climbed onto the guard's back. This meant she could walk at a reasonable pace without looking suspicious. He allowed her to lead the way, since she seemed to know exactly where she was going. She took him down one small street, and then another, moving with a controlled sense of urgency. He could hear shouting coming from the direction of the rue Saint-Antoine, but by now they were several streets south of it. No one they passed gave them so much as a second glance. Jacqueline turned a corner and led him down a street that was dark and deserted. At the end, hidden in the shadows, he could just make out the shape of a small, black carriage.

The driver stomped his foot as they approached and the door swung open. Jacqueline climbed in and Armand followed right behind her. The carriage lurched into motion as he pulled the door shut, and he was thrown back against the seat beside Jacqueline.

"Ooooof! Get off me!" complained a muffled voice from underneath him.

"Forgive me," he apologized as he moved to the seat across from Jacqueline. He squinted into the darkness at the boy he had just sat on. "I don't believe we have met."

"I am Philippe Mercier. I stole that uniform for you," Philippe explained proudly.

"I see," replied Armand. "Then I am deeply in your

debt, Citizen Mercier, for the uniform was most effective."

Philippe shrugged his shoulders, as if stealing the uniform was nothing.

"We are heading straight for the coast," said Jacqueline, her voice thin and tight with nerves. They still had to make it past the city barricade. "It is too risky for us to remain in Paris. The reward for you will be high, and besides, *The Angélique* will be waiting for us off the coast of Boulogne tomorrow night."

Armand nodded. "Have you papers for us?"

"Yes," she replied. "Justin arranged them." She reached under the seat and pulled up a folded pile of clothes and a white wig. "Put these on. You will have to be out of that uniform before we reach the barricade. Philippe can help you."

"Who am I?" he asked as he began to unbutton his jacket.

"Your name is Roland Mougie," she informed him. "You are a bookkeeper from the town of Amiens. You were ordered to Paris on official business, to testify before the Tribunal against Pierre Lacombe, who was charged with participating in a royalist plot. Since you had never been to Paris before, you brought your children with you. Philippe is your son, Georges, and I am your other son, Bernard. They will be looking for a man and a woman, not a man with two boys."

She was changing as she spoke, pulling on trousers and tucking her coarse shirt into them, exchanging her enormous floppy hat for a small woolen cap, into which she stuffed the scraggly ends of her greasy dark hair. He paused to watch her, fascinated. Here she was, orchestrating his escape from prison and flight to England as if it were the most normal thing in the world for her to be assuming false identities and lying her way past guards and barricades. Despite the precariousness of their situation, he found himself smiling at her through the darkness.

"You have done well, Mademoiselle," he stated in a low voice.

Jacqueline stopped buttoning her jacket and looked up at him. His face was hidden in the shadows, but she felt almost certain he was smiling at her. Suddenly she felt shy and awkward.

"I had a very fine teacher," she replied softly.

They completed their transformations in silence.

It only took about fifteen minutes to reach the barricade. It was up to Armand to handle the questions of the guard who inspected their carriage, and armed with his new character, he did so with ease. Jacqueline had been right. The word was out that the one rumored to be the Black Prince had escaped from La Force, but as always there were many carts and carriages leaving the east gate of Paris that evening, and although the guards were thorough in their inspection of their papers, it was clear they were not terribly interested in an older man traveling on official business with two young boys. Even their driver had papers identifying him as having come from Amiens with Citizen Mougie. The cart behind them contained a young man and woman, and that was clearly much more suspicious to the guards. Their carriage was waved through.

Once they were about a kilometer past the gate, Jacqueline allowed herself to relax.

"We made it," she sighed, leaning heavily into her seat.

"So far," agreed Armand. They still had many hours ahead of them before they were safely on *The Angélique*.

"I guess you can let me off here, then," said Philippe nonchalantly. "We're close enough that I can walk back."

"You're going back?" asked Armand in surprise.

Philippe shrugged. "I done my bit," he informed him. "I said I would help Jacqueline get you out, and I did." He regarded Armand seriously. "Now it's up to you to watch out for her."

Jacqueline hesitated. Although the plan had been to let Philippe off once they were safely past the barricade, now that the time had come she was reluctant to honor her agreement. What was going to happen to him when he returned to Paris? she wondered. What kind of life was she sending him back to? A life of stealing, and beatings, and starvation? A life of sleeping in the streets on those freezing-cold nights when he couldn't find a friendly prostitute willing to share her bed with him? Twice he had saved her life. And he had been instrumental in helping her to save Armand's life. She owed him. To simply say good-bye and send him back to the streets was impossible.

"Philippe, I wonder if you might consider coming to England with us," she began hesitantly.

"I don't need your charity," he told her firmly. "I can take care of myself just fine."

Judging by the ugly bruises all over the boy's face, Armand somehow doubted that, but he said nothing.

"No, no, you misunderstand," said Jacqueline quickly. "I don't mean that you should come to England because you need me to take care of you. Quite the opposite, in fact. I want you to come to England because I need you."

He looked at her in amazement. "Is there someone else in England you mean to spring from prison?" he demanded incredulously.

"No," Jacqueline assured him. "It's just that London is so terribly big and strange to me. I never venture out on my own because I know I will get lost."

Philippe looked unconvinced. "I don't know my way around London either," he informed her shortly.

"But you have a wonderful sense of direction," argued Jacqueline. "And you are familiar with getting around a big city. London is just another big city."

"I don't speak English," he stated.

"But you could learn," she pointed out reasonably. "I did not speak English either when I first went there, not a single word, but after a few weeks of study I found I could understand a great deal, and even carry on a conversation."

Philippe hesitated. It was apparent he was at least a little intrigued by her offer.

"You would always have plenty to eat and warm clothes to wear," continued Jacqueline. "You would never have to wonder where you were going to sleep at night. And we would spend much of our time in the countryside, where you could learn to ride."

Philippe shook his head. "I could never pay for that kind of living," he told her. "And I don't want your charity."

"Well, you could work then," she suggested.

"As what? Some kind of fancy-dressed serving boy?" He snorted in disgust, telling her what he thought of that idea.

"You could work in the stables," interjected Armand.

Philippe looked at him in surprise. "I don't ride," he said defensively.

"I am not suggesting you ride," countered Armand. "You would start at the bottom, cleaning out stalls. Then, if you were good and quick, perhaps you would be allowed to try your hand at polishing harness. And if you showed that you were serious, you might work your way up to actually grooming the animals. But all the while you would be watching and learning from the trainers, and taking riding lessons, until one day you might be fit enough to work with the horses themselves. That would, of course, only be once you had proven your ability. Not everyone has what it takes to properly train a horse."

"I could do it," Philippe told him confidently.

Armand studied him a moment. "Perhaps you could," he allowed.

"You would also have to learn to read and write," added Jacqueline, determined that in his new life he would be equipped to carve out a decent future of his own making. "You can work as long as it does not interfere with your lessons."

Philippe thought for a moment. "Very well," he said finally. "I will go with you."

"Thank you," breathed Jacqueline with relief. Satisfied that both Armand and Philippe were now safe and there was nothing more she could do, she settled back against her seat and instantly fell asleep.

Armand stood with his legs braced apart and his hands clasped behind his back, contemplating the churning black water of the English Channel. The air around him was freezing cold and fragrant with the sharp tang of salt. He drew in long, hearty drafts of it, cleansing his lungs of the foul stench he had been forced to inhale for almost a month. He was free. He would not feel completely secure until he was standing on the deck of *The Angélique* watching the coast of France recede into nothing. Until then, he was content to stand here on this beach and listen to the crash of the waves against the rocks and enjoy the vast stretch of ocean before him.

"Where are they?" muttered Jacqueline nervously as she came up beside him and peered out into the darkness.

She had been a bundle of nerves throughout the journey, and the fact that *The Angélique* was not here waiting for them did nothing to ease her fear. So far everything during their trip had gone exactly according to plan. Justin's contacts and Jacqueline's jewels had proven most effective in purchasing dependable assistance. Fresh horses and new drivers met them exactly on schedule, complete with food and drink so they did not have to stop. Twice they had been detained by frozen-looking detachments of the National Guard, who seemed utterly satisfied with their papers. In fact they had made remarkable time getting here, which could account for why Sidney and his men were not waiting for them.

"Are you certain Sidney said he would be here by today?" asked Armand, pulling his gaze away from the ocean to look at her. She was still dressed as a young boy, with her greasy hair stuffed up in a woolen cap, and the exquisite curves of her body hidden beneath coarse, baggy trousers and an ill-fitting coat. She was a far cry from the gloriously feminine vision he had imagined in his fantasy, yet he was certain he had never seen a woman look more beautiful.

"Positive," she replied, her brow furrowed with concern.

"Then he will be here," he assured her. "We just have to wait." He wanted to pull her into his arms and kiss her, but they were not safe yet, and he could not afford to let himself get distracted. He turned to look at the sea again.

Jacqueline shivered and pulled up the collar of her coat. She hoped the ship arrived soon. She was absolutely freezing. The carriage and driver had left immediately after dropping them off, so there was no place for her to sit and be sheltered from the frigid night air. She began to walk back toward the trees on the other side of the beach, looking for a private place to relieve herself before the ship arrived.

It was almost over. Soon she would be leaving her beloved France again, this time for good. She reminded herself that there was nothing left for her here. Her home was gone. The life she had once known was destroyed. Nicolas was dead, so she could not even use vengeance as a reason for returning. France held nothing for her but memories, some good, others hideously painful. She tried not to think of them.

Her sisters were safe, and now so was Armand. Philippe was also going to be part of her new life, and that pleased her immensely. She shook her head in wonder. He was nothing but a street urchin and a filthy, common thief. In her former life as the sheltered and privileged daughter of the wealthy Duc de Lambert, she would not have thought him fit to scrape the mud off her boots. But the revolution had forced her to change her thinking about what made people decent, worthy, and honorable. Honor was not something instantly bestowed upon an individual by the accident of birth or title. People could not be judged solely by their wealth, or titles that had simply been handed down to them. Armand and Philippe had risked their lives to keep her from harm, not for money or personal gain, but because their personal code of honor would not allow them to stand by and do nothing.

With guidance and encouragement, she felt certain Philippe would grow up to be a very fine man. She hoped that in England he would not be judged by his humble beginnings or his lack of a title. She would see to it that he received an excellent education and would ask Armand to teach him about business so he could make a lot of money and tell anyone who thought themselves better than he to go straight to hell.

She was going to have to learn how to make some money herself. It had cost her almost the entire De Lambert jewel collection to pay the exorbitant costs of the bribes, false documents, information, and transportation it had taken to get the three of them here. She was still titled in England, but without money or holdings she was not sure what good her title was, except perhaps to some man looking for the novelty of an escaped French aristocrat for a wife. She and her sisters could not impose upon the Harringtons' generosity forever, and she would have to be able to support them and Philippe until they were old enough to marry. She sighed. Maybe Armand could advise her. He was, after all, very successful at making money.

"Did you really think you could escape me?" drawled a bitter, harsh voice.

No, she thought desperately, it cannot be. Numb with fear, she slowly turned.

Nicolas stood before her, his face twisted with hate and fury. The edge of a bloodstained bandage was exposed beneath the brim of his hat, and a raw gash marked his face from his temple to his chin. Jacqueline opened her mouth to scream. Nicolas slapped his heavy, gloved hand against her lips before the sound got beyond her throat.

"Did you think I would let you get away a second time?" he hissed as he jerked her around and viciously twisted her arm into her back, paralyzing her with pain. "Or did you actually believe you had managed to kill me?" he sneered, his face so close to hers she could feel his breath on her cheek.

She struggled and tried to break free from his hold. His response was to violently wrench up her arm. She let out a cry of pain, but his hand still covered her mouth and no sound escaped.

"If you fight me, I will take great pleasure in hurting you," he warned softly. He released her arm and laid the icy-cold steel of a dagger against her cheek. "And believe me, there is nothing I would like more than to repay you the mark you have so thoughtlessly left me with." He pressed the flat of the blade into her skin. "One quick slice, and your pretty little face will be reduced to a hideous, bleeding mess."

Jacqueline fought to control her panic and tried to think. If Nicolas was alone, she felt confident Armand could outwit him, as long as he did not have to fear for her safety. But if Nicolas held her hostage, Armand would do nothing to endanger her, and that put him at a severe disadvantage.

"I knew you would be going to La Force to free your friend," Nicolas spat into her ear as he continued to hold her. "I got there only moments after the two of you escaped. I anticipated you would be anxious to leave France quickly, so I took a detachment of eight men and left for the coast at once. When we finally caught up to you, I decided to wait until your carriage was gone, and you had no means of getting away other than on foot. Right now your two accomplices are surrounded by the National Guard. A nice surprise for the Black Prince, don't you think?" he drawled sarcastically.

A mixture of fear and defeat churned within Jacqueline's stomach. It was hopeless. Armand and Philippe could never fight off eight armed members of the National Guard. An overwhelming sense of despair gripped her.

"And now we are going to join them," he told her cheerfully, sliding the dagger from her cheek to her throat. "But be warned, Jacqueline. If you make one sound or move I don't like, I will slit your throat open like the belly of a fish. Do you understand?"

Jacqueline nodded.

"Excellent." He took his hand off her mouth so he could wrap his arm around her shoulders and hold the dagger at her neck. They walked together out of the wood and found Armand and Philippe standing on the beach casually staring out at the ocean.

"How touching—two traitors lost in thought as they watch for their ship," sneered Nicolas.

Armand turned to look at him, his brows lifted in surprise. "Inspector Bourdon, what an utterly charming coincidence," he said pleasantly. He frowned as he studied him. "My God, you look perfectly awful. What the devil made that ghastly mark on your face?"

Jacqueline could feel Nicolas tighten his grip on her.

"A little gift from Mademoiselle de Lambert," ground out Nicolas acidly, pressing the point of the dagger into her throat. "But once I have disposed of you and the boy, I shall give her a chance to make it up to me before I return her to Paris for execution."

"Really?" said Armand with interest. He paused for a moment, studying Nicolas, as if trying to decide whether what he was telling him was true.

Nicolas smiled triumphantly. Finally he had his enemies exactly where he wanted them. Jacqueline was trapped in his grip, unable to escape, and too afraid to fight him. And the Black Prince was surrounded by the National Guard, without the slightest chance of getting away. It was a sweet moment, and one he was enjoying immensely.

"You mean to say Mademoiselle de Lambert gave you that hideous-looking gash all by herself?" Armand demanded finally, completely ignoring the rest of Nicolas's threat.

"Forget the damned scar!" snapped Nicolas irritably.

"Well, I am trying to," remarked Armand, "but unfortunately it is just so horribly long and deep and red, well, I am sure you just have to look in a mirror to appreciate it is quite difficult to ignore such a thing." He shook his head sympathetically.

Jacqueline stared at Armand in confusion. She could not imagine what he was trying to do. Here they were, trapped, with *The Angélique* nowhere in sight, and instead of fighting Nicolas or making a final effort at escape, all he seemed to want to do was bait him. What on earth was he doing?

"Unfortunately you have caught us at a rather bad time," continued Armand, his tone light and apologetic. "We were just leaving, actually. I would invite you to join us, of course, but somehow I rather think Mademoiselle de Lambert would prefer I did not, given your past history together."

"The only place you are going is to the guillotine," stated Nicolas bitterly.

"Well now, that is a most generous offer," acknowledged Armand, "especially given how difficult it is for one to get a place on the scaffold these days." He sighed. "Unfortunately, I am afraid I must decline. If you would just be kind enough to release Mademoiselle de Lambert, we will be on our way."

Nicolas scowled. "Are you mad, or just a complete idiot?" he demanded. "I have you surrounded with a detachment of the National Guard. You are all under arrest."

"Really?" said Armand skeptically. "Forgive me, Inspector, if it appears I am doubting you, but would you mind very much showing us these esteemed members of the National Guard?"

"With pleasure," Nicolas replied. "Guards!" he barked.

A moment passed. No one appeared. Armand regarded Nicolas calmly.

Nicolas looked around in confusion. "Guards!" he shouted, louder this time. "Get the hell out here!"

Jacqueline looked at the woods beyond the beach, waiting for the guards to appear. None did.

Nicolas tightened his grip on Jacqueline. "Guards!" he

screamed, his voice tinged with frustration and panic. "Get out here now!"

Another moment passed. No guards appeared.

"It would seem they have been distracted," suggested Armand casually. "So if you will just release Mademoiselle de Lambert—"

"Never!" snarled Nicolas, grabbing her tightly and holding his dagger across her throat. "You and the boy will come with me, or I will kill her right now, is that clear?"

Armand sighed dramatically. "Really, Bourdon, you must try to get over this obsession of yours, before it destroys you completely."

"I am taking you all into Boulogne, where you will be held until an escort can be arranged to take you back to Paris," Nicolas insisted.

"That is most thoughtful of you," acknowledged Armand, "but unfortunately we do not have the time to make another trip to Paris. If you will just take a moment to look beyond that point, you will see our ship has arrived."

Jacqueline stared into the darkness beyond the point. The ghostly silhouette of *The Angélique* was gracefully bobbing up and down on the black waves. A surge of relief rushed through her.

"You will never get on her," snarled Nicolas. "Either you come with me, or I slit Jacqueline's throat here and now." He held her steady and pressed the sharp edge of his dagger against the soft flesh of her throat.

Jacqueline let out a little whimper of fear as the cold steel bit into her. She looked at Armand helplessly.

Armand's expression remained only politely interested, but Jacqueline could see his jaw had tightened slightly.

"I am afraid I have grown weary of your threats and your posturing, Inspector," he informed Nicolas. "You will release Mademoiselle de Lambert immediately, or suffer the consequences."

Nicolas laughed. "And just what is it you intend to

do?" he sneered. "I hold her life in my hands, while you do not even bear a weapon."

"That is true," admitted Armand blandly. He fixed his gaze behind them and nodded. "However, if you do not release her this instant, I shall be forced to order my men to splatter your brains across this beach, which I think Mademoiselle de Lambert might enjoy, but I feel almost certain you will find most unpleasant."

Still holding tightly on to Jacqueline, Nicolas warily turned his head to look behind him. He hesitated a moment. And then Jacqueline felt his grip on her relax as he slowly lowered the knife from her throat.

Without pausing to see what was behind her, she ran over to Armand and Philippe. Armand ignored her, keeping his gaze fixed on Nicolas. She turned and saw a dozen of Armand's men from *The Angélique* standing behind Nicolas, their muskets primed and aimed at his head. Sidney Langdon stood at the center of this impressive rescue party, looking as if he was just dying for Armand to give the order to shoot.

"And now, I regret that we must tie you up and leave you," sighed Armand. "I will ask my men to put you with your friends from the National Guard, however, so that you have some company through the night. I am sure by morning someone will have seen your horses running loose and will send out a rescue party. Until then, I invite you to enjoy the darkness and the cold. I think you will find it not unlike spending a night in La Force, except of course the air here is much more pleasant," he qualified.

"You will never get away with this," vowed Nicolas, his voice thick with fury as Sidney stepped forward and roughly began to bind his hands behind his back. "I promise you, my clever friend, we are not finished. I will not rest until you have been tried and executed for your crimes against the Republic. I will go all the way to England to find you, if need be. I will find you, and I will bring you back here for execution, or I will kill you myself."

"You are certainly welcome to try," replied Armand

cheerfully. "In fact, I sincerely hope you do find the time to make a trip to England. I would relish the opportunity to show you the inside of an English prison. I think you will find they are not quite as overcrowded as the prisons in Paris, but rather unpleasant places to be nonetheless."

Nicolas fixed his gaze on Jacqueline. "You may think you have won, Jacqueline, but I assure you, you have not," he told her. "You aristos are a scourge upon this land, and you will obliterated, do you hear? Every last one of you will be killed, until your blood flows like a surging river that will cleanse France of your crimes. I swear to you, Jacqueline, if it is the last thing I do, I will—"

At that point Sidney unceremoniously stuffed a rag into his mouth, so Jacqueline could not find out whatever it was Nicolas was going to swear. It did not matter. She was free of him forever. She did not doubt that he would be severely punished for losing the Black Prince and the escaped Mademoiselle de Lambert yet again. Perhaps he would even be executed this time. The thought should have pleased her, but instead all she felt was emptiness and sorrow. She was getting away, but thousands of others like her were trapped here and would die. She turned and looked up at Armand.

"Can we go now?" she pleaded softly.

He looked down at her in surprise. He had thought she would want to bear witness to Nicolas's humiliation, and perhaps have the satisfaction of issuing a few choice parting words to him herself. Instead she looked up at him sadly, her silvery eyes filled with weariness and pain. He berated himself for not being more sensitive.

"Of course, Mademoiselle," he returned, his voice gentle and low. He took a step, and then hesitated. He turned to her and slowly offered her his arm.

She laid her hand gracefully upon it and extended her other hand out to Philippe, who was watching Armand's men produce a skiff from a crevice of rock at the end of the beach. Philippe looked at her uncertainly a moment, as though he was beyond such childish comforts as hand-holding. He did not take it, but instead awkwardly lifted his arm to her, trying to imitate what he saw Armand doing. She smiled and laid her hand upon it. Slowly, the three of them began to walk down the beach.

Jacqueline sat before the small stove in Armand's cabin, methodically working an ivory comb through the tangles in her wet hair. The sea was relatively calm, leaving *The Angélique* free to skim quietly over its gently pulsing surface. Jacqueline was grateful for that, because it meant she had been able to languish comfortably in a steaming-hot bath, soaking away her aches and tension as well as the layers of grime she had accumulated during her stay in France. She had soaped her hair three times in an effort to rid it of the red color Justin had put on it, but was not entirely convinced it had all come out. She held up a damp lock and examined it against the soft orange glow of the candles on the table. She was almost certain it was tinged with auburn, but she told herself it could just be the light. She purposefully set to work on another tangle.

She did not know where Armand was.

When they boarded *The Angélique,* he instructed Sidney to take her to his cabin, to bring her clothes, a tray of food, and a hot bath, and to provide her with anything else she might wish for. Philippe had started to go with her, but Armand had told John to take him to another cabin. Philippe protested, but Jacqueline explained to him that he would have to stay in his own cabin tonight, as she wished to take a bath and wanted him to do the same. They argued briefly over the necessity of his taking a bath, but in the end he shrugged his shoulders and allowed himself to be escorted to a different cabin. By that time Armand had disappeared, presumably to issue orders to the rest of the crew before retiring himself.

While she was eating, Sidney returned with a silk and lace nightdress for her to sleep in, and a beautiful gown and cape for her to wear tomorrow. Jacqueline contemplated the exquisite nightdress for several minutes before carelessly tossing it over a chair and rifling through Armand's trunk for one of his soft cotton shirts instead. She did not want to sleep in something that had belonged to his wife, Lucette, or perhaps to one of his many mistresses. Besides, she found his shirts comfortable to wear, and this would be the last time she would have the opportunity to do so. After all, her business with him was completed. She had saved his life, just as he had saved hers. She no longer had to feel guilty for stupidly sending him into a trap. She owed him nothing, just as he owed her nothing. When they reached England tomorrow, they would return to their separate lives and that would be that. She sighed.

The sound of voices arguing in the hall distracted her. Curious, she wrapped a blanket around her shoulders and went to open the door. Philippe was standing with his back to her, having risen from the makeshift bed he had prepared at her doorstep. Armand stood in the hall facing him. He was freshly bathed and had changed into a loose white shirt and charcoal breeches. His hair had also changed color, from black to its usual mixture of brown and copper and blond. He was holding a crystal decanter of red wine in one hand and a single glass in the other, and was looking mildly irritated.

"You'll not disturb her—she needs her rest," Philippe was saying authoritatively as he looked up at Armand, who towered well over a foot above him.

Armand looked at Jacqueline with helpless exasperation. "Perhaps we should ask Mademoiselle de Lambert whether or not she is willing to receive a visitor," he suggested mildly.

Philippe whirled around in surprise. "I thought you might be sleeping," he stammered. "I didn't want anyone to wake you."

Jacqueline smiled. "You are most thoughtful, Philippe, but as you can see I am fully awake. You may return to your cabin now."

He shrugged his shoulders. "Think I'll just stay here

for the night," he told her nonchalantly. "Just in case you need me." He looked meaningfully at Armand.

Armand raised one eyebrow at the impertinence of the young pup and looked at Jacqueline, waiting to see how she would handle this.

"That won't be necessary, Philippe," Jacqueline assured him, feeling slightly embarrassed by Philippe's determination to protect her virtue.

"I don't mind," he replied easily, preparing to settle down once again on his mound of blankets.

Armand looked at her with a mixture of curiosity and amusement. Jacqueline's cheeks grew warm.

"Philippe, I really would prefer it if you would sleep in your own cabin tonight," she told him casually. "You need a good sleep, and you cannot get one sleeping on the floor in the hallway."

"I've slept in worse places," he scoffed. "It won't bother me." He began to shake out his blankets.

Jacqueline raised her eyes in helpless frustration to Armand. He shrugged his shoulders, as if to say this was her problem and she would have to deal with it.

She drew her blanket tighter around her shoulders. "Philippe, I am asking you to return to your cabin," she stated, her voice more pleading than authoritative.

He stopped arranging his bed and looked at her in surprise. "You mean you don't want me here?" he demanded in disbelief.

"No," she replied, her face burning. "I do not."

He looked at her, and then at Armand, who calmly accepted his scrutiny. Finally he looked back at Jacqueline. "Well then," he said, his voice tight with embarrassment. "I guess I'll go back to my room." He quickly scooped up his blankets and pillow and hurried down the corridor.

Feeling as if she was about to go up in flames, Jacqueline turned and went back into the cabin. Armand followed her and quietly shut the door.

Awkward silence gripped the tiny room. Armand went to the table in the center of the cabin and put down the decanter and the glass. He poured a glass of wine and held it out to her.

"Did Sidney bring you everything you need?"

"Yes," she replied, accepting the glass.

"Good."

She could not think of anything else to say. She took a huge swallow of wine, wishing desperately that some words would come to mind.

Armand stood before her, wondering what to do next. He knew what he wanted to do. He wanted to reach out and pull her into his arms, to thread his fingers into her hair and kiss her lips and face and throat and shoulders, to tear that blanket off her and carry her to the bed and caress her all over with his hands and lips and tongue until she was as desperate with need for him as he was for her. Instead he simply stood there, frozen, unable to do anything lest he frighten her.

For weeks now he had tormented himself with images of her, all the while believing he would never see her again. The thought of her had been his escape, had lifted him out of that cell and into a world that was filled with peace, and joy, and life. She did not know it, but she had kept him from going insane. And now that she was really here, warm and alive and vibrant, he just wanted to be close to her, even if that meant all he could do was look at her. He knew he would not be able to bear it if she sent him away. And so he simply stood there, feeling like an awkward, nervous schoolboy, totally in awe of the incredible woman who was before him.

She was utterly, unbearably magnificent. The champagne strands of her hair were shimmering brilliantly against the sapphire wool of the blanket she clutched so primly to her shoulders, as if by holding on to that soft scrap of material she could shield herself from the power of his desire for her. She nervously studied the contents of her glass, her silvery-gray eyes sparkling with the brilliance of the sun upon the sea, her silken skin aflame with the heat of the wine. She overwhelmed him. Not just with her beauty, for he had always known she was beautiful, from the moment he first saw her miniature in Sir Edward's study. When he learned she had been arrested, he swore he would not rest until she was safe from the bastards who sought to destroy her. But he had not known her then. He had simply thought she was young, and beautiful, and innocent, and such a lovely combination did not deserve to be slaughtered on the guillotine in the name of liberty. As with all the other men, women, and children he had saved during his personal war against the Republic, he had thought of her as something abstract, an exquisite work of art that needed protection from the violence and destruction of revolution and war. If he succeeded in saving her and her brother, it was another strike against the government that had butchered his family, and coincidentally, a gift to Sir Edward. Nothing more.

It was not until he sat at the back of the courtroom in the Palais de Justice that he began to realize what a remarkable creature he had come to France to save. She was, of course, far more beautiful in the flesh than any artist could ever have painted her, but he could not fault the artist for that. What he had not expected was her courage, her strength, her fierce, unwavering determination. They could condemn her to death, but they could not destroy her. They could strip her of her home and her belongings, force her to send away her sisters, murder her father, beat her brother almost to death before her eyes, and then throw her into a freezing, dank cesspool to rot for weeks before parading her in front of a furious mob to endure the bitter humiliation of a mock trial. They could do all of that and more, but they could not break her. She was strong, and brave, and willful. She had been raised to be a delicate blossom, forever sheltered in a crystal château, but when her world was shattered she revealed herself to be forged from steel. She was a survivor.

And she had been ready to sacrifice herself for him. She had been safe in England, with her new life ahead of her. Yet she had come back to France and risked her life so he could be free. He had thought she cared only for vengeance, that the force that drove her was the desire to murder her enemy. But when Bourdon stood before her, bound and helpless, she had not so much as spoken to him. She had scarred his face, but a scar was nothing compared with the deaths of her father and brother. Her return to France had nothing to do with vengeance, he realized, and everything to do with him. The enormity of her actions astounded him.

"Why did you come for me?" he asked quietly.

She raised her eyes from the contents of her wineglass, surprised by his question. "I—I should never have asked you to help François-Louis," she stammered. "It was stupid of me not to sense it was a trap."

The mention of her betrothed irritated him, tainted the moment. "Did Monsieur le Marquis reach England safely?" he asked dryly.

Jacqueline winced at the sarcasm in his tone. "Yes. He came to see me at the Harringtons'. That was how I found out you had been captured."

"I see."

He wondered whether she still intended to marry the fool, but he could not bring himself to ask. If she said yes, then he had no business being here. He wondered what story the spineless little fop had given her, to explain how he had managed to escape while the Black Prince did not. He wanted to tell her that the idiot was not fit to touch her, that he was weak and selfish and stupid, that he dallied with other women in prison, God help him, he even wanted to tell her that underneath that ridiculous wig the man was bald. But he said nothing.

"When I learned you had been caught, I knew I had to do something," she continued, trying to fill the awkward silence that stretched between them. "I mean, I had sent you there. I could not bear the thought that you would die because of my stupidity. You saved my life, and I repaid you by sending you into a trap."

"You did not send me there," he informed her. "You hired me to go. I did not have to accept your proposition. It was entirely my choice." He moved a step closer to her, closing the distance between them. "As I recall, you even paid me in advance," he murmured, his voice low and slightly husky. "Remember?"

She felt a hot flush streak from her face right down to the pit of her stomach. She released the blanket she was clutching slightly and took a nervous swallow of wine, thinking back to his terms of payment.

"I remember," she breathed.

He reached out to take the wineglass from her hand and placed it on the table behind him. "Do you know how many times I have relived that night?" he demanded, his voice taut and strained. He held her steady with his gaze.

She shook her head, desperately clutching the corners of her blanket.

He reached out and lightly caressed the soft silk of her cheek. She did not move away, but stared up at him, her eyes shimmering with desire and uncertainty.

"It is strange," he mused as he explored the incredible perfection of her cheek, "it was the thought of you that kept me sane when I was in prison." He began to slowly lower his head. "And now you are here, you are real, and I feel I am about to go out of my mind." He held his lips a breath away from hers. "How is it that you can have such power over me, Jacqueline?"

He said her name with the same languor and care that he always had, caressing the letters as if they were notes in an incredible piece of music. The tenderness and desire in his voice washed over her like a symphony, causing her to reach up and wrap her arms around his neck while pressing her lips to his.

Her response to him broke the last vestiges of his control. He crushed her against him and kissed her desperately, like a drowning man who has just found his first breath of air. She tasted sweet and hot, a mixture of wine and honey, while the delicate scent of her skin filled his nostrils with the essence of flowers. He greedily began to touch her all over, exploring the length of her back, the curve of her hips, the soft swell of her breasts. The sapphire blanket had dropped to the floor, revealing that she was wearing one of his shirts. The oversized garment draped loosely over her shoulders and fell shapelessly below her knees, hiding every lush curve of her body, and yet he was certain he had never seen anything look more sensual on a woman. He could not imagine why she had chosen to wear it, but somehow the intimacy of her electing to cover herself in something of his filled him with pleasure. She trembled against him, pressing her body into his as she released her arms from his neck and began to touch him all over, laying claim to him, grasping his shoulders, kneading his back, threading her fingers into the length of his hair, telling him that she wanted to touch and be touched. He had not expected her to want him so, he had thought she would be reluctant and afraid, but when he felt her moan and press herself against the hardness of his arousal, he knew that he was lost. Without breaking their kiss, he bent down, lifted her high in his arms, and carried her to the bed.

Jacqueline felt herself sinking into the softness of the mattress, and then Armand was covering her with the heavy warmth of his body. He kissed her deeply as he touched her though the soft cotton of her shirt, his fingers deftly releasing the buttons. She felt the garment fall open, exposing her bare skin to cool air, but his mouth was caressing her cheek, her ear, her throat, slowly working its way down to her breast, and she did not feel cold. He was teasing her, drawing circles around the velvety tip with his tongue before taking it into the heat of his mouth. She let out a ragged moan and dug her fingers into the steel muscles of his back, clawing in frustration at the fabric that kept her from touching his skin. He obliged her by tearing the garment open and throwing it to the floor. She sighed with pleasure as her hands roamed over the hard warmth of his muscular back, but by then he was tugging and sucking in gentle rhythm on her other breast and her moan suddenly became deeper and more primal. His hand moved down the flat of her stomach to the curve of her hip, and then he was touching that soft triangle of curls, lightly, gently, teasingly, making her restless with the de-

sire for him to do more. There was a mysterious rush of
liquid heat, and then he slipped his fingers inside her and
began to idly caress the satiny slick folds, still sucking on
her breast. She shamelessly spread her thighs wider and
writhed beneath his touch, holding his head to her breast,
running her hands through his coppery hair and down the
solid steel of his back. His fingers moved deeper, in and
out, mimicking the rhythmic sucking of his mouth, until
her breathing was reduced to a shallow, ragged pant. He
pulled away from her nipple and began to trace a hot path
of kisses down her stomach, she felt his breath hover
against the wet triangle of curls, and then suddenly he was
tasting her, delicately lapping at the wet heat of her, causing her to cry out with a mixture of shock and unbearable
pleasure. Her body went rigid, but his tongue began to
flutter lightly inside her, like the soft beating of butterfly
wings, and the sensation was so incredibly exquisite she
let out a ragged moan and allowed her resistance to dissipate. A flame of mindless desire began to burn wildly inside her as he teased her with his mouth, sending restless
heat from the roots of her hair to the tips of her toes,
stripping her of her inhibitions, causing her to thrash
against the bed as he tasted her quickly and deeply and
thoroughly. And then, just as her breath was coming in
shallow gasps and she was certain she could endure no
more, he stopped, leaving her cold and alone as he stood
and stripped off his breeches.

He lowered himself back onto her, covering her with
his magnificent body, cradling her face between his hands
as he kissed her eyes, her nose, her mouth. She clung to
him fiercely as she opened herself to him, desperate for the
need of him to be inside her, wanting to give him back
some of the incredible pleasure he had given her. He
hovered over her for a moment, all animal power and heat
and fire, and she held her breath as she stared into his
emerald and sapphire eyes, burning with passion and
need. And suddenly, inexplicably, she thought of his pain.
She thought of his mother, and Lucette, and Angélique,
and the little black box in the bottom of his chest with the

lace hankie and the colored ribbons. Her heart constricted, and a tear escaped her lid. He noticed it and looked at her in surprise, as if he thought he had hurt her.

"Jacqueline?" he whispered hoasely. "Do you want me to stop?"

She laid her hand tenderly against his cheek. Then she wrapped her arms around his waist and pulled him down into her, kissing him deeply as she did so.

An incredible wave of pleasure assaulted him as he buried himself inside her. He wanted to stay that way forever, lost in the sweetness of Jacqueline, in her strength, in her softness, in her remarkable ability to make him feel happy to be alive. He began to move within her, slowly, carefully, wanting it to last, but she was hungry for fulfillment and would not tolerate any more gentle teasing. She began to lift her hips to meet him, her hands moving restlessly over his body, urging him to go faster. He obliged her, thrusting powerfully into her as he held her in his arms, kissing her with weeks and months and years of pent-up passion, drinking in her life and her strength, trying to get as deep inside her as he could, as if he believed that every thrust brought him closer to her heart. His hand slipped down to where their bodies were joined and he began to caress her there, until he felt her moving faster against him, until her breathing was in tiny, shallow, desperate gasps, until her body suddenly tightened around him and a soft cry tore from the back of her throat. Then he arched his back and drove into her as far as he possibly could, his whole body alive and straining with power and need, releasing the essence of his desire deep within her. A low groan escaped him as he ground himself into her again, and again, unwilling to accept that it was over. He wanted to stay like this forever, just the two of them and nothing else. He pushed himself into her again, but his body betrayed him with its weakness and he was forced to collapse against her.

He buried his face into her neck and inhaled the scent of roses. He felt her arms tighten around him, and he worried that he would crush her, so he gathered her into his arms and rolled over onto his back, pulling her up so she lay on top of him.

They stayed together like that for a while, listening to the sound of their ragged breathing and the water breaking against the hull of the ship. Armand reached down and pulled the blankets up over them. Jacqueline lay her head against the warmth of his chest and marveled at how she could feel the beating of his heart against her cheek. She felt deliciously invigorated and exhausted. This is the way it is between a man and a woman, she thought sleepily. She wondered if her own parents had known such wonder. She was not sure. She was, however, quite certain that she would never experience such incredible passion with François-Louis. She had never felt anything toward him except a very proper, polite friendship, and even that had been severely strained. She realized she could never marry him now. She had lain twice with a man whose very presence made her blood quicken, who flushed her with warmth just by looking at her, who could take her to the stars and back whenever he touched her. She could never be satisfied with anything less.

"Armand?" she murmured softly.

"Mmm?"

"What do we do now?" she asked, feeling shy and awkward.

He tightened his arms around her and shifted his head to one side. His eyes were closed. "We sleep," he said, his voice already thick and heavy.

"That is not what I mean," protested Jacqueline. She began to lightly caress his nipple. "What do we do when we are back in England?" she asked.

"We go home," he told her, as if the answer was obvious.

"Home?" repeated Jacqueline hopefully.

He nodded sleepily.

A rush of joy filled her heart. She bent her head to kiss him on the lips. "You will not regret it," she swore softly. "We will all be very happy. I feel certain of it." She sighed and rested her head against his chest. "We will make a wonderful family."

Armand opened his eyes in sudden confusion. "What are you talking about, Jacqueline?"

She lifted her head to look at him. "I am talking about when we get married. Suzanne and Séraphine and Philippe will, of course, come to live with us."

He looked at her blankly. "We are getting married?"

"Well, you cannot expect me to live with you as your mistress," she pointed out, feeling a little incensed that he would want such a thing.

"No, of course not," he agreed hurriedly, sensing that he had insulted her, "it's just that—" He stopped, feeling hopelessly confused. He had no idea what he had said to make her think he was going to marry her. He could never marry anyone. He had tried marriage once before, and he had been a hideous failure at it. And his work as the Black Prince was far too dangerous to permit him to take on the responsibility of a wife and children. Surely she would understand that?

"Jacqueline," he began, "I cannot marry you—"

"I don't care if you are not titled," she interrupted fiercely, daring him to contradict her. "According to current French law I am no longer titled either, so that makes us equal, does it not?"

He stared at her in wonder. Was this the arrogant, young daughter of a duc who had so passionately defended her aristocratic status to him just a few months ago? Who believed the rigid hierarchy of the nobility was a gift from God and was therefore not to be questioned? Who had thought of him as nothing more than a hired servant? Who was betrothed to a marquis of impeccable lineage, as befit her station? He was surprised and humbled by the changes in her. But it was not the issue of her title that prevented him from making her his wife.

"Jacqueline, that is not why I cannot marry you," he told her gently. "In a few weeks I shall resume my work as the Black Prince, and I cannot expect you to sit at home and wait and wonder if you will ever see me again. Also, if I had the responsibility of a wife and children, it would affect how I perform my work. It would cloud my judgment, making me less willing to take risks and therefore slower to respond, which could ultimately cost me my life." He reached out and caressed her cheek. "Do you understand?"

She stared at him in silence for a moment. "Are you absolutely mad?" she demanded suddenly, her voice quivering with fury. She rolled off of him, covering herself with the blankets as she did so. "How can you even think of going back there?"

He raised himself up on one elbow and regarded her seriously. "Jacqueline, the revolution grows more violent every day. Robespierre and his followers are trying to crush all opposition to the new order, using appalling brutality. During my time in prison there was talk of the slaughter happening not just in Paris, but all through France. In December alone, two thousand prisoners were executed in Saint-Florent, while others were taken from the prisons at Nantes and Angers and shot like animals. They say three or four thousand perished that way."

"You cannot save all of them," protested Jacqueline weakly.

"The *représentant en mission* at Nantes has a particular taste for cruelty," he continued gravely. "He has decided to supplement the work of the guillotine with what he calls 'vertical deportations.' Do you know what those are?"

"No," she replied, not certain she wanted to know.

"He has his men take flat-bottomed barges and punch holes in the sides of them. Planks are nailed to these holes to keep the boats afloat. The accused men and women are put into them with their hands and feet tied, and the boats are pushed into the middle of the Loire. The executioners then break off the planks and jump into another boat, while the victims stand and watch themselves sink. Those who try to escape by jumping into the river are cut to pieces with sabers."

She stared at him in horror, unable to speak.

He stopped there, not wanting to further upset her. He would not tell her of the so-called republican marriages, in which young men and women were degraded by being stripped completely naked and tied together to die in these boats, much to the sadistic amusement of their executioners.

"I cannot stop my work," he told her.

"Not even for me?" she asked, her voice small and pleading.

He regarded her seriously. "No," he answered. "Not even for you."

She shook her head, trying to understand. Her eyes were becoming blurred with tears. "You have been fortunate to survive as long as you have," she told him. "But they are looking for you, and now they know what you look like. It is only a matter of time before they catch you again. For you to return to France is suicide." She stopped, her voice breaking with anger and fear.

He reached out and gently caught the tear that was trickling down her cheek. "It has always been suicide, Jacqueline," he told her softly. "But in the process, I have been able to do some good. You are living proof of that. And every life I save is penance for those I was not able to help. Do you understand?"

"I know about your wife, and mother, and Angélique," she informed him tearfully. "And I think you have done more than enough to make up for what was never your fault in the first place. There is nothing you could have done to help them, don't you see that?"

He shook his head. "I could have been there to stop them from going," he said simply. "I could have gone instead."

"Then you would have been killed!"

"That is right," he agreed. "I probably would have. But Angélique and Lucette and my mother would have lived."

"But then you never would have rescued all the others whose lives you have saved," she protested. "Don't you see, Armand? You have done enough. There is nothing to be gained by your death."

"The scales are not equal, Jacqueline," he informed her. "And if I can still save a life and hurt the Republic of France in the process, then I will continue to do so. They murdered my family. They threw me into a filthy cell and robbed me of a month of my life. And they continue to slaughter their own people, all in the name of this new utopia, where everyone is free and equal. I will not simply stand by and watch, do you understand?"

She shook her head. "You once told me that I had to put the past behind me and get on with my life. I thought you could not possibly understand what it was to be driven with pain and hatred. Now I know you do understand. I am asking you to put your own past behind you and make a new life. Please."

He stared gravely into her eyes, which were luminous with tears. She did not know what she was asking of him. She did not understand. "I cannot," he said helplessly.

She felt herself begin to tremble with disappointment and fear. She bowed her head so he would not see the tears leaking from her eyes. "Then get out," she said, her voice tight and stiff. "Now."

He did not argue. He rose from the bed and began to dress. He would have done anything to alleviate her misery. Anything except agree to what she was asking of him. He never should have come here tonight. He could see that now. He had done it out of pure selfishness. But he had never dreamed that she would want to marry him. He had hurt her terribly, but he did not know how to undo what he had done. Feeling like anything else he might say could only hurt her more, he stepped into the hallway, cursing himself as he shut the door on the sound of her muffled sobbing.

Chapter 15

"De . . . ship . . . sailed . . . a-long . . . de . . . shh . . . shh . . ." Philippe paused and looked up at Jacqueline in helpless frustration.

"Shore," she told him.

Philippe bent his head and squinted at the black letters on the page. "Shoa-wer," he repeated slowly. "Shoawer."

Suzanne looked up from her exercise book and sniffed in disgust. "I don't know why you are trying to teach him to read English when he doesn't even know how to read French," she commented acidly in English.

"He will learn to read both," Jacqueline informed her sister.

"De ship sailed along de . . . shoawer," repeated Philippe triumphantly.

"*Très bien, Philippe,*" praised Jacqueline. "*Continue, s'il te plaît.*"

Philippe bent his head over his textbook and studied the next line. "De . . . orse . . . ran . . . in . . . de . . . meddow," he read.

"Horse," corrected Jacqueline, emphasizing the *h* sound. "Ho-ho-ho-horse."

Philippe looked at her skeptically. "Ho-ho-ho-horse."

Jacqueline nodded and smiled.

"I don't see why he needs to read and write anyway," continued Suzanne petulantly. "After all, he is only a common stable boy."

Philippe looked up from his book and stared warily at Suzanne. "What are you saying about me?" he demanded threateningly in French.

Suzanne smiled at him sweetly. "Philippe, you know we are not allowed to speak French in the classroom," she scolded in English.

He looked at Jacqueline for help.

"Ignore her, Philippe," she instructed. "Continue with your reading."

He paused to throw Suzanne a final scowl before bending his head again. "Suzanne . . . is . . . a . . . little . . . bi—"

"Philippe," interrupted Jacqueline in a warning tone.

"How dare he!" cried Suzanne, leaping up from her desk.

"Was speaking English," he told her innocently.

"I won't stay another minute in this room with him, the filthy, common peasant!" she shrieked. True to her word she ran from the room, a flurry of pink satin and bobbing blond curls.

"Now, that was not very smart," commented Jacqueline in French.

Philippe shrugged his shoulders. "She thinks I'm beneath her," he said, also reverting to French.

"You don't do much to convince her otherwise," pointed out Jacqueline.

"You never thought I was beneath you," argued Philippe. "You risked your life for me, and you didn't even know me."

"That was different," commented Jacqueline. "Suzanne has not had a chance to outgrow the beliefs she was raised with. She was never allowed beyond the grounds of the Château de Lambert, except after our father was arrested and I had to send her and Séraphine away. In her limited understanding, she believes it is people like you who took her home from her and killed her father and brother. She expresses contempt for you not only because she has been taught that she is better than you, but also because she is afraid of you."

Philippe gave her a doubtful look, obviously not convinced by her explanation.

"I would like you to work at easing her fear, not intensifying it."

He shrugged his shoulders. "I don't mean to scare her."

"I know," replied Jacqueline. "But you do, whether you mean to or not. She is also jealous of my relationship with you, and that is something I must work on. You are part of the family now, and Suzanne must understand that does not mean I love her any less." She sighed. "I realize it has only been a few weeks, but we all have to try to help each other get through this period."

"Séraphine doesn't mind me," Philippe commented, looking over at Jacqueline's little sister. She sat at her desk drawing a picture, apparently oblivious to their discussion. Philippe thought she was as pretty as a china doll, with her white-blond curls spilling over the lace collar of her blue satin dress.

"Séraphine is only six, and has not absorbed as much prejudice and fear," explained Jacqueline.

"That could be," he allowed, rising from his chair and going over to see what she was drawing. "Or it could be that she just plain likes me."

He picked up a pastel crayon from her desk, idly examined it, and then pretended to eat it, much to Séraphine's amazement. He picked up another, and another, and made a great show of dropping them in his mouth and chewing them, all the while slipping them into the palm of his other hand, and from there into the pocket of his new coat. When the last one had disappeared he grabbed his throat, made a terrible gasping sound, and collapsed heavily to the floor.

Séraphine climbed down from her chair and went over to examine him, not too concerned about his health, but curious to see if he was in fact hiding the pastels somewhere. She pried open one hand, and found nothing. She pried open the other, and found a square of folded paper. She opened it to reveal a colorful drawing of a cat chasing a butterfly. She smiled at Philippe and returned to the desk with her new possession. Philippe leapt up from the floor and deposited the missing pastels on her desk.

"Tomorrow I will draw a fine horse for you," he told her. "Would you like that, Séraphine?"

She ignored him and continued with her drawing.

"I am not sure what color to make it," he mused. "I was thinking of bright green."

She looked up at him and scrunched her face together, obviously displeased with his choice.

"No?" he remarked in surprise. "Very well then. How about blue, like your pretty dress?"

She looked down at her dress, as if she needed to evaluate its color. She looked up at him and shook her head.

"Not blue either?" He drew his brows thoughtfully together and pretended to think. "I've got it!" he pronounced suddenly. He hunched down beside her. "There is a little pony in the stables that is a soft gray, the exact shade of your eyes. Why don't you come down to the stables with me this afternoon and take a look at him? If you like the color, then that is the color I will make your horse."

Séraphine nodded brightly.

Jacqueline smiled. Philippe had a wonderful, easy manner with Séraphine. Although she still did not speak, Philippe regularly carried on conversations with her as if she were answering him. He was always trying to amuse her, by acting out little charades in her presence and presenting her with special gifts. Séraphine was the only friend he had made in the Harrington household, other than the men who worked with him in the stables. Laura was convinced he was a thief and was constantly mentioning that something had mysteriously gone missing and then looking pointedly at Philippe. Sir Edward and Lady Harrington had been most reluctant to take what they called "a street urchin" into their home and suggested that he should work full-time in the stables and sleep there as well.

Jacqueline would not hear of it. She had not brought Philippe back to England with her to turn him into a stable boy. He was permitted to work in the stables four hours a day, but only after he had completed his lessons to his tutor's satisfaction, and then spent time with her and the girls practicing his English and learning the proper manners of a gentleman.

In four weeks he had learned enough English to carry on a basic conversation, and enough manners not to embarrass himself in almost any social situation. He had been outfitted in the clothes of a young nobleman and firmly instructed in the rules of regular bathing, which he grudgingly accepted. His dark hair had been trimmed to a neat length at his shoulders and he had been taught to brush it and tie it back with a ribbon. At first glance there was no reason to suspect he wasn't the son of a wealthy aristocrat, except that he looked uncomfortable in his new surroundings. He was quiet and sullen in the presence of the Harringtons, obviously sensing that they did not like him, and not liking them much in return. Since he was not at all accustomed to having to take care with his clothes, they quickly became rumpled and soiled, and he had a habit of constantly pulling at his cravat as if he felt it was strangling him. However, he absolutely loved being around horses. He went riding every day and, according to his riding master, was a natural in the saddle. Jacqueline thought he was adjusting to his new life remarkably well.

She wished she could say the same for herself.

In the past four weeks she had neither seen nor heard from Armand. She had no idea if he was still in England, or if he was already making trips back to France. She had thought several times of writing to him, and then decided against it. She did not know what to say to him, and if he was about to leave for France, he would never reveal such a thing to anyone.

She knew she should try to forget about him and focus on putting her life together. She had returned from France with the last few jewels from the De Lambert jewel collection sewn into her underclothes. They were valuable, but not valuable enough to support herself, her sisters, and

Philippe for more than a year or two. Her plan was to sell the jewels and invest the money, but without Armand to advise her she was lost as to how to go about doing so. She considered speaking to Sir Edward, but he had inherited all of his money and land, and she was not convinced he knew anything about taking a small amount of money and turning it into a fortune. On her own, she was not confident she would even get a fair price for the jewels, and if she were cheated, they would be destitute. And so for the moment she did nothing, living on a mixture of Sir Edward's charity and the severely reduced funds she had sent from France for Suzanne and Séraphine.

"Excuse me, your ladyship, the Marquis de Biret is here and awaits your presence in the small salon," announced Cranfield, interrupting her thoughts.

"*Merci, Monsieur Cranfield*," replied Jacqueline. "Tell him I will be down directly."

Cranfield gave her a small bow and left the room.

"*Qui est le marquis?*" demanded Philippe suspiciously.

"He is my betrothed," replied Jacqueline in English. "The man Monsieur St. James was trying to rescue when he was caught."

"The man who let him be trapped, you mean," clarified Philippe in French, his disgust obvious.

Jacqueline nodded. "So it would seem," she replied. "Philippe, I want you to stay with Séraphine while I go downstairs. You may continue with your lessons until I return."

Jacqueline hurried along the hall to the stairs. Although she had not seen François-Louis since her return, she was still officially betrothed to him. That was a blessing on the one hand, because it had enabled her to refuse all invitations to balls and parties, telling Lady Harrington that she was betrothed and simply did not wish to go out. On the other hand, she had no intention of marrying François-Louis and really should let him know. Given that she no longer had any money, somehow she did not think he would be overly distraught by the breaking of their contract.

She found him standing in the salon with his back to her, staring out the window that looked onto the garden. He wore a striped yellow and green jacket with mustard-colored breeches and a snowy-white wig tied back with a matching green velvet ribbon. Great quantities of lace were blooming out from underneath the cuffs of his jacket. At one time she had thought his attire to be wonderfully fashionable and was pleased that her betrothed took such care with his appearance. Today she found him utterly ridiculous.

"Bonjour, François-Louis," she said coldly.

He turned and smiled at her. "Jacqueline, my love, what a relief that you have returned safely," he gushed in French. He bent low over her hand and pressed a long kiss to it. "When I heard from Sir Edward that you had disappeared, I was absolutely sick with worry for your well-being."

"Really?" remarked Jacqueline. "If you were so concerned, how is it that you have taken over a month to come and see me?"

"I apologize for not coming sooner, but I was staying in the countryside with a friend and only just received word of your return," he replied smoothly. "I came as quickly as I could, my dearest. And how wonderful you look!" he added, stepping away from her so he could better see her.

"We need to talk," said Jacqueline, stepping away from him to look out the window.

"Of course we do," he agreed, moving to stand beside her. "I have spoken with Sir Edward, and he informs me that you were successful in your bid to rescue your friend, which of course I think is wonderful. Tell me," he continued casually, "has the man offered you any kind of remittance for saving his life?"

She turned to him, appalled by the question. "I cannot see that it is any of your concern whether he did or not."

"Come now, Jacqueline," he said easily, "I am, after all, your betrothed, and it is my right to know the details of your finances."

"You trapped him, François-Louis."

He lifted his eyebrows in surprise. "How can you accuse me of such a terrible thing, Jacqueline?"

"Do not waste your breath denying it," she returned darkly. "You knew if you wrote me that letter I would not be able to stand by and do nothing. You struck a bargain with Nicolas, trading your freedom in exchange for the man who had come to save you. And then you came to me, with an elaborate lie about how he was injured and could not go on." She glared at him with unmitigated disgust. "What you did was cowardly and despicable."

He shook his head. "Sweet Jacqueline, is that how you see it?" he asked painfully. He sighed. "I confess, I did go along with Nicolas's request, but it was only so I could be with you again. I was out of my mind, I was so worried about what would become of you and your sisters. I wanted to live, yes, but not for me, for us. The thought of you tormented me day and night, thinking of you being destroyed by your grief for your father and Antoine, and the loss of everything you had once known. I had to get out of there so I could see for myself that you were all right, and if you were not, so I could take you in my arms and dry your tears and absorb at least some of your terrible pain."

He reached out and grabbed her, crushing her against the lace of his shirtfront in a passionate embrace. The scent of sweet cologne filled her nostrils. "You are everything to me, Jacqueline," he told her dramatically. "My life, my soul, my very heart. Without you, I am nothing. How can you be angry with me for trading a stranger for the opportunity to be reunited with you? I love you, my dearest heart, more than life itself. You are everything to me. When we are married, I will worship you like a goddess. You will see what it is to be loved by a man who is enslaved by his devotion for you, who would do absolutely anything to make you happy." Before she could stop him he lowered his head and pressed his lips to hers.

"How perfectly touching," drawled a sarcastic voice in English.

Startled, Jacqueline pushed herself away from François-Louis. Armand stood leaning against the doorway, blandly watching the pair of them as if they were actors performing a little play for his entertainment. "De Biret, I had no idea you were sacrificing me for such a noble cause. I suppose I should have felt privileged to have been a part of it."

François-Louis humbly inclined his head toward him. "I fear I must apologize, Monsieur St. James, for the terrible situation I put you in. I hope you will be able to forgive me?"

"No."

François-Louis sighed. "I understand," he said sadly. "Perhaps one day I can make it up to you."

"I doubt that."

He abruptly shifted his gaze to Jacqueline, as if the marquis no longer warranted his attention. He leisurely looked her up and down, visibly demonstrating to François-Louis that he felt he had the right to do so. She felt herself grow warm under his scrutiny.

"I see you are well, Mademoiselle."

"The marquis and I are almost finished," stammered Jacqueline, her face flushed, her voice tight with embarrassment. "If you would like to wait in the library a few minutes—"

"I did not come to see you," interrupted Armand. "I have some business to conduct with Sir Edward, and then I will be on my way."

"I see," she replied, flinching at his scornful tone. "Perhaps, if it does not inconvenience your busy schedule too much, you might find a moment to speak to Philippe. He has been working very hard at his lessons these past weeks, and I am certain he would enjoy the opportunity to tell you about it."

"I will look in on him," he replied. "Please, do carry on as you were. I believe the marquis was promising to worship you like a goddess when you are married." He swept into a courtly bow. *"Mademoiselle,"* he drawled, his mockery unmistakable. He straightened up and cast a look of absolute loathing at François-Louis. *"Monsieur le Marquis,"* he added, his voice thick with contempt. He turned and left the room.

"That man has the manners of a peasant," commented François-Louis in disgust.

A well of anger boiled up inside Jacqueline. "And just what did you expect him to do?" she demanded furiously. "Accept your pretty little apology for getting him thrown in La Force for a month when he was risking his life to save you? You almost got him killed, François-Louis. Did you think he would shake your hand and thank you for it?"

"I expect him to act like a gentleman in your presence, Jacqueline," he told her firmly. "His anger should be directed at me, not you. I will not tolerate rudeness toward the woman who is to be my wife. He is lucky I did not call him out for his loutish behavior."

Jacqueline sighed. "I do not need you to defend me from him, François-Louis."

"You are my betrothed," he insisted. "You are the daughter of the Duc de Lambert, and soon you will be the Marquise de Biret. I expect men to treat you with the respect you deserve."

"I am not going to be your wife, François-Louis."

He looked at her in amazement. "You are breaking our betrothal?" he demanded.

Wearily she went over to the sofa and sat down. "When you and my father worked out this match, it was a union that made sense," she began. "My father was anxious to find me an appropriate suitor, and since you lived close by and came from impeccable bloodlines, you were an excellent choice. We were uniting the De Biret and De Lambert families, and all the lands and investments that went with them. We did not know each other very well, but neither of us found the other disagreeable, and in time, I am sure, we would have come to care for each other as husband and wife." She stood and began to pace. "But everything is different now. We have been forced to leave our homes and possessions, we don't have any money, and I do not believe that the union of our blood-lines is an adequate reason to go forth with a marriage, since those bloodlines have very little relevance in this country."

He looked at her in dismay. "Jacqueline, dear heart, do you really mean it?"

She stopped pacing and looked at him. "Yes," she told him, feeling a little sad. "I do."

He looked unconvinced. "You really don't have any money?"

"For God's sake, François-Louis," she snapped heat-edly, "if that is all that matters to you, go find yourself a wealthy English girl to marry."

"I wish it were that easy," he commented bitterly, go-ing over to look out the window once again. "These En-glishwomen are a mercenary lot. They are impressed by titles and accents at first, but very quickly they want to know just exactly what it is you have brought with you from France."

"It would seem you have been doing a little investigat-ing," commented Jacqueline dryly.

"Harmless flirtation, my love, harmless flirtation," he quickly assured her.

"You don't need to explain," replied Jacqueline. She was hardly in a position to be critical.

"Perhaps you are right," sighed François-Louis. "Given my limited funds, you would probably do much better to marry some nice, wealthy Englishman."

"Marriage is not at the forefront of my plans."

He looked at her in confusion. "What is it you intend to do?"

"I have a little money left. I am going to try investing it."

"Investing it?" he repeated incredulously. "Dear Jac-queline, you know nothing of investing. What if you lose it all?"

"I will worry about that only if it happens," she re-turned.

"I see." He was silent for a few moments, staring pensively out the window. "Before I go, there is something I think you should know," he said finally, turning to face her.

She looked up at him expectantly. "Yes?"

He went to the sofa and seated himself beside her. "I don't want you to get overly excited, because the information I am about to share with you is probably false, do you understand?" he demanded. "I was not even certain I was going to tell you, and as your betrothed I felt it was my responsibility to make that decision on your behalf. However, since we are no longer betrothed, I feel I must tell you. But remember, this information is coming from an unnamed source, and therefore must be treated with enormous skepticism. Do you understand what I am saying?" he asked seriously.

Jacqueline's heart began to beat a little faster. "What is it?"

"Yesterday I received a message that your brother Antoine may still be alive."

The blood drained from her face. "What?" she managed, her voice barely a whisper.

"It may be lies, Jacqueline," he repeated firmly. "We have no reason to think it is true."

"Who did you hear this from?" she demanded.

"The counterrevolutionary network runs deep, even in England," he replied. "Last week I received a message from a man who would not identify himself and would not reveal how he had come upon his information. He would only say that the Marquis de Lambert was alive and being hidden by friends, in a small farmhouse near the Austrian border. The fellow said he had been gravely ill and was so weak he could not be moved, or else they would have worked to get him out of there."

"Oh my God," breathed Jacqueline.

"It could be lies, Jacqueline," he repeated firmly.

"But it could also be true!" she protested, desperate to believe that Antoine was alive.

"Either way, it doesn't really matter," François-Louis

told her. "The messenger said that the marquis was so ill it was not thought he would survive."

Jacqueline felt a cold chill of despair grip her. "Not survive?" she repeated blankly. She wrapped her arms around herself, trying to make sense of what François-Louis was telling her. "I was told he was dead—that he died in La Conciergerie," she murmured.

"Apparently his jailer thought he was," replied François-Louis. "But this fellow said that when they were taking his body off the cart to bury it, he moaned. Well, peasants are a superstitious lot, and the poor fools who were carrying him were convinced it was the work of the devil, bringing a dead aristo back from hell to haunt them, so they ran off. A couple of counterrevolutionary sympathizers who were assigned to report on the number of bodies buried each day were watching, and they took him to a place where he could be cared for, and that is where he has stayed ever since."

Jacqueline stood up suddenly, her spine rigid with purpose. "I am going to get him," she stated flatly.

He looked at her in disbelief. "Jacqueline, you cannot," he told her. "We do not even know if this information is true, and besides, even if it is true, it would be far too dangerous for you to return."

"But I must know if Antoine lives, and if he does, I must help him to get out of France," she told him.

"You have just returned from a very dangerous mission," he said. "You must not risk your life again for an unsubstantiated rumor."

"He is my brother, François-Louis," she countered. "If he lives, I must find him."

"Jacqueline, I cannot let you do this," he protested. "Why don't you ask Monsieur St. James to go and investigate? I am sure he would be willing to help you in this matter."

Jacqueline thought for a moment. She had asked Armand not to return to France again, for her sake, because it was too dangerous for him. How could she then turn around and ask him to go back? To do so would be enormously selfish and hypocritical. It would be like saying, *Do not risk your life to save those who need your help, unless it is someone who matters very much to me.* He would never respect a request like that. Besides, if Antoine was ill and could not be moved, she wanted to be with him and care for him herself. She would make him strong again, strong enough that he could be moved. If Armand went to France, he would never allow her to go with him, and that might cheat her of her last chance to see her brother alive. No, she could not ask Armand to go.

"I will go myself," she stated flatly. "I do not need Monsieur St. James's help."

François-Louis sighed. "I should have known you would feel this way if I told you," he said. "Since I cannot dissuade you from going, then I will go with you."

She looked at him in astonishment.

"I feel somewhat responsible for having put you in this position, by sharing this information with you," he informed her. "If anything happened to you while I was sitting safely here in England, I should never be able to forgive myself."

"François-Louis, do you know what you are saying?" she asked incredulously. "This mission will be extremely dangerous. Are you certain you want to risk your life for it?"

He swept into a courtly bow. "I am ever your devoted servant, Jacqueline," he told her gallantly. "When do you wish to leave?"

"We will take a coach to Dover tonight," she replied without hesitation. "No one must know of our plans. I will leave a note for Sir Edward saying that I have decided to join you at your friend's house in the countryside. He may not like the fact that I am traveling unchaperoned, but he will have no reason to suspect anything else. We will find a ship to take us to Calais tomorrow."

"I will contact the messenger who gave me this information and find out exactly where Antoine is supposedly being held," offered François-Louis. "And I will arrange for our traveling papers in France. In my flight from Paris to the coast I did make a few useful connections. I think I will be able to get us everything we require."

"Do you need any money?" asked Jacqueline, remembering how exorbitantly expensive the bribes and false papers had been in France.

He smiled and shook his head. "I told my hostess I was expecting some funds in the near future, and she was kind enough to grant me a loan until those funds arrive. I will use that money to pay for the necessary arrangements."

"Your hostess is very generous," observed Jacqueline.

He shrugged. "I am a very fascinating guest," he assured her. "She has reason to be generous."

"I shall be ready to leave at midnight," said Jacqueline, not really caring to know what it was François-Louis was doing to keep his hostess so "fascinated." "Everyone will be asleep by then, so no one will see me leave."

"I will be back with a coach at that time," he assured her, swooping low and pressing a kiss to her hand. He turned to leave the room.

"François-Louis."

He turned to look at her.

"Thank you."

He hesitated, gave her a brilliant smile, and left the room.

The massive oak door swung open slowly, revealing a white-haired butler who regarded him curiously. "Yes?" he asked.

"Monsieur St. James," said Philippe breathlessly, panting with exhaustion from his long ride.

"Mr. St. James is not at home," replied the butler stiffly. He began to close the door.

"*Attendez!*" cried Philippe, slamming his foot inside the door.

The butler looked down at him with raised eyebrows.

"If him not here, I must wait," explained Philippe

awkwardly, searching for the proper English words. "He would want."

"He will not return until tomorrow," said the butler, obviously reluctant to let him in.

Philippe knit his eyebrows together. Tomorrow. Tomorrow. When was tomorrow? he wondered in frustration. Tomorrow. It did not matter. "I must wait," he repeatedly stubbornly.

The butler sighed. "Very well," he said, evidently not pleased. He opened the door and stood to one side. "Come in."

Philippe stepped inside.

"This way," said the butler.

He picked up a candelabra and began to lead him down the hallway and up an enormous staircase. They traveled along a dark corridor until they reached a door. The butler opened it and gestured for Philippe to follow him inside.

Philippe watched as the butler lit several candles around the room, revealing it to be a bedroom. He frowned in confusion.

"You will sleep here," said the butler slowly. "And tomorrow you may see Mr. St. James."

Tomorrow. Tomorrow. Philippe struggled to remember what tomorrow meant. It seemed the butler wanted him to rest here until Armand returned. He was not sleepy, but he did not argue. He nodded. "You tell Monsieur St. James I am here?" he demanded.

"Yes," replied the butler. "Tomorrow." He closed the door.

Philippe threw himself onto the bed, bursting with restless energy. He had ridden for almost three hours trying to find Armand's estate. One of the men in the stables had drawn a map for him, but he was still forced to stop several times along the way to ask for directions. Fortunately people seemed to know the St. James estate. But Philippe found their accents extremely difficult to understand, and directions were not something he had studied in his English lessons. He would have to speak to his tutor about that.

A clock began to chime from somewhere down the hall. Philippe counted nine chimes and cursed. He went looking for Armand as soon as he finished eavesdropping on Jacqueline and the marquis, thinking to tell him right away of their plan. But Armand had left, without even speaking to Sir Edward, which he had claimed was his only reason for being there. Philippe knew he would have to find him, but he had four hours of work ahead of him in the stables, and since he was always supervised as he worked, there was absolutely no chance of him sneaking away with a horse. At six o'clock he started out with his map, thinking it would take only about an hour and a half to reach Armand's estate, and then the two of them could head back to the Harringtons' and stop Jacqueline from leaving at midnight, or at least go with her. But the roads were dark and unfamiliar, and it had taken him twice as long to find this place, only to learn that Armand was not even here. If he did not return soon, they would have no chance of stopping Jacqueline.

He laced his fingers behind his head and sighed. He was extremely weary. Although he loved to ride, he seldom went out for more than an hour or so. His whole body was stiff and aching. He groaned and closed his eyes. Perhaps he should use this opportunity to rest. As soon as Armand returned they would be heading out once again. He could only hope that for the return trip they would take his carriage.

He was awakened by the sound of glass shattering. He opened his eyes and instantly leapt from the bed, preparing to defend himself. He looked around in confusion. The candles had gone out, telling him that he had been asleep for at least two hours, possibly longer. A feeling of panic assaulted him. He swore softly and went out into the hall to see if Armand had returned.

The muffled sound of someone cursing was coming

from the end of the corridor. Philippe moved toward the sound, thinking to ask whoever it was if Monsieur St. James had come back. He came to a closed door with light spilling out from underneath it. He raised his fist and rapped firmly on the door, only to be rewarded by the sound of something shattering against it.

"Get away from there, do you hear me?" demanded a furious, alcohol-thickened voice.

Philippe hesitated. He was sure the voice was Armand's, but experience had taught him that an angry drunk was not to be trifled with. He cleared his throat.

"It is Philippe Mercier, Monsieur St. James," he said in French. "I must speak with you immediately."

Silence. Philippe waited.

"Did she send you?" the voice demanded suspiciously in French.

"No, Monsieur. She does not know I am here."

Silence again. Philippe began to wonder if Armand had heard him.

"Come in, then, for God's sake," Armand snapped irritably.

Philippe twisted down the handle and opened the door. The heavy, sweet stench of whiskey immediately filled his nostrils. He blinked and looked around the room, which was a shambles of overturned furniture, broken glass, empty bottles, and spilled liquor. Armand was sitting in an armchair before the fireplace, holding a bottle of amber liquid in his lap and moodily staring at the dead coals. His jacket, waistcoat, and cravat were carelessly strewn across the floor, along with books, papers, and smashed figurines that had evidently been foolish enough to get in his way. His wrinkled shirt was rolled up at the sleeves and largely unbuttoned; his coppery hair had come loose from its ribbon and spilled wildly on his shoulders. He looked like a common drunk, not at all unlike the men who passed out in the cheap cafés in Paris and then got tossed onto the street when the owners wanted to close.

Armand looked up and tried to focus on Philippe. He had no idea how long he had been in here. Time had ceased to mean anything. All he knew was that from the moment he had seen Jacqueline kissing De Biret, had heard that fool driveling on about how it would be when they married, he had been overcome with a rage so painfully intense nothing but alcohol could begin to numb it. One drink. That was all he meant to have. But one drink was useless, and so he allowed himself another, and another, until finally he decided that if he was going to drink he might as well allow himself the pleasure of a roaring good drunk. But the alcohol did not set him free. Instead it trapped him, forcing him to confront his rage, intensifying it, filling him with loathing for himself, for Jacqueline, for France, for the world.

He was a failure. He was a bastard. He had been an unfit son, an unfit husband, and an unfit father. He had not been able to keep his family safe, and so they had been killed. And though it went completely against every rule he now lived by, he had purposefully seduced Jacqueline. And then he had rejected her, which sent her right back into the arms of her marquis. Of course. After all, De Biret was titled. He was worthy of her. As for himself, he still had to make up for his sins. That was a life-long sentence he had given himself. Falling in love and marrying again did not factor into it. And so now he was alone, free to continue to go to France and wage war against the demons of his past, not caring if he lived or died. Except that suddenly he did care, and that realization terrified him.

As Philippe took in the state of the room and the number of empty bottles, he realized Armand had been here all along. He had obviously informed his butler that he did not wish to be disturbed, and his butler, aware of his drunken state, had no wish to violate that order.

"Come over here and have a drink," ordered Armand.

Philippe shook his head. "I don't drink."

"Neither do I," said Armand darkly. He tilted his head back and took a long swig from the bottle. The liquor trickled down the sides of his mouth and dripped onto his shirt. He raised his arm and wiped his mouth on his sleeve.

"Monsieur St. James, Jacqueline needs your help," began Philippe, desperately wondering how Armand could do anything for Jacqueline in his current drunken state.

"Is that so?" sneered Armand. "What's her problem this time? Does she have another suitor who needs rescuing?"

Philippe ignored the bitter sarcasm in his voice. "No," he replied. "But I overheard the marquis giving her some disturbing information when he visited her today—"

"Ah, the marquis," interrupted Armand mockingly. "This must be serious." He took another slow swig from his bottle.

"The marquis told her he received a message that her brother might still be alive," continued Philippe, "and Jacqueline decided she would return—"

"I should have killed him," interrupted Armand, his voice deadly calm.

Philippe looked at him in confusion. "Jacqueline's brother?"

"He was touching her," growled Armand furiously, re-creating the scene in his mind. "The bastard was pressing himself against her and kissing her, showing her how it will be when she marries him. And she was *letting him.*"

"Monsieur St. James, I don't think now is the time to be discussing the marquis," pointed out Philippe. He did not like the way Armand was speaking of Jacqueline.

Armand took another long mouthful of whiskey and stared thoughtfully into space, completely oblivious to Philippe's presence. "Won't he be surprised on their wedding night," he drawled scornfully. His lips curved into an ugly smile.

His meaning was unmistakable. "Shut up," choked Philippe, feeling his stomach tighten.

"I had her first," boasted Armand, his voice a mixture of bitterness and triumph.

"*Shut up,*" commanded Philippe, clenching his jaw with anger.

"At first she thought I was beneath her," muttered Armand, ignoring him. "The noble daughter of a duc was far too good for the untitled likes of me. But once she lay naked in my bed, she was only too willing to spread those long, aristocratic legs—"

Philippe's small fist crashed into Armand's jaw, snapping his teeth together and sending his brain spinning. He shook his head and stared at the boy in astonishment. "What the hell—"

"Shut your filthy mouth, you *goddamn bastard*!" Philippe blazed, his whole body trembling with rage. "You don't know anything about her, and you aren't fit to touch her, do you hear?" He stood before him, his hands balled into fists, fighting the impulse to strike him again. "She risked everything for you. Her life, her jewels, her future—everything. She never cared what happened to her, only that you got out. Nothing else mattered."

Armand stared at him, dumbfounded.

"Did you ever see her home?" Philippe demanded furiously. "It was far grander than this place. But they took it away from her. They destroyed it. She walked through it like a queen. She didn't cry. She didn't say a word. Because all she cared about was getting her jewels so she could use them to get *you* out.

"She hates it here," he continued, his voice beginning to shake. "She never goes out. She never sees anyone. Maybe she was not much better off when we were in France, but she was different then. Do you know how I know she was different?"

"No," said Armand, his mind swimming with alcohol and yet suddenly deadly serious. "How?"

"She never cried in France," Philippe told him.

"She cries?" he asked hoarsely.

Philippe's eyes narrowed. "You made her cry that night on *The Angélique*," he said accusingly. "You used her, and you made her cry. And she has cried every night since." He turned away from him in disgust. "She isn't going to marry the marquis," he sneered. "He isn't nearly good enough for her." He turned to look at Armand.

"And neither are you," he spat, his voice thick with contempt.

Armand stared at him in wonder. This young, abused, thieving urchin, who had ever reason to hate the aristocracy with his entire being, was passionately defending Jacqueline. And why not? She had saved him from a life of violence and misery. She had seen beyond his filthy exterior, and taken him off the streets of Paris and made a life for him that held some hope. But more than that, she became his friend. From the beginning she made it clear that he was not a servant, but part of her family. He was humbled by the boy's devotion to her. And he was humbled by Jacqueline's devotion to him. She had changed a great deal since that first day he had seen her on trial for the crimes of her class.

"You are right," he admitted softly. "I am not nearly good enough for her."

"I came here because I thought you could help her," continued Philippe, his voice still taut with anger. "At this very moment she is leaving for the coast, to take a ship to France and find her brother. I hoped you would be able to stop her, or at least go with her to make sure she was safe. But look at you," he said with disgust. "You could not even make it to the stables, let alone to France. I would have been better to just follow her myself. I never should have come here." He turned to leave.

"Wait," called Armand, desperately trying to comprehend everything Philippe was telling him. "You say she is returning to France?" he repeated, hoping he had misunderstood.

Philippe turned. "She is on her way to Dover right now," he informed him.

"Alone?" demanded Armand, pulling himself up out of his chair and fighting to keep his balance.

"The marquis is with her," replied Philippe.

Armand knit his brows together and frowned. François-Louis was going with Jacqueline to France? But why? Philippe had said something about Jacqeline's brother being alive. But that was impossible. Wasn't it? He was not sure. What he was sure of, even in his drunken stupor, was that the marquis was not the kind of man who risked his life for others. If he was returning to France with Jacqueline, somehow he must believe that in doing so he was not placing himself in any grave danger. But that was pure foolishness. Wasn't it? What would make him think he would not be arrested and imprisoned the minute he stepped onto French soil? And if he really wanted to help Jacqueline, why didn't he just go to France alone and get her brother for her? If he cared for her as much as he claimed, why risk her life by taking her with him?

Understanding dawned on him like a wave of icy water. "My God," he breathed in horror. "It's a trap." The room began to spin.

Philippe looked at him in bewilderment. "How do you know?"

Armand shook his head impatiently, unable to explain. "Call the butler," he ordered, desperately trying to keep the room steady. "Tell him to bring coffee. Some food. Get the carriage ready. We must leave tonight. We have to try to stop her before she gets on a ship. *Move.*"

"Oui, Monsieur," replied Philippe hastily, surprised by the sudden change in Armand. Perhaps he was not quite as drunk as he appeared. He turned to fetch the butler.

An agonizing groan prevented him from reaching the door. He whirled around just in time to see Armand's eyes roll up into his head as his massive frame collapsed heavily onto the floor.

Chapter 16

Icy rain lashed against Jacqueline's cheeks as she stood on the deck watching the misty gray coast of France loom mysteriously in the distance. Her beloved country looked dark and peaceful as it stretched languidly before her in the soft evening light, but Jacqueline knew better than to be deceived by its tranquil beauty. The France that lay ahead was violent and cruel, more cruel than she could ever have imagined. Once she had believed the madness would pass, that reason and justice would quickly return to the country that counted among its sons some of the finest artistic, scientific, and philosophical minds the world had ever known. But that time was not at hand. In this dark hour, brutal terror and oppression reigned supreme. She prayed to God that Antoine would not fall victim to it a second time.

She was certain he lived. From the moment François-Louis had spoken the words, the secret belief she had buried deep within the depths of her heart was set free, filling her with a fire of brilliant hope and ruthless determination. She would stop at nothing to get him out. She would find him, care for him until his strength was sufficiently restored, and then take him away from those who sought to destroy him. This time she would not fail him. She would get her brother safely out of France, or die in the attempt. There was nothing in between.

Suzanne and Séraphine would be overjoyed when they saw their brother again. She smiled at the thought, pushing the possibility of failure far from her mind. Suzanne had always adored her older brother, and it was possible that when he returned she would no longer feel jealous and threatened by Jacqueline's relationship with Philippe. Maybe Séraphine would even begin to speak again.

And what would Armand think? He would be furious with her for returning to France, of that she was absolutely certain. And he would be angry that she had gone with François-Louis. He had obviously been enraged to find them locked in that embarrassing embrace. By what right had he reacted so? she wondered angrily. After all, he held no claim on her. He had allowed her to make an absolute fool of herself over him, and then he had rejected her. He made his choice. He chose to maintain a life of danger and intrigue over starting a new life with her. Not once in the weeks since they arrived in England had he visited her or made any attempt at contact. It was as if she had simply ceased to exist for him. Then he suddenly showed up and was furious becuase he found her listening to her betrothed's declarations of love. What on earth did he expect of her? Did he think that after being with him she should shroud herself in black and enter a convent? Or did he think she should wait for him, however many years it took for the revolution to end or for him to slay the demons of his past so he could get on with his life? She was not sure. She sighed. Armand despised François-Louis, and the sight of her in the arms of the man who almost got him killed undoubtedly infuriated him. She was sorry for that. If he had only been willing to wait, she would have tried to explain that it wasn't as it seemed.

She adjusted the bonnet of her dark cape over her head in an attempt to better protect herself from the rain. She knew she should go below, but for the moment she wanted to stand here and watch the country she had come to both love and hate slowly emerge through the veil of rain. There had been no time to dye her hair or affect a disguise of any sort, but Jacqueline hoped that her simple attire would keep her safe from suspicion. François-Louis had traded his customary fancy dress for a decidedly unfashionable outfit of rough brown wool, similar in style and cut to the drab brown clothes Nicolas was so fond of wearing. When he had gone below he was still wearing his fine wig, but he assured Jacqueline he did not intend to wear it when they disembarked from the ship.

Surprisingly, François-Louis had proven to be an invaluable asset thus far on their journey. His decision to go with her was decidedly uncharacteristic of him, and at first she had worried he would prove to be a great liability. But to her surprise he organized every facet of their trip down to the smallest detail with amazing competence. From arranging their transportation to the coast, to chartering a private vessel once they reached Dover, to the false traveling documents he somehow managed to procure for them to use once they set foot in France, Jacqueline was amazed by his unfamiliar show of concern and resourcefulness. She realized perhaps she had judged him unfairly.

The ship anchored some two kilometers from the shore. Jacqueline went below to warm herself briefly and fetch her bag before meeting François-Louis on deck and allowing him to help her into the small skiff that would unobtrusively take them across the water. He was most gallant as he assisted her, fussing over her comfort and safety, and painfully reminding her of the difference between him and Armand, who never treated her like a weak, fragile female. True to his word, he had removed his silvery-white wig. A length of smooth brown hair protruded from underneath his dark felt hat, and Jacqueline wondered why he chose to cover such a fine color. She was becoming accustomed to seeing men and women without wigs in England and was starting to find the custom of wearing them rather odd.

They landed north of the town of Calais, thereby avoiding the necessity of going through the checkpoint set up by the National Guard where all newcomers were required to submit their traveling papers and passports for examination. When they reached the shore they set out at once on foot toward the town. Once there they would hire a coach to take them southeast, to the small farm near the Austrian border where Antoine was hidden.

François-Louis had managed to secure detailed directions from the messenger before they left for Dover. If all went well, they would reach the house within three or four hours. A heady mixture of excitement and fear began to stir within her. Soon she would be with Antoine.

The town of Calais was hundreds of miles from the great city of Paris, but its remoteness did not make it any less revolutionary. The rough-looking men who walked the streets were dressed in the simple garb of the sansculottes, wearing their soiled red caps pinned with tricolor cockades like a defiant badge of honor. Men and women alike glared at everyone around them with harsh distrust, their beady, hawkish eyes alert to everything, as if searching for an opportunity to pounce. Jacqueline suspected it did not require much more than a wayward look to have someone accuse you of being a traitor or a spy. She kept her eyes down and quickly moved along beside François-Louis, anxious to be off the treacherous, narrow streets and in the relative safety of a coach.

They came to a busy inn that had several coaches of various sizes waiting outside of it. Jacqueline pulled her hood low over her head as they entered the smoky place, which was thick with the stench of alcohol, unwashed bodies, and burned food. François-Louis guided her to a small, filthy table, sticky and red with spilled wine.

"Stay here," he instructed as he looked about awkwardly. It was obvious he was not used to being in places like this any more than she. "Order some food if you like. I am going to make some inquiries about hiring a carriage."

She watched with concern as he walked over to the counter. He began to speak with a thin, miserable-looking man who was busy setting up a tray with dirty wet glasses and a bottle of cheap red wine. The man appeared to ignore François-Louis, except he nodded every now and then, demonstrating that he was not deaf but simply unwilling to extend the courtesy of giving a patron his full attention. Such niceties were not necessary under the new Republic, and therefore could be considered suspect. She sighed and pulled her gaze away, looking to see if there was someone who might be willing to serve her some food. She was extremely hungry, and since she did not want to stop once they started out, it was best to eat something now.

"Welcome back, Jacqueline," drawled a harsh, mocking voice.

Jacqueline froze. There was a painful roaring in her ears as the identity of that voice settled on her consciousness. A flash of heat and cold rendered her horribly nauseated. She swallowed, willing herself to turn, but somehow unable to make her body cooperate. It was as if her mind thought that as long as she did not acknowledge him, he might simply disappear, allowing her to get on with her mission.

"Come now, you can do better than that," taunted Nicolas as he stepped around to face her. "Aren't you going to at least say hello?"

Slowly she raised her eyes to him. He stared back at her, his dark expression a terrifying mixture of triumph and hatred. She noticed the dreadful scar she had inflicted upon him still looked bloodred against his ashen skin. She wanted to scream, but what use would that be? She swallowed, willing herself to stay calm.

"Your silence is most uncharacteristic," observed Nicolas dryly as he pulled out a chair, dusted it lightly with his gloved hand, and seated himself before her. "I suppose you are somewhat surprised. Tell me, did you really believe I would permit you to get away, especially after our last encounter?" he demanded.

"I never wanted to see you again," managed Jacqueline, her voice shaking.

Nicolas shook his head. "That was most unrealistic of you, Jacqueline," he informed her. "Given our history, I would expect you to know that I am not a man who gives up easily. And since our last meeting, I have been ordered by the Committee of Public Safety to make it my sole mission to capture you and bring you in for execution. That is the only way I can salvage the considerable damage you and your friend have done to my otherwise spotless career. If you are not returned, I will be charged with treason."

Jacqueline stared at him, still unable to believe that he was here. How could he have known she was coming? How could he have known she would be landing here, on this day, and coming to this inn to find transportation? She was loath to accept the only explanation she could find. She cast her eyes down, shrinking into the depths of her cloak as if she felt it could offer her some protection from the reality that surrounded her.

"Ah, here comes your noble marquis," sneered Nicolas.

Jacqueline looked up to see François-Louis walking toward her, flanked on either side by two members of the National Guard. The patrons of the inn were staring at him. He was not being held in any way by the soldiers, and his expression was resigned and calm. Her heart sank.

"Why?" she managed brokenly when he reached her, wondering how he could possibly betray her so. "Why did you do this?"

He shifted his gaze uncomfortably from her to the floor and back to her. "I—I desperately needed the money," he said simply, his blue eyes embarrassed and pleading, as if he thought she should understand.

She stared at him in utter disbelief.

"I have nothing, Jacqueline," he continued defensively. "I thought you had the jewels, and that we would marry and get on rather comfortably. But when you broke our betrothal and told me you had nothing anyway, I knew I had no alternative but to go along with Bourdon's offer."

Her heart constricted with pain. Her betrothed, a man who had once sworn she was everything to him, who had promised to give her anything to make her happy, was trading her life for money. "And Antoine?" she whispered, her voice barely audible over the curious hush that had descended on the room.

He looked at her, his face twisted with deep, genuine regret. "I am truly sorry, Jacqueline," he answered softly.

The pain that washed over her in that moment was awesome, suffocating, unbearable. "You bastard!" she shrieked, leaping up from the table and clawing viciously at his face with all the rage and frustration and horror that suddenly exploded within her.

The two soldiers halfheartedly tried to restrain her, obviously not too concerned about the sight of one aristo attacking another. Jacqueline ignored them and remained focused on François-Louis, much to everyone's entertainment. He raised his hands to protect his face and so she switched her attack to his head, tearing off his hat and wig in the process. She stopped and stared in confusion at the brown hair that dangled from her hand. The entire room roared with laughter. She looked up at François-Louis, whose shiny bald head was nearly as red as his outraged cheeks.

"Enough of this!" ordered Nicolas, although it was obvious that he was taking no small amount of pleasure in the sight of seeing François-Louis publicly humiliated. "Take them outside to the carriage."

Jacqueline bit her lip and drew her cloak protectively around her, trying to regain some control. The two soldiers positioned themselves on either side of her and escorted her through the rough-looking crowd to the door. Nicolas and François-Louis followed behind.

"Send the traitorous bitch to the guillotine!" shouted a burly man who glared at Jacqueline as she walked by, his filthy, unshaven face contorted with malicious pleasure.

"To the guillotine! To the guillotine!" chanted the crowd enthusiastically as they lifted their glasses into the air in mock salute.

She held her head high as she walked past them, unwilling to let them see her fear. A scrawny-looking girl with dirty, matted hair reached out and grabbed at her cloak, tearing her hood down and exposing her to the crowd. One of the guards roughly shoved the girl out of the way, sending her sprawling onto the floor. The crowd cheered. Jacqueline breathed a small sigh of relief. Whatever was to happen to her, Nicolas had obviously ordered that she was not to be molested by the mob, and she was grateful for that.

A carriage was waiting for them outside. Jacqueline climbed in first, followed by François-Louis and Nicolas. She moved as far away from both of them as the constraints of the vehicle would allow.

"You did well, Citizen," commented Nicolas as the carriage lurched into motion, purposely not using François-Louis's title. He reached deep into his coat and pulled out a swollen leather purse, which he tossed heavily at him. "Here is part of your payment," he told him. "The rest has been set up for you in an account in your name in London, as we agreed. You are free to return to England. If you stay here, I cannot guarantee your safety. Do you understand?"

"Yes," replied François-Louis with a nod. He slowly closed his hand around the purse.

"How much did you sell me for?" demanded Jacqueline bitterly.

François-Louis looked at her uneasily.

"Come now, Citizen, tell her what she is worth," taunted Nicolas. "After all, she has a right to know."

François-Louis swallowed. "Eight thousand pounds."

Jacqueline stared at him in disbelief. "Eight thousand pounds?" she repeated, certain she could not have heard right. A man with the lavish spending habits of the Marquis de Biret would go through eight thousand pounds within the year—two years at the very most.

"Rather cheap, I thought," commented Nicolas pleasantly.

"Your negotiating skills must be very poor," commented Jacqueline, her voice dripping acid. "I would think you could have held out for a great deal more."

François-Louis said nothing.

"And to think this was the man you chose over me," taunted Nicolas with heavy sarcasm. "What a pity."

"What is a pity is that I did not make certain you were dead when I left you bleeding on the floor of the Château de Lambert," spat Jacqueline.

"That was rather fortunate for me," agreed Nicolas, idly stroking his scar. "What was unfortunate was this mark you so carelessly left me with. I have yet to repay you for that." He looked at her meaningfully.

Jacqueline glared at him, unwilling to betray any of her fear. "Lay a hand on me and I will tear open the other cheek," she promised vehemently.

The back of his hand smashed viciously against her jaw, causing her to utter a cry of pain and knocking her back against the soft padding of the carriage seat.

"Jesus Christ, Bourdon, is that necessary?" demanded François-Louis, his blue eyes round with shock.

Nicolas rapped on the ceiling of the carriage. The vehicle came to a stop, and Nicolas threw the door open.

"Get out," he ordered, glaring at François-Louis.

François-Louis looked at him in surprise. "But I thought—"

"My business with you is finished," interrupted Nicolas. "You are of no further use to me. Now get out."

The marquis cast a look of apprehension at Jacqueline, as if he was suddenly worried about what Nicolas might do to her once he was gone. "Look here, Bourdon, you must give me your word as a gentleman that you will not—"

"I don't have to give you anything," sneered Nicolas, "especially where Mademoiselle de Lambert is concerned. You sold her to me, remember?"

"I agreed to bring her back to you," conceded François-Louis, "but not so that you could—"

"What I do with her now is none of your concern," interjected Nicolas. "What you should be concerned about is getting out of France before somebody decides to arrest you and throw you back in prison. Do I make myself perfectly clear?"

François-Louis looked worriedly at Jacqueline. "Jacqueline, I swear to you, I never wanted it to end like this," he said apologetically.

Jacqueline looked at him in disgust. "I hate you."

He lowered his eyes. "I don't blame you." He climbed out of the carriage and the door banged shut.

The carriage lurched into motion once more.

"Where are we going?" demanded Jacqueline after a while. "Back to Paris?"

"Not just yet," replied Nicolas. "You will be staying in the local prison for a time."

"Why?" she asked. "I would have thought you would want to take me back as quickly as possible so you can parade me before all your corrupt accomplices on the so-called Committee of Public Safety."

"You will be seeing them soon enough," Nicolas assured her. "But you are only part of the package. I intend to present you and your friend the Black Prince together, and then I intend to watch you both be executed together."

A wave of unease crashed over her, making her feel dizzy. "You will never catch him, Nicolas," she assured him, feigning more conviction than she felt. "You might as well tell the driver to make speed for Paris now."

"Oh really?" returned Nicolas. "I disagree. I think he will come after you, and when he does, I intend to see to it that he is arrested and taken to Paris for execution."

Jacqueline forced a shallow laugh, terrified by the prospect Nicolas was describing. "He won't come after me," she scoffed lightly. "He only saves those who can afford to pay him a handsome reward. Since I no longer have any money, he will have no interest in rescuing me. You had best focus your attention elsewhere if you hope to catch him."

"From what I understand, Armand St. James has no great need for money," he countered easily.

Jacqueline stared at him in blank surprise.

Nicolas smiled. "I decided it would be beneficial to better understand the man who has been plaguing France for almost two years," he informed her. "De Biret was only too willing to give me his name as we began our negotiations. But to capture your enemy, it is not enough to simply know who he is. One must understand what motivates him. A little investigating revealed him to be the grandson of the former Marquis des Valentes, whose daughter, Adrienne, ran away to marry an English commoner named Robert St. James. Further investigation showed that Madame St. James returned to France in 1792, with her daughter-in-law, Lucette, also a French citizen by birth and the daughter of a silk merchant imprisoned at the time because of his counterrevolutionary sympathies, and her granddaughter, Angélique. The two women were clearly aristo émigrés, and they made no secret of their royalist sympathies, which was enough to convince a jury they should all be executed for treason."

"Of what crime was the child guilty?" demanded Jacqueline, feeling sicker with every passing moment. "She was an English citizen, and far too young to be considered a threat to your precious French Republic."

Nicolas shrugged his shoulders. "She was guilty by her association with her mother and grandmother," he replied easily. "At any rate, contrary to what you would have me believe, it would appear this Black Prince of yours does not do his rescuing for money. It seems to me his reasons for saving nobles facing execution are far more personal."

"Maybe so," allowed Jacqueline indifferently, as if this was all news to her. "Nevertheless, you are grasping at straws if you think he will come after me. First of all, he knows nothing of my trip here. I have barely seen the man since we returned to England some weeks ago. And since our last meeting was far less than amicable, I have no reason to believe he will find out about my disappearance anytime soon, much less decide to risk his life to come after me. You might just as well send me on to Paris and be done with it," she suggested practically. The idea that she was being used as bait to lure Armand into another trap was too horrible to bear.

"You seem unusually anxious to be executed," observed Nicolas dryly. "Could it be you are in love with this man, and are sacrificing yourself in a noble bid to protect him from being captured?"

She gave him what she hoped was a scathing look of

insult. "Really, Nicolas, permit me to remind you that I am the daughter of Charles-Alexandre, the Duc de Lambert, and formerly betrothed to the Marquis de Biret. Do you honestly believe I could fall in love with a commoner?" She forced a haughty laugh, as though the mere idea was too ridiculous to be taken seriously.

Nicolas stared at her intently. "You risked your life to rescue him once before, Jacqueline," he pointed out.

She sent him a withering look. "That was a matter of honor, something I do not expect a man like you to understand," she snapped frostily. "I felt responsible for his arrest, since I had unwittingly played a part in it. Monsieur St. James, on the other hand, has played no part in my return to France and, since I do not have the means to reward him, will have no interest whatsoever in trying to help me. You are wasting your time."

He steepled his fingers together as he sank back against his seat and smiled. "We shall see, Jacqueline," he replied calmly. "We shall see."

"She has been arrested."

Armand felt a sickening rush of black, icy fear surge through him, but he was careful to remain composed in front of his men. *He said arrested, not executed.* "When?" he demanded curtly.

"Yesterday," reported John. "As soon as she got here."

Stay calm, he told himself furiously. Get the facts. "How?"

"An inspector from Paris arrested her in a tavern," replied Andrew, another of Armand's crew who spoke fluent French and had been sent ashore to investigate. "Apparently she and the marquis were there trying to hire a coach."

The bastard was waiting for her and she just walked into him, unsuspecting as a lamb. Stupid, stupid, stupid. He shoved his anger aside, struggling to keep focused. "And the marquis?" he demanded evenly.

"He was taken out of the tavern with her, and they got into the same carriage, but he is not being held where she is. No one seems to know what happened to him," replied John.

"No doubt the spineless cur is on his way back to England," offered Sidney furiously.

"No doubt," agreed Armand. At the moment he did not give a damn where De Biret was. "Where is Mademoiselle de Lambert being held?"

John leaned forward on the table in Armand's cabin and unrolled a rough map he had drawn. "There is a small prison, here, near the edge of the town," he began, pointing with his finger. "It is only a single story, and probably holds two or three cells at the most."

Armand studied the small box drawn on the map. "What's it made of?"

"Stone," replied Andrew. "The walls are over a foot thick."

"Any windows?"

"One," answered John, "but it's small and heavily barred. Not even the boy could fit through it," he added, casting a glance at Philippe.

"I could try," offered Philippe, anxious to be of help.

Armand shook his head. "What about guards?"

"That's the real problem," stated Andrew. "The place looks like it's ready for battle. We counted more than a dozen soldiers posted around the building and surrounding area."

Sidney frowned. "That doesn't make any sense," he stated. "Why would they need so many men to watch over her? She's only one unarmed aristocrat."

"Why is she there at all?" added Philippe. "If he wants her executed so much, why didn't he take her back to Paris right away?"

"Why indeed?" mused Armand. He looked at John. "Any word on when they will be moving her to Paris?"

"Some say immediately. Others say she is to be held in Calais indefinitely. No one really seems to know."

Armand leaned back in his chair. He had hoped to

arrange an ambush of her coach while they were on a deserted stretch of road. That would have been fast, quiet, and efficient. Breaking her out of a heavily guarded prison in a small town where she was the focus of everyone's attention was going to be much more difficult. He clenched his jaw in frustration. Obviously that was what Nicolas was counting on.

"I have a bad feeling about this," muttered Sidney. "It's as if he's waiting for something, like he knows you are going to show up in some disguise to try to save her, and when you do, no matter who you are, he'll be ready for you."

"Another trap?" asked Philippe.

Armand began to drum his fingers idly on the surface of the table. "It certainly looks that way," he replied.

Philippe looked at him curiously. "What are we going to do?"

Silence reigned for a moment as his men waited for him to answer. Armand continued to drum thoughtfully on the table, carefully weighing his options.

Suddenly he smiled.

Chapter 17

Cold, gray light filtered through the tiny window across from Jacqueline's cell, indicating the day was finally coming to an end. She sat on her bed and calmly stared at the light, taking comfort from it, for it heralded the beginning of nightfall. This evening would be her third caged in this barren, frigid cell.

It would also be her last.

She knew what she was about to do was a terrible sin, but in a world where nothing made sense anymore, she hoped that God would somehow find it possible to forgive her. The only thing she knew for certain was that she could not allow Nicolas to use her as the bait with which he would snare the Black Prince. Her own death was inevitable, but Armand's was not. If, when he finally learned of her disappearance, he decided to come after her, he would have no way of knowing he was walking into a trap. Perhaps he would be wary and cautious, but regardless of how careful he tried to be, Nicolas had the upper hand as long as he held her prisoner. She could not go to her death knowing she had caused the death of Armand, and with him the deaths of all the innocent people whose lives might otherwise have been saved had he lived.

It was not such a terrible thing to die, she reflected. After all, she could take comfort in the fact that Suzanne and Séraphine were safe, and Philippe was in a new world in which he would never know hunger and where he could make his own future. She hoped Armand would take care of him when she was gone, for she knew Sir Edward and Lady Harrington would not. She realized she should have written some kind of note expressing her last wishes, but she had left in such a hurry she had not thought to do so. Anyway, the children were safe, and that was enough. She could join her father and Antoine in peace.

Her hand idly traced the narrow contours of the dagger hidden in her petticoat. Before she was placed in this cell the guard thoroughly searched her cloak and bag, and smiled with satisfaction when he discovered the pistol she had hidden deep within an inner pocket of her cape. Feeling smug with his find, the fool did not think to examine her further. Before leaving for Dover, she had stitched a small pocket into her underskirt and placed a six-inch dagger inside it. She took comfort from the solid feel of it beneath her clothes. Over the past two days she had spent many hours imagining how it would feel to plunge that pointed shaft deep into Nicolas's heart.

Tonight she would find out.

She smiled.

Oh yes, Nicolas had to die. That was part of the bargain she had made with herself. Nicolas would come to her cell, thinking to find her a helpless victim. And when they were alone, she would pretend to accept his disgusting advances. But when his guard was down, and he was congratulating himself on how cleverly he had reduced the untouchable Jacqueline Marie Louise de Lambert to a defenseless, desperate prisoner begging him for mercy, she would draw out her dagger and drive it deeply into him, through fabric and skin and muscle and bone, piercing his lungs and heart and whatever other organs she might be fortunate enough to reach, until the blood spilled from him in a heavy flow and his eyes grew wide with shock and horror. And then, when he lay utterly dead upon the filthy cold floor, she would take the knife from his back, wipe it clean against his shirt, and use it to slash her wrists to ribbons.

She would not give this evil Republic the satisfaction of murdering her in a public forum. She would cheat them of their desire to make an example of her. She would not die a victim, but a victor. She could only pray that God would understand.

She calmly rose from the bed and went to the table where the guard had left a pitcher of water. She poured some into her hands and splashed it against her face, taking pleasure in the sharp, stinging cold it brought to her skin. She patted herself dry with the rough wool of her cloak. Then she pulled the pins from her hair and took her time running her comb through the honey-colored strands, quite accustomed by now to its shoulder length. She did not have a mirror, but she was able to sweep the pale mass up into a reasonable arrangement and fasten it in place with pins. Then she rinsed her teeth with water and carefully smoothed her hands over the wrinkles in her gown. She wanted to look her best when Nicolas arrived.

"Guard!" she called, looking out the grille of her cell door.

An unshaven soldier in an ill-fitting, filthy uniform appeared after a moment. "What is it?" he demanded irritably.

"I wish to speak with Inspector Bourdon," Jacqueline told him. "Can you send for him?"

"What do you want to see him for?"

"I have some information I think he will find of great interest," replied Jacqueline evasively. "It is urgent that I speak with him at once."

The guard looked at her curiously. "What's so urgent?"

Jacqueline shook her head. "This information is only for Inspector Bourdon."

The guard scowled. "You better not be wasting his time." He turned and disappeared into the next room.

Jacqueline smiled with satisfaction. She reached down among the layers of her underskirt and pulled out her knife. She reverently caressed the icy blade of steel before carefully placing it underneath her pillow. Then she seated herself upon the bed and prepared to wait.

. . . .

The window across from her cell had become a sheet of black by the time she heard a key scraping in the lock. She rose from the bed and stood in the darkness, struggling to appear relaxed as the door slowly swung open.

Nicolas narrowed his eyes, trying to make out her form in the shadows. "Bring a candle in here at once," he snapped.

The guard hastily returned with a two-tiered candelabra, which he placed upon the table. The smoking yellow flames cast an eerie glow over the tiny cell.

"Will there be anything else, Inspector?" the guard asked.

"Go and wait outside," ordered Nicolas abruptly as he threw his hat onto the table. His dark eyes locked onto Jacqueline, burning with intensity. "The citizeness and I have important business to discuss."

The guard retreated into the next room. Jacqueline listened as the front door opened and then banged shut.

Good.

"And so, my sweet Jacqueline, we are finally alone again," stated Nicolas, his voice low and menacing as his eyes raked over her.

"I wondered why you have not come to see me," returned Jacqueline softly.

He looked at her warily, wondering at her mood. "My duties to the Republic come before even you, Jacqueline. In anticipation of your friend's arrival, every soldier and citizen here has been instructed to bring anyone suspicious directly to me. Unfortunately, scores of men and women have been detained for questioning, which has taken all of my time these past two days."

Jacqueline managed an amused laugh. "You are wasting your time, Nicolas," she assured him. "I have already told you, he will not come for me."

"I think you are wrong, Jacqueline," he stated with deadly certainty. He slowly began to remove his gloves. "He will come, and when he does, I will be ready for him."

No Nicolas, you will not be ready for him. You will be dead. She smiled.

Nicolas threw his gloves to the table and looked at her curiously. "You seem in unusually good spirits, considering your situation."

She shrugged her shoulders, a mannerism adopted from Philippe. "I know my days are limited, and I have decided there is nothing else to do but try to enjoy them."

He frowned, obviously not convinced. "You expect me to believe that?"

Jacqueline sighed and shook her head. "Poor Nicolas," she cooed sympathetically. "Always working. Always suspicious."

He began to undo the buttons on his coat. "Either being locked in this cell has addled your brain, or you think you have discovered some way of escaping." He tossed his coat onto the table. "Let me assure you, you will not escape me this time."

She took a step toward him and casually raised her hand to brush a black strand of hair off his face, a gesture so openly intimate he could not control his expression of surprise.

"Perhaps," she whispered softly, "this time I do not wish to escape."

He stared at her as if she had lost her mind. Jacqueline laughed inwardly, empowered by her newfound ability to confound him. She moved her hand to his cheek and lightly traced her finger over the scar she had inflicted on him, fighting to control her revulsion. *He is going to die,* she reminded herself as she looked up into his eyes, dark and cruel and yet obviously fascinated.

Nicolas grabbed her hand and wrenched it away, squeezing her wrist so painfully she was forced to cry out.

"What game is this you are playing, Jacqueline?" he snarled. He jerked her into him and wrapped his other arm around her, imprisoning her in his grasp.

"No game, Nicolas," she protested, fighting to control her fear.

"Why then this sudden show of familiarity? Do you think I am fool enough to believe you want me?"

"I don't give a damn what you believe." She wrenched her hand free from his grasp and clamped it around the back of his neck. Then she pulled his head down and planted her lips firmly against his, pressing herself against his body as she did so. She felt him hesitate, as if he was unsure what trick she played upon him. She moaned softly, trying to make it seem as if she was enjoying it, struggling with the revulsion spreading through her body.

Suddenly Nicolas tightened his arms around her and began to return her kiss, forcefully, greedily, roughly running his hands over her to demonstrate that he was the one who was in control. Jacqueline pretended to respond as she took a step back toward the bed. He followed her, not relinquishing his grip, hurting her with his touch, which was demanding and brutal. She whimpered with pain as he squeezed her breast, and Nicolas let out a low growl of animalistic pleasure. In that moment Jacqueline realized that this was how he experienced fulfillment; not in the giving and sharing of gentle, exquisite pleasure as Armand did, but in the savage domination of a woman who was not enjoying his touch. A rush of nausea and fear raced up her spine. Soon it will be over, she reminded herself. She tried to move closer to the bed, but instead of following her he grabbed her shoulders, twisted her about, and roughly shoved her against the wall. His hand probed the neckline of her gown and wrenched down in one vicious motion, ripping open the fabric and exposing her breasts to the cold air.

Jacqueline gasped and tried to raise her hands to cover herself, realizing she was losing control of the situation. "Nicolas, I—"

"Shut up!" he spat as he grabbed her breast and began to squeeze. "Did you think I would be gentle and dignified when I finally had you?" he demanded sarcastically. He lowered his head so his lips hovered over hers as his other hand began to wrench up her skirts. "I am no gentleman, Jacqueline, or have you forgotten? That was why you rejected me in the first place, remember?" He ground his mouth against hers, pinning her to the wall with his body while his hand fumbled at the front of his trousers.

Jacqueline whimpered and struggled to break free from his hold, but he was far too powerful for her. A wave of terror churned violently within her as she felt his hand probing between her thighs. She had made a ghastly mistake, and now she was about to pay for it. Her mind reeling with fury and despair, she twisted her face away, closed her eyes, and opened her mouth to scream.

"Once again I see I have come at an inopportune moment."

Nicolas froze, as if he could not quite believe he had heard the voice.

Her heart pounding violently, Jacqueline opened her eyes.

Armand was casually leaning against the doorway of her cell, with an armed guard standing behind him. His expression seemed mild, as if the little scene he was witnessing was no more than he had expected. He was not wearing a disguise, but was simply dressed in a dark jacket, white shirt, and breeches, over which he wore an enormous black coat. He looked at her calmly, with only the slight tightness of his jaw giving any indication of the staggering fury that was boiling wildly within him. Then he fixed his gaze on Nicolas.

"I really think you should let her go, Bourdon."

Nicolas snorted with contempt and moved away from her.

Jacqueline let out a sob of crushing anguish as she pulled together the torn pieces of her bodice. Her heart was bleeding with an agonizing mixture of love, relief, and terror. There was no escape for either of them, she realized painfully. Armand had been captured in his bid to rescue her. Now they would both be executed.

"It would appear, St. James, that you have walked right into my trap, just as I knew you would," sneered Nicolas triumphantly as he adjusted his clothes.

Armand shrugged his shoulders. "And it would appear, Bourdon, that you have not yet learned to control your obsession for Mademoiselle de Lambert," he returned mildly.

"Where did you find him?" demanded Nicolas of the guard, ignoring Armand's remark.

"He walked up and said he was the Black Prince and he understood we were looking for him," explained the guard. "We figured he must be crazy, but he insisted on seeing you."

Jacqueline stared at Armand in confusion. Why on earth would he do something as foolish as that?

"It is truly fascinating, the absurdity of human nature," remarked Armand with amusement. "Practically every man, woman, and child who comes into Calais is being detained and accused of being the Black Prince. Yet when I walk in and say 'here I am,' no one takes me seriously." He turned his head to look at the guard. "It is almost insulting, you know," he informed him.

"I don't give a damn," snarled Nicolas impatiently. "You have been captured and that is all that matters."

Armand looked startled. "Captured?" he repeated, as if the idea was news to him.

It was Nicolas's turn to smile. "What would you call it?" he demanded mockingly.

"I have turned myself in of my own accord, in the hopes that we could work out some sort of arrangement," replied Armand.

"What sort of arrangement?" demanded Nicolas.

Armand began to idly adjust the folds of his cravat. "It is really very simple. I am offering you a straight exchange. A life for a life, if you will."

"Which means?"

"I am offering you myself, the Black Prince, in exchange for Mademoiselle de Lambert's freedom." He looked up from his cravat. "If you wish, you can create some grand tale about how you cleverly snared me to tell all your cronies on the Committee of Public Safety, and I will go along with it," he offered generously.

Nicolas laughed. "Tell me, St. James, just why is it you are so concerned about Jacqueline's life?"

Armand shrugged his shoulders. "I am not accustomed to having my work undone. Not after all the trouble I went through to rescue her in the first place." He turned his attention back to the guard. "You really should have seen my disguise, it was absolutely brilliant," he assured him.

"You were saying," interrupted Nicolas impatiently.

Armand looked back at him in surprise, as if he had forgotten he was there. "Oh yes. Well, after all that work, it seems a waste that it should be for naught. It is I your government really wants anyway."

"How touchingly noble," drawled Nicolas sarcastically. "Unfortunately, I am not interested in your offer. I now have both of you, and therefore see no need to bargain with you over anything." He motioned to the guard. "Lock him up."

The guard stared at him and did nothing.

"Lock him up, you damn fool!" growled Nicolas.

The guard remained where he was.

Armand appeared to be preoccupied with removing a fleck of lint from his coat. "You must forgive him for being somewhat less than enthusiastic about your order." He sighed. "Unfortunately, he works for me." His coat apparently in order, he looked up at Jacqueline. "Mademoiselle, would you be kind enough to step out of your cell?" he asked politely.

Confused, Jacqueline hesitated and looked at the guard. Andrew winked at her. Incredulously, she went to the bed, removed the dagger from under the pillow, and grabbed up her cloak. She gave Nicolas one final look of sheer, unmitigated hatred before stepping out the cell door.

"Do you think she meant to use that dagger on you?" asked Armand curiously.

"Guards!" roared Nicolas at the top of his lungs. "Guards!"

The front door of the prison crashed open and six uniformed soldiers came rushing into the room.

"Arrest all of them," ordered Nicolas furiously. "Lock them up."

The soldiers did not move.

Filled with unease, Nicolas looked at Armand.

Armand shook his head sympathetically. "Unfortunately, they all work for me as well. Your men have been temporarily relieved of their duties."

"You will never get out of Calais alive, St. James," Nicolas assured him bitterly.

Armand sighed again. "I wish I could say it has been a pleasure, Inspector Bourdon, but I must confess I am beginning to find our meetings rather tedious." He stepped back and motioned to the guard behind him. "Forgive me for taking the precaution of tying you up," he apologized as the guard went into the cell. "But I do wish to discourage any plans you may have to follow us."

"I'll see both of you dead," snarled Nicolas. The guard stuffed a rag in his mouth.

"Farewell, Inspector," said Armand pleasantly when the guard had finished tying him up. "I do hope your superiors are understanding when you explain to them how you lost your prominent prisoners yet again." He swung the cell door shut and turned the key.

Jacqueline stood numbly amongst the raggedly dressed soldiers, many of whom she now recognized from the crew of *The Angélique,* including Sidney. She clutched her cloak against her chest and tearfully looked up at Armand, still shaken from her ordeal.

He moved toward her and reached out to take her cloak, which he wrapped protectively around her. "I have come to take you home, Jacqueline," he whispered softly.

The knife she had been holding clattered to the floor. He bent low to pick it up.

"Listen to me, Mademoiselle," he said, his voice calm and soothing as he looked down into her tear-filled eyes. "I am now Inspector Garnier, and I have been sent here by the Committee of Public Safety with a detachment of

men to escort you to Paris for execution. Do you understand?"

Jacqueline nodded. Outside she could hear the cries of
a restless mob.

"When we walk out this door, you are a prisoner under my guard. You must conduct yourself accordingly. Do
you understand?"

She cleared her throat, fighting to control her fear.
"Yes."

Armand looked at her with approval. "Good. I will
hold on to this for you," he added as he slipped her dagger into his boot. "I don't believe you will be needing it."

He made a circular motion with his hand and the
guards immediately assembled around her, forming a protective wall. Armand moved ahead of them and opened
the door, leading the impressive contingent outside, where
three more guards and a dozen horses awaited, along with
an irate assembly of men and women carrying a variety of
weapons and torches.

"What's happening to her?" demanded a furious
woman with a heavy pistol tied to her waist.

"Where are you taking the bitch?" screeched another.
The torch she held revealed she was missing most of her
teeth.

A burly man purposefully gripped a musket between
his black-stained hands, looking like he would shoot on
the slightest provocation. "Where's the other inspector?"
he shouted.

A young boy of about twelve glared at her, his little
face contorted with hate. "Are you going to kill her
now?" he shrieked.

This suggestion drew a round of bloodthirsty cheering.

Armand calmly raised his hand to silence them. "I am
Inspector Garnier," he informed them. "I have been sent
here by the Committee of Public Safety to relieve Inspector Bourdon of his prisoner. I will escort this treacherous
aristo to Paris, where she will be executed for her crimes
against the Republic." His powerful voice rang with authority. "Anyone who tries to interfere will be treated as a

traitor." He glowered at the crowd, as if daring one of them to try. And then he raised his fist triumphantly into the night and shouted: "Liberty, equality, fraternity, or death!"

The mob broke into a wild roar of approval. "To the guillotine! To the guillotine! Liberty, equality, fraternity, or death!"

Armand motioned to the guards and they moved forward with Jacqueline, leading her to a horse. She climbed up as the guards quickly mounted their own horses and formed a protective ring around her. Armand took the lead, guiding them through the ragged crowd, which was now screaming and cheering and dancing wildly, their weapons and torches bobbing gaily up and down as they watched Jacqueline being led away, presumably to her death.

They rode for some half hour, taking the road that led south of Calais to Paris. A few stragglers from the group followed them to the edge of the town, raucously chanting and singing, but the night was dark and cold and eventually they grew weary of their excursion and turned back. When Armand and his men were quite sure they were not being followed, they turned off the road and headed toward the water.

Jacqueline's heart was racing with anticipation as they reached the beach. She slipped down off her horse, closed her eyes, and deeply inhaled the sharp salt air, cleansing her mind and her body and her soul as she did so. In that moment she realized how much she had come to love the sound and scent of the sea. She wrapped her arms around herself and searched the darkness for the silhouette of *The Angélique*. It took her a moment, but finally she saw it, gracefully waiting for her on the black water some kilometer from the shore. She sighed. The first time she had seen that ship she had hated her, because she was stealing her away from the country she loved. Now the sight of her filled her heart with joy. *The Angélique* had come to take her home.

Armand had come to take her home.

He was giving orders to his men, instructing them to cut the girths of their saddles before sending their horses galloping off into the night. Four men were moving a huge skiff out from behind a jut of rock and into the water. Armand strode over to the skiff and looked around in exasperation.

"Where the hell is the boy?" he demanded furiously. All the men paused to search the shore.

"He should be here," said John. "He was told to stay here and watch the boat."

"Jesus Christ," cursed Armand in frustration. "You men take Mademoiselle de Lambert to the ship, and then two of you come back in the smaller skiff for me and the boy. Move."

Without question or hesitation, everyone began to assemble around the skiff and climb in. Everyone but Jacqueline. Armand walked over to her.

"Philippe is here?" she asked, frantically hoping she had misunderstood, that they were referring to some other boy, even though she realized that was horribly selfish of her.

"He insisted on coming with me," replied Armand, wishing to God he had not agreed to let him. "But I will find him, Jacqueline. Trust me."

She nodded, clutching her cloak. "I will stay and help you."

"No," he replied, shaking his head. "You are going to take that boat over to *The Angélique* and wait for me there," he ordered firmly.

He was staying here. Alone. For a moment she was unable to breathe, so overwhelming was the sudden wave of fear that washed over her. She knew that even now they might be looking for him. And this time the entire town knew what he looked like. The fear bloomed into terror, and the terror froze her to the spot. "I will go with you," she declared stubbornly.

He stood before her, helplessly aggravated by the precious minutes they were wasting. It was only a matter of time before someone discovered Nicolas in the cell, or the soldiers of the National Guard who had been abandoned in a barn on the edge of Calais. Once they were found, all hell was going to break loose, and there was no way of knowing whether that would be in a few minutes or a few hours. There was no time to argue with her, and no way in the world he would permit her to stay. "I will find him, Jacqueline," he insisted flatly. "I promise. Now get on that boat."

It was impossible, what he was asking her to do. Surely he could see that? Numbly, she shook her head.

He let out a sigh of frustration and reached out to grab her, intending to carry her to the goddamn boat. But to his surprise she let out a cry of absolute anguish and threw herself against him, burying her face in his chest and sobbing so painfully he thought her heart would break.

"Do not leave me," she pleaded brokenly, her voice shaking with emotion. "If you stay, then I must stay, too. Please don't make me leave without you. I—I cannot be without you." Her sobs became louder, deeper, more tearing. "I love you," she whispered, her voice so ragged with pain he barely heard her.

He stood there and held her, overwhelmed by the raw desperation of her words. Of course he had known she loved him. He had known from the moment she appeared in his cell at La Force, a magnificent, rescuing angel, ready to sacrifice her life in the hope that he might live. He had known then, and he had treated her love carelessly. He used her and left her, telling himself he did not need her love nearly as much as he needed to continue his quest for vengeance. But he had been wrong. He needed her love, and he needed her, more than anything in the world. Once again, he would have done anything for her in that moment. But he would never allow her to risk her life again. If anything happened to her, he felt certain he would go mad. He gently cupped her chin with his hand and lifted her tear-streaked face to look down into the silvery depths of her eyes.

"Listen to me, Jacqueline," he ordered, softly caressing

her cheek. "You wound me with your lack of faith. I have told you I will find the boy, and I will. And then I will come back to you. Do you understand what I am saying?" he demanded.

She shook her head and buried her face deep against his chest.

"I love you, Jacqueline," he told her, his voice hoarse with emotion. "I have always loved you. From the moment I saw your miniature in Sir Edward's study, I knew you were something magnificent and rare. I thought my life was over then. I didn't care if I lived or died, which is probably why my rescues were successful. But you changed that. You made me care about something more than death and revenge." He wrapped his arms tightly around her and rested his chin on her head.

"When you disappeared, I felt as if my world had shattered all over again. I realized I no longer cared about having vengeance on this damned revolution. I have something far, far more precious to care about. You. And when we get home, I will shower you with my love, Jacqueline. I will wrap you in it and protect you with it until you are healed and we can both put the past where it belongs—in the past."

She shuddered with an agonizing mixture of joy and fear and continued to cling to him like a lost child.

"But before we can do that, you must trust me," he continued, taking her face in his hands. "And you must show me that trust by getting into the boat and going with my men to the ship. I cannot risk having you with me. If something happened to you, it would cripple my ability to act. Do you understand?" he demanded softly.

"Promise you will come back to me," she sobbed, tears flowing down her face as she struggled to accept what he was asking her to do.

He gave her a tender smile. "I promise to come back to you, Jacqueline. Always."

He bent his head low and captured her lips with his. Their kiss was deep and long and desperate, he seeking to fill her with the strength and power of his love, she seeking to hold him with her for as long as she could. Finally Armand broke the kiss and gently set her away from him. He took her arm in his and led her to the skiff.

"Sidney, you are to see that Mademoiselle de Lambert is safely aboard *The Angélique* before coming back for me and the boy, is that clear?" he demanded as he helped her into the boat.

Sidney regarded him seriously. "Aye, Captain."

Armand nodded, and the men in the skiff began to powerfully pull their oars, guiding the heavy boat into the rough water. Armand stood on the shore and watched them a moment. Then he turned and began to walk along the beach toward the road they had taken from Calais. Jacqueline sat in the boat and stared at his dark form as it grew smaller, silently praying for God to keep him safe and let him find Philippe.

Suddenly a horse appeared, carrying not one but two figures. As they thundered along the beach toward Armand Jacqueline realized it was Nicolas, holding Philippe a helpless prisoner in front of him. Fear stabbed into her heart. She screamed. The crew stopped rowing.

"Shoot him!" cried Jacqueline.

"We cannot," replied Sidney in frustration. "He is using the boy as a shield, and besides, our weapons are useless this distance from the shore."

Armand calmly watched Nicolas approach. He had drawn his pistol, but as Nicolas drew near he could see that he also held a pistol, and it was pointed directly at Philippe's temple. Nicolas reined in his frothing mount some ten meters from Armand, and the two men warily assessed each other.

"I give you two seconds to drop your weapon, St. James," ordered Nicolas, "or I will blow the boy's head off."

Armand did not hesitate. His pistol fell onto the sand.

"He is not armed—we must turn back!" cried Jacqueline in horror.

Sidney hesitated a moment, obviously reluctant to disobey Armand's orders.

"They will be killed!" she insisted, her heart pounding in terror. "We must turn back!"

"Head toward the shore," ordered Sidney.

Nicolas watched the boat filled with armed men change its course and begin to row toward the shore. "If your men return, it will be to see your dead body, and I promise you, whatever happens, I will make sure Jacqueline does not live." His voice was deadly serious.

Armand turned to look at his men. "Continue to the ship," he shouted harshly across the water. "Under no circumstances are you to return here, is that clear?"

The boat stopped. Slowly it resumed its course toward *The Angélique*.

"Now then, Inspector," said Armand calmly, "I would ask that you release the boy. It is me that you want, and I will be happy to turn myself over to your custody if you let him go."

Nicolas smiled. "Tell me, St. James, how is it that you are always so damned polite?" he drawled sarcastically. "I mean here you are, about to die, and yet you still manage to act so ridiculously civilized. Is that your aristo blood showing?" he wondered acidly.

Armand shrugged his shoulders. "I myself have never felt that titles and bloodlines had anything to do with being civilized. After all, titles give men power, and power can make men extremely uncivilized, as you yourself can attest to."

"Shut up," snapped Nicolas. "Remember, I am the one holding the gun." He held it close to the boy's head and watched Armand, fully enjoying the incredible sense of power the moment was giving him. "You are just like the Duc de Lambert," he sneered. "Always so polite. Always so civilized. Pretending to treat men like me as equal, when in reality he saw me as nothing more than a serving dog. He was happy to take my advice, to use me for my financial brilliance, without which his fortune would have collapsed like a house of cards. I built his fortune up from the brink of ruin. And in return he paid me a paltry salary while inviting me to be a constant guest at his château. He introduced me to the finest foods and wines, splendid artwork and magnificent furnishings, lavish gardens and ridiculous clothes, whetting my appetite for a world he knew I would never be able to afford."

"Forgive me," interrupted Armand, "but if you were as brilliant at business as you claim, surely in time you could have built your own fortune."

"Over the course of a lifetime, perhaps," mused Nicolas. "But I had nothing to get started with, and I was impatient to lead the life I had watched for years as an outsider. And of course, before the revolution, merely having money did not open the doors to the finest social circles in France. You still did not have the rights of the nobility. They were very careful to keep those to themselves."

"And so you sought to marry Jacqueline."

Nicolas smiled. "With her as my wife, they would have been forced to open their doors to me," he replied. "I wanted her the first moment I saw her. Of course she was only fifteen at the time. I had to wait, and watch as she grew from an innocent young girl into an incredibly desirable woman. I tried to be nice to her. I did not want to scare her. I wanted her to genuinely like me."

Armand lifted one eyebrow. "I don't think you have been very successful in that area," he remarked.

Nicolas scowled. "She thought I was beneath her," he spat contemptuously. "She did not share her father's newfound philosophies concerning the equality of men. She had learned the lessons of her class too well, and was loath to give them up."

"Sometimes to change you need to grow," suggested Armand, thinking back to Jacqueline's narrow opinions when he first met her. "She could not grow while sheltered in the Château de Lambert."

"I could not wait for her to grow anymore," spat Nicolas. "There were already a dozen mincing fools sniffing at her door. I had to go in to Charles-Alexandre and make my claim on her."

"Very romantic," commented Armand dryly. "I am amazed she turned you down."

"She did not get the chance to," replied Nicolas. "Her father laughed in my face, and then turned around and betrothed her to that spineless idiot."

"Now that is something we can both agree on," stated Armand. "De Biret really is a spineless idiot."

"I knew he would desert her at the first hint of danger," sneered Nicolas. "And I was angry at the duc for humiliating me. So I arranged for him to have a little rest at the Luxembourg."

"Which ultimately led to his execution."

"That was unfortunate," admitted Nicolas. "Sometimes the outcome of these things cannot be predicted."

"And then you arranged for the arrest of her brother, Antoine."

"It was necessary," replied Nicolas. "I told Jacqueline that if she would only become my mistress, I would protect her and her family. But she foolishly refused my offer."

"Imagine that," commented Armand. "And in retaliation, you planted false letters in her home and denounced Antoine, which led to his arrest and subsequent death."

"I merely meant for his arrest to be a show of strength," protested Nicolas defensively. "Once she agreed to my terms, I would have cleared his name and had him released."

"But you did not anticipate Jacqueline getting herself arrested in the process."

"No," he admitted. "She was always so controlled and elegant. It never occurred to me she would attack a member of the National Guard."

"Her brother was ill, and the soldiers were beating him," pointed out Armand. "But of course, again that was something you did not anticipate."

"Sometimes the soldiers take brutish pleasure in their orders," Nicolas allowed.

"As do the men who lead them."

Nicolas scowled. "And then she was sentenced to

death. I had been cheated of having her. That was not acceptable. And then, just as I was finally about to have what should have been mine all along, you came in. You stole her from me, and in doing so did irreparable damage to my career. I had let both the treacherous Mademoiselle de Lambert and the Black Prince escape from my grasp. I can tell you, I paid for that mistake. I knew that to redeem myself I had to get you back. But when I trapped you, I could not prove to the Committee of Public Safety that I had actually snared the Black Prince. It was not until Jacqueline broke you out of La Force that they decided to believe me. I was told to either capture you, or be tried and executed for treason."

He shifted in his saddle, still holding tight to Philippe, who was watching Armand closely, silently waiting for some kind of signal.

"I do hope you understand, therefore, that I cannot allow another escape. My own life is at stake. Which is why I cannot take the chance of returning you to Paris for execution."

"Of course, I understand," said Armand reasonably.

Jacqueline sat rigidly in the skiff watching the two men. She could not hear anything, but the darkness had faded to the cold, gray light of morning, revealing Nicolas on his horse with his gun at Philippe's head, and Armand, unarmed, facing him.

"It really is a pity it has to end this way," Nicolas commented sympathetically. "You would have made a wonderful spy for the revolution, had you decided to work for us."

"You will excuse me if I am not flattered," returned Armand.

Nicolas sighed. "Farewell, Black Prince." He moved his pistol from Philippe's head and pointed it at Armand.

With a cry of rage Philippe threw himself as hard as he could against Nicolas's arm, knocking him backward. They both lost their seat on the horse and slid off into the sand.

"Run, Monsieur, run!" Philippe shouted as he scrambled to his feet and sprinted toward Armand.

Nicolas let out a snarl of fury and aimed his gun at Philippe. "You little bastard!"

Armand raced forward, grabbed Philippe, and threw him out of the way just as the pistol exploded. Shots echoed across the water, but they did not reach the shore. He could hear Jacqueline screaming. He looked up at Nicolas, who was smiling triumphantly. He made no move to shoot again. Armand frowned in confusion.

And then he felt it.

A searing, burning, icy pain gripped his chest, hot and cold at the same time, excruciatingly painful, and yet not so painful at all. He looked down in disbelief, wondering how he possibly could have been hit and feel almost nothing. Hot scarlet blood was seeping through the white of his shirt, quickly soaking it and flowing into his jacket.

Suddenly he felt dizzy and nauseated. He was vaguely aware of Jacqueline's agonized screams. Nicolas was laughing. He tried to focus on those sounds as he dropped to his knees in the sand.

Nicolas stepped toward him, his face a mask of bitter victory. "And so we witness the death of the infamous Black Prince," he drawled mockingly. "How utterly tragic, to come to such an ignoble end."

Armand forced himself to remain focused as he approached. His chest was tearing him apart with every breath. The need to lie down was overwhelming, but he made himself stay erect. Just a few more steps, he told himself as he felt for his boot. *Come on, you goddamned bastard.*

Nicolas took another step toward him. "Let's not take all day, St. James," he mocked. "Unless you would like me to shoot you again."

"You are most considerate," managed Armand weakly, "but I believe once is enough."

Nicolas took another two steps toward him. "Are you sure?" he drawled sarcastically.

The icy cold steel of Jacqueline's dagger filled his

palm. With bitter determination he wrenched it from his boot and hurtled it through the air. "Positive," he rasped.

Nicolas stared in bewilderment at the handle sticking out of his chest. He put his hand on it and looked at Armand in disbelief, as if he thought it was a trick. Then he let out a pathetic whimper of rage and fell forward onto the sand, driving the shaft of steel deeper into his heart.

Armand grunted with satisfaction and moved to get up. An excruciating current of pain shot through his body, robbing him of his ability to think. His legs gave way and he collapsed onto the sand.

"Lie still, Monsieur," ordered Philippe, his voice small and taut. He leaned over and began to undo his shirt. "Let me see how bad it is."

Armand groaned and closed his eyes, desperately wishing for a drink. His last thought before blackness hit was that somewhere in the darkness, Jacqueline was still screaming.

"We have to go back for him!" she wailed hysterically, her eyes blinded by tears, her hands clawing desperately at Sidney. "He is not dead—we have to go back for him and Philippe!"

"We cannot," replied Sidney gravely. "Look."

Jacqueline raised her eyes to the shore and her heart froze. Against the soft, smoky peach light of morning, a regiment of soldiers on horseback were thundering along the beach toward Armand and Philippe. There were more than twenty of them, and behind them was a mob of men and women carrying knives, muskets, and pistols, shouting and firing randomly into the air.

"Oh my God," she whispered brokenly.

"To go back would be suicide," said Sidney. "Once we got close enough to shore, we would probably kill our fair share. But we are a sitting target in this boat, and ultimately we would all be killed. I cannot allow that, Mademoiselle. Armand would never sanction such a decision. My orders are to take you safely to the ship, and return to England."

"But we cannot leave them there," protested Jacqueline, weeping openly.

Sidney clenched his jaw and looked away from her. "We have no choice."

He gave the order for the men to resume their course toward the ship. The men were painfully silent as the skiff began to cut swiftly across the water.

Her heart shattered into a thousand pieces, her mind insane with grief, Jacqueline watched numbly as Philippe stood to face the revolutionary guards who surrounded the lifeless bodies of Armand and Nicolas.

Chapter 18

"See that fat cloud over there? That one is a fine chariot which is going to swoop down from the sky and take me away to my first ball," announced Suzanne dreamily in French to Séraphine. "And I shall wear a gown covered in diamonds, and my hair will be arranged into a thousand curls, all glittering with sapphires and rubies."

Séraphine lay on the grass and studied the cloud, her expression somewhat skeptical.

"It's true," continued Suzanne defensively. "And my dancing slippers will be made of gold, and I will carry a fan of lace and pearls."

Séraphine looked at her sister thoughtfully, as if she was trying to imagine her in such an outfit.

"And I will meet a handsome prince," continued Suzanne, "all dressed in silver, and he will beg me to marry him the moment he sees me, and take me away to live in his silver castle where nothing bad ever happens." She lay back against the warm grass and stared at the cloud. "That is what is going to happen when I am older." She closed her eyes and tried to picture her gown. "Jacqueline, how old were you when you attended your first ball?"

Jacqueline pulled her gaze away from the distance, only vaguely aware that her sister had spoken to her. "Pardon?"

"Your first ball," repeated Suzanne. "How old were you?"

"I don't remember," she replied vacantly.

"What about your first time to the theater?" Suzanne persisted.